T0194273

DESIRES OF THE SOUL

ANDREA E. MCKINNEY

authorHOUSE

AuthorHouse™
1663 Liberty Drive
Bloomington, IN 47403
www.authorhouse.com
Phone: 1 (800) 839-8640

Published by AuthorHouse 06/16/2016

ISBN: 978-1-5246-1313-6 (sc)
ISBN: 978-1-5246-1311-2 (hc)
ISBN: 978-1-5246-1312-9 (e)

Library of Congress Control Number: 2016909214

Print information available on the last page.

Chapter One

————— ❧❧ —————

THE SET UP

I

t was a bright sunny summer day. The cool breeze whispered to the seagulls gently in the air. Her name was Chelsea McQuire. When she finished the salad that she had prepared for herself when she got home, she began her walk as she did every day to fill the rest of her lunch hour. She had hurried home on her lunch break so that she could eat her lunch and take a walk on her favorite beach in Marshalls Bay. She hopped in her sedan and drove the three blocks to her beach house to have lunch and then drove the three blocks to walk on Marshall's Bay beach. After she parked her car when she arrived at the beach she slipped out of her heels to make her way to the shore for her walk. She had locked up her cottage and could leave directly from the beach to her place of work after she was finished walking. She had packed a bag of bread crumbs for the seagulls to eat while she walked on her favorite beach. She loved the way the sand felt between her toes and the way the waves splashed against the shore. A boy was playing catch with his golden retriever and he threw the tennis ball into the surf as the dog chased after it. Then the dog gripped it in his mouth and returned it to the boy. Girls laid out in skimpy bikinis on towels along the way.

It put her at ease and gave her peace because she knew every inch of this beach that she called home. She was a beautiful blonde with long flowing hair and she walked the shores of the beach that she adored every day at this time on her lunch hour from work. She watched the children play in the sand, making sand castles and playing without a care in the world. She watched the seagull's fly overhead. She tossed a few broken pieces of bread in the air for the birds to eat from the bag of bread crumbs that she had packed for just such an occasion. She delighted in the fact that the birds could catch the pieces of bread in midair. This was something that she loved to do because the birds were always true to her. They always seemed to know when she was coming. She always made sure she had plenty of bread crumbs to share with the seagulls.

While she was walking along the shore she could feel the surf hit her toes. She was paying attention to the children and the seagulls while she took her treasured walk along the shore of Marshalls Bay beach. She dreamt of the day when she too would have children to take to that very beach and watch them play in the pearly white sand. The mother of the children called them to their blanket to feed them their lunch. Watching this made Chelsea's heart ache for her Prince Charming.

She owned a charming little two-bedroom cottage just a few of blocks from the shore. One day she hoped to share this beach house with the man of her dreams. Then she could take her own children to the beach and teach them how to swim and build sand castles in the sand. She looked at her watch and found that it was almost time to get back to work. She had to hurry because her lunch hour was almost over. So she quickly made her way back to her car, unlocked the door, and jumped in to head back to her place of work, Trinity bank. The beach was along the shores of Tallahassee, Florida. Her cottage near Marshalls Bay beach was just a few minutes down the road from the bank where she worked.

Many wealthy people banked at this establishment. The decor alone attracted the wealthy. Mr. Joseph Eldridge, the owner, was a kind old man. Many who patronized the Trinity bank knew Mr. Eldridge personally and highly respected him. He was a fourth generation banker, and he knew quite well how to run a successful bank. He was a faithful man and was a regular attendant to Sunday services with his wife Eleanor.

Chelsea was unaware that she was being watched every day when she made her precious walk along the shore of Marshalls Bay beach. Frank Snow sat in his rented van alongside of the road. He took pictures of her with the high powered lens on his camera so that he would know every inch of her by heart. He could download the pictures onto his high tech laptop to edit and print so that they could be hung on the walls of this temporary residence. He was also able to get her in full motion with the movie setting on his camera. He could just download the video surveillance to his high powered laptop and add it to his collection at his leisure. He had become accustomed to the way that she moved when she walked and the sound of her voice on the recorder when they taped her calls. He didn't realize it yet but his heart already belonged to her.

He knew her routine like the back of his hand. Chelsea was a creature of habit and he used this to his advantage. He had nefarious intentions. He smoked a cigarette while he watched her make her way down the beach and innocently feed the seagulls. He thought she was a beautiful sight and he was very happy that she would be the one that fit into his plan. Every day he sat in different rented vehicles watching her take her treasured walk along the crowded beach. He traded in the vehicles each day so she wouldn't notice that he was watching her. He would soon get to know her very well, because he intended on using her in his plan. Chelsea walked down the beach as though she did not have a care in the world. This pleased Frank because he knew she would be an easy target.

When she headed back to her sedan and hopped in she made her way back to the Trinity bank. Frank threw his cigarette butt out the window and started the engine to the van. He would follow her to her place of work so that he could keep close tabs on her from a distance. He followed her back to the Trinity bank and parked his van. Then he waited for her to exit her vehicle, so that he could take one more picture of her as she entered her place of work.

After college Chelsea had already achieved her employment goals. She worked in a bank of high caliber and had a very lucrative career. She was the vice president, third only to the president of the bank who was also her best friend Ms. Felecia Grey and Mr. Eldridge who was the owner of the establishment and treasured her as an employee as well. She was very comfortable in her current position. She knew that she was secure in the job that she held.

When Chelsea returned from her lunch break she said a quick hello to Harold the security guard and Cheryl the banks greeter then climbed the stairs to deposit her purse in her office. She then entered Felecia's office and asked, "How was your lunch break, Felecia?"

Felecia was a shorter version of beauty. She was a brunette but always kept her hair in a tight fashionable haircut. Her biggest assets were her breasts. She didn't like a hairy body, so she paid to get a brazilin wax every week religiously. She had an appointment to get her Brazilian that evening after work. Her breasts were quite large for her size and she was very proud of them. They were a natural asset and she knew the men went wild for them. She had a very strong sexual appetite and she did not have a problem finding sexual partners when she turned on the charm.

Felecia was sitting behind her desk going over the daily books as was her job. She too had just returned from her lunch break. She knew full well that Chelsea had spent her lunch break walking the shores of her favorite beach.

"Well, it was lovely. Mr. Eldridge took me out to a very nice lunch to go over last month's balance sheet, I was pleased to tell him that we are in the black once again. How was your walk?" Felecia asked

"It was very relaxing. Where did you go for lunch?"

"That upscale Italian restaurant, Luigi's. It's one Joseph's favorite restaurants."

"How is Mr. Eldridge feeling?"

"He is doing quite well considering his recent heart attack."

Chelsea knew of Mr. Eldridge's latest scare with his heart. He was a very wealthy man with a lot on his shoulders. Since the heart attack he had scaled down his hours and he depended more and more on Felecia and Alice his secretary than ever before. He began coming in at the hour of 10 am and often left the bank early to please his wife Eleanor.

Then Chelsea inquired "Do you think Mr. Eldridge should be back to work so soon?" Chelsea went on to say "He seems quite capable of doing his job, but we better keep an eye out for him just in case. He has cut back on his hours to accommodate the risk to his health"

"Yes, that's a good idea, we don't want him having another heart attack on our watch." Felecia replied.

Then Chelsea excused herself and went back to her own office. After Chelsea and Felecia were back in their offices Frank moved the rented van to a place where he could see Chelsea's office as well as Felecia's easily through their large picture windows, on the walls, in their offices.

He kept close tabs on Chelsea and Felecia while Jonathan his brother listened in on the tape recorded conversations that he could pick up from the ladies offices. Jonathan Snow was also Frank's partner in crime. Jonathan kept tabs on Felecia by listening in on the tape recorders that picked up every conversation that each woman had within the confines of their offices. Both women were part of the plan. Jonathan spent most of his time listening to the tape recorders that shared the information with the Snow brothers when the ladies were in their offices. Jonathan was trying to figure out a way to break the banks security codes on both Felecia and Chelsea's computers and decode their passwords so that he could download the money that they intended on stealing from the Trinity Bank in Marshall's Bay.

The Snow brothers would soon bug their homes and have complete access to everything the two women said within the confines of their homes as well. They had many pictures and a lot video of Felecia and Chelsea as the women busied themselves with their duties for the bank. Frank was busy taking as many pictures as he could get with his long-range camera as the two women worked diligently in their offices. Neither woman suspected a thing.

Frank Snow was also keeping track of the armored truck deliveries and logging the information onto his tablet to send to Jonathan who was keeping track of this through a spreadsheet on his computer. Jonathan was extremely well versed in computer technology and had bought the latest and best computer just for this occasion with the money from their last heist. This is because the armored truck delivered the money on a rotating drop schedule. This meant that the armored truck made its drops on different days and times rotating the drops every day.

Jonathan had spent the last two months studying the times and days of these drops so they could choose the best day and time to rob the bank and the armored truck. He had found a program that helped him download the armored truck schedules as well so that there could be no errors on the day of that the plan was to take place. He had matched the download to the log that Frank had been keeping of the armored truck drops. This was to insure that there would be no mistakes made on the day that the plan was to go through.

By this time he knew every move that that the armored trucks made on their delivery route that delivered the Trinity banks money and took the deposits to be processed. Frank Snow was pleased that he was able to get this information and it had only taken time to gather the information that gave him the tightly guarded schedule of the armored trucks.

Jonathan was to be Felecia's newest mate. This was all part of the plan. Frank would seduce Chelsea and get as much information out of her about what was going on inside the walls of Trinity bank. They were both quite handsome and knew how to treat a lady and get what they wanted. Jonathan's job was to keep tabs on both women through the bugs. He counted on his brother to get him around in his rented vehicles. When Frank couldn't take him where he needed to go, he just called for a cab to take him where he needed to go.

Felecia lived alone as well but she had a three-bedroom house close to the bank in an upscale neighborhood in the residential district in town. Like Chelsea she only had to drive a few minutes to get to work. She was a successful woman and didn't feel the need to get married anytime soon like Chelsea did. Felecia was not as much of a creature of habit as Chelsea was, but she enjoyed her nightly trip to the gym. She was a bit harder to follow and keep tabs on, but Jonathan was up to the task. The Snow brothers would make their move soon.

The bank was secure as far as Mr. Joseph Eldridge knew. Each and every day that he came into work Felecia made sure that the picture windows above the door were free of window shades, so that Mr. Eldridge could rest at ease. No one knew that Anthony Alvarez had ulterior motives. Though he had been an employee for only two short months, he was proving to the Snow brothers that he was worth his weight in gold, or so they thought.

Mr. Eldridge thanked Alice for her services that day and told her that he was on his way home. It was almost 4 o'clock and time to head for home before he overdid it. "Goodnight and watch your health carefully. Mr. Eldridge, we don't want a repeat performance", she said as she waved good bye. Then she packed her things to leave as well. Alice was fond of the elevator.

Then Mr. Eldridge went to Felecia's office and said "Well, Ms. Grey the Mrs. will have my hide if I put in any overtime. She's assured to keep me on my toes about my health. So I'm going to call it a night and I wish you a good weekend."

"That's a good idea Mr. Eldridge you take good care of yourself, we don't want to see you have another heart attack. You can count on me to take care of things for you. I'll close up for the night."

With that, Mr. Eldridge turned on his heel and left Felecia's office heading for the elevator to leave the building. Then he entered Chelsea's office to say goodnight to her before leaving.

"I will see you on Monday Ms. McQuire, time to call it a night". Mr. Eldridge said,

"You have a restful weekend Mr. Eldridge. Good night, I will see you on Monday" Chelsea knew that Mr. Eldridge was growing weary of all the interest in his health so she stayed away from the subject when she said goodnight. Then he turned to leave her office for the weekend. He took the elevator to the first floor and said a quick goodnight to Mark and Ken then he went to his son's office and said good night as well. He told him that he would see him at home soon. He then said his good byes to both Cheryl and Harold and left the building, feeling quite confident that Felecia had everything under control.

Anthony Alvarez was the newest employee and the Snow brother's mole. He watched Mr. Eldridge intently while he made his rounds. He wanted to keep close tabs on him so that he would know when he was ill again if that happened again, which might benefit him. Felecia was anxious to get ready for the date that she and Chelsea had set. She knew there were only a few hours left before she would be sweating like she liked to.

The tellers had to count their drawers and then hand their bags over to Felecia to deposit into the vault for the weekend. She stopped by Mark Patterson's office to say goodnight. She went into Ken Steven's office and asked if he was ready to assist with letting the tellers go for the night. He was ready and told her that he was right behind her. Chelsea was already waiting by the door for the employees to finish counting their drawers for the day. She had already let all the loan officers out for the weekend.

Until Monday the money bags would rest in the vault waiting to be reconciled behind the secure doors of the combination lock that held the banks money. During the week she went over the reports that the tellers had made out before they left for the night. On Fridays she locked the money bags in the vault for the weekend until she could check the balances of the teller's money bags and balance their tapes. Then she would make her report for the armored truck and bag up the deposits that the armored truck would take away then as well. This was a procedure that she was assured to regret in the near future.

Chelsea chatted with Harold about his weekend plans while she waited. He divulged that he was going fishing with his son this weekend. Chelsea was happy to hear that Harold had plans.

Ken Stevens oversaw the tellers and helped Anthony Alvarez with his drawer. He was having a hard time balancing and this was making Felecia a very anxious. With the help of Ken Steven's, Mr. Alvarez was able to get his drawer to balance. Then he was let out of the bank for the day. With everything secure Chelsea already let the rest of the employees go for the weekend one by one. Then Felecia went back up the stairs to her office, she had a feeling that Anthony Alvarez was going to be a problem and she didn't like those thoughts. She then went to Chelsea's office and asked if she was ready to lock up the vault for the weekend.

"Ready when you are." Chelsea replied. Then both ladies went to the vault to lock it up.

Felecia secured the money behind the combination lock. The vault could only be accessed by using both women's keys and Felecia shared the only combination to the vault with Mr. Eldridge, which tightly held Mr. Eldridge's money.

Felecia, Chelsea and Mr. Eldridge all had keys to the front door. The vault couldn't be opened or closed without both women's keys and Felecia's combination on the door that held all the money. Everyone knew this and it was up to Anthony Alvarez to see to it that the Snow brothers had access to the vault.

Chapter Two

GETTING TO KNOW THE BANK'S EMPLOYEES

The bank was a beautiful building. It was owned by Mr. Joseph Eldridge, a billionaire who trusted Chelsea explicitly. The bank stood alone close to the outskirts of the small town of Marshalls Bay. It had beautiful pillars at the front entrance. There were seven steps that stretched across the front entrance to the banks enormous front doors. It was an old Victorian building. The glass doors that opened up into the lobby when you walked into the bank and were always sparkling clean. When you entered the establishment you were greeted by the banks luxurious interior. Light green wall paper adorned the walls with hundred dollar bills as their only accent around the upper edge of the wall. The color of money, one would say. The lobby had green plush carpet with a light green plaid pin striping throughout the entire building. This helped to keep it from showing every little thing that made to the floor during the work day before it could be vacuumed again that night. This color was chosen because Mr. Eldridge loved the color of green. All of the desks were cherry wood with leather chairs for comfort. The greeter's desk was the nicest of all. The greeter's name was Cheryl Ratcliff and she had a personality of patience and held a caring attitude. After all, firmpressions were important to Mr. Eldridge. He counted on Cheryl Ratcliff to greet his customers and she never failed to accommodate every one of them and treated them with the best care possible.

The bank was a two-story building. The offices that held the president Felecia Grey and vice president Chelsea McQuire were on the upstairs level. Mr. Eldridge also had an office upstairs alongside the two trusted women. Their offices could be reached by either using the staircase or the elevator. Chelsea and Felecia chose to use the stairs every day because they liked to stay in shape. Chelsea's boss and best friend, Felecia Grey, had just returned from lunch as well. There was also an office for Mr. Eldridge's secretary, Alice Ridgemont, who he trusted explicitly as well. She saw to it that Mr. Eldridge didn't overdo it in his daily chores while watching the bank's activities.

Mr. Eldridge hired his trusted longtime friend Harold Snipe as his only security officer. It was a mistake that Mr. Eldridge would regret in the future. He wore a uniform and held a small .22 caliber gun on his hip. The customers were put at ease and they thought that their money was safe with him in charge. Harold helped Chelsea open the bank in the mornings and closed the bank at 4 o'clock every day. He was a gentle man and carried his job with authority. When he was finished helping Chelsea let the employees in in the mornings he took his post at the front door and took his job seriously. When the day was done he helped Chelsea let the employees out for the evening.

The lobby was adorned with green velvet ropes that led a labyrinth line to the tellers. There was an island that held deposit slips, pens, other forms to be used by the customers and brochures of the banks many benefits that were offered to each customer in the center of the lobby. Cheryl's desk was cherry wood as well with a leather high back chair for her comfort. Cheryl was under Chelsea's charge. The pens that had the banks logo on them and were for the customers to take as mementos and to use for their banking needs. There were also comfortable chairs where customers could sit and wait for a banker in a lighter shade of green, if they needed more help than a teller could offer or they needed a loan officer. Each individual teller window was lined with gold trim and the ceiling was trimmed in gold as well around the edges above the $100 dollar bill accents. Each new customer was greeted by Cheryl Ratcliff who was specifically assigned the task of making them feel at home while they attended to their banking needs. It was also her job to make sure the island was stocked at all times. Cheryl had to keep a good attitude so that the customers would feel welcome when they entered the Trinity bank.

As a line formed and the customers were treated with the highest respect by each teller. Each teller was chosen for their professional personality. Anthony Alvarez had passed the test and had gotten hired recently. He was in cahoots with the notorious Snow brothers. The tellers were meant to put the customers at ease with their banking needs so they had to be efficient in their chosen jobs. Only one teller was proving that his position at Trinity bank was beyond his capabilities. Mr. Anthony Alvarez as a new hire was to help customers at the teller window. He was having a hard time understanding his duties lately because the pressure of the upcoming events were rubbing his nerves raw. Felecia Grey was growing weary of his incompetence.

Part of Chelsea's job was to oversee the managers of the bank, Ken Stevens and Mark Patterson. She was quite good at delegating responsibility. She had a good head on her shoulders and made a good team with Felecia. Along with any bank there was a sign to tell the owner that everything was good for the day. There were two picture windows above the door. If the shades were drawn it meant that there was a problem. If the shades were open it meant that everything was in order. Mr. Eldridge watched these two windows very carefully as he entered his establishment every day. Any sign that there was trouble and he would be on the phone to the police in a moment's notice.

Ken Stevens was married with two children. His wife Amanda was one of the tellers. They were both trusted employees. Mark Patterson was gay. He had a domestic partner named Clark who worked as an aerobics instructor. Clark held aerobics classes on Monday, Wednesday and Friday nights at the Al Star Gym. Ken and Mark knew their jobs well and treated their employees with the highest amount of respect. There were cameras watching every teller to make sure that their job was done with integrity. There were also cameras mounted in all four corners of the lobby. Nothing that went on in the bank went unnoticed by the spies in the sky.

There were six tellers in all. Ken Steven's wife Amanda who had been with the bank for many years and had gotten her husband his job at Trinity bank. Matthew Burch was a fresh graduate from the Union University in Tallahassee Florida. Kristin Mayes had held her post for several years as well. Thomas Underwood was another trusted employee who had been with the bank the longest as a teller. Kathy Richmond was new but had proven to be a trustworthy employee and Anthony Alvarez who had worked at the bank for two months and the jury was still out on him. He was in cahoots with the Snow brothers and he had been making mistakes which was not acceptable to Felecia. She was growing weary of his presence at the bank.

Of the six tellers, Mr. Eldridge trusted Amanda Stevens the most. Mr. Eldridge had a four-way television screen in his office to watch the actions in the lobby and a six way television screen that watched the tellers every move. The tellers knew they were being watched, but they did not mind because they knew it was necessary for the bank's integrity.

Mark Patterson oversaw all the bank's loan officers. There were four loan officers. There was Cynthia Marks, who was also gay so Mark and Cynthia saw each other on common ground. Richard Eldridge was Joseph Eldridge's eldest son and he was being groomed for management at a later date. Samantha Smith who had proven to be a very trusted employee and Justin Banks had been with the bank for many years and held the second longest post at the Trinity Bank. Mr. Eldridge's secretary, Alice Ridgemont, had been his trusted employee for many years and he trusted her with his life. She was the one who had found him in his office when he had had his recent heart attack. The ambulance was called and his life was spared because of her quick action.

Chelsea made herself comfortable in the chair in Felecia's office so that they could have a conversation about the managers and employees. Felecia would tell her trusted friend and colleague of the events that the bank was undertaking. Loans had to be processed, tellers had to be watched very closely because they handled the money and were the first thing that the customers encountered after Harold and Cheryl greeted them when they did their business at Trinity bank.

The two managers on the floor helped the employees when they needed to. If there was any trouble, Ken and Mark were very levelheaded and could handle any situation that came their way. They were both managers who were well versed in the banks procedures and they both handled their employees with respect and a caring attitude.

Jonathan had heard that Mr. Alvarez was not one of Felecia Grey's favorite employees through the wires in Felecia and Chelsea's offices. Felecia would give him an evaluation the next time that he made a mistake. The only thing that he had going for him was that he was always on time when he came to work. But he always arrived after 8 am so he didn't know about the time locks which would interrupt the Snow brother's plans to rob the bank and the armored truck when the time came. Little did Felecia know that Anthony would become dispensable in the near future.

"All of the employees are doing well, though the jury is still out on Anthony Alvarez. He's been having trouble balancing lately. Ken is watching him closely so that he will learn the routine better although he should know this by now." Chelsea reported. Felecia was not pleased to hear this news.

Chelsea was still concerned that Mr. Eldridge wasn't up to the task of running the bank on his own. So she was especially on guard for his welfare. She cared very deeply for her employer as she did the president of the bank.

With the meeting coming to an end Chelsea asked Felecia "Are you going to the gym tonight?"

"Of course it's Friday night. What better night and place to get a hot and sweaty suitor to play with."

The two women giggled and Chelsea asked "Do you mind if I join you tonight, I can use some hot and sweaty action?"

"Maybe we should check out Clark's aerobics class?"

"That sounds like a great idea. Let's do it. I will call him and verify what time the class is. I hear it starts at 7 o'clock at the All-Star Gym down town."

Little did the women know that Anthony Alvarez had planted a bug in both of the ladies offices on the sly. One day Anthony made an excuse to be in Felecia's office for a trivial reason, at which time he planted a bug at the corner of her desk when he stood as he leaned on her desk to show her something about the report that he was giving her. He also managed to distract Chelsea with a trivial reason and planted a bug in the same place on her desk by simply leaning in on her desk planting the bug just under the corner edge.

Jonathan Snow monitored the conversations that the girls had that fell within the confines of their offices. He also had found a way to hack into the banks website with his high tech laptop. He just needed to get close to Felecia and Frank needed to get just as close to Chelsea. This was so that Jonathan could seduce Felecia and Frank could seduce Chelsea and the men could use the time when the women were asleep to search for their passwords on their home computers. Frank had learned that they both took work home with them from time to time and worked on the banks website with their home computers. He had learned this from the conversations that he had heard through the tapes. It would only be a matter of time before Jonathan had the password information to hack into the deepest crevices of the banks website and have access to the banks funds.

Now the Snow brothers knew of their plans to meet up at the gym for the aerobics class tonight. All Frank had to do is show up for an aerobics class and do a little sweating himself. Jonathan wasn't interested in taking an aerobics class so he would be introduced to the ladies after the class. Chelsea excused herself and went to her office. She busied herself with her own obligations for the bank. Felecia busied herself with the books. Neither woman suspected that they were on the way to meeting the two men that would change their lives forever.

Felecia picked up the phone and called down to Mark Patterson's office. Mark answered "Hello, this is Mark Patterson Trinity bank, how may I help you?"

"Mark this is Felecia"

"Yes Felecia what can I do for you?"

"Chelsea and I were wondering if it would be all right if we joined Clark's aerobics class tonight?"

Mark said "Of course Clark would be honored to have you join him, the class starts at 7 o'clock and it's at the All-Star Gym on 5th and Broadway down town. I have to tell you he gives you quite a workout. Although I can't make it tonight."

"Thank you, I know where that's at, we will be there tonight then. See you on Monday."

Felecia hung up the phone noting that Mark would not be present in the class that evening. He was not as much of an exercise buff as his partner was, but he kept in shape in other ways.

Working out was something that Felecia enjoyed very much. An aerobics class would be just the thing to get her heart pumping and possibly meet a new stranger who might just prove to be Mr. Right for the night. So at 4:30 Felicia left her office, and used the stairs to go down to the lobby to check on things and see to it that the loan officers had been let out for the weekend and the vault was secure. Chelsea locked the doors behind each one as they left for the day. Then she waited while the tellers started closing up their drawers. Each teller ran their tapes to be reconciled on Monday. She took their money bags into the vault from the tellers to put away for the weekend. Then she locked up the vault tight for the weekend.

All of the tellers had balanced that day except for Anthony Alvarez. He was beginning to make stupid mistakes because he knew what was about to happen in just a couple short weeks on the Friday before the big Labor Day weekend.

Felecia told Chelsea as they walked over to the vault to close it up tight for the weekend. "One more thing before I go, I spoke to Mark and Clark's aerobics class is definitely at 7 o'clock, so wear your aerobics gear and be ready by 6:45 and I'll pick you up at your house."

"That sounds great to me I'm looking so forward to a good, hard work out." Chelsea said excitedly.

Felecia knew that Chelsea could let herself out. So, she closed the blinds to the picture windows, as was her routine, and they left for the night. The Snow brothers were unaware of Felecia's sign to Mr. Eldridge which would make their job just a little harder in the end. It was up to Anthony Alvarez to give the Snow brothers this information but Mr. Alvarez didn't know this fact because he always showed up just in the nick of time every day and he was so anxious about his new post that he simply didn't notice that Felecia closed the blinds every evening and opened them every morning after all was determined to be fine for the day. Chelsea wasn't far behind her, she was anxious to get to the gym and work out.

When Frank Snow saw both women leaving, he quickly started his van and waited for Chelsea to get in her sedan and leave the parking lot. He had called Jonathan using his disposable cell phone at the apartment to ask if the ladies had made any plans for the evening. Jonathan said they were planning on attending an aerobics class at 7 o'clock at the All Star Gym on 5th and Broadway down town. So he stopped by the apartment and changed into an outfit befitting an aerobics class, made himself a light sandwich to eat and headed for Chelsea's cottage to wait for Felecia to pick up Chelsea and give her a ride to the aerobics class. He would eat his sandwich while he waited for the girls to head out for the class. These two women had no idea what they were in store for with the Snow brothers.

Jonathan Snow had spent time in prison for armed robbery. He was no stranger to firearms or nefarious business. Frank Snow was in very good shape and would be able to pull off an aerobics class with ease. Frank had avoided the long arm of the law when he had pulled previous jobs. So he hadn't spent any time in jail and had no record to speak of. However that really didn't matter because Jonathan had made fake I.D's for both of them under assumed names with new social security numbers and new drivers licenses.

"All we have to do is get close enough to these two women to gain their trust." Frank said to Jonathan as he entered their dingy apartment. Jonathan called his attention to the fake ID's for his approval. \

"So I'm Christopher Fields. That sounds like a trustworthy name. Thanks bro." Frank Said as he added the new ID to his thin wallet.

"So who are you?" Frank asked.

"Mr. Randy Withers. I shall be known as Randy from now on." Jonathan replied as he showed Frank his new ID and snickered.

Frank didn't carry much with him in his wallet. Just a simple prepaid credit card that he could access the money with, his ID's and a few various notes that he had saved over time. He didn't like clutter so he tried to keep his wallet free of too much unnecessary items.

As handsome as Frank was, he felt that there should be no problem getting Chelsea to fall for him. Then all he would have to do is find a way to get Felecia interested in Jonathan. Jonathan on the other hand wasn't quite as muscular as Frank was. But he was up to the challenge of getting Felecia to fall for him all the same. He was arrogant and knew he could pull it off.

As Chelsea entered her cottage, she was met by her pet cat. She fed the cat and fixed herself a quick meal. Then, she threw a French braid in her hair and put on her cutest aerobics gear to get ready for the occasion. She also packed an outfit to go out in, so that they could go to have drinks just incase they met a handsome suitor who might be just the one to fill her lonely nights. She was anxious with anticipation for what might come of the evening. It had been a long time since she had been out with a gentleman.

Frank Snow was a smooth as they came. Chelsea just wanted to meet her Prince charming. Felecia on the other hand, was more of a one night stand kind of woman. After all, she already had the house and the career what did she need a man for other than to get sweaty with once in a while? The two women were excited about the evening's plans. And they were anxious with anticipation about who they might meet in the aerobics class. They had heard that Clark was a wonderful instructor.

Chelsea made herself a quick sandwich and ate it before she dressed for the Gym. She figured she would just take a shower after the class when they were finished. At 6:45 pm sharp, Chelsea heard a knock at the door. She was ready. Saying goodbye to Misty her pet Siamese, she opened the door to Felecia and greeted her with an excited "Hello, are you ready to meet our handsome strangers?"

"As ready as I'm ever going to be, let's go."

Felecia pet Misty when she came into Chelsea's cottage. Chelsea was ready to go so she locked her cottage up and got in Felecia's sports car. They were off to Clark's aerobics class to meet a potential handsome stranger. They were very excited about getting a good work out for the evening as well.

Chapter Three

A NIGHT AT THE GYM

Frank Snow had gone home and learned that tonight was the night that the plan would start. Jonathan filled him in on the latest plans for the ladies. He had to get dressed for the aerobics class and then drive to Chelsea's cottage and wait for Felecia to pick Chelsea up. He knew what time they would be leaving for the gym and he had looked up the All Star Gym on his iphone so his GPS had been programmed and he knew where the gym was he just wanted to make sure that he arrived on Chelsea's heels. He wanted to become indispensable to her. Now he knew where they would meet as well. But he wanted to keep a close eye on her, so he decided that following them to the gym would afford him the best advantage over her there.

So he hopped into his new SUV which he had traded in the van for and headed for Chelsea's cottage. He parked down the street just out of sight so that he could follow them from a safe distance. When Felecia got there he made sure he would be ready when they were. When they left the cottage he followed them as they headed for the gym, so that he would arrive at the same time and be able to take the same class with them. He didn't know which class they would be taking because he didn't know what Clark looked like or know his last name so Frank went to the gym and inquired at the counter as to where Clarks class was. He had rented the car that he liked the best, a blue SUV, because he knew that he would keep this one for the rest of the time he would spend in Marshalls Bay.

Chelsea had fed Misty before Felecia got there. She picked out her cutest aerobics gear and was satisfied with how she looked. She packed a bag with clothes for a night out as well. Felecia had made herself a light sandwich before she left to pick up Chelsea. She was also dressed in her cutest aerobics gear and had packed an outfit to wear after the aerobics class as well. After Felecia picked Chelsea up she pulled in to the All-Star Gym and parked her car, promptly at 6:55 pm. Both women hurried out of the car and Felecia locked the doors.

When Frank got to the gym he followed both women into the class that Clark was leading tonight. The gym was neat and tidy as anyone would expect. Clark's aerobics class was in a mirrored room off to the right of the entrance of the gym. There was no need to check in because Clark was already aware that the women were attending this class for the evening. Frank checked in and began to stretch in anticipation of a good work out. Clark saw that he had signed in as Christopher Fields. He was pleased to have him in the class. He was attracted to Frank but his heart belonged to Mark.

Clark was primed for a good work out. Felecia and Chelsea greeted him saying hello and thanking him for allowing them to take this class for the evening.

"Make yourselves at home, just pick a spot where you feel most comfortable." Clark told the ladies

Both women agreed that being in the front of the class would give them the best exposure to any man who might be interested in them for the evening. When Frank noticed that the women had chosen a place at the head of the class, he quickly moved his position so that he could be closest to Chelsea.

"Okay everyone, let's get ready to sweat" Clark said in an excited tone of voice.

Clark was very good at his job and he was in very good shape. Felecia could see what Mark saw in him. He set a good example for the class that he held. He then began to lead the class in a series of stretching movements.

He told the class "We don't want to pull a muscle so we must always stretch before we begin."

After a few minutes of stretching he then turned on the music that was very upbeat and led the class in a heart pounding series of exercises.

Frank tried to get as close to Chelsea as possible without tripping her. He accidentally bumped into her on purpose on several occasions. Chelsea noticed that he was a very handsome and muscular man. She was in the hopes that she might meet up with him at the juice bar after the class.

When the class was over, Chelsea and Felecia thanked Clark for his excellent choice in aerobic exercises. Felecia said "It really feels good to get such a heart pounding workout I will feel the burn tomorrow."

Clark laughed and commented "Well I aim to please, you two have a good night and come again anytime."

"Thank you Clark we will do that." Then they said good night to Clark and headed for the juice bar.

Frank busied himself with stretches after the class, so that he could keep tabs on both women before they left.

When the women left the class and headed for the juice bar, Frank wasn't far behind. Chelsea and Felecia chose a seat at the bar where they could be noticed easily by any handsome stranger. They parked their gym bags by the bar stools on the floor. They ordered a glass of juice and discussed the class and how good it felt to get such a good workout.

Frank made his move. He approached the two women with ease. He then commented to Chelsea in particular "Wow, what a great workout, is this seat taken?"

To this Chelsea replied "Why no, help yourself."

Frank then began a conversation with Chelsea telling her "I'm terribly sorry I bumped into you so many times, I can be quite a klutz at times"

Chelsea replied "Oh don't worry about it, we all make mistakes."

Then Frank said "Do you come here often?"

"Well, actually, this was my first time."

"Well, you look like you do this every evening, as a matter of fact you are quite beautiful if I may say so?"

"Why thank you, my name is Chelsea McQuire, how do you do?" Then she added "What might your name be?"

Frank replied "I'm Christopher Fields, it's very nice to meet you. What is your friend's name?"

To this Chelsea replied "Oh, I'm so sorry. Please forgive me, this is Felecia Grey my close friend and business partner."

Frank then said "It's so nice to meet two such lovely ladies, how do you do Felecia?"

Felecia was on guard, because he was alone, but she still replied "Why thank you and it's nice to meet you Christopher, do you have a friend?"

"Why yes, I have a very close business partner who would find you very attractive."

Both women giggled, because they both felt like they had met their intended handsome stranger that they had set out to meet that evening. Frank then told the women that he was about to meet with his partner after showering. He asked "How would you both like to go out for a drink later and meet my friend?"

Felecia replied "That sounds wonderful. Where would you like to meet?"

"I know of a quaint little tiki bar just up the road. Why don't we meet there say around 9 o'clock?"

Chelsea replied "Sounds great, it will give us a chance to shower as well and a drink sounds wonderful. I know the place you are speaking of."

"Well, ladies it's time to get to the showers I'll see you there at 9 o'clock then. It was very nice to meet you and I look forward to introducing you to my friend." He directed this last statement to Felecia.

Then Frank headed for the showers as he had said previously to make it look as if he was telling the truth.

The women finished their drinks and headed for the showers themselves. Christopher to them, seemed to be just the right type of gentlemen that they were looking for. Chelsea was very attracted to him. They were both filled with excitement about their new encounter. It had been a long time for Felecia and she was a little bored with pleasing herself. So she looked forward to meeting Christopher's friend that night at the tiki bar. Both of them showered quickly and got dressed in the clothing they had brought for a night on the town. They both looked spectacular, because both of them had chosen a simple black mini skirt and glittery tank top to show off their legs and hidden assets. Chelsea was as much of a lady as she appeared, she wore a bra under her tank top with matching panties, Felecia didn't. The one difference between the two ladies skirts was that Felecia's was Skin tight and short and Chelsea's was flared and knee high.

When they finished getting dressed, they jumped in Felecia's car and headed for the tiki bar. They wanted to arrive early so that they could get a good booth that would seat four and be in the back corner for privacy.

When Frank and Jonathan arrived Felecia noticed them first. She liked what she saw in Jonathan. She was attracted to him right away. Frank had rid himself of the smell of stale cigarettes with a mint and the cologne he always wore. He wore the patch on to ward off cravings for the night. He didn't want the lady of his desires to know that he smoked. At 8:45 Frank and Jonathan entered the bar.

"There they are. And they're early. I like that." Felecia said to Chelsea, and she gave a little wave to entice them into coming over to the booth that they had chosen.

Felecia was pleased with Jonathan's appearance. He wasn't quite as muscular as Christopher was, but he would fill the need in her all the same. Both men were dressed for a casual evening out. But Jonathan wore snake skin cowboy boots, as they were his favorite. The two men looked around and noticed Chelsea and Felecia as soon as they entered the tiki bar. Frank waved back and they both headed for the booth that the women had chosen. Frank was pleased that they had chosen a secluded booth in the corner. This would make their intentions much easier. They made their way over to the booth. Frank said "Good evening ladies, this is my business partner Randy Franklin" as he reached the booth.

Then Christopher sat as close to Chelsea as he could get without getting to close right off the bat. Randy sat next to Felecia but made sure that he didn't get too close to her either, he wanted to give the impression that he was the shy type at first. *I could get used to this guy, those boots really look sexy'* Felecia thought as Christopher introduced her to Randy.

"Nice to meet you ladies." Randy said as he sat down, directing his words to Felecia.

Felecia started to feel herself responding to Randy and his cowboy boots and a shiver went through her body when Christopher introduced Randy because of his boots. They really turned her on and she was very attracted to him. It had been a long time since she had had any action in the bedroom. His appearance excited her and she responded as she felt a tingle go down her spine. Both men had rehearsed their roles with these two women many times in their dingy little two bedroom apartment down town. They would have to secure a hotel room at the upscale hotel on the beach soon so that they could impress their two newest conquests soon. The waitress came by and said, "Hello, what will you be having tonight?"

Christopher turned to Chelsea and asked "What would you like to drink my lovely lady?"

"I would like a long island iced tea," Chelsea replied, which was her favorite drink.

Christopher then turned to Felecia and asked her "And what will you be having tonight beautiful?"

Felecia answered "I'll take a rum and cola to get the night started."

Then Christopher asked Randy what he would like. "What a coincidence that's my favorite drink Felecia, make that two rum and cola's and thank you Chris, I'll get the next round."

Then Christopher told the waitress that he would like a dry martini shaken with two olives. The waitress scribbled their orders on her pad and scurried off to fill them. Chelsea was impressed with Christopher's choice in drinks. It showed her he had class.

To make polite conversation, Christopher asked Chelsea "What do you do for a living?"

Chelsea replied "Oh we both work at the Trinity bank. Felecia here is the president and I am the vice president."

Christopher smiled and said, "That's a pleasant surprise. I was hoping to find a new bank. You see, ladies, we are both in precious gems. And we are in need of a good bank to deposit some of our merchandise."

Chelsea asked "What kind of merchandise are we talking about?"

Christopher then told her that he needed a safety deposit box to secure some rough cut diamonds and rubies that they had recently acquired. Randy was busy making eyes at Felecia, which Felecia didn't mind at all. Christopher interrupted Felecia and Randy and asked Randy what his thoughts were about using the Trinity bank for their needs.

Randy replied "Well, what a nice surprise that we should meet two such lovely ladies who are in just the business that we are in need of."

Christopher then said, "I think we should pay the bank a visit on Monday and see for ourselves, however you'll have to give us directions as we are new in town."

Chelsea chimed in and said, "Oh I'll be happy to give you directions before the nights over."

Then the conversation turned to more pressing matters like personal information.

Christopher asked Chelsea "Do you go out often?"

To this Chelsea replied "Well, I don't get much of a chance to get out"

"But you are such a lovely lady it's a shame that you don't already have a boyfriend." He then went on to say "Lucky for me though."

They both laughed. Then the music began to play. There was a live band playing at the tiki bar that evening. The waitress brought their drinks and Christopher paid in cash. This impressed both Chelsea and Felecia because Christopher gave the waitress $100 bill and told her to keep the change. According to Felecia and Chelsea this man must be wealthy to be able to throw that kind of money around so casually. The waitress was overjoyed and hoped for more as the evening drew on. Christopher was beginning to crave his habit by now but he tried to hold it at bay with the patch. He bit his lip when the latest craving hit him. Once the music started it became harder to have a conversation. So Christopher asked Chelsea if she would you like to dance? Chelsea answered "Of course that sounds great, I love this song."

So Christopher and Chelsea got up and started moving their hips to the beat of the music. They both enjoyed dancing together very much. Randy and Felecia were happy to be left alone at the table. They slowly inched closer together to make it easier to hear each other and to be able to touch each other when the time was right. Randy moved in closer and asked as politely as he could in her ear. Another shiver came with this question because he nibbled on her neck as he got close to her ear.

"So, how long have you known Chelsea?"

With passion in her eyes she responded. "Oh we went to college together. She was hired first at the bank and she got me my job. We were both promoted from there."

Randy then asked a series of trivial questions to keep Felecia interested until Christopher and Chelsea returned. He managed to gently brush his arm against hers and this sent Felecia's sexual appetite soaring. Randy inched closer and closer to Felecia as the night drew on. When Randy touched her she felt herself respond to his touch. She started to feel moist under her mini skirt. She shivered again and inched closer to him. Then they had their first kiss. It was a light kiss and he didn't linger. His sexual appetite was soaring as well, she would be a pleasure to seduce when the time came. They both enjoyed each other's company. Randy was certain that he had Felecia under his spell at least for the night.

When the song was over, Christopher and Chelsea returned to the table and Christopher waved for the waitress to return because it was time for a refill. The dancing had made him crave his bad habit even more. However it was Randy's turn to impress the two women this time. He ordered another round and did the same with another $100 bill. The waitress was ecstatic. She had hit the jackpot tonight. These two men were trying really hard to impress their ladies and she was benefitting from it immensely. After all the gentlemen had to impress these ladies because it had to look as though they had money. The gems that they intended to deposit in the safety deposit box were nothing more that cubic zirconia crystals and red glass made to look like rough cut rubies. But they looked close enough to diamonds and rubies to fool their intended audience, if need be.

When Chelsea finished her second drink she said "Wow, I'm really feeling those drinks, I better slow down a bit." To this Felecia added "Me too, I'm driving tonight."

Christopher said "I understand sweetheart, as you wish."

Then he slowed down and said "I had better watch it as well, I am driving too."

But Randy didn't have to drive so he ordered another rum and cola when the waitress came by again. Another song started and it was a slow song this time.

Christopher asked Chelsea "May I have this dance?"

To this Chelsea replied "Of course, let's go."

Christopher held her hand and gently placed his other hand on her lower back, then he drew her close to him. She rested her head on his chest and felt his muscles under his shirt. This made her tingle all over. He wanted to give the impression that he was the kindest gentleman that she had ever met. Then they began to slowly sway to the music together.

As the night wore on, the songs strung together. Everyone but Randy switched to cola's and water so that everyone would be safe for the evening. Randy wasn't concerned about drinking too much. He had plans of going home with Felecia. So he continued to order rum and cola's throughout the evening. Christopher and Chelsea wore a hole in the dance floor and Randy and Felecia grew closer and began kissing when Christopher and Chelsea were dancing. Randy asked her everything he could think of to hold her interest, when all she wanted was to get him home and jump in the sack. She hoped Chelsea could find another ride home because she wanted to bring her handsome cowboy home with her to be alone with him and get between the sheets as soon as possible.

Another song came on that Chelsea just loved. She thought to herself, *this guy is the real deal. He can dance, he works out and he's wealthy, I can't believe my luck tonight.* For Felecia, all she was interested in was a roll in the sack. But she was growing very fond of Randy with each passing moment. She couldn't wait to get him out of those clothes and cowboy boots and ravage him. Those boots really turned her on.

When the next song ended Chelsea said "I need a break, do you mind if we sit this one out?"

To this Christopher replied, "Of course, just let me know when you are ready to hit the dance floor again."

The men wanted to spend as much money on their intended targets as possible. So Christopher called the waitress over one more time and ordered a cola for himself and asked if Chelsea wanted another long island iced tea.

She said "Why yes, thank you kind sir."

Felecia was nursing a glass of water.

Then he asked Randy, "Are you ready for another?"

To this Randy replied "Of course, I'm not driving tonight." After this last drink Christopher chose to hold off drinking for the rest of the evening but Felecia ordered a cola twice to keep a drink in front of her at all times. Between the two men they must have spent at least a $700 on drinks that night because they tipped the waitress generously and Randy had a refill each time the waitress came by. But that was chump change compared to the big score that was to come. The clock struck 1:45 am and the lights came on in the bar. The bartender called last call in the busy little tiki bar.

Christopher asked Chelsea "May I take you home tonight, my lady?"

Chelsea saw that look in Felecia's eyes and asked "What about your friend?"

Christopher asked Randy if he needed a ride home and Felecia jumped in and said "I'll be happy to give him a ride." With a twinkle in her eye she winked at Randy, and the two couples went their separate ways.

Chapter Four

THEY GET TO KNOW
EACH OTHER

In the car on the way to Felecia's house, Randy rubbed her leg and held her hand to let her drive them to her house safely. He held her arm gently by the elbow and slowly kissed it starting at the fingers until he made it to her shoulder. Then he ran his fingers through her hair and smelled it. Her scent turned him on. She held his other hand and brought it to her lips and kissed him lightly on the top of the hand. This sent tingles down Randy's spine. Her scent only encouraged him to press on.

He nibbled on her ear and whispered "You are so sexy, I can't wait to get you to your house."

As he reached over and began to run his fingers up her abdomen to her breast then he pulled up her tank top to expose her rather large breasts. He bit her earlobe lightly and she responded to his this with a moan. She tilted her head to give him more access to her ear lope. He ran his hand up her skirt and felt her naked delicate area. She was smooth and this turned him on more than he could take. He began stoking her gently and slowly inserted his fingers into her one by one. She moaned being sure to keep at least one eye on the road.

"Wow I don't think I can make it to your house beautiful. You feel so good to me."

Felecia moaned again and gunned the gas pedal to get them to her house as fast as possible, she grew goose bumps all over her body when he touched her. Felecia raised his hand again to suck on his extended index finger. He shivered again from her lips on him. She had set him at ease.

Randy felt the electricity between them and responded by leaning over and sucking her on the nipple slowly while she drove them to her house.

She said "You're gonna have to stop that or I'm gonna have to ravage you right here and now."

"Just get us to your house so I can make you feel like a real woman." He nibbled on her earlobe, then he slowly moved to her neck again while he whispered this into her ear.

His desire was a rush of heat. This excited Felecia and she gunned the gas pedal again to get there as fast as she could. When Felecia got Randy to her house she opened the garage with her garage door opener and pulled her car into the garage and hit the button to close the garage door again to give them some privacy. When they were inside the garage she shut off the engine. Then he pushed her skirt up to her hips so he could see her smooth delicate parts.

"Oh God you are so sexy" He said as they began another fiery kiss.

She reached for his engorged member while it throbbed and demanded to be released from the zipper in his pants. He didn't want to let her out of the car before he finished exciting her. He began to roll her erect nipple with his index finger and thumb with his other hand. He was hot for her and would do anything that she wanted him to do.

When she was satisfied for the moment she opened the car door wide and turned to him with hazy look in her eyes. He winked at her and opened his door and got out. Then he walked around to her side of the car and pulled her from the car and held her close. They steadied themselves as they stood kissing feverishly. She jumped on his hips and he laid her over the hood of the car. She seemed very delicate next to him. She held on tightly to his neck while they walked to the back door. He carried her to the door. She ripped at his shirt to expose his chest and abdomen. The buttons on his shirt went flying. She wanted to feel his naked chest against her breasts. He pushed her tank top above her breasts once again.

He pushed her against the door while giving her a fiery kiss. She tingled all over while he did this. Before she got out of the car, she grabbed the keys from the ignition of her car. For all the intensity between them, their desire was a rush of heat. She climbed off of him and turned around to unlock the door. She fumbled with the keys while he pulled her tank top over her head again. Her back was exposed. Then while she fumbled for the right key he came up behind her and ran his tongue down her spine. This made her hot and wet. When she turned to him after she found the right key she wrapped her arms around his neck and they began another intense kiss. In a fit of passion she wrestled out of her skirt. He pushed her up against her door in a passionate rage. After she found the right key and unlocked the door. She arched her back in ecstasy and exposed her nipples so that he could suck on them. She was completely naked and he loved every minute of it.

"Oh God I love that" She exclaimed.

He pushed her up against the door harder and she fumbled with the doorknob to let them in. While he pressed her against the door it gave way and they fell in through the doorway on to the floor. Then he kicked the door closed leaving a distinct boot mark on the door. He was pleased with her best assets. Randy then kicked off his boots as she ripped at his jeans. She had to release his throbbing member that was imprisoned behind that zipper on his pants.

He then licked one nipple and rolled the other nipple between his index finger and his thumb once again. She loved this and it showed in her response. While they lay on the floor in front of the door he licked her lips gently and lingered in her delicate area. He had been watching her breasts bounce around while she moved at the tiki bar all night long. He was pleased by this. He then made his way up to her mouth while licking and kissing her body along the way. The kiss that they shared was meltingly hot. She loved the way he tasted after he had licked her in her delicate areas.

This is sent Felecia's hormones soaring. She felt her body respond to his. She was wet and a shiver went down her spine again. He joined her body while he shoved his maleness into her as hard and as deep as he could. This was how she liked it. As unpredictable as the evening had gone she loved every second of his touch on her. He couldn't wait any longer. He tingled when she found his throbbing manhood. She couldn't be more pleased. His engorged member was ready for action. The next thing Felecia knew he was moving in and out of her and she was on the verge of another series of orgasms. He rode her long and hard right there on the floor and she enjoyed every second of it. Randy filled her up when he came and she could feel every ounce of it.

After she came and he pulled out he whispered in her ear, "I want to taste you again"

He moved down into position and began licking her gently between her legs. Her private parts were shaped like a heart and he delighted in this. When he got to her delicate area he spread her lips apart and started licking her. She had another orgasm from this and offered to help him regain his hardness for her. Desire this strong couldn't be denied.

She wasn't a woman who gave herself freely to just anyone. She had a very strong sexual appetite but she was careful about who she slept with. She enjoyed the feel of him next to her. She then began licking his throbbing manhood and he grew hard in an instant.

"Ready for round two?" she asked.

He reached out and fondled her nipples which made Felecia's skin tingle. She felt another series of orgasms hit her hard. Again she arched her back and pushed her erect nipples to the sky for him to suck on while she let out a moan. He then picked her up while kissing her and biting her lip gently as she directed him to her bedroom. They fell onto the bed and got into position. The passion was intense. He thrust his throbbing manliness into her once again.

"Oh God I love that. More please." She exclaimed.

He moved back and forth slowly to see just how many times he could make her cum. The two of them went at it all night long. They didn't even take a break to have a drink of water to refuel. He was as pleased with her as she was with him. When the passion wore them out, they passed out in each other's arms and fell asleep.

Christopher was a perfect gentleman with Chelsea. He was starting to feel the effects of going without his favorite habit as another hard craving hit him. He asked her where to go, even though he knew the route by heart.

"Why does your vehicle smell like stale cigarettes?" She asked.

"Oh my business partner smokes and he insists on smoking in my vehicle, does it bother you sweetness?" He asked.

"No I guess not, you have a life too, so I will just deal with it. Sorry you have to put up with that. You seem like such a nice man." She replied.

Chelsea directed him as he drove, and when they passed the bank she pointed it out. When they got to her cottage Chelsea invited Christopher in for a night cap and he cheerfully accepted. She fixed them each a glass of white wine. They talked more about how well he did as a precious gems salesman. And she shared her personal information freely.

Chelsea offered Christopher a seat on the couch. Then she sat close by him being careful to act like a lady and not get too close. Misty was scarce for the evening. This didn't even faze Chelsea because she was so wrapped up in Christopher. Normally her cat would be all over her dates, but her cat knew something was not right with this man. So she kept her distance and waited for his departure in the bedroom keeping a careful watch from the door of the bedroom. She didn't even try to meet Chelsea at the door when she came in. She had sensed something was up from the minute the doorknob turned. Which was odd because her faithful cat was always underfoot.

Christopher asked Chelsea, "Well my princess, may I have your phone number so that I can call you up properly and ask you for a date another time?"

Chelsea was waiting for this question. She said, "Of course."

Then she went to the phone in the kitchen and picked up the pen that she kept by the phone. She grabbed a piece of paper from the note pad that she kept by the phone. Then she wrote her number on the piece of paper. She gave it to Christopher in hopes that he would call right away and ask her out before the weekend was over.

As the night grew into the wee hours of the morning, Christopher, not wanting to go too fast, said to Chelsea "I had better get going, I know you need your beauty rest, my beautiful princess."

Chelsea was swept off her feet by her handsome stranger. This was exactly what she wanted. She thought to herself, *I could really fall for this guy, what a night it has been.*

Then Christopher said, "It's past my bed time, but I hope to see you again real soon."

And with that Chelsea walked him to the door and allowed him to kiss her on the hand.

Then he said, "Goodnight sweet princess, it was a pleasure meeting you tonight."

She replied "The pleasure was all mine, good night sweet prince."

Then she closed the door then went to her bedroom to see why Misty had been so scarce all evening.

She stroked her cat on the head and said to Misty, "Well I hope you liked him because I sure did."

Then Chelsea undressed and put on her night gown, tired from a night of dancing and a little woozy from the drinks that she had consumed. She knew she would pay for it in the morning, but to her it was all worth it. She then climbed into bed and thought of whether or not he would call the next day.

When Frank left Chelsea's house he left a rose and a note under the windshield wiper of her sedan. The note said, Tonight I met a dream come true, I only hope it was the same for you. Then Frank jumped in his SUV and drove back to their dingy little two bedroom apartment to take account of the evening's events. The minute that he got into his vehicle he tore off the patch. He lit a cigarette as soon as he was out of sight. When he got home he noticed that Jonathan wasn't anywhere to be found. He laughed to himself *'That bastard did it again. He always jumps in head first before the time is ready.'* He made a call to Chelsea to say good night before he readied himself for bed. She was excited that he had called so soon. When the phone rang she was in hopes that it was her knight in shining armor.

She answered the phone with a groggy "Hello?"

Christopher then said, "Hello my princess, I just wanted to say goodnight before I got into bed myself."

She giggled and replied "Well you almost caught me asleep."

He then apologized, to which she said, "Oh no, I don't mind I had a great time tonight, I hope to see you again real soon."

With that Christopher asked her "Do you have any plans tomorrow?"

Chelsea replied "Why no, I was just going to spend the day sunbathing on my favorite beach. It's just up the road" After that Chelsea asked, "Would you like to join me, we could have a picnic on the beach?"

Christopher responded, "That sounds like a wonderful day. I would love to join you."

"Okay, it's a date then, come by around 11 o'clock and I'll be ready. We can make a day of it."

Christopher then said, "I'll be there at 11 then. Get some sleep my princess, Goodnight."

Chelsea said "Goodnight sweet prince, I'll see you tomorrow."

They both hung up the phone, and Chelsea dreamt of a life of luxury with Christopher by her side. Then Frank stripped down to the buff and jumped into bed, having dreams of the successful night that they had had. He lit another cigarette to calm his cravings for the night before he drifted off to sleep.

Chapter Five

A DAY AT THE BEACH

Chelsea slept like a baby, and awoke at 10 o'clock. It had been a long night. She was a little tired and a bit hung over but she would press on for her date with her prince. She let Misty out, so that she could get some fresh air and she noticed the rose and note on her windshield. She quickly grabbed her bathrobe and threw it on, then she raced to her car to see what the note said. She read it and agreed that that it had been a success for her as well. She was taken by surprise by the note and the rose but it only made her want him more. She would cherish this note forever she thought. It will be a good story to tell their grandkids she decided as another passing thought of them being together for life came to mind.

Then she quickly ran back into the house and got ready for her day of fun in the sun with Christopher. She had slept late and it was almost time for their date. So she quickly made a pot of coffee and then jumped in the shower and washed her beautiful long hair. Then she threw another French braid in her hair to keep it under control while the day progressed. She put on her new bikini and threw on a cute matching sun dress. She then called for Misty and the cat came running and jumped into her arms, a trick that Chelsea loved about her dear cat.

Then she made sure to pack a bag with sunscreen, two towels and a blanket to sit on. She threw her sunglasses on her head. She then brought out her picnic basket and packed it with the necessities for the day. She made two chicken salad sandwiches and some peanut butter celery sticks then she sliced up an apple and put some water in the baggie so that the apples would stay fresh. She wanted them to have enough snacks to last the day. Lastly she added a box of crackers and sliced up some cheese to munch on throughout the day. Certain that she had packed enough items to keep them from going hungry for the day, she carefully placed the items in zip lock bags individually and then she added a bottle of wine and a cork screw to open the wine with and then strapped in the two wine glasses to the lid of the basket. She also strapped the wine to the lid as was intended. She made sure that there were napkins and paper plates. She was satisfied that she had made a nutritious lunch. She wanted to make sure that she was prepared for her date with Christopher.

Before he left the apartment Frank had one last cigarette then he put a patch on his hip under his swimming trunks. He ate a mint and dowsed himself with cologne. Then he packed an ice chest with sodas and headed out the door. He stopped at the store and bought a bag of ice to keep their drinks cold during the day. He arrived at her cottage promptly at 11 o'clock as they had agreed. When she opened the door she couldn't believe how handsome he looked in the daylight. He wore a simple tank top and his swimming trunks with flip flops. She would be proud to sport him at her favorite beach.

She greeted him with a smile and said "Hello, so nice to see you. The beach isn't far from here." She added "I have packed us a picnic basket just for such an occasion."

"Well hello to you too my darling, I'm so excited that I get to spend the day with you. I brought us some sodas as well, Shall we?"

"Well I packed a bottle of wine to go with lunch, I hope you don't mind."

"No, not at all, we'll have the sodas after the wine, they won't go to waste."

She was pleased that they were set for a day at the beach. And he motioned for her to come along with him. Chelsea said to Christopher, "Thank you for the rose and the note and I agree"

Christopher was pleased with this comment and replied, "Well you make me feel so happy I just wanted to tell you so."

She giggled then grabbed her bag and he grabbed the picnic basket that she had prepared just for them. This would be a real treat for her because it would be the first time that she would not be sunbathing alone.

Felecia wasn't into sunbathing. Chelsea usually enjoyed the sport by herself. He had sprayed an air freshener in the SUV to disguise the stale smell of cigarette smoke. They hopped in his rented SUV and headed for the beach just a few blocks down the road. She didn't notice the smell of stale smoke this time.

After three blocks she told him. "This is it, Marshalls Bay beach" and pointed to the entrance to the parking lot.

They unloaded themselves, her bag, the picnic basket and the cooler from his SUV. Then they found that the beach was rather crowded but they were able to find a spot that was a little secluded, so that they could have some time to themselves. The first thing she did was take off the sundress to show him her new bikini. He was almost taken aback by her beauty.

He commented, "Your quite beautiful my dear, I'm so glad to have met you last night."

"Why thank you kind sir and likewise I'm sure."

He then removed his tank top, to which she commented, "You're quite muscular do you work out often?" He also had a very nice rippled abdomen.

He said "Well, I enjoy keeping in shape."

She returned the comment with "Well, it really shows and you look great yourself."

Then they laid out the blanket that she had packed. He was only wearing his swimming trunks now. It was clear he took pride in his appearance.

She asked him "Would you care to get a little wet before we lay out?"

"Why not, that sounds like a great start to a great day".

They then took a quick dip in the ocean and playfully splashed each other. He dove under the water and came up right beside her and she was pleased that she had invited him on this excursion.

He asked, "May I kiss you, I've been wanting to do that since I met you?" As he came up close to her.

She was impressed that he acted like such a gentleman and said, "Of course, I have been waiting for you to ask." Then they embraced while they waded in the ocean waters. They kissed lightly and then he pulled away so as not to give her the impression that he was after her for more than the simple kiss that he had asked for.

Then they returned to their blanket and dried off with the towels that Chelsea had brought. And then they began to apply sunscreen.

Chelsea put her sunglasses on and she said to him, "I have never had anyone to apply my sunscreen to my back before, thank you so much."

"My pleasure, my lady, anything for you." He delighted in being able to rub her down with the sunscreen. Then she asked, "Do you need help as well?"

"Yes, do you mind?" He replied

"Of course not, we don't want to get a burn, just a tan will do."

After they were prepared for their day of laying in the sun, they laid down on the blanket and made themselves comfortable.

The cravings started again for Christopher but he shrugged it off so as not the give her the impression that he was as much on of the edge as he was. As the day went on they talked about things to come and Chelsea's dream she wanted to have a family one day and bring the kids to this very beach to teach them to swim. This was a dream come true for Chelsea. She never thought she would meet such a nice and handsome man that she had so much in common with. Christopher was careful to keep the conversation on her so that he could really get to know her. He wanted to keep his activities as private as possible.

At noon, she opened the picnic basket and loaded a paper plate with a sandwich and a couple of celery sticks as well as a couple of apple slices that she had prepared for them in the basket.

Then she handed him the plate and he said "Thank you, my lady."

She then made a plate of the same for herself and placed it on the blanket beside her. She then unhooked the wine glasses and brought out the bottle of wine.

She picked up the cork screw and turned to him and asked, "Do you mind opening the wine?"

He happily said "Of course not, sweetheart" and she handed him the bottle of wine along with the cork screw.

Christopher opened the bottle of wine and filled the wine glasses that she held out for him to fill. They ate their picnic in the sun and enjoyed

each other's company for the day. This couldn't have worked out better if Christopher had planned it himself.

After lunch he was really feeling the cravings of his beloved cigarettes, but he shook them off as they were not a part of his plan. He was a very disciplined man and he wouldn't let a bad habit interrupt his time with this woman. Then they took another swim and she swam out a little farther than he was used to.

She yelled to him, "Come on, the waters great" so he swam to her side and embraced her tightly in the water so that he could feel her close to him. Then they swam back to the shore, dried off again and laid out in the sun enjoying the day.

Around 1 pm she asked, "Would you like some cheese and crackers to go with your wine?"

"Thank you. You really know how to treat a man." After the crackers he was really craving his bad habit but just like before he held it off to impress her. The wine had brought the cravings on.

The day was a success and both of them were pleased with the way things were going. Baring his rather uncomfortable cravings for his bad habit.

At 2 o'clock they finished the last of the wine. Then Christopher offered Chelsea a soda.

She said "Yes that sounds lovely." She thanked him for it and he opened the can of soda for her.

By 2:30 they were ready for another swim. She said to him, "I'll race ya to the water,"

Then she jumped up and dove in the surf. He chased after her and they played in the water for a while and enjoyed each other's company. Around 3 o'clock Chelsea offered Christopher some more cheese and crackers and he offered her another soda from the ice chest. She graciously accepted. It was a little snack to help ward off any hunger pangs that he might have before his dinner tonight. He was impressed with her hospitality on the beach. '*She would make a perfect mate and victim.*' He thought to himself, '*It's too bad this has to be this way because she is really a nice lady.*' He did actually have a little a heart after all. But a plan was formed and had to go through with it under any circumstance with his brother Jonathan. It meant retirement. He would just have to enjoy his limited time with her.

They were both starting to get tired from a day in the sun. So when the clock struck 4 pm Christopher made an excuse that he had a business dinner to attend and told her that he had a wonderful time with her today.

He asked "When can I see you again? I really must get going for the evening, because I already have business plans."

She replied, "Well I can't say I'm not disappointed, I was hoping that we could spend some more time together."

"Don't worry my princess I will make time for you later in the evening if you're free."

"Yes I am, what time did you have in mind?"

"Well the business meeting should run a couple of hours, I'm sorry I can't take you out to a special dinner, but maybe we could meet up for a night cap around 9 o'clock, does that sound good?"

She nodded her head and said, "I would like that very much, do you want to meet at my cottage again?"

"That sounds like a great plan, I will meet you there at 9 o'clock then tonight."

Then they packed their stuff up to leave the beach. It couldn't have gone smoother in Christopher's opinion. He was getting closer to her than he ever expected to in such a short amount of time. He had to regroup with Jonathan to see what had happened with him and Felecia since he hadn't made it back home before he left for the beach. He had to make sure that things were going smoothly with Felecia as well. So the business dinner that Frank spoke of was with his brother Jonathan that evening and their business associate Henry Cornwell, aka none other than Anthony Alvarez to the ladies. They had planned it that way so that they could make further plans on how to get as close to these two women as possible.

Christopher dropped Chelsea off at her cottage and gave her a peck on the cheek. He said his goodbyes quickly because he was preoccupied with the plans he had with his brother and he was really craving a cigarette by this time.

Chelsea said "Goodbye, I had a lovely time today, and thank you for spending the day with me."

"My pleasure, I will see you at 9 o'clock." With that he walked her to the door gave her a peck on the cheek and turned on his heel then headed for his vehicle in her driveway.

He then jumped in the SUV and started the engine and backed away giving Chelsea a wave as he left. He then tore at the patch and lit a cigarette when he was sure he was out of her eyesight. He drove off with a sparkle in his eye. Chelsea was in heaven. She let herself into her cottage and was greeted by Misty.

She said to Misty, "I think I have met Mr. Right," then she stroked her cat and Misty was pleased that Chelsea was home alone this time.

Chapter Six

THE INTRIGUE BUILDS

Felecia woke to an empty bed. She heard the shower and guessed that Randy had helped himself. Little did she know that he had bugged her whole house while she slept. She made her way to the kitchen to make them some brunch. It was almost 11 o'clock and she had some eggs on hand for just such an occasion. She scrambled up the eggs and threw some bacon in a frying pan. She then grabbed a couple of glasses and went to the refrigerator. She filled the glasses with orange juice and put them on the table in front of each chair. She did have enough food to keep them from going hungry this morning but she would have to go to the store soon if they continued to see each other. Then she grabbed a couple of slices of bread and put them in the toaster. The toast quickly popped up and she filled two plates with the eggs, bacon and toast that she had made. She buttered the toast and set the plates on the table alongside of each glass of juice.

She heard the shower water turnoff and made her way back to the bedroom. She peeked in the bathroom and said to Randy, "If you're hungry I made us some brunch."

To this Randy replied "That sounds great tiger, you were wonderful last night." He then stepped out of the shower, grabbed a towel and wrapped it around his waist. Then he made his way over to her and wrapped his arms around her and kissed her gently.

She said to him "I'll need a shower next, I hope you didn't use up all the hot water cowboy." Then she giggled.

He winked at her and replied "Of course not, I knew you would be next. But what do you say we get dirty again first?"

Felecia couldn't believe her handsome cowboy had such a strong sexual appetite. "We need to eat brunch before it gets cold first" Felecia replied then winked at him.

Randy answered "Of course, I can't wait to see what you have prepared, all that activity has made me very hungry." And he winked at her again.

He threw on his boxer shorts and she led him to the kitchen so they could enjoy the meal that she had prepared. He told her "This looks great, I'm starved."

"Well, we had quite a workout. You should be hungry." She giggled. They ate their brunch and playfully kept up the banter between them while they ate.

"Well I'm ready for a shower now, care to join me?" She said after they were finished eating.

To this Randy replied "Lead the way."

Felecia slipped out of her robe and turned on the water. Randy slipped out of his boxer shorts and joined her in the shower. They embraced each other and he became hard instantly from the feel of her up against him with water caressing their bodies. It was time for another round.

She picked up the soap and began to rub it on his chest so that they would slide together in unison. She loved the way that he felt with her naked body up against his. She felt vulnerable to his charms. Then she stepped under the shower and got her hair wet. Next she wrapped her arms around his neck and kissed him gently on the lips. He responded to her kiss and his manliness grew under her charms. She reached for him and she opened her lips for him to enter her. Then she began to move slowly so that they could reach an orgasm together. Desire moved slowly down his spine and this sent him tingling from her touch. Her desire for him rapidly crept up on her. She felt him inside of her again and this made her tingle all over. She rested her foot on the molded seat in the shower.

Having sex standing up in the shower was just as fun as it was in the bed or on the floor in front of the back door. *'I wonder how many places we can have sex in this house.'* She thought to herself. She thought of the passion that they had shared when they had sex on the floor in front of the back door.

She moved in motion with him gently, with him inside of her again and again. It didn't take long for her to have another series of orgasms. While she tightened around his engorged male part he exploded. Her orgasm gripped him tightly. They both came together and enjoyed every second of it.

She said to him. "How do you do that to me? You make me feel so good." The shivers that went her spine had returned with the new encounter in the shower. They had sex so long in the shower that they ran out of hot water. She didn't mind because he did make her feel like a real woman.

When they were satisfied he pulled out of her and allowed her to rinse off. He stepped under the shower water to rinse himself off once again. She washed her hair in the cold shower water then soaped up and washed her body off. This calmed them down for a few minutes.

She loved the way he made her feel and she didn't know if that was a good thing or not. Then she turned the water off and stepped from the shower. She grabbed a towel and dried herself off then twisted the towel around her hair in a on her head. Then she grabbed her silk bathrobe and wrapped it around her body.

"You look great fresh out of the shower tiger." He told her from the doorway of the bathroom.

She said "Thank you, you're not so bad yourself."

He loved that she was so easy to please sexually. Her appetite for sex was something that he had never experienced before in a woman. He was almost sorry that he was going to have to betray this woman in the end. But not that sad, he would play with her as long as it took to finish the plan that was set in motion now.

It was almost noon and Randy told her "I really have to get going tiger. Can I see you again?"

To this she replied "I look forward to it, when do you think you might be available again?"

"Well I have a business dinner tonight but we could meet afterwards, say around 9 o'clock."

She agreed and the date was set. "Where do you want to meet up?" She asked innocently.

He said "How about if I come over here and ravage you again." He then moved towards her and embraced her and gave her a passionate kiss. The towel fell off of her head and her hair fell around her face.

She said "I really must get dressed."

He told her. "I think I'm going to call a cab and give you some time to rest up for tonight."

She agreed and went to her nightstand for the phone. She then opened the drawer in her nightstand and pulled out the phone book.

"Here ya go." She said to him as she handed him the phone book.

"I had a wonderful time last night and this morning too. I can't wait until 9 o'clock to see you again so that I can do the things that you like and make you cum over and over again tiger." He told her while he dialed the phone number to the cab company.

Then he winked at her and ordered a car to pick him up from her house. He had to ask her for her address and he made a mental note of the address because he planned on spending a lot of time with this woman before the plan was over.

The Rolling Cab Company answered the phone and he then made an appointment for them to pick him up. She picked through her drawer for a thong and then went to her closet for a sun dress. She slipped into her thong and put the dress on and sat down beside him on the bed. She then began brushing the tangles out of her hair and left it to dry on its own. He repeated the address to the cab company. He counted on rides from cabs and his brother to get him where he was going. That way he could drink anytime he wanted to, baring his brothers demands that he not drink so much while they conducted business.

They chatted more while they waited for his cab to arrive. He knew he had to get back to the apartment or Frank would have his hide. It was only a short time later that cab honked its horn outside her driveway. He wrapped his arms around her and said "Well I guess that's my cue. It's time for me to go now, but I look forward to another eventful evening with you at 9 o'clock."

Then she told him "Goodbye cowboy, wear your boots tonight, they turn me on." and she watched as he got into the cab.

He gave a quick wave as the cab drove away. She closed the door behind him and thought to herself *what a great night.* She would need a nap before he returned. She was worn out from all the sexual activity they had shared. But she was happy nonetheless. She only hoped that Chelsea was as happy with his business partner.

Felecia wasn't one to keep animal's, she liked her life to be free of obligations. Except for her home and her car, she didn't care to take on further obligations that would strap her down. She was a free spirit and loved being that way. Anything that she felt she needed from a man, she knew she could get from a handyman or a welcome stranger like Randy. She didn't dream of getting married and having children like Chelsea did. She enjoyed being single and took comfort in the position that she held at the bank.

Chelsea was her best friend, but they couldn't be two more different personalities. She decided to lounge around for the day alone in her home waiting for Randy to return. But before she did that she had to run to the store to pick up some provisions for the evening and the morning after. She made a list for the store and left her house in her sports car with visions of the passionate night that she had spent with her handsome cowboy. She loved his nick name for her. It made her tingle inside.

She planned on taking a nap so that she would be prepared for another round with Randy tonight when he got there. She thought it was time again for her weekly waxing because Randy liked it so much. So she made a mental note to set up an appointment for her next waxing. She then picked one of her favorite novels from her book shelf and settled in to read for a while. She laid down on the couch and began reading her book. After reading a couple of chapters she drifted off to sleep because she was exhausted from her night of passion with her cowboy.

Jonathan made it back to their apartment where he had all of the electronic equipment he needed to monitor both women's every move. With the bugs set at Felecia's house, he could monitor her anytime he wanted to or needed to. It was only a matter of time before Frank got the chance to do the same inside of Chelsea's cottage. Frank was pleased that the plan was set in motion and coming together so well.

He waited patiently for Frank to return from wherever he had spent the day. But, he began listening in on Felecia because he had the technology to listen to her every move now. He was pleased with himself that he had accomplished what they would need to get the job done. He only hoped that Henry Cornwell was going to be as true to them as he seemed to be. He was their inside man at the bank. He began to get bored with the noises that came from Felecia's house because he could hear her snoring and he knew that she was resting. So he took a nap and rested up for his meeting with his brother later that night. He was exhausted from his encounter with Felecia as much as she was. He would need all of his strength to match her sexual appetite tonight.

Frank returned to the apartment at 5 o'clock. He opened the door with his key and entered the apartment with a cigarette in his mouth. He noticed that the electronics were left on while his brother rested in his room. He also noticed that he could hear a one sided conversation that Felecia was having with Chelsea on the phone. He was pleased that his brother was able to plant the bugs that he had planted. It was only a matter of time before he would do the same in Chelsea's cottage. He smoked his cigarette and turned up the volume so that he could hear more clearly. Then he went to his brothers room and saw him lying there alone half naked, dressed only in his boxer shorts.

Frank slapped his leg, and said loudly "Wake up cowboy, we got work to do, do you realize that both of them are on the phone together right now, isn't it your job to monitor the situation?"

Jonathan stirred and turned over in his bed. He said "Well hello to you too, where the hell have you been all day?"

Frank answered "I spent the day with Chelsea getting close to her what happened to you last night?"

"Well, most of it is none of your business, but let's just say the plan is in motion."

Frank countered with "That's good, let's get ready for dinner with Henry, he'll be meeting us at 6 o'clock with more information."

Jonathan smirked and said "That weasel had better come through, our plan depends upon his knowledge of the bank."

Frank returned with "Just get up and get dressed for dinner and then get in there and start listening to what you're supposed to be listening to."

To this Jonathan sat up in bed and rubbed his eyes. He didn't even get dressed when he went into the living room where the electronics were alive with the voices of Felecia listening to Chelsea go on about her evenings events. It was a one sided conversation but Jonathan understood most of what was being said. He listened in for a few minutes and was pleased that Felecia was keeping quiet about their night's events. All she would say is she liked him and they fit well together. Chelsea knew all too well what this meant so she didn't push it.

Chapter Seven

—❦—

THE BUSINESS DINNER

Chelsea couldn't wait to tell Felecia about the day in the sun with Christopher. So she called Felecia as soon as Christopher left. She picked up the phone and dialed Felecia's number. The phone rang several times. Felecia was still napping but she stirred when she heard the phone ring.

She answered it with a groggy "Hello?"

Chelsea said "Hello to you, Felecia it's me Chelsea. I couldn't wait to call you and tell you how wonderful Christopher is."

Felecia answered still in a fog she said while yawning "What time is it?"

"It's 10 after 6 did you have a long night?"

"I had a great time with Randy all night long."

Chelsea asked "So, do you like him?"

"We fit very well together, I'm seeing him again tonight, he has some business dinner to attend to then he's coming over here so we can spend some more time together."

"He must be having a meeting with Christopher, because he said the same thing. And we are meeting at 9 o'clock for a late night cap as well."

"That's what time I expect my cowboy to return." And they both giggled.

"Well, do you want to step out for dinner tonight?" Chelsea asked Felecia "It seems as though we're both going to be alone tonight to eat."

"That sounds great, where do you want to go?"

"I feel like having Mexican how about La Comida, say around 7 o'clock?"

"That sounds great." Felecia replied "I'll pick you up "

"Well, I'll let you wake up a little, you sound sleepy."

"Okay then, I'll see you at 7 o'clock. Goodbye for now."

"Goodbye I'll see ya at 7 at your house." They both hung up the phone.

Chelsea jumped in the shower to wash the sunscreen and sand off of herself for tonight's dinner with Felecia. Jonathan was a little worried that Felecia might divulge crucial information about the time she had spent with him. But based on the conversation that he had just heard it seemed as though she would keep quiet about the details of their evening.

Jonathan listened further to see what his latest conquest was up to after the phone call. He now knew where and when they would be dining for the evening. He was pretty proud of himself for being able to set up the bugs as planned. Frank finished his shower while Jonathan listened to the conversation that Chelsea and Felecia were having. He needed to wash the sunscreen and sand off before his dinner plans.

Jonathan yelled to Frank "Hurry up man, we don't want to be late. Henry is supposed to give us more information about the banks website and his password so that we can have partial access to the banks information tonight."

Frank shouted from the shower "Don't worry so much, you did your job. Let him do his."

Frank stepped from the shower and lit another cigarette he noticed that it was almost 5:30 and Jonathan was right. He needed to get a move on so that they weren't late for the dinner with Henry Cornwell. Henry Cornwell aka Anthony Alvarez worked at the Trinity bank with Felecia and Chelsea. They had hired him at the bank a couple of months ago when the Snow brothers put the plan in motion. He was to play a key role in the Snow brothers plan. This is why he took the job at Trinity bank in the first place.

He had been hired after an employee had fallen ill from the food that he had eaten with Jonathan. Jonathan had befriended him when they first started casing the Trinity bank. He had taken this employee to lunch and spiked his food with rat poison. His guest fell ill rather quickly and ended up in the hospital. Jonathan visited him in the hospital regularly at lunch time and ate with him. He spiked his food each time, so the doctors were baffled as to what was wrong with him. He just kept getting sicker and sicker.

Henry had proven himself to be a trusted partner so far, however Frank worried about his brothers temper. If Henry so much as said one wrong thing, Jonathan might just knock his block off. Henry Cornwell was born in New York City. He was had two brothers and his mother was his only surviving parent. His dad had died when he was 10 and his misspent youth was without the influence of a father figure as his mother had never remarried. A good friend of his had introduced him to the Snow brothers. He was a petty criminal who was looking for a big payoff. When the Snow brothers offered to include him in this job he was ecstatic. He didn't have any experience in the banking field but he thought he could learn it. *'After all everyone lied on their resumes didn't they?'* Henry thought to himself as he got ready for dinner with the Snow brothers.

Frank grabbed the towel to dry himself off and threw it around his waist. He then asked Jonathan "What do you have against Henry anyway?"

"I just don't trust him. Okay? Plus I'm not pleased about splitting the proceeds three ways. But we need somebody on the inside, so he'll have to do, for now."

"That's right," Frank said while he got dressed and lit a cigarette then rested it in the ashtray. "We can't afford to make any mistakes and things are going smoothly so far, just chill out and give the guy a break. We need him."

"I am on board with having him as a partner as long as he doesn't screw anything up. If he does I'll take him out."

That was a statement that Frank didn't want to hear. Jonathan was perfectly capable of pulling the trigger on Henry if necessary. Henry needed to understand his life was in jeopardy if he double crossed the Snow brothers. Frank decided to make him aware of this possibility at dinner.

Since it was closing in on 6 o'clock, Jonathan turned to Frank and asked "Do you really trust this guy?"

Frank said "Well I may not trust him with my life but he is all we have in place at the moment. We need him so don't be talking about taking him out so soon."

Jonathan smirked and said "He's just a pawn, do we really need him once he's given us what we need?"

Frank picked up his cigarette that was resting in the ashtray, took drag and blew the smoke in his brother's face then said "Don't be thinking anything other than the plan right now. We need him so keep your emotions in check."

"Okay, I'll put up with a little weasel as long as we have to, Felecia on the other hand, I could spend hours with her."

Frank replied "What did you two do last night anyway."

"I don't kiss and tell, but I have to say she is quite the tiger."

"You amaze me, it's never enough for you."

"Oh, mind your own business. I have needs and she's pretty damn good at filling them." Then he went on to say "I'm meeting up with her again tonight at 9 after our meeting."

Frank replied "I'm meeting Chelsea at 9 o'clock as well."

Jonathan told him "I know I heard all about it while they were talking on the phone,"

Frank listened in to hear Felecia say "Christopher seems to be quite smitten with you."

And Jonathan repeated this to Frank who answered "Well, I know how to treat a lady and she responded very well. By the way good job getting the bugs set in Felecia's house, it will only be a matter of time before Chelsea's cottage is bugged as well."

"Okay bro, just get them set up."

With that Jonathan laughed, and headed for his room to get dressed for the evening. Frank crushed his cigarette in the ashtray and headed for his bedroom to get dressed as well.

At 5:45 Frank and Jonathan jumped in Frank's rented SUV and headed for the seafood restaurant that they had chosen for their business meeting. There was no need to rent different cars now that they had gotten close to the girls, so Frank kept the rented SUV for their only mode of transportation. Frank had another cigarette on the way to the restaurant. Henry was waiting for them when they got there.

Frank looked at Jonathan and said "See he's punctual and I'm sure he can be trusted. Just let me do most of the talking."

"Okay bro, it's all yours I can't stand the little weasel."

Then Frank parked the jeep in the parking lot. They both stepped out of the jeep and Frank stepped on his cigarette putting it out on the ground. Then they headed for the restaurant. Jonathan was on guard because he did not trust Henry one bit. However, he gave his word to his brother so he held his tongue even though he wanted to just slap the little bastard right upside the head.

As they approached Henry at the restaurant. Frank said "Hello, how are you tonight?"

To this Henry replied "Hello, I'm bit nervous, but I'm prepared."

"Then let's go to the restaurant and get down to business."

Henry didn't so much as get at a hello out of Jonathan. This put him on guard even more. Jonathan thought to himself *What have you got to be nervous about we're taking all the risks.* But what Jonathan didn't understand is that Henry was necessary as an employee of the Trinity bank. He was their inside man. They needed him just as much as they needed each other.

As they entered the restaurant, the hostess came up and asked "Will it be three for the evening?"

Frank nodded and said "Yes a secluded booth please."

The hostess turned on her heel and said, "Right this way please."

The three men followed her to a vacant corner of the restaurant. This would be perfect. There were no other customers around to listen in on their conversation.

Frank slipped the hostess a $100 bill and said, "Do you mind keeping this area clear for the evening?"

The hostess said, "Of course not sir, it will be my pleasure." And she walked off, happy to have a $100 tip. There were only four other booths nearby. Keeping the area clear shouldn't be a problem. Frank lit another cigarette and took a drag before they could order dinner.

The waitress returned and handed them each a menu and asked them "Can I get you gentlemen something to drink? And do you need an ashtray?"

To this Frank replied "We'll all have iced tea, thank you very much. And yes please to the ashtray." He didn't want either Jonathan or Henry to get drunk during their meeting.

When the waitress left, Frank asked Henry "Well, what have you got for us?"

Henry replied "Well for starters, Harold Snipe sits by the door every day. He's the lone security guard for the bank." This was useless information because the heist would be done through the wires on the internet.

Henry continued, "He's always watching. He holds a pee shooter on his hip but I really doubt he knows how to use it or has good aim he's very old. Then Mr. Eldridge has been coming in around 10 o'clock since the heart attack."

"Okay Henry but what about security on the website. What do you have for us about the security on the computers?" Frank asked with a smirk on his face. "What else do you have for us?" He wasn't getting the information that he needed from Henry so he was getting agitated with him.

Henry started to reply but the waitress interrupted with their drinks and the ashtray. Frank thanked her and told her they needed another minute to order, so she left them to look over their menus. Jonathan already knew this information from the conversations he had been monitoring in Felecia's office. He thought to himself, *'just what I thought, he's useless.'*

Frank watched his brother closely, he knew that Jonathan would take Henry out at the drop of a hat. So he was careful to ask his next question. He had to get down to the brass tax.

Frank told Henry "Now you understand that we are counting on you and accidents can happen if things don't go our way." Henry swallowed hard and looked at Jonathan, he knew exactly what Frank meant and who would do the bidding.

Jonathan was getting annoyed at Henry for trying to give them information that wasn't useful. So he picked up his menu to decide on what he wanted.

The waitress returned with their drinks and asked "What will you be having tonight, have we decided yet?"

Frank ordered for all of them. "We'll all take the seafood platter, thank you sweetheart." And he put his cigarette out in the ashtray that the waitress had brought him. The waitress nodded and made a note on her pad with her pen. She also picked up the dirty ashtray and told Frank that she would be back with a fresh ashtray right away.

She then said "Will there be anything else that I can get you for this evening."

Frank smiled and replied "No ma'am. We'll just take the seafood platters and a refill on the iced tea. Thank you." So the waitress scurried off to fill their order, replace Frank's ashtray and refill their iced teas. Jonathan noticed that the waitress had a nice set of knockers and thought of Felecia. This made him smile, which put Henry further at ease.

"What about the website, what's your password so that we can access the banks backdoors?" Frank asked Henry, picking up where they had left off.

Henry said "Well, my password is BERMUDA123. Its where I want to settle when this is all over." Henry added. "Ms. Grey and Ms. McQuire have their own passwords and it will take some digging to figure out their passwords. But with a high powered computer with a good software package you could decipher the password for both ladies on your own. Do you have a good computer? I can suggest a good software program if you haven't picked one out yet." Henry told the Snow brothers.

Taking all this in and tucking it away for the future, Frank replied "Okay, we will be paying the bank a visit on Monday to deposit some merchandise in the safety deposit boxes. Where are they in the vault?"

"Well the vault is behind my station. When you drop off your merchandise just look for the big barred door on the left when u walk into the vault. But if you are planning on hacking into the computers you that is useless information." Henry replied

Jonathan smirked when Henry said this. He knew that they would be hacking into the Trinity banks computers with his high powered laptop that was resting at the apartment now.

Henry got nervous again, "The door inside the vault that is held tightly closed with a combination that only Ms. Grey and Mr. Eldridge are privy to." Henry forgot to tell Frank about the $500 that each teller received every morning. This would be crucial information when it came to downloading the exact amount that they would be taking during the heist.

Frank looked Henry straight in the eyes and said "Good work that will be very helpful information when we enter the bank on Monday." Jonathan still wasn't impressed with this man. Most of the information that he told them, they already knew or was useless from the conversation that he had been monitoring between Chelsea and Felecia's offices. Although he was unaware that there were 18 employees in all, he had to hold his tongue, as he had promised his brother. He really didn't need to know how many employees there were in the bank at any given time.

The waitress soon arrived with their dinners. Jonathan was happy to have something else to concentrate on. They all dug in and ate their meal. The hostess was true to her word. She had kept their area clear of other customers so they were free to talk amongst themselves.

"Is there a security wall or firewall that blocks the banks website from theft that you know of?" Frank asked Henry after he swallowed a bite of food.

Henry was still chewing his first bite, and this question caught him off guard. He swallowed hard and said "Well, um, I really hadn't thought about that. I'm sure there must be. The software that we use to secure the money is BankSecure, we like to call it BS, but that's just a joke between the employees at the bank. If u get a copy of this software you will have an easier time getting into the banks computers."

"That's good information. That means that we should be able to access the banks deepest crevices if we can get ahold of the ladies passwords. But don't worry we have a very good password decoding software package so we should be fine. We should be able to access the banks money with ease and transfer it to our bank account when we get those passwords.

All it will take is a good flash drive to copy the information on their computers while they sleep."

Henry got nervous again. "So you will just be needing the banks passwords and you will be extracting the banks money through the internet?"

"Yes that is correct Henry there won't be any casualties because we won't be going into the bank?"

"Nobody said anything about casualties. I sure hope you're not planning on killing anyone?" He asked Frank directly.

Frank told him "We'll do what we have to do. But like I said, we will download the money into our account probably over the labor day weekend." Henry waved off a sigh of relief. He wasn't sure just how far these two men would take their plans.

The waitress came back to replace Franks ashtray and refill their glasses with iced tea. She asked "Can I give you gentlemen a refill on your drinks?"

Henry chimed in "I'll take some more please and thank you very much." The waitress smiled and nodded.

Then she turned to Frank and Jonathan and asked "How about you two gentlemen, do you need a refill?"

Jonathan said "No, I'm fine."

Then Frank smiled and said to her, "Just a little to top it off, thank you." The waitress filled both Henry and Frank's glasses with the pitcher of iced tea. Then Frank said to her "We'll be needing the check soon, and thank you for your quick service." Frank said as he lit another cigarette.

The waitress smiled and said "My pleasure, can I interest you in desert?"

"No thank you that will be all." And the waitress deposited the check on their tabled and turned and left them to their conversation.

Frank place another $100 bill in the receipt book. The bill only came to $75, but Frank wanted to catch her eye and leave a big tip. So when he put the money in the receipt book he winked at her and she winked back at him. Then she came by and smiled when she picked up the money.

"Thank you sweetie. Keep the change hun." Frank told her as she picked it up.

"Oh thank you kind sir, please come again real soon, okay?"

"Will do hun, thank you again." Frank told. Then she winked at him once again. Frank enjoyed watching her walk away. At the moment his heart belonged to Chelsea but there was always the times when they were not together. So he decided that he would return and get her phone number for a change of pace one night.

Frank smiled. Henry had given them as much good information as he could at the moment. Now it was up to his brother Jonathan to break the code and decipher the ladies passwords so that they could help themselves to all that money. Frank was pleased with the information that Henry had provided for the evening, although it was light.

"Well, that sounds like a good plan. I couldn't have planned it better myself." Frank said as he lit a fresh cigarette and stood to leave the restaurant. He blew grey smoke in Henry's face as they left the table.

Chapter Eight

LADIES NIGHT OUT

Felecia picked Chelsea up and they headed for La Comida as planned at 6:30 pm. Chelsea was anxious to tell Felecia all about her time spent with Christopher. Felecia wanted to keep as much of the details about her encounter with her cowboy as quiet as possible, so she let Chelsea go on about her time with Christopher willingly. They were seated in a booth in the corner so they could be as graphic as necessary when they talked. After they were seated, Felecia asked Chelsea to tell her all about her handsome stranger. Chelsea was happy to tell all.

Chelsea started by telling Felecia about how the night ended.

"Well" Chelsea said, "He was a perfect gentleman the entire night. I invited him in for a night cap and we had a glass of wine together."

Felecia smiled and asked, "Did he try to make a move on you?"

Chelsea replied, "No, not at all, he was a perfect gentleman, like I said."

Felecia held her tongue about the events of her evening with her cowboy.

Then Chelsea said, "He asked for my phone number then he left and I got ready for bed."

The waitress interrupted them. "What can I get you ladies to drink?" The waitress said with a gruff tone of voice as she handed them both a menu. Felecia was taken aback by her demeanor.

Chelsea said "I'll have a long Island Iced tea please."

Felecia said, "And I'll take a rum and cola."

"I'll be right back with your drinks ladies." And she left them to fetch their drinks.

Felecia could tell Chelsea was smitten with Christopher. They both looked over their menus.

"Oh that Tostada Salad looks great I think I'll have that." Chelsea commented. Felecia was still going over her menu when the waitress arrived with their drinks.

"You ladies ready to order yet." The waitress said as she approached their table again.

Felecia could feel the tip dropping with each sentence that this waitress said. "I'm not quite ready yet, could you give me a minute?" Felecia replied in an intense tone of voice.

"Sure thing, I'll be back in a minute then," She then turned to walk away and left them alone to decide on their meals.

Felecia commented "I don't think that waitress knows how to be hospitable."

Chelsea felt a little uncomfortable but said, "Well maybe she's just having a rough night."

Felecia replied, "I'll show her a rough night, wait till its tip time."

Chelsea laughed nervously then said, "Well you have to admit she is efficient."

Felecia said to this comment "I can get efficient anywhere I go. Maybe I'll have the burrito combo," She said to change the subject. Then she waved for the waitress to return. This waitress was in for it for upsetting Felecia. No one rushed her when she was hungry.

The waitress returned and said, "What can I getcha?"

Chelsea chimed in quickly and said "I'll take the Tostada Salad with ranch dressing on the side, please."

The waitress noted Chelsea's order on her pad and turned to Felecia and asked, "And what'll you have ma'am?" Felecia bit her tongue from the comment she wanted to make and said instead, "Just give me the burrito combo with extra cheese"

"Sounds great ladies I'll be back with your orders in a few minutes, just let me know if you need a refill on those drinks." And she turned and left them to talk amongst themselves.

Felecia said, "Now that was a little better, but she still hasn't earned her tip."

Chelsea said, "I think she's just very busy, it's crowded in here tonight."

Felecia smirked and took a sip of her drink. "So go on." Felecia said to Chelsea.

"Well, then I had just gotten in bed and he called to say goodnight." Chelsea beamed with pride because she was certain she had found prince charming.

Felecia said "Is that it, you seem so excited?"

Chelsea returned with, "Oh I haven't even gotten to the best part yet." Felecia couldn't wait to hear what her prince charming had done next.

Chelsea went on, "We made plans to have a picnic at the beach and then when I woke up, when I let Misty out I saw a rose and a note on my windshield." Chelsea was just beaming with pride while she said this.

Felecia asked, "What did the note say?"

"Oh that's the best part, it said 'Tonight I met a dream come true, I only hope it was the same for you' He's a poet too, isn't that sweet?" Chelsea was admittedly smitten with Christopher. Felecia could tell she had lost her friend to this guy. She only hoped they were as true as they seemed. Felecia held her reservations despite the evening of pleasure she had spent with Randy.

"Then when he showed up to take me to the beach, he looked so good. I could barely contain myself." Chelsea went on to say.

The waitress arrived with their meals and had the same attitude as before. "Here ya go girls, dig in while its hot."

As the waitress turned and walked away Felecia said "That's it. This waitress should not be serving food anywhere."

"Why don't you let me treat tonight?" Chelsea said. Not wanting to make the situation worse, and knowing that when Felecia got a burr under her saddle she was not easy to calm down. "Let's just enjoy our meals?" Chelsea said.

"Fine with me, but you better not tip her big."

Chelsea replied "Don't worry so much, she's just busy." And they began eating their meals.

"What's got you so upset anyway?" Chelsea asked Felecia. "Didn't your evening turn out the way you had expected?" She continued.

Felecia said, "No, not at all, I had a great time with my cowboy, I can't wait to see him again tonight. Things went perfectly we had a great time and he's exactly my type."

"Well then smile wouldja?" Chelsea commented. Chelsea decided to just drop it as she knew she would get nowhere since this waitress had already gotten on her bad side.

So she went on about her date with Christopher. "Well" Chelsea said, "Then we went to the beach and spent the day sun bathing. He's really handsome in swimming trunks. He asked me if he could kiss me and I let him, and we had a picnic in the sun." Felecia was happy to hear that Chelsea had such a great day and night with her prince charming. She only hoped that they were the real deal.

Then Chelsea said to Felecia, "Well I am gonna have just one more drink, promise not to say anything to our waitress?"

Felecia nodded and Chelsea waved the waitress over to their table. "I could use another drink and please get my friend here another as well."

The waitress smiled and said, "Sure thing, They're on their way."

Felecia needed to loosen up a bit in Chelsea's opinion so she thought another drink just might do the trick. They continued chatting about the events of the evening and the day that Chelsea had spent with Christopher. Felecia kept quiet about her most of her time with Randy except to say that she had a great time with him and they fit well together. She knew that Chelsea was head over heels for this guy and she didn't want to spoil it for her by having a sour attitude. Besides she had her own evening to look forward to which would bring much pleasure her way. She counted on her cowboy making her feel like a real woman again and again tonight as well. About the only thing that Felecia would admit to was that she loved his snake skin cowboy boots, she said they turned her on.

Chelsea got embarrassed with that and just said, "That's great, I know how much you like those. It's good that he can make you so happy."

When they finished their meals and drinks Chelsea waved the waitress over. She asked "Can you get us our check please?"

As the waitress approached the table she was cheerful for once in the evening and said "Sure thing honey, comin right up."

Felecia cringed and said "What do you see in that woman anyway?"

Chelsea commented, "Like I said, it's busy in here tonight and she's probably having a hard night. You really gotta loosen up a little, she deserves a good tip."

"Do what you want, I wouldn't tip her much at all. She shouldn't be waitressing anywhere, but I'm not going to worry about it now since you're paying and I have my cowboy to make me happy tonight." Felecia said, before the waitress walked back up and placed the receipt book on the table.

Then the waitress said "Thank you girls for comin in, and come again anytime"

"Thank you and we will" Chelsea said. Then she went on to say "See she's friendly, she deserves a tip. I'm glad I'm paying and not you or you would stiff her, I know you would." They both agreed that that's exactly how Felecia would have handled it. But Chelsea had stepped in and taken charge of the situation so that her friend couldn't treat the waitress with anymore disdain than she already had. Just to spite Felecia and her attitude Chelsea wrote in a generous tip on the receipt, then she slid her credit card into the slot and replaced the receipt book on the edge of the table.

It was closing in on 8 o'clock and Chelsea wanted to get ready before Christopher came by. Felecia felt the same way, so they said their goodbyes and promised to keep each other posted as to what went on that evening. After all the guys had said they were going to pay the bank a visit on Monday and make a deposit. They didn't want to cost their employer any money. So Felecia took Chelsea home to get ready for her date with her handsome stranger. Felecia headed straight home after dropping Chelsea off to get ready for her cowboy.

Chelsea let Misty out of her cottager once again when she got home from the restaurant. She counted on her cat's instincts when Christopher came by. If Misty was standoffish she would take her time getting to know him. If Misty warmed up to him, she knew that she had a green light as far as her cat was concerned and then all she would have to do is get the green light from her mother as well before she would make a decision as to whether or not to get close to him.

Felecia was looking forward to spending more time with her cowboy. Those snakeskin cowboy boots really turned her on. She knew that her night would be filled with passion. Randy was due to show in less than an hour. She had been to the salon earlier in the day and had gotten her Brazilian, so she was as ready as she would ever be to see her cowboy tonight. She was smooth and soft to the touch. She knew that this turned him on too. So she decided to increase her trips to the salon to twice a week so that she would remain smooth for him always.

Frank and Jonathan were thick with anticipation to get to know Chelsea and Felecia. Although Frank had not spent the night with Chelsea yet, Jonathan was well on his way to downloading Felecia's data on her home computer soon with his flash drive. He knew that all he needed was about a half hour to gather all the information that he would need on his flash drive to hack into the banks software and transfer the stolen money into an offshore account.

Chelsea on the other hand, would be just a little bit harder to fool because she was not ready to spend the night with Christopher yet. However, Felecia was the banks President and held the most crucial information on her computer. Chelsea's wasn't as important as Felecia's was.

Jonathan would bring a fresh flash drive with him tonight so that he might be able to download the information off of Felecia's computer tonight while she slept. He would just set the alarm to vibrate on his watch and it would wake him in the middle of the night to get to work.

Chapter Nine

PHONE TAG, YOU'RE IT...

Jonathan called Felecia at 6 o'clock to keep in touch with her for the night. Felecia was at the gym so the answering machine picked up. "Hello, it's me, I'm not here, leave a message, Beep." The recorder said to Jonathan.

"Hey darlin, I miss you tonight, I can't wait to see you again, give me a call and we can chat later 555-8890" He heard the machine click off and he hung up. He just couldn't stand being away from her for even one night. She was definitely growing on him.

"What the fuck are you doing? You can't leave her this phone number. We supposed to be staying at the Regency. We better get over to the hotel room so that you can give her that phone number."

"You're right, we better get over to that hotel room and call her back. Then I will give her the right number, I'll just blame it on being new to town and all. Is that okay with you?"

"Well we better get a move on, the class only lasts an hour and she will probably call right away when she gets home."

When Felecia got back home from the gym, she noticed the light blinking on the answering machine. So she pushed the play button and listened to the messages. There were three messages for her. One from her cowboy, one from her mother, and a wrong number. She decided that she would call her mother and Randy back after her shower. She got ready to take a shower and but prepared some dinner to eat before she hopped in the shower.

Frank and Jonathan needed to get to the hotel room to call her back. Jonathan didn't want the number to the apartment to show on her caller

ID. So he waited until they checked into the hotel and went to room 504 to call her back. They left the dingy apartment and headed for the store then the Regency hotel.

Christopher offered to cook for Chelsea tonight at the hotel rom. When they arrived at the Regency, Frank checked them in under the alias Christopher Fields. He thought that this should dispel any confusion in front of the ladies.

Felecia waited patiently for Randy to call her back after the aerobics class that she had just attended had ended. She headed for the bathroom to wash the sweat off of her body. She had taken Clarks aerobics class again and it felt so good to work out. And a hot shower was just what she needed. She turned on the water then undressed then stepped under the water and dipped her head under the shower head. She then soaped up and rinsed off then stepped from the shower dripping wet.

She grabbed her towel just as the phone started to ring. It was Randy calling from the Regency. She ran for the phone and picked it up on the third ring.

"Hello" She said a little out of breath.

"Hey tiger, I missed you earlier. How are you tonight?" Randy said cheerfully. "I wanted to see you tonight." He told her.

"We are staying at the Regency and here's the correct number. Do you have a pen?" He asked. "Yes go ahead," She said happily. "It's 555-2232 room 504. That's the direct line to the hotel, just ask for room 504 and they will transfer you right up to me. Hey Christopher and Chelsea want to know if we want to have drinks and go dancing on Saturday night. What do you say, wanna go?" Randy asked Felecia,

"That sounds terrific, then we can have a late night romp in the hay." She giggled.

"Okay then, I will tell Christopher and set it up. I can't wait to see you again. Did you get your work out in?" He asked,

"Yes I did and it feels great. When can I see you again?" She asked.

"Well Christopher and Chelsea have plans tomorrow night, what do you say we get together then? Maybe I can show you our hotel room and you can help me break in the bed in my room." He replied in a seductive tone.

She giggled again and said, "I can't wait, I will talk to you tomorrow then cowboy." Then they said their good byes and hung up the phone.

Chelsea walked in the door to the phone ringing. She hoped it was her handsome prince calling. She unlocked the door and let herself in, then answered the phone slightly out of breath.

"Hello" She said into the receiver.

"Hello beautiful, I wanted to see how your day went."

"Hi Christopher it's so nice to hear from you so soon. I can't wait to see you again."

"I can't wait either, how was your day?" Christopher repeated.

"It was ok, we are having some trouble with one of our employees." Christopher knew she was talking about Anthony Alvarez.

"What did this employee do sweetness?"

"Oh he had trouble with a customer then his drawer wouldn't balance, you know bank stuff."

"Oh ok, what are you going to do about it? Is everything okay" He asked.

"I don't know yet, that would be up to Felecia. But I would give him another chance if it were me." Chelsea replied. "Ken Stevens will have the pleasure because he is his immediate supervisor, Felecia threatened to fire him herself though. So I am just waiting to see if he screws up again. If he does Felecia said he's getting the ax."

"Well let's just hope the poor guy doesn't mess up again. What's his name princess?" Christopher asked.

"Anthony Alvarez." She responded, "It just stinks because I know it's coming, and I hate to be the bad guy. So I'm dreading what's going to happen next."

"Cheer up sweetness, it will all work out. Do you want to do anything tonight?" Christopher asked,

"I have laundry to do, so I better wait tonight. You kept me busy all weekend and I didn't get any of my chores around the house done. So I better stay in tonight and get it done. I will miss you though." She said with genuine sadness in her voice.

"That's okay sweetheart, I'll go catch a show with Randy, I hear Felecia is busy tonight as well."

"Okay, that sounds good" She replied,

"When will I be able to see you again," he asked.

"In a couple of days, I'm really excited about Friday night." She cooed.

"That sounds great, I look forward to it." Then they said their goodbyes for now and hung up the phone.

Frank and Jonathan discussed the Henry situation after they called the girls and settled the plans for the night. "Now what do we do? Felecia means business. When she gets mad she gets what she wants." Jonathan said with a tiny bit of fear in his voice.

"I sure wish I could keep her. She's just my type." It was the first time Frank had ever seen his brother buckle under the charms of a woman.

"What do you mean, I thought you wanted to take him out. This is your perfect opportunity." Frank replied as he blew grey smoke into the air.

"Yeah I know, but I wanted it to be on my terms, I didn't want the girls getting involved."

"Oh you really are falling for this chick aren't you? You better take a few days off to regroup and refocus on the plan." Frank said.

"I am focused, I just didn't expect to have to take him out so soon. We still need him." "I know, but if Felecia fires him, what can we do, he's a liability then. We will have to take him out."

"Okay, my pleasure, but let's keep the girls out of it as much as possible."

"So be it." Frank said as he smashed another cigarette in the ashtray.

Chelsea opened a can of cat food and Misty came running as the scent of her food floated in the air. She brushed up against Chelsea and walked around in circles at Chelsea's feet. Chelsea put the cat food in Misty's dish and fed her. She then set about fixing herself dinner. She thought a bowl of spaghetti sounded good so she took some hamburger out to defrost and readied the kitchen for her to cook. While the meat was defrosting in the microwave and the water was boiling for the noodles, she went to the bedroom and gathered her dirty clothes to separate them for the wash. She then went to the laundry room and started a load. Next she headed for the kitchen and began cooking the meat. She made little meatballs to brown in the pan. When they were all cooked she poured some spaghetti sauce over the meatballs and put the noodles in a bowl.

Then she called her mother to ask her about their dinner plans. She dialed her parent's number and her Father answered the phone. "Hello" He said into the receiver.

"Hi daddy, how are you doing?"

"I'm pretty good sweetheart. Retirement agrees with me. How are you my love?"

"Oh daddy I'm bursting with joy. I have met the kindest gentleman and I want you and momma to meet him Friday night. I wanted to talk to mom about the menu."

"Oh so we get to meet him on Friday do we? What does he do? Tell me all about him sweetheart." He said.

"Well he's a precious gem salesman. We have been seeing each other for a week now."

"Well I just hope he treats you right sweetheart. Here's your mom." He said while handing her mother the phone.

"Hi sweetheart, how are you?"

"Oh momma I think I met mister right. I want to bring him over to your house at 6 o'clock to have dinner on Friday night. Does that sound okay?"

"Well yes it does, I would love to meet the man who has stolen my daughters heart. What did you have in mind for dinner."

"Well you know how much I love your meatloaf roll. Would you make that?"

"Of course dear. Whatever you want. I look forward to meeting him. It's an old recipe that has been passed down to me and I think it will do just the trick." Her mother said, then they said their goodbyes and hung up the phone with the dinner plans set for Friday night.

Her mother made out the shopping list to make her famous meatloaf roll and made plans to make the meatloaf roll with mashed potatoes to go with it. This was always a crowd pleaser. Chelsea knew that he would love it and she would enjoy that her mother was making it for him. She missed her prince tonight. She was really growing fond of him now. She couldn't believe her luck. He seemed perfect for her as far as she could tell. She still had this nagging feeling that Misty had provoked, but she brushed it off for now and decided that she would just take things slow and see where they went. For now she was as happy as she could be. She would get her Mothers opinion of him and decide whether or not she should continue to see him after that.

Felecia headed for the kitchen to fix herself something to eat. Her fridge was close to being bare, she hated cooking. So she made a bowl of canned soup for dinner and declared the night a success. She was exhausted from all the sexual games her and Randy had played. She really needed a couple of nights off to regroup. She wanted to get to bed early to be rested up for tomorrow's day. She thought of the mistakes that Anthony Alvarez was making and decided that he had to go. She would have a talk with Mr. Eldridge tomorrow about him and ask whether or not she could fire him this week.

Frank stayed in the hotel room incase Felecia called. He would just tell her that Jonathan was asleep if she called. Jonathan spent the night in the apartment so that he could listen in on what was being said between the girls that night, which is something that he had grown fond of doing and why he decided to stay in the apartment that night instead of wait for Felecia to call back. Frank fixed some dinner and Jonathan ordered Chinese food to have at the apartment. Jonathan was famished and he always loved Chinese food. He thought about what to do with Henry. Jonathan took out his revolver, he liked looking like a cowboy too so he carried his pistol with him just incase he needed it. He called Frank in the hotel room to discuss the plan further. So he dialed the number to the Regency hotel.

Frank answered the phone with a seductive tone because he thought it was one of girls calling.

"Hello." Came the voice of his brother.

"Hello Frank Its me Jonathan." Jonathan said to his brother. "What's up" Frank asked.

"Well I just wanted to talk to you about Henry. I'm getting nervous that he may get fired and that would not be good at all. What do you think?"

"Well he may not be the brightest light bulb in the box but he's all we have in place at the moment. So put the revolver away and stick to the plan for now." Frank said this with a tone of authority. "Why don't we wait and see what Felecia does first. I don't want any blood shed unnecessarily."

"I'm dying to take that idiot out. First we have to split it three ways. Then we have to put up with his incompetence. Next you'll be singing him lullaby's to put him to sleep at night and tuck him in. Quit babying him and let me do it." Jonathan said with authority.

"Look when Felecia makes up her mind about it we will make up our minds. Got it! Now focus on the plan." Frank snarled at Jonathan.

"Alright, but I'm gonna call her back tonight and question her about her day, maybe she will give me a sign or something so I will know what's going on with that."

"You do that and then we will make a plan for Henry." Frank said with disdain. He really didn't want to hurt anyone. But Henry was screwing up. Jonathan was anxious to take him out and the pressure was building. The time was getting near.

The phone rang at Felecia's around 8 o'clock, she answered with a groggy hello. "Were you asleep tiger?"

"I was just dosing off, what's up cowboy?"

"Well I missed you tonight and wanted to talk to you a little."

"Okay, what did you want to talk about?" She said as she woke up a little.

"I was wondering how your day went. It can't be easy being the boss over so many people. How was your day?"

"It was just another day, I'm getting ready to fire one of my tellers because he's incompetent, but that's about it."

"Really, what did he do?"

"What didn't he do is the question. He's just not getting it. He's been with us for a couple of months and things just are not going well with him."

"Oh okay, well I'm sure you know how to handle him, you are my tiger you know that don't you?"

"Why that's an awful sweet thing to say, yes I am and you are my cowboy." She said with a handful of doubt.

She was growing board with him and she doubted that she would keep him after this weekend. She really enjoyed the sex but relationships aren't built on sex alone. Besides she was growing weary of his insecurity.

"You sounded like you were about to go to sleep, why don't I let you go so you can get your beauty rest." Randy said into the phone.

"Okay, thanks for calling again, I did miss you tonight but I had other pressing matters to attend to. I will see you soon cowboy."

"Goodnight tiger." Randy replied and they both hung up the phone.

"Well she's gonna do it." Jonathan turned Frank and told him. "Okay, then we better take him out. We meet up with him again tomorrow at lunch. Then we will take him up to the old Bayou Rd. and take him out tomorrow. We will just have to do without him." Frank said with a somber tone. He really didn't like this part of the job. He had a heart after all and he was a bank robber not a murderer.

"You know this changes the plan." Jonathan said to Frank. "I know, I know, now we have to call him and pick him up. We will just say that you only know the way to the restaurant and don't know how to give him directions, new to town and all. Then we will take him out to lunch and ply him for any last bit of information and then take him for a ride and you can do whatever you want to him."

"He should do well sleeping with the fishes." Jonathan said with a smirk.

"Oh would you knock it off, you know I don't like that thing and I don't like killing." Frank said as he pointed at the revolver on the table.

Jonathan reached for his gun, and said, "I can't wait to hit him, I didn't want to split anything with him anyway."

"Just make the call." Frank snarled at Jonathan again. So Jonathan dialed Henry's number and he picked up on the first ring.

"Hello" He said with a touch of fear in his voice because he recognized the phone number on caller ID on is phone.

"Hello Henry, its Jonathan. We need to change the plans for tomorrow. We will pick you up for the ride to the restaurant and take you back home. You better be ready at noon. We will be by to pick you up then." Jonathan spit out at him with disdain in his voice. Henry was taken aback that Jonathan had called instead of Frank. He so didn't like Jonathan. But who was he to question their plan. So he went along with it anyway.

"Great, thanks, we'll see you tomorrow at noon, don't be late!" Jonathan hung up the phone with that said.

"See you can be nice to him when you want to be." Frank said sarcastically.

"What other plans will we have to change because of this idiot." Jonathan remarked as he walked into the bathroom and relieved himself without closing the door.

"We will have to be in and out before the customers get there for one thing. And now I think we should be there before the employees get to work." Frank replied

"We will just have to depend on the ladies for information. We should plan on tying up the early birds and say at 8:00 am and make them open the vault to let us into it and Felecia can let us into the cash room. What do you think of that?" Frank asked Jonathan. They knew nothing of the time locks on the doors.

"I really hate the idea of taking my tiger hostage but if it has to be done then so be it. I'm just glad it's you who will be holding the gun on my tiger, it's too late for attachments now." Jonathan said with a hint of sadness in his voice.

"You have really fallen for her haven't you?" Frank asked

"No I'm just having fun, when the time comes you can count on me." Jonathan replied. "I better be able to count on you. Everything depends on it." Frank said angrily.

"So what else are we forgetting?" Jonathan asked.

"I won't know that until we talk to Henry tomorrow. He may have forgotten to tell us some important detail." Frank said.

"Well I hope the idiot gets it straight tomorrow and I will take pleasure in removing him from our little partnership." Jonathan said with a smile as he twirled the barrel of his gun.

"Would you put that thing away, it makes me nervous!" Frank told Jonathan.

"Alright tough guy, I'll put it away for now. But I can't wait to use it on Henry. Thanks bro for the all clear on this."

"Oh this isn't gonna be pleasant why are you smiling like that. Sometimes I wonder about you. It's a wonder we haven't gotten caught before this based on your penchant to kill." Frank replied. "You act like you want to get caught" He continued.

Jonathan interrupted and said, "Wait just a minute, I haven't done anything that would put the plan in jeopardy yet have I? What makes you think I can't control my temper?" Jonathan asked angrily,

"Well put that damn thing away then, and no you haven't, so let's keep it that way." Frank spat back at his brother.

Jonathan did as Frank asked and holstered his gun. He didn't need his brother anymore uptight than he already was. Frank lit another cigarette and blew grey smoke in Jonathan's direction.

"When do you see Chelsea next?" Jonathan said to change the subject.

"Friday night she's taking me to dinner at her parents place." Frank replied.

"That's great, maybe you can get into her pants finally after you are done with dinner." Jonathan said with a smirk on his face.

"I'm not after that right now. I have my head in the game. All I'm thinking about is the plan right now. So get you mind out of the gutter wouldja?" Frank replied.

"I can't get enough of my tiger, I will see her Friday too then, if she will let me."

"You almost sound whipped brother of mine." Frank said and smiled.

"Oh don't go thinking that, I'm just having fun with this one. She really is a tiger, and I can't get enough of her at the moment. But when the time comes I will let her go just like we agreed." Jonathan replied.

Neither of them would admit that they had fallen hard for both ladies. It would be harder than they expected to betray these two ladies when the time came. For now they decided on their own that they would keep their true feelings to themselves and stick to the plan.

Since things had changed so drastically, they would need their heads about themselves to make the plan work. They had everything in place for now,

"Maybe we should move up the date that we plan to rob the bank." Jonathan suggested.

"First we should take into consideration that the armored truck schedule shows that there will be an 8:15 am delivery the Friday before Labor Day weekend. The armored truck will deliver the money that comes on that Friday before Labor Day to replenish the banks funds for the next week and pick up the deposits for that week. So we should rob it on the Friday before the big Labor Day weekend, since Henry will be out of the picture this week."

They thought this should be an easy pull, but this time they got their hearts involved and that could lead to complications. The original plan was to pull the heist on the Monday before Labor Day weekend which was coming up in two and a half weeks. Frank thought and thought all night about all the possible scenarios. He wanted to be prepared. They would take Henry out tomorrow and then stick like glue to the ladies until the Friday before Labor Day weekend in two and a half short weeks.

The plan had to be fool proof. They would have to lock Felecia up in the vault before they left the bank with the money in hand. Frank was really upset about having to betray Chelsea this way, but the plan came first. They had too much wrapped up in the plan to let it go now. The Trinity bank was their next target. Little did the ladies know they were being set up by their handsome suitors.

Frank had been chain smoking all night while they talked about the plan. He would be glad when this was over so that he would calm down a little bit and cut back on his smoking. His lungs were starting to hurt from all the extra smoking that he had been doing. He was up to two packs a day which was twice the amount he usually smoked. Then they would head for parts unknown with their stash in hand and live out their lives on some sunny beach somewhere. This would be their last heist, and he wanted it to go well. That is why they used an inside man this time. With all the other banks that they had robbed, the plans had been different each time to throw off the cops. But it had never included such beautiful women that they would need to get so close to.

They thought about it more and Frank realized that they would be losing their inside man. Who would tie up the hostages and send them over to Jonathan to watch over them? Then Frank thought about his friend Charlie Wright. He was in South Carolina out of work right now but he could take a late flight and be in place right away. They would just need to get him hired by Felecia and then he could tie the hostages up when they showed up for work. Then take them into to the conference room right by the door for Jonathan to watch over them.

Frank smoked one last cigarette before he went to bed. He would just tell the ladies that their third partner had had a cigarette in the hotel room and that is why it smells of stale smoke. This was a fact that Jonathan was not pleased with. Frank enjoyed his last cigarette of the day. Hell he enjoyed every cigarette, but the end of the day and bed time was his favorite time to smoke. He finished his last cigarette of the day and headed for his bedroom. Felecia hadn't called but it was nice to sleep in a nice bed for once. They would go over the tapes to see if the girls had called each other and spoke of anything important. He was growing weary of that dingy little two bedroom apartment that they had set up for this job. He would be happy to let that part go.

He stripped down to nothing and hopped into bed, then dialed Chelsea's number. He so enjoyed talking to her at the end of the night and tucking her in so to speak.

"Hello, prince charming," came the voice on the other end of the line.

"Hello princess, I just wanted to say goodnight before I turned in for the night."

"Well I'm glad you called, I so enjoy hearing from you just before I go to sleep."

Christopher smiled and said, "You make me smile too beautiful. I can't wait for Friday."

Chelsea was excited about Friday night as well. "I can't wait till Friday either. I only hope you enjoy what mom cooks." She said to him in a sweet voice.

"Oh I'm sure whatever she cooks will be fine my lady, you just keep my plate warm for me and I will be there at 5:45 to pick you up. By the way, I have another business meeting tomorrow night, so I can't see you until Thursday would you like to go to lunch or maybe a movie that night?" He asked.

"We all have things to take care of as well, so I can't wait to see you until Thursday night then." Chelsea replied.

Christopher was pleased that Chelsea didn't have a problem waiting until Thursday to see him, he needed a little distance right now to stay on track. They had a job to do and an unpleasant part of it was tomorrow.

"I will see you Thursday then my lady, and I can't wait to see what your mother cooks for us." Christopher replied.

"Well, will I talk to you tomorrow?" Chelsea asked.

"Of course, I can't go a day without at least hearing your voice babe. Get some sleep now and I will talk to you tomorrow."

"Goodnight sweet prince," She cooed into the phone.

"Goodnight sweetness," he said back to her. And they both hung up the phone then faded off to sleep.

Chapter Ten

THE MORE TIME THEY SPEND

Frank had raced home to see if Jonathan had spent another night with Felecia. When he walked in the door and saw his brother's bed was empty, he knew exactly what he was up to. He lit another cigarette and headed for the recorder to listen in on the two of them. He didn't hear anything so he figured they must have worn themselves out. But he was pleased nonetheless, because the closer Jonathan got to Felecia and the closer he got the Chelsea, the better chance they would have carrying through with their plan.

He undressed and jumped into bed, knowing full well that he would not see his brother again until tomorrow. He took another drag then blew the smoke out and put his cigarette out then jumped into bed and closed his eyes then fell fast asleep after saying goodnight to Chelsea, knowing that the plan was put in motion and it was just a matter of time before he would get closer to her. He knew that his brother was working Felecia just the same. He was pleased with himself for being able to plant the bugs in Chelsea's cottage so they could keep closer tabs on both women. He just needed to bug her phone as well. That was a job for the next visit to her cottage. He knew she had two phones, one in the kitchen and one in the bedroom. So all he had to do was plant the bugs while she was in the bathroom. A task he was sure he could pull off the next time they were at Chelsea's. He would just make sure that she drank enough to make her have to use the restroom more than once.

Randy stirred around 3 am, and wandered into the kitchen for a drink of water. Felecia awoke when he removed himself from the bed because he unwrapped her arms from around him. "Where ya goin' cowboy?" She whispered into the night.

"Don't you worry your pretty little head, I'm just going for a drink of water. Can I get you anything?"

"Nah, all I need is you for tonight. Why don't you come back to bed and see what I have to offer you again?" Felecia whispered back to him with a hint of seduction in her voice.

Randy replied "You have worn me out, but I'm up for anything that you have to offer. I'll be right back" Then he slipped into the kitchen and got himself a drink of water. As she stirred every time that he left the bed, he considered himself lucky that she had stayed asleep while he planted the bugs.

He returned to find Felecia laying naked across the bed ready for another round of play. He snickered and jumped into bed. He was ready to ravage her once again. Just the sight of her heart shaped mound turned him on. He grew hard almost immediately. She gently stoked him and made him harder for her. He kissed her neck and then he made his way down to her breasts, where he spent some time sucking on her nipples once again. He knew this aroused her and he wanted her to be as wet as possible when he entered her again.

She opened her legs and he put his fingers inside of her and ran his tongue around her lips and began sucking on them. She grabbed his throbbing manly member once again and began stroking him and then she moved into position and he slowly inserted him inside of her from behind. They moved in unison together and enjoyed every second that they spent together in bed. She climaxed again and again, this man could make her cum just by looking at her it seemed. Randy felt her grip him and he began to cum as well each time she climaxed. She shook with delight and fell back asleep after they were finished. He collapsed on top of her and fell fast asleep as well.

In the morning, Felecia and Randy jumped in the shower and had another round with the suds covering their bodies. She got wet under the shower head and reached for his erect member. Then he rubbed soap all over her delighting at every curve of her beautiful body. She really took pride in looking her best. When she lifted her leg and placed her foot on the seat in the shower he inserted his fingers into her and found her G-spot. This sent her into another series of orgasms and she let go once again. After she came she helped him regain his composure and then she slid him inside of her once again. They moved back and forth together while he was inside of her. She moaned again and arched her back while tingles went down her spine.

"You make me feel so good." She said to him while he plunged himself deeper inside of her. She climaxed with this movement and she gripped his engorged member once again. They decided that they were made for each other in bed. She would really hate to see him go when the time came.

When they were wore out from the passion that they had shared, they both moved one by one under the shower head and rinsed off. The then turned the water off and stepped from the shower. They made sure that they didn't lose the hot water this time. She grabbed a couple of towels as well and tossed him one. Then they quickly got dressed and Felecia threw on her robe and headed for the kitchen. She was famished and she knew her cowboy would be as well.

Felecia loved to be naked so she didn't even try to get dressed, she just threw her silk robe around her as she chatted nonchalantly with Randy as he wondered around her house in his boxers. She prepared them a tasty breakfast because they had to get going for the day. Randy had the appointment at the bank with Christopher and Felecia was looking forward to showing him her office. He wore his boxer shorts around her house all morning as they got to know each other better. This was the plan that Frank and Jonathan had made before they got to know these two women. So Randy didn't feel the slightest bit of loyalty to this woman because he knew in the end she would be his victim. He had to get as close to her as he could emotionally, because the plan depended on it.

Around 7 am Randy told Felecia "Well hot stuff, I had better get going, we have a long day ahead today and you have worn me out."

Felecia laughed and said "I didn't hear any complaining coming from you last night or this morning."

Randy laughed along with her, but he knew it was time to go. So he asked her "Do you mind if I call a cab again?"

Felecia replied "Sure cowboy, when will I see you again?"

Randy said "Well, we were planning on stopping by today at the bank. We have some gems that we need to secure."

Not wanting to talk about business Felecia just brushed off his comment and moved in closer to him wrapped her arms around his neck and gently kissed him, She bit his lip gently and asked "When might I see you privately again?"

This was so unlike her but she was really starting to like this man which in Felecia's opinion wasn't a good thing. Randy grabbed her and said "Just soon as I can tiger." Then he kissed her gently and pulled away to ask for the phone.

"Here ya go cowboy, don't be a stranger."

"Oh I wont, you can count on that." Then he dialed the cab company, a number he now knew by heart, and asked for a cab to pick him up from her house once again. When the cab arrived he left her house but he turned around and gave her a quick wave before he jumped into the cab.

Felecia waved back and watched him leave as he drove away in the cab. She was completely satisfied by this man and wanted more as soon as she could get it. But she was patient, she knew she would see him again very soon, and then they would cum together as one once again.

In the morning Chelsea anxiously awaited on the call from Christopher that would take her on her date to the movies with him tonight. She had already called the Cineplex this morning to see what was playing instead of waiting on him to choose the movie. She wanted it to be romantic so she picked a romantic comedy that she wanted to see. She also did this so she would have a time in mind that he could pick her up for their date together. As the clock struck 7 am the phone rang. She knew it was him calling for their morning chat.

"Hello" she said to him as she answered the phone.

"Good morning beautiful," Christopher said into the phone.

"I called the Cineplex and I know just the movie I want to see. What do you think about a romantic comedy?"

"That sounds just like you and I would be delighted to spend the night with you watching a romantic comedy together. What time does it start?"

"8 o'clock. Is that okay?" She asked him.

"That's perfect, it gives me just enough time to hop in the shower and come over and pick you up before the show begins."

She giggled and said. "I can't wait to see you again"

Christopher replied "Well baby I can't wait to see you either. I am so looking forward to spending the night with you."

She giggled once again and said to him, "You are such a sweet man."

"I'll see you around 11:30 to make our deposit of gems at the bank, then we can look forward to our evening tonight. What do you say we take you and Felecia to lunch after we make our deposit?"

"Of course, I can't wait to see you again today and I would love to have lunch with you today. I will tell Felecia when I see her at work." Chelsea said. They said their goodbyes and hung up the phone.

Felecia readied herself for work. She was a little worn out but she could handle it. Randy was proving to be a great bed partner. She had a big smile on her face as she locked her door and jumped in her sports car to leave for work. She wanted to impress Randy, so she wore a tight fitting dress suit that complimented her breasts. She didn't want to encourage sleazy work attire so she kept it simple and pulled her short hair back into a bun. She made the short drive to the bank so that she could get the money ready for the tellers for the day.

Chelsea couldn't wait for Christopher to see where she worked. She was filled with excitement. When it was time to go, she picked up Misty and gave her a light kiss on the forehead. "When are you going to meet my prince, missy? I trust your judgment, I need your input. Please stick around tonight so you can meet him?" Chelsea chatted to Misty as Misty jumped from her arms and strutted away with her tail in the air. Chelsea thought to herself, '*I wonder if she is trying to tell me something by not being around.*' It was the first time she had doubted her prince. "Maybe I should listen to you, missy. I guess it's time to invite him over to meet mother so I can get her opinion." She said as Misty strutted away.

Chelsea then fed Misty and headed for the door. She locked up her cottage tight and jumped in her sedan. She was a little uneasy about the way Misty was acting around Christopher. But she brushed it off because she liked him so much. *'How could he possibly be bad for me?'* She thought to herself as she made her way to the bank.

Chelsea wanted to have Christopher over to her parent's house for dinner soon. She decided she would bring it up when he called next time. She didn't think bringing it up when they came to the bank today was a good thing, so she decided to wait to ask him over to meet her parents. She was so excited that he was turning out to be everything that she wanted, or so she thought. She couldn't wait to introduce him to her parents. He had no idea that she was planning this but he would go along with whatever she wanted to get closer to her.

She had to work today but she also wanted to plant the seed of meeting her parents as soon as possible. She wondered if it was too soon and questioned Misty's behavior once again. But she wanted to introduce him to her parents really bad. She knew that her mother would give her, her opinion on the situation. She hadn't slept with him yet as was her style. She never jumped into bed with anyone this soon. But with Christopher it all seemed so easy to get close to him and he was such a gentleman that she was sure that he was everything that she wanted.

Just then the phone rang. "Hello prince charming, how is your morning going?"

"Well hello sweetness, I'm having a good morning so far. It's better now that I am talking to you. How did you sleep?"

"I slept very well with visions of you dancing around in my head. You know I dreamt about you last night." She cooed.

"Well I hope it was a good dream then."

"Oh yes, it was a very good dream. We were in bed and we made love and it made me feel so secure in you that it made me want you even more."

"That's great sunshine. I love that you dream about me."

"I have a question for you." She said to him seriously.

"What is it sweetness?"

"Well things seem to be going so well for us I was thinking it would be nice to introduce you to my parents. I would so like you to meet them? What do you say we make dinner plans on a Friday night?"

"Well that sounds terrific sweetheart. I would love to meet your parents."

"I normally wouldn't ask this soon but I have fallen for you pretty hard. It seems like I can't get enough of you my prince."

"Well I think that's a good thing princess." He told her in between drags. He blew grey smoke into the air and smoke came out of his nostrils.

"Okay I was thinking this Friday, what do you think?"

"Sounds good princess, I can't wait. I will let you go for now and I will see you at the bank soon."

"Okay I will see you at the bank around noon. Goodbye for now sweet prince."

"Goodbye for now baby." And they hung up the phone.

Chapter Eleven

PREPARING TO MAKE
THE DEPOSIT

Frank lit another cigarette and let himself into their two-bedroom apartment. He had run to the store to purchase his beloved cigarettes. He found Jonathan listening in on Felecia and Chelsea's conversation.

"So we have lunch plans today, huh" Jonathan said as Frank walked in the door.

"Yes how did your night go" Frank replied.

"It was great, thanks for asking bro, and how was your night?"

"A success as usual." Frank replied, then went on to say, "We're supposed to meet them at 11:30 and rent a safety deposit box and put our fake gems in the box for safe keeping. They won't know the difference because they look just like real diamonds and rubies but as you know the rubies are just red glass and the diamonds are cubic zirconia stones."

"Excellent, what about the bugs?" Jonathan asked

"Safely planted at Chelsea's. I will get the phones next time I am alone in her cottage. Did you get he bugs set at Felecia's?" Frank asked his brother this while putting out his cigarette in the ashtray.

Frank was content to not know what went on between Jonathan and Felecia so he didn't push it when Jonathan told him, "Yes the bugs are in place and as far as Felecia and I, let's just say we fit well together. Let's just stick to business. When do we meet up with that Cornwell again?" Jonathan asked

"In a couple of days. Give it time. We need to know the girls better. Just be patient." Frank replied

"Oh I can take this kind of patience any day of the week. She's a real tiger." Jonathan commented.

Frank walked over to listen in on the conversation that the two women were having at their office. He lit another cigarette and let it rest in the ashtray on the table that held the recorder. He was pretty proud of himself for his handiwork and Jonathan's as well, he was even impressed with Henry's handiwork for planting the bugs in the ladies offices. It was safe to say that these women would have no idea what they were in for when the time came to rob the bank. Frank picked up his cigarette and took another drag then he went into his bedroom because he wanted to leave the surveillance to Jonathan. Frank took another drag and blew grey smoke into the air filling his bedroom with smoke once again. Jonathan listened intently to the conversation that the two women were having, while Frank readied himself for their meeting. Jonathan was pleased that Felecia was keeping the events of their evening to herself. After all, he didn't like to kiss and tell anything and he liked a partner to do the same.

Frank came out of the bedroom in his boxers with his newest cigarette hanging from his mouth and said "I really hate to betray Chelsea, she is such a sweet lady."

"Oh c'mon now don't let your heart get involved, you can be a real sucker for the ladies sometimes." Jonathan replied.

"Don't worry, I got it, you don't worry about me she's just beautiful that's all. Under different circumstances I could really fall for this lady."

"Well, we need to stick to the plan so keep your head straight, wouldja?" Jonathan said sarcastically. Frank took another drag and blew the smoke into the air towards Jonathan.

Frank thought of Chelsea frequently throughout the morning. Frank headed for the ashtray and took one last drag then smashed the cigarette out. Frank had started to chain smoke because it was the only way to keep his emotions in check. Jonathan could tell his brother was preoccupied with this chick because he was chain smoking, a habit he had when a woman was involved that he liked.

"It's a shame that I couldn't meet her under different circumstances, because she's just the type of woman that I would like to settle down with." Frank replied *'I'll just have to enjoy the time I get to spend with her now.'* He thought to himself again. Not wanting to let Jonathan know what he was thinking Frank lit another cigarette.

"You know those things are gonna kill you one day." Jonathan said to his brother.

"Oh mind your own business." Frank replied. "I can think of a few things that you should refrain from doing as well. So don't push it."

"Oh really, and what might that be." Jonathan retorted.

"Well for one thing you have a penchant for drinking. Can't you go just one meeting without it?"

"My drinking is nothing compared to your smoking, and what about the second hand smoke and I can't believe that that chick hasn't caught you yet."

"Well I guess we both have habits that we could work on. Maybe after the heist I will either cut back seriously or quit all together." Frank told his brother. Jonathan just smirked when Frank said this, he knew his brother would probably never quit smoking those disgusting things.

"It won't be soon enough for me." Jonathan commented under his breath, not wanting to upset Frank.

Then Frank came out of his bedroom dressed in a suit and tie to look the part they would play today. At 10:30 am Jonathan got dressed and readied himself for the meeting at the bank. Frank lit another cigarette. He would have to go to the gym soon to work out his muscles so that he could stay in shape for Chelsea. He didn't want her thinking that he was a slouch when it came to exercise. So he planned to attend the same gym where he had met the ladies last Friday night. He knew that he was going to have to secure a hotel room soon so that he could keep up appearances with Chelsea. A double suite would do just fine at one of the finest hotels on the strip.

After he dressed he entered the living room to find Frank listening in intently on the two girls in their offices.

"Well, are you ready for lunch today Felecia?" Chelsea asked.

"Of course, I just hope he wears his cowboy boots again." Felecia replied. "I'm a sucker for those boots that he wears."

"You must really like him then," Chelsea replied.

"Oh he's just fun to spend time with, another guy will come along in due time." Jonathan heard what Felecia said and he was disappointed to hear this because he wanted to make sure that Felecia was seeing only him. He would have to step up his time with her so that she would fall for him and the plan would come together. Little did he know that if he tried to get too close to her or spend too much time with her she would pull back and he might just find himself kicked to the curb.

"Anything good?" Frank asked his brother.

"I am worried about Felecia falling for another guy, so I have to make sure that I stick to her like glue so that the plan goes through without error."

"Don't worry so much, you heard it yourself that she likes you and we're seeing them for lunch. Just relax a bit and take it slow with her so that you don't scare her away." Frank replied as he took another drag and blew grey smoke into the air.

"You don't understand, she is the love em and leave em type of woman. I really need to stick close to her to keep her in my sights to make for the plan go through."

"Okay, if you are worried take her to a restaurant for dinner tonight and stick as close to her as you can," Frank replied.

"Don't worry bro I gotta plan to keep her close." Jonathan said to Frank.

Frank took another drag of his cigarette then he said "Well I'm sure that Chelsea is well under my spell," then he continued "It's almost time to go"

Jonathan had been sitting around in his boxer shorts in their apartment all morning while he listened in on the ladies conversations. He didn't hear anything new, but he was sure that they were going to divulge precious information that will be crucial to their plan eventually.

Since there was no need to take pictures of the girls any longer and rent various vehicles, Frank stood back and looked at all those pictures of his beloved Chelsea and had second thoughts for just a minute. However he had already set the plan in motion and Jonathan was counting on him, so he couldn't have Chelsea even if he wanted her.

Jonathan depended on Felecia, Frank and cabs to get him where he was going. He liked the freedom of not driving all the time. That way he could drink when he wanted to. Frank planned on heading to the Regency hotel that afternoon and renting a two bedroom suite, to keep up appearances. He would have to pack a suitcase and bring his briefcase to this hotel room so that Chelsea would see that he was what he said he was. He would be able to blame his smoking in the hotel room on his silent partner as well.

At 11:15 Frank asked Jonathan "Are you ready to go yet?"

Jonathan replied "I've been ready for an hour now." But Jonathan was wearing a button-down shirt and jeans, not exactly the attire that two businessmen would be seen wearing while they were doing business.

Frank told Jonathan "Go get dressed into something more professional, so we can look the part you idiot."

"Don't talk to me that way, or you'll be sorry."

"Just get dressed now!" Frank demanded "It's almost time to go. We don't want to be late."

"Alright already, I'll put on something less casual, but I'm wearing my cowboy boots. Felecia really likes them."

"Whatever bro, just get dressed into something more appropriate." Frank demanded.

Frank crushed his cigarette out in the ashtray on the desk. Jonathan retreated to his room to get dressed in a more professional outfit. Frank lit another cigarette while he waited for Jonathan to get dressed into something less casual. He smoked his cigarette down in minutes while he waited for his brother. In a just a few minutes Jonathan walked out of his room dressed in a blazer, tie and slacks, and his signature cowboy boots. He knew this would catch Felecia's eye.

Frank then put his cigarette out in the ashtray and put another patch and some cologne on, then he popped another mint in his mouth. Then they exited the apartment locked it up and headed for the bank.

Chapter Twelve

THE DEPOSIT

Frank was holding a briefcase that held the fake precious gems so he could look the part. As they approached the bank, Frank pulled into a parking spot and they jumped out of the SUV and headed for the doors of the giant building that lay in front of them called Trinity bank. As they entered, Harold the security guard opened the door for them and greeted them with a smile.

Jonathan said under his breath to Frank, "There they are, God she's beautiful."

To this Frank whispered back "Just keep your mind on the task at hand, wouldja!"

Cheryl greeted them cheerfully next. She said, "Hello, may I help you two gentlemen?"

Frank replied "Hello my name is Christopher Fields and this is my business associate Randy Franklin, we have appointment with Ms. Felecia Grey and Ms. Chelsea McQuire at 11:30."

Cheryl was the sole support for her ailing husband. So she took her job very seriously. She was a little overweight but she was trying to lose the extra pounds. She replied "Oh then have a seat right over here in one of our chairs and I will call them to the lobby." As she pointed to the green chairs.

They both retreated to the chairs in the lobby and took a seat. She had been restocking the island when the men came in. So she greeted them from there. When she had determined what they wanted she scurried back to her desk to call Felecia and Chelsea down to the lobby.

She dialed Felecia's extension and when the phone rang in Felecia's office she answered her and said, "Yes Cheryl, what is it?"

"Well there are two gentlemen named Mr. Christopher Fields and Mr. Randy Franklin here waiting for you and Ms. McQuire. They say they have an 11:30 appointment with you. Should I show them up to your office or do you want to just come down and meet them in the lobby?" Cheryl asked her,

"Oh yes, we were expecting them. We'll be right down. Thank you Cheryl."

Cheryl got up from her desk and waddled over to Christopher and Randy "They'll be right down in just a minute, may I get you a cup of coffee?" Cheryl asked.

"No thank you ma'am, we'll just wait for our appointment." Christopher said as a craving hit him hard.

Soon Felicia and Chelsea came walking down the enormous staircase from upstairs in their offices. They greeted Christopher and Randy with a kind hello. "Are you ready to see the safety deposit boxes gentlemen?" Felecia said as she winked at Randy while noticing the boots.

"Why yes, we have our merchandise safely tucked away in my briefcase."

Felecia felt herself getting wet and she tingled all over at the sight of those cowboy boots. "Well, come right this way, and we'll show you to a box."

The armored truck made its delivery on a rotating drop schedule. This meant that the armored truck made their drops on different days and different times to avoid any possibility of being robbed. The rotating drops of the armored truck would determine what day and time the money would be delivered and it would determine when they would rob the bank as well. Frank had been watching the bank for several months and had been keeping track of the armored truck schedules on a tablet that he carried with him at all times. They knew the armored truck and ladies schedules well by now.

Frank knew the schedules well. He studied his notes on the drop days and times at the apartment earlier that morning. They had decided that the best time to rob the bank would be in just three short weeks on the Friday morning before the long Labor Day weekend. The armored truck drop for that week was on Friday morning at 8 am before the big Labor Day weekend. This would ensure that the bank had enough money for the week following Labor Day. The bank would need those funds to cater to their customers that week. This would mean that the money would be dropped off and it would be delivered on that Friday at 8 am. Or so they thought. The deposits would be held until the armored truck delivered the next order from Felecia. Frank had decided that the drop that the armored truck made would be the biggest pull yet. Watching the schedule had afforded Frank the information that they needed to plan the heist on this day. Jonathan would simply download their take on that weekend and transfer it to an offshore account that he had set up recently. This is why they picked this weekend to rob the bank.

They still had lots of money left over from the other robberies that they had pulled off previously. They had almost a million each saved up from the past jobs. They had discovered through the wires in Felecia's office that the drop for that Friday would be around $200,000 plus the weeks deposits and the money in the armored truck. The amount had been doubled from normal days to keep up with the banks demands. The money that they would take away from this pull would set them for life. They had calculated that this job would warrant them at least a $500,000. Frank had been studying the banking functions and had learned how to manipulate the offshore accounts that would give them enough money to live their lives out without interruption on some sunny beach hiding with the money.

Felecia and Chelsea came walking down the stairs coming from their offices. "Well hello gentlemen, Are you ready?" Felecia asked as they approached the men.

"Yes, so nice to see you this morning, you look wonderful." Randy said to Felecia.

"Thank you cowboy, right this way then, lets go to the vault." Felecia replied.

Chelsea said good morning to the men and winked at Christopher. Just as Henry had told them, Felecia and Chelsea led them to the vault which was right behind his station. Henry or Anthony to Felecia and

Chelsea, didn't even look away from his customer to see what the Snow brothers were doing. He knew exactly what the plan was. The ladies unlocked the vault with their keys and Felecia used her master key to let Christopher and Randy into a safety deposit box in the vault after they filled out the forms allowing them to rent this box.

Christopher noticed a combination door to the right of the safety deposit boxes.

"Is that where the money's kept?" Christopher asked Felecia nonchalantly.

"Oh yes we keep the money under a combination lock just on the other side of that door."

Randy nodded in agreement and seemed to take this in casually.

Christopher told Chelsea, "We'll be needing some privacy now if you don't mind ladies."

"No not at all," Chelsea replied "We'll leave you two to make your deposit, just let us know when you're ready to lock it up."

"Sure thing babe." Randy replied

"We'll just be a minute. Are you ladies ready for lunch yet?" Christopher asked.

"Of course, we just have to get our purses upstairs." Felecia replied.

"Why don't you let us show you our offices after you finish with your business in here?" Chelsea chimed in.

"That sounds great. We will be just a few minutes." Christopher replied as another craving hit him.

When Felecia and Chelsea left the room, Christopher scolded his brother

"Will you please stick to business cowboy! We need to focus on the plan right now!" He said under his breath in a firm manner.

When Christopher finished depositing the fake gems in the safety deposit box, Randy poked his head out of the vault and called for the ladies to return. Chelsea and Felecia walked back into the vault and inserted the master key into the safety deposit box to lock it up.

"All finished?" Felecia asked.

"Yes, we thank you for your time ladies. Now let's get a look at your offices." Christopher said

"Great, come right this way then." Chelsea replied. And they all exited the vault after Chelsea and Felecia inserted their keys to lock up the vault tightly.

"Don't worry gentlemen, your merchandise is safe in our vault. C'mon up stairs we'll show you our offices."

Anthony Alvarez kept a wary eye on Randy as he walked past him when he exited the vault. Randy watched Anthony closely to see if this idiot was going to screw things up for them. He gave Anthony the evil eye as they walked past him. He seemed to be doing his job as the plan was coming together nicely.

The ladies led them upstairs to their offices.

Chelsea turned to Christopher and said "We like to take stairs to keep in shape, there is an elevator which Mr. Eldridge and his secretary use but Felecia and I like to use the stairs. We didn't think you would mind."

Christopher smiled and said, "Of course not, I like physical exercise, I plan to go to the gym tonight." He cringed as another craving hit him.

Randy smirked and looked at Felecia's ass as he walked behind her while going up the stairs, he responded to the sway of her hips.

As he grew harder he moved in closer to Felecia to whisper in her ear, "I'm getting hard baby. Get us to your office fast so I can sit down." He tried to keep it at bay but this woman had him wanting her more and more each time he saw her.

As they reached the top of the stairs the first office was Chelsea's. Chelsea said, "Well here's me, Felecia's is just next door" Christopher entered Chelsea's office and sat down in the light green chair across from her desk. Chelsea moved behind her desk and sat down as well. Felecia and Randy entered Felecia's office and had a seat too.

"So what do you think?" Chelsea asked "I think I'm in love with a very powerful and beautiful woman." Christopher replied

"Oh my, that's a word I hadn't expected to hear so soon. But I like it just the same." Randy was busy making small talk with Felecia until the clock struck noon.

"I was thinking" Chelsea replied. "What do you think about having dinner with my parents this Friday night? I would love for you to meet them. My parents mean everything to me and I would like you to meet them as soon as possible." She realized that she had already brought this up but she wanted to secure the plans for that Friday night.

"Well that sounds great sweetheart. You said this Friday night? What time did you have in mind?"

"Well we usually eat around 6 o'clock, would that work for you?"

"Yes of course I look forward to it." Christopher replied.

When the clock struck 12 Felecia said "Well let's get a move on cowboy, I noticed you wore my favorite boots."

"Why yes I did, thank you for noticing tiger, I can't wait to get you alone again."

Felecia blushed and said "Well we do have a lot in common and I do enjoy our time together."

Randy smiled and looked Felecia straight in the eye and said "You make me horny as hell tiger,"

Felecia could feel herself getting wet again and this comment gave her goose bumps but she had to hold her composure for the rest of the day. "You have to stop that for now, please. Or I may just cum right here on the spot."

"I would like that" Randy replied with an evil grin on his face.

"All the same I have work to do, so let's go to lunch." They stood and headed for the door.

Felecia and Randy walked into Chelsea's office and asked "Are you two ready to go yet?"

Chelsea replied "Is it that time already? I had lost all track of time."

Christopher smiled and said "You make me lose track of time as well, my lady."

Felecia said "Well let's get a move on we only have an hour, you know how Mr. Eldridge likes us to be punctual."

"Yes of course. Let's go, you said you were in the mood for Mexican right Christopher?"

Christopher replied "Yes I can eat a burrito or two where did you have in mind?"

"Well, there's a place called Amigo's. You should like it. It's very quaint and it's just down town." Chelsea said.

"Then it's settled, let's go" Felecia replied.

Another craving hit Christopher hard but he held his composure yet again. He was growing weary of these constant cravings now when he spent time with Chelsea.

Chapter Thirteen

LUNCH WITH THE LADIES

They all left the ladies office's and headed down the stairs and out of the front doors. Felecia and Chelsea said goodbye to Cheryl and told her that they would be returning at 1 o'clock. Anthony Alvarez watched them leave the bank and bit his tongue, he wanted to be a bigger part of the plan, but he was scared of that Jonathan. So he kept his distance and did his job as planned so as not to upset Jonathan any more than he already had. He could tell that Jonathan didn't like him the other night at dinner, so he planned to keep his distance from Jonathan as much as possible. They said goodbye to Harold then Christopher always being the gentleman, opened the doors for the ladies and let them go first.

Then they all hopped into his rented vehicle and he drove them to the restaurant. Chelsea gave directions along the way while she noticed that distinctive smell of stale smoke.

"Why do you let that guy smoke in your car?" Chelsea asked.

"Well he is as heavy smoker and I try to get the smell out when I have time but he usually doesn't listen to me. He just has this bad habit that we have to put up with until we get rid of the gems that we deposited today."

"Okay well if that's the way it has to be, would you please try to disinfect it before you pick me up?" She asked directly.

"I have been princess. That smell lingers."

"Oh well at least we are together for now." She replied.

When they got to Amigo's, Christopher parked the SUV close to the entrance so the ladies wouldn't have far to walk. Again, being the gentleman he opened the doors for the ladies. The patch wasn't working very well this time at all. He thought to himself, '*Maybe I should try the gum.*' Then he made plans to pick up the nicotine gum and some regular gum just incase Chelsea asked for some.

The hostess greeted them and asked "Will that be four for today?"

Christopher nodded and said, "Yes, please. We would like a booth in the corner."

The hostess said "Right this way please, you should be comfortable right here." And she led them to a corner booth as Christopher had asked.

She gave them each a menu and asked "What can I get you to drink?"

Christopher ordered an iced tea and asked Chelsea what she would like to drink.

Chelsea said, "I'll take an iced tea as well."

Then the hostess turned to Randy and asked him what he would like. Not wanting his brother to order for him again Randy said "I'll take a beer. Whatever you've got on tap."

Christopher wasn't pleased with his brother for ordering a beer during lunch but the ladies were present so he bit his tongue. Then the hostess asked Felecia what she would like to drink?

Felecia said "I'll take a soda please." And the hostess said "Very well, your waitress will be along shortly."

They chatted amongst themselves until the waitress arrived. When the waitress approached their table she was pleasant and smiled a lot. This made Chelsea very happy because she knew how Felecia could be when she didn't get her way in a restaurant. The waitress arrived and asked if they were ready to order and they all chose a meal that made them happy. Then the waitress made a note on her pad, and asked if there was anything else she could get them. She had brought a bowl of tortilla chips and salsa when she had arrived.

Felecia chimed in saying "Do you have any guacamole dip for the chips?"

The waitress said "I'll be right back with that for you." And she turned on her heel and left them alone to talk amongst themselves.

Christopher was really fighting off cravings by this time and regretted his bad habit. Then the waitress returned with the guacamole dip and their drinks quickly and Felecia was pleased. Felecia said, "I'm sure glad we picked this restaurant, the help is much better than the last Mexican restaurant we ate at." Chelsea cringed. She knew a tirade was coming from Felecia about that waitress at La Comida. But Felecia left the comment at that.

Randy asked "What do you mean tiger?"

Felecia said, "Oh it's nothing, we just had a bad waitress last time we had Mexican food. No problem here though,"

Christopher turned to Chelsea and said, "You look beautiful as usual, if I may say so myself," Chelsea blushed and thanked him for the compliment.

The waitress came back to take their order. She asked what they wanted to eat. They put their orders in and she made a note on her note pad and trotted off to fill it. They made small talk while they waited for their food. They were getting to know each other very well.

After a few minutes the waitress arrived with their meals and they all dug in. They all enjoyed the company and the meals. Christopher, always the gentleman, asked Chelsea if she was ready for that night. Chelsea replied between bites, "Well I am and I can't wait to be with you again."

Christopher asked if she would like to see his hotel room tonight. He said, "I didn't want to be presumptuous and invite you over before, but I think we can quit with the formalities now."

Chelsea said, "Well I would love to see where you are staying, although you are welcome to save on the hotel bill and stay with me."

Felecia was taken aback by her offer, as they still didn't know these two men very well. But they had proven to be everything that they claimed to be so far.

"Well darlin, I wouldn't want to impose. I'm sure Randy can find something else to do tonight while we see your movie and visit our hotel room. Randy winked at Felecia with a slight grin knowing what he would be doing that night.

Christopher said "I don't want to give you the wrong impression, we have a two bedroom suite with a living room area and a kitchenette. Why don't I cook for you tonight? Say around 6 o'clock?"

Chelsea smiled and said, "Of course that sounds lovely. I'll be there at 6 o'clock sharp. Where are you staying?" Christopher got uncomfortable because he hadn't rented the room yet.

They had rented the apartment on a 30 day month to month agreement, and they would keep the apartment so they could use it in their plan. They would give it up after they pulled the heist and headed for parts unknown, it would serve as a wonderful hiding place when one of the guys seduced the ladies in the hotel room. He told her that they had a room at the Regency hotel. He was hoping that she wouldn't ask for the room number so he added "How about if I come pick you up tonight?"

Chelsea said "Well I don't want you to trouble yourself I can drive myself."

Christopher replied "Oh it's no bother, I like to treat you special, plus this way you can help yourself to as much wine as you want."

Chelsea said, "Well it's a work night and I won't be drinking to heavily tonight, but I thank you for the ride. I'll see you tonight at 6 o'clock then at my house."

Christopher was relieved that he didn't have to give her a room number because he hadn't rented it yet, so he played it cool while he felt a sigh of relief inside. Another craving hit him hard as he was finishing his meal. He would really have to invest in the gum.

Randy watched Felecia carefully and said, "What about you tiger, how about a date tonight?"

Felecia answered, "Well yes that sounds great, you can come over to my house and we can have a little fun ourselves."

Chelsea knew what that meant, but she held her tongue. The waitress interrupted and asked if she could get them anything else. Randy said, "Yes I'll take another beer. Hell I'm not driving." And Felecia let out a little giggle. Frank gave his brother a dirty look for ordering the second beer. The waitress scurried off to fetch him his beer. She came back in minutes with his order. Randy was unfazed by his brother's attempt to scold him.

When they finished their meals and the waitress approached the table with the check. She asked "Will there be anything else?"

Christopher said, "No that will be all, and thank you ma'am." Then he wrote a generous tip on the receipt and left his credit card in the receipt book, he then placed it on the edge of the table.

Felecia said, "I don't think I will ever return to La Comida again, this place is much better."

Randy asked, "What happened at La Comida?"

Chelsea chimed in saying "Oh nothing, we just had a bad waitress, but the food was good."

"Well the help here is nice so I have no complaints," Felecia commented.

When the waitress returned to retrieve the credit card, she was pleased to see such a generous tip from Christopher. She quickly processed his credit card and returned his card and receipt. The guys let themselves out of the bench seat and stood and Christopher said, "Ready ladies?" Then the ladies scooted across the bench seat and they let themselves out of the table while the men stood in wait for them.

"Oh yes, it's time that we got back to the bank. You know how Mr. Eldridge likes us to be on time when we return from lunch." Chelsea said.

Felecia was busy making eyes at Randy when Chelsea practically bumped into her as she headed for the door. Randy was getting to Felecia and in Felecia's eyes this was not good thing.

Chelsea said, "Thank you for lunch Christopher and I look forward to dinner tonight."

Christopher smiled and said, "My pleasure sweetheart, we better get you two back before it's too late."

They all walked out of the restaurant, with the hostess in tow saying, "Please come again and good day to you."

They all loaded into the SUV and Christopher started the engine. Felecia thought she smelled cigarette smoke in his vehicle. "Why does your car smell like cigarettes Christopher?" She asked him.

"Oh you noticed. I had hoped you wouldn't smell that. Our other business partner smokes and we gave him a ride when we had our last meeting."

"Oh that's not good, I wouldn't let anyone smoke in my car."

"Well we let him smoke in here. I tried to get the smell out but it's really hard to get the smell out of a vehicle when a cigarette is smoked in it." Frank added.

Frank was a bit miffed at his brother for drinking during lunch, but Randy could care less how he felt about it, although he knew he would hear about it later. When they reached the bank, Christopher pulled into a parking spot and turned the engine off.

Felecia said, "We can walk from here," But Christopher insisted on being the gentleman and walked them to the door of the bank.

Felecia said, "I'll see you tonight cowboy, come by about 6 o'clock. Okay? I feel like pizza tonight. We can order a pizza or something like that. How does that sound?"

"You got it babe I'll be there on time." Randy replied,

They said their goodbyes and agreed to meet up at 6 o'clock.

Christopher said, "I'll pick you up at 6 o'clock tonight, does that sound okay princess?"

"Of course, I'll be ready then."

"I'll see you tonight." Randy said to Felecia and the guys descended the steps and headed for the SUV. They hopped in it and drove off as the ladies watched them drive away.

Frank tore off the patch again just as he got out of eye sight and he lit a cigarette. He blew grey smoke out of the window. Felecia and Chelsea entered the bank and greeted Harold as he opened the door to let them in, then they said hello to Cheryl as they walked by her desk.

Cheryl said, "Did you have a good lunch boss?"

"Why yes we did, thank you very much," Felecia told her. And the two ladies walked up the stairs to their offices to finish their work day.

Frank had dodged a bullet and almost got caught with his smoking.

Jonathan commented, "See I knew those damn cigarettes were gonna bite us in the ass."

"We got through it didn't we? Now I can smoke in the car without them finding out that I smoke. We just blame it on our third partner." Frank said happy that that was out of the way now.

When Frank and Jonathan got back to the car Frank tried to be bossy with him about the two beers he had drank at lunch. But whatever

Frank was saying went in one ear and out the other. He could care less what his brother thought about a coupla beers at lunch. The plan was in place and he knew he was getting laid tonight. So he just brushed off what Frank was saying with a smirk.

Frank took another drag and pulled into their apartment complex parking lot and told Jonathan "I'm gonna let you off here, I need to go rent a hotel room at the Regency. You behave yourself and just listen to what they have to say for the afternoon. I'll be back soon."

Jonathan let himself out of the car and unlocked the their dingy apartment. Frank pulled away and drove to the Regency hotel. It wasn't too far from Chelsea's cottage. He chain smoked the entire way there.

When Frank arrived he went to the check-in counter and asked for a two-bedroom suite with a kitchenette. The clerk asked him how long he would be staying. Frank replied "Just a coupla weeks will be fine."

"Well we thank you for choosing the Regency sir, and have a pleasant stay. We have a pool, a bar, a gym and a restaurant for your pleasure." The clerk said.

Frank thanked the clerk and headed for the elevators. He took the elevator to the 5th floor where his room was. Then he went to the room that he rented, number 504. It was perfect. He needed to make it look like he had been living there awhile so he unpacked his belongings and put it into the dressers. He then messed up the bed in both rooms to make it look like they had been staying there the whole time.

He then left the room and went to the grocery store to pick up the necessities for the dinner that he was going to make for Chelsea that evening lighting another cigarette along the way. The first thing he looked for was the nicotine gum. He wanted to ward off any cravings that night. He knew how to make beef stroganoff, so he bought the necessities for a meal of stroganoff and asparagus with Hollandaise sauce. He thought this would make a nice meal for the two of them that evening. He also bought a bottle of wine at the local outlet store. He wanted it to look as though he was prepared for their meeting tonight. He returned to room 504 and stocked the fridge with the sour cream, and asparagus that he would need to make tonight's dinner. Then he dropped the stew meat into a large zip lock bag to marinate the meat with red wine. Then he added the bag of marinating stew meat to the fridge to keep it cold. He put the bottle of wine in the fridge and chilled the wine glasses in the freezer. He also bought a couple of candles at the outlet store which he set out on the table for ambience. He would bring a CD player later so that he could put on some mood music as well. The room was all stocked and ready to go, so he headed home to their grubby little apartment.

Once again he walked in on Jonathan listening in on a Felecia and Chelsea in their offices. Frank walked in with a cigarette hanging out of his mouth again. He was happy that his brother was at least staying focused on the task at hand. Jonathan loved listening in on Felecia and Chelsea's conversations. It was the second best part of the job as far as he was concerned sleeping with Felecia was number one in Jonathan's book. He couldn't wait to meet with his tiger that evening. Frank walked up to the recorders and listened in as well, smoking a cigarette the whole time.

"Would you put that damn thing out, it's a disgusting habit. I'm surprised she hasn't caught you yet." Jonathan said angrily to his brother.

Frank just shrugged off the comment and put the cigarette out in the ashtray on the desk.

Jonathan said "Well you could at least keep it to yourself, and move this damn thing." As he pointed to the ashtray.

Frank replied. "I'll be just fine thanks, move it yourself." Then he retreated to his bedroom to get ready to pick Chelsea up.

Chapter Fourteen

ANOTHER ENCOUNTER

At 5:45 pm Jonathan called a cab and scheduled pickup for 5:50 pm to take him over to Felecia's house. Frank was busying himself at the hotel room with the amenities that he would need for the evening. He had brought a CD player and some mood music, to set the mood for the night, from the apartment. He started the stroganoff and set it to simmer while he ran to Chelsea's house. He also put the asparagus in the steamer on the stove, so that dinner would be ready when they got there at 6 o'clock. He only had 20 minutes to pick Chelsea up and get her back to the hotel room before the food burned. His timing had to be perfect. He hoped that Chelsea would be ready when he got there. At 5:50 pm Frank locked the door to room 504 and hopped on the elevator then pushed the button to the lobby. He exited the elevator when it reached the lobby and headed for the exit door of the hotel. He walked to his SUV and jumped in. He then started the engine and backed out of the parking space. Then he pulled onto the Boulevard which would lead him to Chelsea's cottage.

Jonathan readied himself for his encounter with Felecia that evening as well. He made sure to wear his cowboy boots because he knew that this turned her on and he loved to wear his snakeskin cowboy boots as often as possible.

When the cab arrived at their apartment to pick Jonathan up, he heard the horn honk in anticipation of his arrival. He locked up their two-bedroom apartment and headed for the cab that was waiting for him. He hopped in and told the driver the way to the Felecia's house. In just about 5 minutes he arrived at her door. He exited the cab and paid for his ride, then the cab driver drove off.

He then walked to Felecia's door and rang the doorbell. "Just a minute" he could hear Felecia saying from behind the door. She was ready as well. She opened the door in her silk bathrobe with nothing on underneath.

Randy had a big smile on his face when he greeted her "Well hello tiger, looks like you're ready for me." He said to Felecia

"I'm always ready, c'mon in cowboy, make yourself comfortable." She said with a smile on her face. Then they embraced and they kissed feverishly while he kicked the door closed. This sent shivers down her spine. She loved a take charge man and he was proving to be just that. Once again she hopped on her cowboy and wrapped her legs around his waist. She sucked on his lips and rolled her tongue around in his mouth while he carried her to the kitchen table.

"How about we get adventurous and do it on the table in the kitchen?" He said in between kisses as he carried her to the kitchen. He knew the way and wasted no time getting them there. He laid her on the table gently and hovered over the top of her still kissing her lips while he explored her breasts and tummy with his hands.

"Oh God, more please." She exclaimed as his kiss made her tingle in her tender spots.

He then undid her robe and exposed her finely toned body. While he did this he slipped out his cowboy boots then his pants. She pushed his jeans down past his butt and reached for his burning desire for her. He slid his shirt over his head and discarded it. Then he continued exploring her body with his hands. He spread her smooth lips and stoked her gently. He loved her the bare heart that her tender spots looked like in the dim candle light. He was gentle with her this time.

He wanted the kiss to linger and make her want more. She arched her back and let out a moan as he inserted his fingers into her. Her nipples were erect and ready for action. When he inserted himself into her she felt the first of many orgasms that she would have that night. She counted on sharing the electricity between them. When he could wait no longer he shoved his manly member into her. She spread her legs wider to let him enter her all the way. She thought he was the perfect size for her. He began sucking on her nipples because he knew this would turn her on. She became wet instantly and craved him with a passion. She began stroking him and kissed him on his smooth chest.

Then he moved in and out of her as gently as he could until he could hold it in no longer. His throbbing member began to grow even harder with each thrust. She began to quiver as the climax hit her hard. He was just as good gentle as he was hard and fast. She exploded after about 20 minutes of sharing their passion together.

He said to her "That took some time, are you holding back for me to make it last?"

She giggled and said "Oh there's more where that came from, cowboy."

He continued to move seductively in and out of her. It wasn't long before she had another orgasm and gripped him when she climaxed. The feel of her gripping him tightly made him climax as well. Then he gently kissed her rippled tummy and licked her all the way up to her breast before he made it to her nipples which were still erect with anticipation. A bead of sweat ran down the side of her face, he loved the taste of her sweat. She pulled him close then licked the sweat from his brow, she loved his taste as well. She began to sweat lightly across her forehead as well. He gently licked the sweat off of her forehead.

"Oh you feel so good to me," She whispered as she climaxed again.

It was a good this time as it had been every other time before. The kitchen table held them well. She had this in mind when she bought this dinette set. When he pulled out he pulled up his pants and picked her up off of the table. "You wore your cowboy boots again, I really like that. Please let's do it again with your cowboy boots on this time, cowboy."

"Yes ma'am. Anything you want is good with me." He said as he began to put his cowboy boots back on.

They kissed passionately after he put his cowboy boots back on. She loved how he looked in them, she especially liked how he looked in only his cowboy boots. She would do anything for him when he wore his cowboy boots. She reached for him and helped him grow hard again for her. She was excited by those boots. She just couldn't hold back anymore.

She pulled him close and begged him the make her cum again. He was all too happy to oblige.

He found her mound and stroked it gently while she stroked him to make his manhood grow for her. Then he put his fingers inside of her which gave her goose bumps all over again. He wiggled his fingers around inside of her and she moaned again. Then she arched her back once again and pointed her erect nipples towards the sky so that he could access them easily. He rolled one nipple in between his index finger and thumb which sent her into a series of orgasms once again. She loved the way this man made her feel. She knew that she would have to dump him soon but she didn't want to let him go just yet. He was turning out to be everything that she wanted in a man. However, all they seemed to do was have amazing sex together. She knew it had to end soon. When they wore themselves out he held her tightly on top of the table.

When they were finished she said to him, "Would you like some dinner before we continue this?"

He replied "Well that sounds great what did you have in mind."

Not being a gourmet chef she said "Let's order a pizza. That way we can have another round before the delivery guy gets here."

"That sounds great to me tiger, get the phone book I'll order us something good." So she handed him the phone and the phone book that was in the kitchen. He began to look for the closest Pizza Parlor that delivered. He found one and dialed the phone.

He then made the order. "Yeah I'll take a large pizza with mushroom and sausage and anchovies on the side. Is that all right with you tiger?" He asked Felecia with the phone to his ear.

She said "That sounds great. Just don't expect me to eat those anchovies I like fish but not on pizza"

He hung up the phone and carried her to the living room. He laid her on the couch and began licking her from her ankles to the lips between her legs. He lingered at her lips for awhile sucking on each one gently. Then he made his way to her breasts. He fondled her breasts and flicked at her nipples. She responded very quickly to this action. His grew for her once again. He was rock hard for her. She stoked him gently and sat up next to her on the couch. They spent some time just feeling each others touch on each others body. As she sat up, he reached for her again. He moved in closer and inserted himself into her once again on the couch this time. He was really beginning to like this lady. As soon as he was inside of her they moved together in unison until the climax hit them hard again. She gripped him with her delicate parts once again and this made him cum as well.

Then they cuddled on the couch, holding each other until the food arrived. They made small talk while they waited for the pizza. Randy knew that what they were saying was being recorded. He would have to erase that part of the tape before Christopher was able to hear it. He didn't want his brother, knowing about his pillow talk. Felecia had picked up a six pack of beer for tonight's antics earlier in the day. So she went to the kitchen to grab two beers while they waited for the pizza to be delivered.

The doorbell rang about 15 minutes later. Felecia went to the kitchen and threw on her silk bathrobe. Then she went to answer the door while Randy retreated to the bedroom to put something on. She gave the delivery guy $50 and told him to keep the change. Then she closed the door behind her and locked it. She walked into the kitchen with the food. Then she grabbed a couple of plates from the cupboard. Randy rejoined her in the kitchen after he heard the door close behind the delivery guy. He had slipped into to his boxers again. They sat down at the table and each took a bite of pizza. Jonathan put the anchovies on his slice, Felecia didn't. They drank their beer while they chatted some more.

"You are really good in bed. You must have a lot of girlfriends to be this good in bed." She told him.

"Well I could say the same thing to you. But I know differently." They both giggled with that said. When he said this he reached out and grabbed her hand and kissed it.

Randy had become accustomed to wearing only his boxers and cowboy boots when they were together. When they were through eating, they retreated to the living room to chat. She was proving to be just what he liked. And he would really miss her when the time came.

"Ya know I can't get enough of those cowboy boots." She said to him with a tone of seduction.

"Would you like me to leave them on from now on?" He asked with an evil grin on his face. He knew how much she like his cowboy boots and he would do anything that she asked to please her. He didn't have much time to share with her and in the end he would betray her. He knew her well by now and decided that her attitude towards sex suited him well and would work to his advantage as they followed through with their plan.

Christopher readied himself for his encounter with Chelsea. He smoked one last cigarette and then brushed his teeth and dowsed himself with cologne. Then he put another patch on his shoulder. He made sure that he had plenty of gum to chew of both kinds incase Chelsea asked for a piece. He had registered at the hotel as Christopher Fields. It was a mistake that would cost him later. He used his alias just incase the ladies came looking for them while they were away. Once he had the gum in his pocket he knew that he could keep his habit under control. If he needed to chew some gum he would just excuse himself to the restroom and insert a piece of nicotine gum in his mouth so she wouldn't become suspicious. He stopped at the store to pick up some flowers and inserted a poem into the flowers.

Christopher arrived at Chelsea's house at 6 o'clock sharp. He was dressed in a new light blue button-down shirt and dark blue slacks. He wore the shoes that he and worn to the bank that very day. He wanted to give her the impression that he was well off and didn't need anything from her but her love. When Chelsea heard the doorbell ring she rushed to open the door to her prince.

Christopher said "Well hello sweetness," then he handed her the flowers once again and they embraced as he entered her cottage.

"You're gonna spoil me if you keep this up." She said with a grin. Then she headed for the kitchen to put the flowers in a vase and give them some water. She noticed the poem and read it out loud to him. She was so impressed with his ability to be so romantic. The poem said 'You make me smile, I would walk a mile, To be with you, And see you too, You make me feel so good, I want to make you feel like you should, please be mine, I will wait till the end of time. She said "You make me feel the same way," Then she smiled at him.

She loved being spoiled this way. Chelsea was wearing a pink spaghetti strap sundress and white sandals. She had thrown another French braid in her hair just for the occasion.

He said to her "You look beautiful again my dear, I am the luckiest man on the planet."

"Oh stop, you're too kind."

"Well, you are beautiful. I can't help myself".

"Are you ready to go, I just need to lock up. Where is that cat of mine." And she looked around for Misty so that she could be sure that she had not slipped out while she wasn't looking. "Where did that cat go this time anyway," Chelsea said as she headed for the bedroom. She found her hiding in the closet and she bent down to pick her up to show Christopher. But Misty was quicker and ran away.

"Well, I guess she's going to be stubborn, she can be that way sometimes. Sorry you had to miss her once again. Let's get a move on I'm hungry, and I can't wait to see how well you cook."

Then Chelsea grabbed her purse and they headed for the door. She locked her door behind them and they jumped in his rented SUV. He drove them to the Regency Hotel. When they got there they took the elevator to the fifth floor. When the elevators doors opened they headed to room 504.

While she searched for her cat, Christopher smiled and winked at her and told her about the dinner that he had prepared for them. "You're going to like what's on the menu tonight, how does stroganoff and asparagus with hollandaise sauce sound?"

"Sounds delicious where did you learn to cook like that?" Chelsea replied.

"Oh, it's an old family recipe that my mother taught me before she passed away. I like to cook it because it reminds me of her. I do miss her so sometimes." He said with a sigh. He was becoming a great actor. "I left it cooking when I came to pick you up." He continued.

"Well we better hurry then we don't want it to burn." Chelsea replied

"Oh, I put it on simmer and planned it so that would have a good 20 minutes before that would happen." Chelsea was pleasantly surprised and a little impressed.

They exited her cottage and she locked up. He held the door open for her as she got into his vehicle. Chelsea would find Misty when she returned and secure her inside, this set her mind at ease. He cat knew her surroundings outside quite well.

Christopher went around the front of the car to the driver side. He hopped in and started the engine. He had tried to freshen up the vehicle as well so she wouldn't smell the odor his bad habit that he had left behind, but the smell just lingered. So he just claimed that their third partner had taken a ride and smoked in his car once again. He backed out of her driveway and merged onto the Boulevard and headed for the Regency Hotel.

Chapter Fifteen

DINNER IN ROOM 504

It wasn't far to the hotel so he knew that his food would be cooking slowly while he was out. As they pulled into the driveway of the Regency, he chose a parking place that was close to the door so that she would not have to walk very far. He said to her, "Hold on I'll be right there." And he jumped out of his side and walked around the front of the vehicle, then opened her door for her.

She said "Thank you, kind sir, you are such a gentleman."

Christopher smiled and commented on her beauty once again. Then a craving hit him so he thought to himself that he would have to excuse himself as soon as they got into the hotel room and put some gum in his mouth. He only hoped that it would work to dispel his cravings.

They walked through the doors of the Regency and entered the lobby. He showed her to the elevator and pushed the button for the fifth floor. They rode the elevator and got off when the doors opened. Then they walked just down the hall to room 504. He used his card key to let them in and allowed her to enter first.

"Wow fancy. I like it." She said with genuine appreciation.

Then he said "Well it's home for now."

"That smells delicious, thank you for inviting me and cooking for me." Chelsea commented.

"Randy can be somewhat of a slob when he wants to be." Christopher said as he closed Randy's bedroom door.

Chelsea replied "Oh, I don't mind this is home to you right now. It wouldn't be home if it didn't look lived in."

"Well, it certainly is lived in, I just wish he would pick up his things. It's a good thing there's a door to hide it. It's kind of embarrassing. I asked him to clean up. But he's gone and that's all that matters for now." Christopher said with a grin.

Then he checked the food on the stove and decided that he would be able to serve her in just a few short minutes. He decided to hold off on the gum until after dinner because the craving had passed for the moment. He would need to chew some after they ate so he would just slip into the bathroom and insert a new piece into his mouth then. He needed to start the hollandaise sauce. Then he asked her "Would you like some wine? I've got some chilled in the refrigerator."

"Oh, that sounds lovely. I would love a glass of wine. Thank you." Chelsea said in response to his question.

"Dinner is almost ready, why don't you have a seat and I'll get you that wine." Christopher said to Chelsea as she sat down at the table.

"Don't mind if I do, my prince. You even bought candles how romantic." Christopher had lit the candles before he left so they would set the mood as they came in. They were scented candles so the hotel room smelled like lavender. She enjoyed the scent of the candles. Christopher chose lavender to relax her and set her at ease. He had read somewhere that lavender had this effect on people.

Christopher said to Chelsea as he grinned. "Well, I wanted you to have a good time tonight." Then he poured her chilled glass of wine and handed it to her. He then walked over to the T.V stand and turned on the CD player to put some mood music on for ambience.

Chelsea was feeling right at home in his hotel room. He poured himself a glass of wine as well as he started melting the butter for the hollandaise sauce. He busied himself in the kitchen checking on the stroganoff and steamed vegetables to make sure that they were still cooking and not burning. He then made the hollandaise sauce. In the end his timing couldn't be better. Dinner was ready so he turned everything off as she watched him from the table in amazement. She couldn't believe that he could cook this well.

"It all smells so delicious. Was your mother a good cook then?" Chelsea asked

"Yeah, she could cook up a storm and she taught me well. I have to admit, it is one of my many talents." He told her as he grabbed the plates from the cupboard. He then set some silverware on the table along with the plates so that they would be able to eat the delicious meal that he had just prepared. He put the stroganoff in a bowl and set asparagus in another bowl. Then he poured the hollandaise sauce in yet another smaller bowl. Then he carried each of them to the table and set them in front of her.

"It all looks very good. You are quite the chef." She told him with pleasure.

He said "Well let's dig in and see how well I did. Nothing seemed to burn while I was out so it should be pretty good."

"I'm starved" Chelsea replied "I can't believe you made all of this."

"Well momma taught me right, and besides, you're worth it my lady."

Then they filled their plates with food and dripped the hollandaise sauce over their asparagus. They cleaned their plates and made small talk while they ate.

He asked her "So do you like horseback riding?"

She replied "Well, I haven't tried it yet but it sounds fun. What did you have in mind?" Christopher smiled and said "I've always wanted to ride a horse along the beach with the most beautiful woman in the world and you would fit that bill. What do you say we rent some horses this weekend and go for a ride?" Chelsea was filled with excitement

"Oh that sounds so fun. Let's do it. I can't wait." He smiled and winked at her while he dabbed the corner of his mouth with his napkin. "Then it's a date. Say on Sunday around noon? What do you think?"

She smiled and replied "I think that sounds like a date to me. I look so forward to it. Now I can't wait for the weekend."

Christopher smiled and said "You really are a dream come true." Then another craving hit him hard after the meal, so he excused himself to the restroom and inserted a piece of gum in his mouth. He proceeded to flush the toilet so as to make it seem like he had used the facilities. Then he came out of the restroom and offered Chelsea a piece of regular gum so as not to throw her off. He told her that he liked fresh breath after a meal, so he always carried gum to freshen his breath. This only made him more endearing to her.

She accepted the gum and then he said, "We better get a move on if we're going to make that movie,"

Christopher replied "Ready when you are," and they made small talk about their past on the way to the movies. Christopher's version was mostly fiction but Chelsea didn't know the difference.

Randy stirred around 9 pm. He unwrapped Felecia's arms around his chest and got up and went to the kitchen for another beer. He was thankful that Felecia hadn't caught him planting the bugs, considering the fact that she woke up every time he left the bed. He grabbed two just in case she woke up and was thirsty as well.

She woke to find him gone once again. She thought to herself, '*This has got to stop. I'm starting to like this guy and miss him when he's gone.*' As she had this thought he walked into the room with the two beers in his hand.

"Hey there tiger, wanna beer, I just got up because I was feeling thirsty." He said

"That sounds great, now come back to bed wouldja?"

"Oh, don't worry I'm not going far." He said with a grin. Then he handed her the extra beer

Then she took a swig. "Ahh, that's good after a little nap. Ready for another round cowboy? Come on over here and make me happy again." She said with an evil grin on her face.

He walked over to the bed and sat down on the edge. She was barely covering her nudity. Her breasts were uncovered and this sent his hormones soaring. He also knew what was just underneath those covers, and it made him hard as a rock again.

"You wear me out tiger, I can't wait for another round though, c'mere and let me lick you."

As she pulled the sheet off of her and spread her legs he put the bottle of beer on the nightstand and positioned himself. He licked her gently and she came once again in his mouth. "You're gonna hafta wait for me tiger, I need some lovin too." So Felecia positioned herself so that she could put him into her mouth while he licked her once again. She took him completely in her mouth and moved gently in and out and she made him climax once again. However this one lingered and he felt it down to his toes.

"I want you inside of me." She whispered into the darkness

"Here I come tiger, just let me turn around." He said to her with passion in his voice.

As he turned around she kissed him down the side of his chest. He liked this and didn't want her to stop. He entered her once again and began to move in and out of her body. She was wet with anticipation. He had removed his pants but had put his cowboy boots back on just for her. She smiled when he did this.

"C'mere cowboy I want you inside of me." She whispered into the night. He spread her clean lips apart once again and licked her delicate area. Then he began to suck on her. This excited her and she moaned lightly this time. He moved in closer to her and inserted his fingers into her once again. He loved the way she felt with his fingers inside of her.

After some time he started to feel the bulge of his maleness. "I cant wait any longer tiger. Here I come. And he ripped at his zipper and released his bulging manhood then inserted himself into her once again. She arched her back once again and pointed her erect nipples to the sky. He loved it when she did this. He began fondling her breasts. She felt the climax hit her hard as her entire body began to tingle.

"Here I cum cowboy, oh my GOD. You are wonderful." She exclaimed into the darkness. She enjoyed every minute of way he made her feel. They knew they were good together and didn't want to stop so they just kept going until they wore themselves out once again and collapsed in each others arms.

Felecia fell asleep once again after they were finished with their sexual antics. Randy also fell asleep and was happy that he could make her cum so easily. He wondered if she was thinking of other guys while they were having sex. But he put that thought to rest because he knew that she was with him now and that's all that mattered.

At midnight Felecia woke up startled. She placed her hand on his shoulder and shook him gently. "You know I have to work tomorrow, cowboy,"

He responded to her again and said "Well, if u say so, what time is it?"

"It's midnight and I have to be up at the crack of dawn.

"Well, what do you think? Should I call a cab?"

She smiled and said "I'm gonna miss you. But yes I do have to work tomorrow." And she handed him the phone and the phone book once again.

He told her "Oh don't worry darlin' I know the number by heart by now." Once again he dialed the number to the Rolling Cab Company and he told them where to come to pick him up.

Felecia hopped out of bed and threw her silk rope around her. Randy began getting dressed, He removed his cowboy boots to be able to put his pants on then he put his cowboy boots back on like she liked him to do. He wanted her to remember the cowboy boots when she thought of him.

He said, "By the way, what do you say we get together again real soon."

She smiled and said "How does tonight sound? Same place, same time?" She said with a grin.

"That sounds awesome tiger. I'll be here at 6 o'clock again tonight then.

"We could order Chinese this time, what do you say?" He said with a smirk on his face, that was the look she loved the most about him and she told him so,

"How do you do that with your face like that? It really turns me on, cowboy."

He smirked again and told her "Well, it's just my look tiger, I can't help it if it turns you on but I'm glad, that makes me happy. So what do you say to the Chinese tonight?"

"Whatever you would like is fine with me cowboy." She replied.

They heard the honk of the cab, as it drove up to her house and stopped in front of it. "Well I guess that's my cue tiger, I'll see ya tonight. You know you haven't even given me your phone number yet may I have it please?" He asked.

"Sure, I'll write it down for you." She said then wrote it quickly on a piece of paper. Then she slipped it in his pocket when she stood to walk him to the door.

"Call me sometime." She said seductively.

He was pleased that he was able to get her phone number from her knowing that she was the love um and leave um type of lady. He was certain that he had made his mark on her and that she was not going to stray before he was through with her.

He put his boots on and headed for the door, but turned to find her right behind him. They embraced and kissed passionately one more time before she opened the door to let him out. The horn of the cab sounded again. He then released her and opened the door.

When he got in the cab he waved goodbye and said "I'll see ya tonight tiger." As he drove off she waved back and winked a goodbye.

Then she closed the door and locked up for the night. She took off her robe and hopped in bed naked. She liked to sleep nude just like Randy did. She thought to herself *'I could really fall for this guy, I wonder what he thinks of me?'* And then she drifted off to sleep with the alarm set for 6 am.

Christopher and Chelsea spent the evening getting to know each other better and enjoyed the movie she had picked. When the movie was over he asked "Would you like to go back to my place for a nightcap before I take you home?"

"Of course, lead the way." She was pleased with the selection of music that was playing when they entered the room 504. She told him so several times. The gum did the trick, he didn't have another craving all night. He had chosen the mint flavored nicotine gum just incase she wanted to kiss. After that he poured them both another glass of wine while they chatted on the couch.

Around 11 o'clock she started to feel the wine hit her and she said "Boy I'm glad I'm not driving, are you ok to drive babe?"

Christopher smiled and said "Oh I feel fine, don't you worry your pretty little head I'll get you home in one piece."

Then she said "Well you know it's getting kind of late and I do have to work tomorrow. I don't need to have a hangover during work hours. So we better call it a night. If you don't mind?"

"No problem sweetness, I'll just get the door for you." Then they exited his hotel room and headed for the elevator. He pushed the button for the lobby and the elevator doors rang open.

They entered the elevator and rode it to the lobby. Then they exited the Regency and he opened the door of his SUV to let her in. Then he walked around the front of it and let himself in the driver side. He was feeling a little bit of the wine but he did have a high tolerance for alcohol and he didn't have far to drive. So he wasn't worried about getting caught driving drunk. He had everything under control as far as he knew.

He said to Chelsea, "Hey I wonder if Randy and Felecia would like to meet up and go dancing this weekend? What do you think princess?"

Chelsea smiled and said "That sounds wonderful, we could go out on Saturday night, and ride the horses on the beach on Sunday."

"Well I think we now have plans for the weekend, I will check with Randy when I get home." Christopher said as he pulled over in her driveway. "Don't get out my lady. I will get that for you." She waited while he walked around the front of his SUV once again to open her door. She was really liking his gentlemanly ways.

"What about Friday night. I would really like to meet your parents?"

"Well make the plans and we will have dinner at your parent's house on Friday night. What do you think?"

"Oh that sounds wonderful. I so look forward to you meeting my parents."

"Then it's settled. What time do you want to meet with them?"

"Well we usually eat at 6 o'clock. I will check with my mom and confirm the time and get back to you." Chelsea replied.

Then he got out of the car and went around the front of to open the door for her and she hopped out. "I wonder how Felecia and Randy did tonight." Chelsea said as they walked to the door. She fumbled with her keys a little then she found the right one. She slid the key into the lock and opened her door. "Well I guess that's it for the night, I had a great time tonight." Chelsea said with a grin.

Christopher had nonchalantly taken his gum out of his mouth and had thrown it out the window while he drove her home in anticipation of a kiss. "May I kiss you again?" Christopher asked.

"Of course you can you don't have to ask anymore. I want to kiss you, I want to do much more, but I think we should wait on that."

"Now we have plans for the whole weekend, I'm so excited." They embraced and kissed gently.

When he pulled away he smiled at her and said "Well I'll leave you to get your beauty rest my lady, I look forward to the weekend." Then he said goodbye and turned on his heel and headed for his jeep. She stood in the doorway and watched him drive away and waved as he left her standing there.

He was pleased with himself that the night had gone so successfully. The minute he got out of eye sight he ripped the patch off and lit a cigarette. He blew grey smoke out of the window while he drove himself home. He wondered if Jonathan would be in the apartment when he got back. *'Probably not,'* he thought to himself. *'He's such a dog. I hope he's not getting too attached to this woman because they would betray them in the end.'* He thought to himself further. When he arrived at their apartment he noticed that the lights were out. This could only lead him to the conclusion that Jonathan was still at Felecia's house. He parked the SUV and got out and let himself into their shabby apartment. And just as he had thought, Jonathan was still at Felecia's.

He had smoked the first cigarette so fast that he got a head rush from it. He went to the table and turned on the recording device and switched over to Felecia's house to see what was going on within the confines of her walls. He then took another drag and listened in. He heard them moaning and quickly turned it off because he didn't want to listen to his brother having sex once again. Then he let himself into his own bedroom and stripped down to the buff. Next he made one last phone call before he finished his cigarette and closed his eyes for the night. He would have to erase this call because he had planted the bugs in the phones while he was at Chelsea's that night. Now every base was covered.

He dialed Chelsea's number as he knew it by heart now. He heard the phone ring a couple of times and then she picked it up and said "Hello, I knew you would call."

He snickered and said "Hello sweetheart, I just wanted to make sure you were all tucked in and ready for bed."

"Well, thank you for checking up on me. I'm fine and I like that you called me this late, however I do need to get some rest now so I have to go. Goodnight sweet prince." She said into the phone

"Goodnight sweetheart sleep well." And they both hung up the phone.

He put his cigarette out then he drifted off to sleep knowing full well that he had Chelsea held tightly under his charms. He knew his brother would be stumbling in at some late hour of the night or early morning. He only hoped that Felecia had the common sense not to jeopardize her position by being late the next morning.

Chapter Sixteen

OPENING THE BANK

Felicia awoke at 6 am and wiped the sleep from her eyes. She felt a little sleepy from her long night with her cowboy. She got out of bed and headed for the kitchen to make some coffee. She started the coffee pot and then went to the bathroom to take a shower. She washed her hair and soaped up so she would be clean for the day. Then she turned off the water and stepped from the shower grabbing a towel and drying herself off. She wrapped a towel around her head and grabbed her makeup bag to apply her makeup for the day. She threw on her silk bathrobe and went back into the kitchen to get a cup of coffee. Then she went back into the master bath that she had in her master bedroom. Then she took out her blow dryer and styled her hair. Next she went into her bedroom and picked out an outfit to wear to work that day. Then she went back into the kitchen to have make some breakfast. She put some bread in the toaster and waited for it to pop up. When the toast popped up she buttered it and put some jelly on it so that it would be ready for her to eat.

She felt a little bit hung over but she was ready for work nonetheless. She finished her toast and coffee and grabbed her purse then headed out the door for the bank. It was 7:50 am and she wanted to get to work on time so that she could make sure that the money was ready for the tellers when they arrived before 8:30 am. There was a time lock on the banks doors and vault that unlocked everything at 8 am sharp. The time locks also locked the doors to the Trinity bank at 5 pm. This was a fact that Anthony Alvarez didn't know and couldn't tell the Snow brothers because he never showed up early. They would be very upset with him if they knew that he had missed such a crucial detail.

Chelsea's alarm went off at 6 am as well. She felt a little hung over from the wine, but she knew she could carry on through the day. She wiped the sleep from her eyes and stroked Misty because she was laying right beside her. Then she got up from bed and went into the kitchen to make some coffee. She then went into her room and picked out an outfit for the day. Next she went into the bathroom and turned the water in the shower. She undressed and stepped into the shower and cleaned herself up. She washed her long hair then turned off the water and rung her hair dry, then she grabbed a towel. She dried herself off with the towel then put the towel around her head to keep her hair out of the way while she got ready.

She then went into the bedroom and got dressed into the outfit she had chosen for the day. Then she returned to the bathroom and applied her makeup and dried her hair. Next she threw a French braid in her hair to keep it held up tight for the day. She loved having long hair and enjoyed wearing it in a French braid the most. Deciding that she was ready for the day she went into the kitchen and put a bagel in the toaster. While the bagel was cooking she opened a can of cat food for Misty and poured herself a cup of coffee. The bagel popped up and she slapped some cream cheese on it generously then took a bite. Then she added cream and sugar into her coffee to take the bitter taste away.

When she was through with her bagel she decided that she was ready for the day. She thought of Christopher often. It was 7:50 am so she decided to leave for the bank. She bent down to stroke Misty on the head once again and kissed her before she left her cottage. Then she locked up her cottage and jumped in her sedan then pulled out of her driveway and headed for the bank.

At 7:55 am Felecia arrived at Trinity bank and waited for the automatic locks to unlock the doors so that she could let her employees in for the day. Felecia waited for Chelsea to arrive so that they could open the front doors. Then Felecia and Chelsea could open the vault and Felecia could count the money bags for the tellers. Chelsea wasn't far behind her arriving at 7:57 am because Chelsea's cottage was just a few minutes farther away then Felecia's house was. They greeted each other cheerfully for the morning.

They waited for the time lock to unlock the doors as Harold, Cheryl and Alice arrived at the same time. At 8am sharp the locks let out a loud click. Which allowed Felecia and Chelsea to unlock the front doors. She let all of them in and Chelsea and her went to the vault and opened the door then Felecia used her combination on the door that held the money. She then grabbed the money bag from the day before and began to count out $500 for each teller. Then she took the receipts for each tellers drawer from the day before and took them to her office to reconcile the money bags that they had taken in on the previous day. After all the tellers had arrived Felecia gave the tellers back their bags from the previous day. They were to reconcile the receipts from the day before and return all of their receipts. As a rule the tellers had to be there before 8:30 am to reconcile their money bags from the day before. This was yet another security measure.

They each balanced for the day before so all Felecia had to do was secure the deposits for the armored truck bags for them to pick up after the tellers reconciled their money bags. Felecia was pleased that all of her tellers had balanced, she was especially happy that Anthony Alvarez had balanced. It was one less thing to worry about for Felecia. Each teller had a drawer and as they arrived they were supposed to count out the money in their bank bag to double check on Felecia's count. Then they were to put their fresh money bags away in their drawers and give Felecia the reconciled receipts from the previous day. This was yet another security measure that they took each day. Felecia was never wrong with her count so if the teller had a hard time balancing it was a mistake on their part not hers. This was one detail that Anthony had forgotten to tell the Snow brothers at their meeting. He grew especially nervous about their next meeting. He was worried that he might forget a crucial detail that the Snow brothers had counted on him to supply.

Harold had been a trusted security guard for Mr. Eldridge for many years. He had been protecting Mr. Eldridge for almost as long as Alice had been his secretary. Mr. Eldridge trusted him implicitly. Chelsea said good morning to Felecia and all three employees then helped Felecia open the great bank. The loan officers were at their desks and had turned on their computers to begin their work day. Harold took his post near the door. Cheryl busied herself by restocking the island with pens, deposit slips and all the necessities that the customers would need for the day. Then Cheryl went into the break room and made a pot of coffee with the industrial sized coffee pot, for the other employees. Alice headed straight for the elevators to go upstairs and put her purse away. She then came back down the in the elevator to get a fresh cup of coffee after waiting about ten minutes for the coffee to brew.

The tellers were to arrive no later than 8:30. This was a detail that Antony had forgotten to tell the Snow brothers the other night as well. But it would give him something to tell them on their next visit. Alice was always punctual as Mr. Eldridge liked. When Mr. Eldridge arrived she would be sure to get him a cup of coffee as well. Alice said thank you to Cheryl for making a pot of coffee.

"It really smells good, you are such a good hostess."

Cheryl blushed and said "Thank you, help yourself. It's almost ready."

Cheryl spent the morning making sure the pot of coffee never ran out. Ken Stevens and his wife Amanda were the next to arrive at 8:15 am.

Amanda greeted Harold and said good morning to him. "Smells like you've got the ball rolling on the coffee. I think I'll have a cup." She said

He then turned to his wife Amanda and asked her if she would like a cup of coffee.

Amanda replied, "No thanks, I had one before we left the house. One is enough for me. Thanks though honey." Then Amanda pecked Ken on the lips and went to her station to wait for Felecia to count out her money bag to put it in her drawer. Mark Patterson arrived next at 8:16 am, right behind the Stevens. Chelsea and Harold waited at the door to let each employee in as they arrived for the day. Chelsea said good morning to them as they filed in for their morning duties. Harold just nodded and grinned as the employees arrived.

Ken Stevens got his cup of coffee and retreated to his office then busied himself with his daily duties and waited for his tellers to arrive. Matthew Burch was the next to arrive at 8:22 AM. He said good morning to Harold and Chelsea then Cheryl and went to his station to wait for

Felecia to give him his money bag to count out and put in his drawer. Amanda Stevens had no trouble counting her drawer and putting it away. So she busied herself with her other duties while she waited with Mathew for the day to begin.

Thomas Underwood was next right behind Matthew. He said good morning to Harold, Chelsea and then Cheryl and went straight to his station as well and waited for his money bag to count it. Kristin Mayes showed up at 8:25 AM. It was closing in on 8:30 am and Chelsea was getting a little bit nervous that one of the tellers might be late. Kristin said Good Morning to Harold, Chelsea and Cheryl and went to her station to wait for her money bag so that she could count it then deposit it in her drawer. Kathy Richmond was next right behind Kristen at 8:26 am, Chelsea opened the door for her as well and said a happy good morning to her.

As Kathy walked by Cheryl's desk, she greeted her with a smile and said "Good Morning Cheryl." She said.

Then, Anthony Alvarez arrived at 8:27 am. He was in a somber mood because he knew what was about to happen in the future. But he went to his station all the same to wait for his money bag as well, as he did every day that he had been working at the bank. After all the tellers were in place and had balanced their money bags for Felecia, they put their money away in their drawers. She then handed each teller their receipts for the day before to reconcile and double check Felecia's reconciliation. Felecia went over to the picture windows above the door and opened them up. This was to give Mr. Eldridge the sign that all was good with his bank for the day.

The loan officers didn't have to be in their offices until 9 o'clock. Still Chelsea stood by the by the door alongside of Harold, waiting for the other four employees to arrive. Mark Patterson said good morning to Harold and both ladies and then he went straight for the break room to make himself a cup of coffee. At 8:40 am Cynthia Marks arrived and said good morning to Harold and Chelsea, and then he said good morning to Cheryl as she walked by her desk. Then she stuck her head into Mark's office and said good morning to him. Next she retreated to her office and busied herself with her duties. Justin Banks arrived at 8:45 am. Chelsea opened the door for him and let him in the bank. She smiled at him and said "Good morning Justin, nice to see you."

He replied "Well thank you and same to you as always." Harold nodded to him and smiled. Harold liked Justin because he was always nice to him and he had been there the longest of the men. He then walked past Cheryl's desk and gave her a wink and said hello.

At 8:55 am Samantha Smith arrived. She said hello to Harold and Chelsea. Then she greeted Cheryl when she walked past her desk. She then went straight for the break room for a cup of coffee before she retreated to her office. Cheryl went into the break room to start another pot of coffee for the rest of the employees. The last one to arrive was Mr. Eldridge's son Richard. Richard still lived with Mr. and Mrs. Eldridge at home. He was a recent graduate of the Union University in Florida. He was being groomed for Marks job when Mark left the bank the next year to pursue other interests. Mark had given his notice a year in advance because he was planning a 4 month trip to the Swiss Alps with Clark. He would worry about further employment after he got back. Maybe he would return to the bank and maybe he would choose a new career path. He just hadn't decided yet. To him this was a once in a lifetime opportunity and he wasn't going to let a job hold him back. So he told Mr. Eldridge of his plans and Mr. Eldridge began grooming Richard to replace him. Richard arrived at 9 am exactly.

As Richard arrived Chelsea unlocked the front doors for the customers. They began streaming in. Chelsea went upstairs to her office after all the employees were accounted for. Felecia had already made her way upstairs and busied herself with the books while she waited for Mr. Eldridge to arrive. But it was hard to stay focused with images of her cowboy dancing around in her head.

The bank was buzzing with the business affairs of the customers to the bank. Mark Patterson called a meeting with his employees at 9:30 am. He had some new procedures that Felecia and Mr. Eldridge had put together especially for the loan officers. Mr. Eldridge felt that the loans were down and wanted more from his employees. Mark stressed this point several times during the meeting.

At precisely 10 am Mr. Eldridge arrived and noticed that the picture windows were open which meant all was in place for the day. He then entered the building and said a cheerful hello to Harold and Cheryl. Cheryl replied "Well good morning Mr. Eldridge, you look great today."

To this Mr. Eldridge said "Well thank you Cheryl, I have been feeling much better lately."

Harold said "Good Morning sir."

It was the only greeting that he gave for the morning besides the smile he gave to Justin. Justin kind of reminded him of his own son. This is why Harold liked Justin. Then he walked to the elevator to go to his office upstairs. He headed into his office and got settled in. He was not in a good mood this morning because loans had been down and he had been losing money. He wanted the changes that he gave to Mark to take place right away.

Mr. Eldridge was a kind old man. Alice had been his trusted secretary for the past 30 years. She was loyal to him to a fault.

"Good morning Alice." He said as he popped his head into her office.

She looked up and said, "Well good morning sir, don't you look good today. These shorter hours must be helping."

"Well I feel much better," He replied, "I'm counting on this bank running smoothly and I treasure everyone of my trusted employees."

Alice then said to him, "Well let me run down and get your coffee so you can settle in for the day." Cheryl had kept a fresh pot of coffee going until Mr. Eldridge arrived.

"Thank you Alice, I will see you in a minute then." And with that Mr. Eldridge made it to his office put his briefcase away and sat down in his luxurious chair behind his massive desk to wait for his coffee. He turned on his computer and began the task of watching over his bank through his monitors.

Alice went to the elevator and rode it down to the lobby. She took pride in treating Mr. Eldridge with respect. He had been a very good boss to her for many years. She made her way to the break room and poured Mr. Eldridge his cup of coffee. She then added one sugar cube and stirred until the sugar melted, which was exactly how Mr. Eldridge liked it. She then rode the elevator back upstairs to Mr. Eldridge's office with his coffee.

"Here you are Mr. Eldridge, just how you like it." She said as she entered Mr. Eldridge's office.

"Why thank you Alice, you are always on your toes with me."

"Oh Mr. Eldridge you are a great boss, how could I not be?" She said with a grin. Then she turned on her heel and left his office to busy herself with her duties.

At 10:30 am Felecia made her way to Mr. Eldridge's office to go over the books with him. He was pleased with the results of the balance sheet. When they were finished and had gone over all the details that told then about the goings on of the bank she stood to leave. The Trinity Bank was open for business and all of the employees that Mr. Joseph Eldridge loved so much were all in place working diligently to run his great bank.

Chapter Seventeen

MORE SURVEILLANCE

Felecia headed for the kitchen to fix herself something to eat. Her fridge was close to being bare, she hated cooking. So she made a bowl of canned soup for dinner and declared the night a success. She was exhausted from all the sexual games her and Randy had played. She really needed a couple of nights off to regroup. She wanted to get to bed early to be rested up for tomorrow's day. She thought of the mistakes that Anthony Alvarez was making and decided that he had to go. She would have a talk with Mr. Eldridge tomorrow about him and ask whether or not she could fire him this week.

Frank stayed in the hotel room incase one of the girls called. He would just tell Felecia that Jonathan was asleep if she called. Jonathan spent the night in the apartment so that he could listen in on what was being said between the girls that night, which is something that he had grown fond of doing. It was also why he decided to stay in the apartment that night instead of wait for Felecia to call back. Frank fixed some dinner and Jonathan ordered Chinese food to have at the apartment. Jonathan was famished and he always loved Chinese food. He thought about what to do with Henry. Jonathan took out his revolver, he liked looking like a cowboy too so he carried his pistol with him just incase he needed it. He called Frank in the hotel room to discuss the plan further. He dialed the number to the Regency hotel. Frank answered the phone with a seductive tone because he thought it was one of girls calling.

"Hello." Came the voice of his brother.

"Hello Frank it's me Jonathan." Jonathan said to his brother.

"What's up" Frank asked.

"Well I just wanted to talk to you about Henry. I'm getting nervous that he may get fired. I want to make sure that we are in control of him. What do you think?"

"Well he may not be the brightest light bulb in the box but he's all we have in place at the moment. So put the revolver away and stick to the plan for now." Frank said this with a tone of authority. "Why don't we wait and see what Felecia does first. I don't want any blood shed unnecessarily."

"I'm dying to take that idiot out. First we have to split it three ways. Then we have to put up with his incompetence. Next you'll be singing him lullaby's to put him to sleep at night and tuck him in. Quit babying him and let me do it." Jonathan said with authority.

"Look when Felecia makes up her mind about it we will make up our minds. Got it! Now focus on the plan." Frank snarled at Jonathan.

"Alright, but I'm gonna call her back tonight and question her about her day, maybe she will give me a sign or something so I will know what's going on with that."

"You do that and then we will make a plan for Henry." Frank said with disdain in his voice. He really didn't want to hurt anyone. But Henry was screwing up. Jonathan was anxious to take use that gun on him and the pressure was building. The time was getting near.

The phone rang at Felecia's around 8 o'clock, she answered with a groggy hello. "Were you asleep tiger?"

"I was just dosing off, what's up cowboy?"

"Well I missed you tonight and wanted to talk to you a little."

"Okay, what did you want to talk about?" She said as she woke up a little.

"I was wondering how your day went. It can't be easy being the boss over so many people. How was your day?"

"It was just another day, I'm getting ready to fire one of my tellers because he's incompetent, but that's about it."

"Really, what did he do?"

"What didn't he do is the question. He's just not getting it. He's been with us for a couple of months and things just are not going well with him."

"Oh okay, well I'm sure you know how to handle him, you are my tiger you know that don't you?"

"Why that's an awful sweet thing to say, yes I am and you are my cowboy." She said with a handful of doubt.

She was growing board with him and she doubted that she would keep him after this weekend. She really enjoyed the sex but relationships aren't built on sex alone. Besides she was growing weary of his insecurity. Which was so unlike him, but it annoyed her none the less.

"You sounded like you were about to go to sleep, why don't I let you go so you can get your beauty rest." Randy said into the phone.

"Okay, thanks for calling again, I did miss you tonight but I had other pressing matters to attend to. I will see you soon cowboy."

"Goodnight tiger." Randy replied and with that said they both hung up the phone.

"Well she's gonna do it." Jonathan turned Frank and told him. "Okay, then we better take him out. We will meet up with him again tomorrow at lunch. Then we will take him up to the old Bayou Rd. and you can use that hand cannon you love so much tomorrow. We will just have to do without him." Frank said with a somber tone. He really didn't like this part of the job. He had a heart after all and he was a bank robber not a murderer.

"You know this changes the plan." Jonathan said to Frank. "I know, I know, now we have to call him and pick him up. We will just say that you only know the way to the restaurant and don't know how to give him directions, new to town and all. Then we will take him out to lunch and ply him for any last bit of information and then take him for a ride and you can do whatever you want to him."

"He should do well sleeping with the fishes in the bay." Jonathan said with a smirk.

"Oh would you knock it off, you know I don't like that thing and I don't like killing." Frank said as he pointed at the revolver on the table.

Jonathan reached for his gun, and said, "I can't wait to hit him, I didn't want to split anything with him anyway."

"Just make the call." Frank spit out at Jonathan again. So Jonathan dialed Henry's number and he picked up on the first ring.

"Hello" He said with a touch of fear in his voice because he recognized the phone number on caller ID on his phone.

"Hello Henry, its Jonathan. We need to change the plans for tomorrow. We will pick you up for the ride to the restaurant and take you back home. You better be ready at noon. We will be by to pick you up then." Jonathan said snarling at him with disdain in his voice. Henry was taken aback that Jonathan had called instead of Frank. He so didn't like Jonathan. But who was he to question their plan. So he went along with it anyway.

"Okay, I'll be ready at noon tomorrow then." Henry replied.

"We'll see you tomorrow at noon, don't be late!" Jonathan hung up the phone with that said without even saying goodbye to Henry. Henry was getting a bad feeling about the Snow brothers, but he was more greedy than scared of them so he just shrugged off Jonathan's attitude to nerves.

"See you can be nice to him when you want to be." Frank said sarcastically.

"What other plans will we have to change because of this idiot." Jonathan remarked as he walked into the bathroom and relieved himself without closing the door.

"We will need to get need to know Henry's password and he will need to direct us on the banks software for one thing. I think we should bring the laptop so that he can help us navigate the banks website clearly." Frank replied.

"Yeah I agree bro. We will bring the laptop then and ply him for information before we take him on his little trip down to the bay." Jonathan added.

"We will just have to depend on the ladies for information. What do you think of that?" Frank asked Jonathan.

"I really hate the idea of taking money from my tiger, but it has to be done. I'm just glad we don't have to use guns this time and we don't have to hold her hostage. I like her, however it's too late for attachments now." Jonathan said with a hint of sadness in his voice.

"You have really fallen for this chick, haven't you?" Frank asked

"No I'm just having fun, when the time comes you can count on me." Jonathan replied.

"I better be able to count on you. Everything depends on it." Frank said angrily.

"So what else are we forgetting?" Jonathan asked to change the subject.

"I won't know that until we talk to Henry tomorrow. He may have forgotten to tell us some important detail." Frank said.

"Well I hope the idiot gets it straight tomorrow and I will take pleasure in removing him from our little partnership." Jonathan said with a smile as he twirled the barrel of his gun.

"Would you put that thing away, it makes me nervous!" Frank told Jonathan.

"Alright tough guy, I'll put it away for now. But I can't wait to use it on Henry. Thanks bro for the all clear on this."

"Oh this isn't gonna be pleasant why are you smiling like that. Sometimes I wonder about you. It's a wonder we haven't gotten caught before this based on your penchant to kill." Frank replied. "You act like you want to get caught" He continued.

Jonathan interrupted and said, "Wait just a minute, I haven't done anything that would put the plan in jeopardy yet have I? What makes you think I can't control my temper?" Jonathan asked angrily,

"Well put that damn thing away then, and no you haven't, so let's keep it that way." Frank spat back at his brother.

Jonathan did as Frank asked and holstered his gun. He didn't need his brother anymore uptight than he already was. Frank lit another cigarette and blew grey smoke in Jonathan's direction.

"When do you see Chelsea next?" Jonathan said to change the subject.

"Friday night she's taking me to dinner at her parents place." Frank replied.

"That's great, maybe you can get into her pants finally after you are done with dinner." Jonathan said with a smirk on his face.

"I'm not after that right now. I have my head in the game. All I'm thinking about is the plan right now. So get you mind out of the gutter wouldja?" Frank retorted.

"I can't get enough of my tiger, I will see her Friday too then, if she will let me."

"You almost sound whipped brother of mine." Frank said with a smirk on his face.

"Oh don't go thinking that, I'm just having fun with this one. She really is a tiger, and I can't get enough of her at the moment. But when the time comes I will let her go just like we agreed." Jonathan replied.

Neither of them would admit that they had fallen hard for both ladies. It would be harder than they expected to betray these two ladies when the time came. For now they decided on their own that they would keep their true feelings to themselves and stick to the plan.

Since things had changed so drastically, they would need their heads about themselves to make the plan work. They had everything in place for now,

"Maybe we should move up the date that we plan to rob the bank." Jonathan suggested.

"First we should take into consideration that the armored truck schedule shows that there will be an 8:15 am delivery the Friday before Labor Day weekend. The armored truck will deliver the money that comes on that Friday before Labor Day to replenish the banks funds for the next week and pick up the deposits for that week. So we should rob it on the Friday before the big Labor Day weekend, since Henry will be out of the picture this week."

They thought this should be an easy pull, especially since they would be robbing the bank behind the scenes. but this time they got their hearts involved and that could lead to complications. The original plan was to pull the heist on the Monday before Labor Day weekend which was coming up in a week and a half. Frank thought and thought all night about all the possible scenarios. He wanted to be prepared. They would take Henry out tomorrow and then stick like glue to the ladies until the Friday before Labor Day weekend in two short weeks.

The plan had to be fool proof. Frank was really upset about having to betray Chelsea this way, but the plan came first. They had too much wrapped up in the plan to let it go now. The Trinity bank was their next target. Little did the ladies know they were being set up by their handsome suitors.

Frank had been chain smoking all night while they talked about the plan. He would be glad when this was over so that he would calm down a little bit and cut back on his smoking. His lungs were starting to hurt from all the extra smoking that he had been doing. He was up to two packs a day which was twice the amount he usually smoked. They would head for parts unknown with their stash in hand and live out their lives on some sunny beach somewhere after the heist. This would be the last one, or so they though. Frank wanted it to go well. This is why they used an inside man this time. With all the other banks that they had robbed, the plans had been different each time to throw off the cops. But it had never included such beautiful women that they would need to get so close to.

They thought about it more and Frank realized that they would be losing their inside man. Then Frank thought about his friend Charlie Wright. He was in South Carolina out of work right now but he could take a late flight and be in place right away. They would just need to get him hired by Felecia and then he could get all the rest of the information that the Snow brothers would need to make this heist go well.

Frank smoked one last cigarette before he went to bed. He would just tell the ladies that their third partner had had a cigarette in the hotel room and that is why it smells of stale smoke. This was a fact that Jonathan was not pleased with. Frank enjoyed his last cigarette of the day. Hell he enjoyed every cigarette, but the end of the day and bed time was his favorite time to smoke. He finished his last cigarette of the day and headed for his bedroom. Felecia hadn't called but it was nice to sleep in a nice bed for once. They would go over the tapes to see if the girls had called each other and spoke of anything important. He was growing weary of that dingy little two bedroom apartment that they had set up for this job. He would be happy to let that part go. He stripped down to nothing and hopped into bed, then dialed Chelsea's number. He so enjoyed talking to her at the end of the night and tucking her in so to speak.

"Hello, prince charming," Came the voice on the other end of the line.

"Hello princess, I just wanted to say goodnight before I turned in for the night."

"Well I'm glad you called, I so enjoy hearing from you just before I go to sleep."

Christopher smiled and said, "You make me smile beautiful. I can't wait for Friday."

Chelsea was excited about Friday night as well. "I can't wait till Friday either. I only hope you enjoy what mom cooks." She said to him in a sweet voice.

"Oh I'm sure whatever she cooks will be fine my lady, you just keep my plate warm for me and I will be there at 5:45 to pick you up. By the way, I have another business meeting tomorrow night, so I can't see you until Thursday would you like to go to lunch or maybe a movie that night?" He asked.

"We all have things to take care of as well, so I can't wait to see you until Thursday night then." Chelsea replied.

Christopher was pleased that Chelsea didn't have a problem waiting until Thursday to see him, he needed a little distance right now to stay on track. They had a job to do and an unpleasant part of it was tomorrow.

"I will see you Thursday then my lady, and I can't wait to see what your mother cooks for us." Christopher replied.

"Well, will I talk to you tomorrow?" Chelsea asked.

"Of course, I can't go a day without at least hearing your voice babe. Get some sleep now and I will talk to you tomorrow."

"Goodnight sweet prince," She cooed into the phone.

"Goodnight sweetness," he said back to her. And they both hung up the phone then faded off to sleep.

Chapter Eighteen

THE PLAN COMES FIRST

Frank was miffed at Jonathan for bringing up his smoking when Jonathan had just as bad a problem with his drinking and attitude. Jonathan always had at least a beer in hand when he was at the apartment and he really did love his beer on a nightly basis. He had a very high tolerance for alcohol so he wasn't concerned about making mistakes because he had a few beers in him. He was just waiting for the day when he could enjoy a cocktail on the pearly white beaches of the Caribbean or some other tropical paradise of his choosing whenever he wanted. They would have enough money to keep them happy for the rest of their lives after this heist by living abroad cheaply. And after all if the money didn't last, all they had they had to do was pull another heist to replenish their funds.

However, Jonathan had taken some computer programming classes at the local community college when they were in New York this last time. Jonathan was prepared for this heist and he felt that it would be the easiest heist that they had pulled yet. After all they were experienced bank robbers but this was a new way to get the job done. None the less Jonathan was looking forward to this heist because it seemed as though it would be the easiest one yet.

Frank stormed out of his room on his way out. "I gotta go to the store bro."

"What, we need to keep tabs on them. Why is this surveillance only up to me?" He asked angrily, "Shouldn't you be a part of this too?"

"No you can keep tabs on them and I will be right back." Frank told Jonathan firmly.

"Yes sir." Jonathan spit back at his brother. So he plugged in the head phones and put them on and listened to the offices of the two ladies that they would betray. Frank was out of cigarettes and didn't feel like arguing with his brother over going to the store for more.

The tapes caught every word that the ladies said within the confines of their offices. So he just listened in so learn what today's plan was. "It's lunch time, want to grab a bite," Chelsea asked as she popped her head inside Felecia's office.

"What did you have in mind, and don't tell me that you want to talk about Anthony again."

"No I don't want to talk about him anymore I know your mind is made up. I wanted to try Chinese food today, there's a restaurant just downtown. What do you think?" Chelsea asked.

"That sounds good, I could go for some Chinese food" Felecia said then she continued, "What about your walk on the beach at lunch?"

"I can go one day without it." Chelsea replied.

"Okay let's go then, but no mention of Anthony, I'm already upset that I have to wait to give him the ax until Mr. Eldridge gets well and returns."

"Don't worry, I know your mind is made up. Let's just have a pleasant lunch. Okay?" Chelsea said with a smile.

"Lets go then." Felecia said as she pushed her chair back and stood. She grabbed her purse from her drawer and they left for the stairs. They said good bye to Cheryl and Harold as they left the bank for lunch.

At 1 o'clock Chelsea and Felecia returned from lunch satisfied. When they returned, Felecia noticed that Anthony was not back yet. *'Boy this guy really knows how to screw up,'* She thought to herself. They climbed the stairs and retreated to their offices. Felecia couldn't get Anthony out of her head. She would much rather be thinking about how much fun it was to have sex with her cowboy but there was business at hand. Chelsea thought of Christopher to keep her mind off of the situation with Anthony. Little did they know that they would be sealing Anthony's fate by firing him. If they had known this, Chelsea wouldn't have had anything to do with it.

The day dragged on but ended on a high note. The loan department was seeing more loans and this would please Mr. Eldridge. His plan was working. He had offered their customers lower rates on home loans and car loans and the customers responded well. At the end of the day Anthony was relieved to find that his cash drawer balanced for once. He was safe at the bank for another day. He would be sure to be early tomorrow. He had no idea that he was finished at the bank for good. He was afraid of the Snow brothers and he didn't know how they would react if he got himself fired. It was a thought he banished from his mind for now.

At 4 o'clock the loan officers left for the day, including Richard Eldridge, even though he had come in late. He was concerned about his father's health so he headed straight home at 4 o'clock right behind him. He decided that his mother would need some help at home and he had some chores to do for his father. Making his father happy was most important to him right now with all the things that had gone wrong with Anthony for the past few weeks. He wanted to ease his father's mind and help him as much as possible to make him happy.

Felecia went down to the lobby to help the tellers with their money bags. She was a little happier that Anthony needed no help tonight, but she still had it in for him all the same. When the tellers all balanced and then ran their tapes for her to go over in the morning, the money was put away. Chelsea let them out of the bank one by one. Then Felecia locked the combination that held the money in the vault. Then Chelsea and Felecia inserted their keys to lock the vault for the night. Then they made their way to the front doors. Felecia closed the drapes in the picture window as she did every night at this time. Then the two women left the bank for the night.

Chelsea was hoping to at least talk to her handsome prince tonight. Felecia was growing weary of waiting for her cowboy and she had lost interest in him. But she knew if she was going to have a fun time this weekend she would need her rest. So when she got home, she ate a piece of left over pizza and had a beer for dinner then settled in to read her book for the night.

Just then the phone rang. It was Randy, checking up on her.

"Hello" She said as she answered the phone.

"Hello to you tiger, how was your day?"

"Well hello stranger, I miss you and I don't know if that's a good thing or not." She said with a smile.

"Oh it's a good thing." Randy cooed into the phone.

"Mr. Eldridge was ill today so I couldn't fire that employee I wanted to."

"Oh that's too bad, when do you think you will be able to finish the job?" He asked nonchalantly.

"Just as soon as Mr. Eldridge is feeling better and back to work."

"Oh and how long might that be?" He asked.

"Soon I hope. I don't know how much more of this employee's incompetence I can take. I would just do it, but Mr. Eldridge has the last say, so I have to wait. Plus I'm concerned for his health, he recently had a heart attack"

"Well tiger, how about we have dinner tomorrow night? And maybe a little fooling around? What do you say?" He asked.

"Oh that sounds wonderful, what did you have in mind?"

"We could break in my bed at the hotel and eat something there. I could order room service. What do you think?"

"Sounds wonderful cowboy, on one condition, you have to wear your cowboy boots." Felecia said as she felt herself getting wet again just talking to him about his boots.

"You got it tiger. I love that you love my boots."

"They turn me on cowboy. What can I say."

"Well I will wear them for you. Do you want to come by here or shall I send a cab?"

"Oh I can drive, you're at the Regency right?"

"Yes room number 504. Say about 6 o'clock?"

"Sounds great, I look forward to it." She cooed into the phone.

They said their goodbye's as the date was set. They both hung up the phone and she got back to her reading. She would spend this weekend with him then she would dump him on Sunday when he's ready to leave.

Misty greeted Chelsea at the door when she let herself into the cottage. She bent down and pet her cat affectionately. Then the phone rang and she grabbed it on the first ring.

"Hello," She said into the phone.

"Well hi there beautiful. How was your day?" Christopher asked as he replied.

"Better than I expected." She went on to say, "Mr. Eldridge the bank owner didn't show up today, so Felecia couldn't fire that employee. Which was a relief to me, because I have to do the firing."

"Oh that's too bad, but at least you have another day to wait. When might he be back?" Christopher asked as he blew grey smoke into the air,

"Well normally Ken Stevens would fire him because he is the boss over the tellers but Felecia is really mad at this guy so she has made her mind up. She is waiting for the all clear from Mr. Eldridge before she fires him. So we don't know that yet. He wasn't feeling well, so when he is better I guess."

"Can Felecia wait that long?" Christopher asked knowing full well what the answer would be. This little bump would cost them.

"Yes she has to, its not up to her. Mr. Eldridge has the final say. And I'm worried about Mr. Eldridge."

"Oh well then I guess you're off the hook for a while, and I'm sure your boss will be okay princess." Christopher reassured her

"Thank you babe," She said to him. "Yes I will have to wait until he returns at least." She replied.

"How was your day?" She asked. "We just relaxed today, but we have a meeting tonight. Although I wish I was seeing you tonight instead." He told her as he blew smoke out of his mouth and into the air.

"But I will call you tonight after I get in."

"Oh I can't wait to hear from you again, I miss you so much."

"We will be together tomorrow night babe, but I miss you too." He said as grey smoke exited his nostrils.

"Well I better get going if I want to get to my meeting on time. Have a great evening babe and I will call later," He told her. Then they said their good byes and Chelsea went about the business of feeding her cat and making dinner for herself.

Chapter Nineteen

DOWN AND DIRTY WITH
FELECIA AND RANDY

It was 4 o'clock on Friday night finally. Chelsea had anxiously awaited introducing Christopher to her parents and having dinner with him at her parent's house. Felecia and Chelsea had had a busy day at work. Chelsea just wanted to get home so she could get ready for Christopher and dinner at her parent's house. Felecia couldn't wait to see Randy's hotel room and play around some more.

At 3:55 pm Chelsea popped into Felecia's office and asked "Are you ready to lock up?"

Felecia looked up from her books and said, "Wow its already time to go, I had lost all track of time. Yeah let's go. I want to see my cowboy as soon as possible."

She was still having regrets about her cowboy and she had wished she had a new interest that she could replace him with. So she would spend the weekend with Randy because she didn't have anyone to replace him yet.

They headed down the stairs to the lobby to let the employees out and lock the door. Felecia oversaw counting the teller's bank bags and Chelsea waited with Harold at the front door so that they could let the loan officers out at that time.

The business at hand went smoothly tonight. Felecia was happy that Anthony had had no problems balancing. This was a record for him as of lately. He had balanced two days in a row now. Felecia was beginning to have doubts about firing him, but she knew that it was only a matter of time before he started screwing up again, so she held her reservations for now.

Anthony left the bank on time tonight. Chelsea let the tellers out one by one as they finished balancing their drawers. She was getting anxious and wanted to leave a little early to get a jump on their dinner plans. At 4:45 all the tellers had been accounted for and Chelsea let Harold and Cheryl out of the bank and locked the doors up tight. Felecia was excited about her night with her cowboy as well, so she didn't mind leaving the bank early either that night.

They left the bank and locked it up for the night. The time locks would kick in at 5 o'clock and lock the bank up tightly until 8 am Monday morning. They said their goodbyes and left for their cars. Then they left the parking lot and headed for home.

After she pulled into her driveway and pulled her car into her garage, Felecia let herself into her house and quickly hopped into the shower so she would be clean for her cowboy. Then she put on a sexy camisole and matching silk shorts and slipped on a light over coat. Then she left the house and locked it up tight. It was almost 5:45 and she wanted to catch him by surprise so she hopped in her sports car and headed for the Regency hotel.

She was growing tired of Randy and hated to tell Chelsea but Chelsea just didn't understand how Felecia worked when it came to men. She wouldn't understand Felecia's sudden change in men this time either when Felecia found a replacement for Randy.

When she got to the hotel, she went straight to the check in counter and asked where room 504 was. The clerk pointed her in the right direction and she was on her way. She began to tremble when thoughts of Randy came to mind. She would miss Randy when he was gone.

At 5:55 she knocked on the door to room 504. "Just a minute" came the voice from inside. Then the door swung open and Randy stood there in his boxer shorts and snakeskin cowboy boots.

"Well hello tiger, I have missed you." He said as he reached out and pulled her into the hotel room. He closed his mouth around hers. She had felt passion before but never this intense. She loved the way it felt in the beginning of a new romance. A new romance would be a nice change from Randy and would keep her satisfied.

She was always ready to go and as she jumped on his hips she was as ready as she ever would be. "I have missed you too cowboy," She whispered into his ear. "Where's your bedroom?" She asked seductively as she wrapped her legs around his waist.

"Oh its right this way, let's get this party started," He said as he kissed her neck.

This desire had engulfed her before. This felt so familiar to her. When she spent time with him it seemed as though time stopped. He carried her to his bed and gently laid her down on it. He then noticed that she was wearing sexy underwear under her over coat. He got hard instantly and she smiled passionately. Then she reached for him and started stroking him gently. He slipped her camisole over her head and started sucking on her nipples. Then he slipped out of the boots that she like so much so that he could slip out of his boxer shorts. "No don't take them off." She exclaimed. "I wanted you to keep them on. They are so sexy."

"Don't worry darlin, I will put them back on. Just be patient and give me a chance tiger." He told her in between kisses.

"Okay then my cowboy, I really love those boots."

She made her way down to his manhood and began sucking on him and made him even harder for her. He moaned as she licked him gently to make him as hard as possible. He exploded in her mouth. She tasted his sweet nectar and she was overjoyed at the way he tasted.

"My turn." She said happily. So he slipped his boots back on and scooted up closer to her on the bed. She slipped out of her shorts and he positioned himself between her legs and began licking her delicate parts. She began to quake almost instantly. He was happy that he could make her cum so easily.

She positioned herself so that she could lick him gently while he licked her. This would help him stay hard until she was ready for him to enter her. Next she moved to her hands and knees and turned around and he inserted himself into her from behind. He began to move in and out of her and she moaned in ecstasy. She felt for her delicate parts and stoked her herself gently. They moved along to the mood music that Randy had put on just for this occasion using the CD player that Christopher had brought to the hotel room. He had set the mood with the light jazz music in the CD player. They came together once again, then they collapsed into each others arms.

"That was awesome, you are so sexy tiger." He told her.

"You're quite sexy yourself cowboy." She whispered to him with a slight hint of regret.

"What do you say we order some room service and go for round two?" Randy asked her.

"Oh I could eat, and another round sounds wonderful. You make me feel so good cowboy."

"You make me hard every time I think of you tiger. Let me get the menu." He said and left the room for the menu in the kitchen.

He returned and asked "What do you want to eat tiger?"

"You, but a burger sounds good too," She replied with a giggle.

So Randy picked up the phone and ordered two cheese burgers with fries and a six pack of beer. The clerk on the other end of the phone took the order and said, "That will be right up sir." Then Randy hung up the phone and headed for the bedroom where Felecia was waiting patiently. He sat down on the bed and just took her in for a moment. He couldn't believe that he had found this chick and how well they fit together. He would miss her when the time came. Little did he know it was going to be sooner than he thought because she was steadily growing bored with him.

Even though the sex was good with Randy, he wasn't the best she had ever had. She was still searching for the perfect mate. Randy thought he had met his perfect mate. He knew he would let her go soon but his passion for her only grew with each passing day.

"Well dinner is served in a few minutes."

"That's great, I really like your hotel room," She said to him, "Wanna fool around a little before the food gets here?" She asked while she spread her legs apart under the sheets.

"Of course, I can't get enough of you. C'mere tiger let me make cum again," He said as he scooted up the bed to be next to her. He gently rubbed her leg and made his way to her delicate parts. He inserted his fingers and she was ready for him once again. She moved slowly along with him and came when he moved his fingers inside of her once again. Randy loved this about her. He was hard as a rock again, so he moved over to get on top of her and inserted his engorged member into her and they began to move in unison again. It wasn't too long before they both came together again. Randy was glad that Christopher had other plans tonight. He was getting tired of just going over to her house to fuck.

A knock came at the door, "Room service," The voice said from behind the door.

Randy threw on his boxer shorts and said, "I'll be right there." Then he turned to her and said. "I'll be right back, don't go anywhere."

She giggled and said "I can't get enough of you either cowboy, I ain't goin anywhere for a while anyways." With that Randy kissed her gently and headed out of the bedroom to the door.

The food arrived in covered plates. He brought the plates into his bedroom.

"I don't want you to move, so lets eat in bed, what do you think tiger?"

"Sounds good to me cowboy, just bring it over here."

So Randy brought Felecia her plate and a beer. Then he settled into the bed next to her.

"I ordered a six pack of beer, I didn't think you would mind."

"Oh I don't have to work tomorrow so another beer sounds good to me." She commentd

"Great then lets enjoy these and if we need more we will just order more from room service. I think they close at 10 pm though, so we might want to order more than a six pack next time, okay tiger?" He asked her.

"That sounds good to me cowboy, let's get drunk." She said with a slight giggle.

And with that they dug into their food. Felecia wasn't a good cook and hadn't had a good meal in a few days. She was famished and gobbled up her burger in a hot second. "How did you know I like cheese on my burgers?" She asked between bites.

"Well I just thought you would like it. Good guess, huh?" He replied.

"You are getting to know me too well mister, I will have to start calling you my boyfriend if you don't watch it." She said as she smiled and leaned over to kiss his neck.

He simply shrugged that comment off and took another bite of his burger. "Want another beer?" He asked after they finished their meal.

"Yes of course, and get back in here wouldja." She said with a twinkle in her eye.

"Ready for another round tiger?" He asked as he took her plate away.

She smiled and said "Ready when you are cowboy. C'mere and let me lick you."

This excited him once again and he began to get hard. "I'm comin darlin', here's your beer and let me lick you too."

They got into position and she took him entirely into her mouth and began sucking on him. He began licking her and in no time they were in the throes of another orgasm. She stroked him gently to keep him hard and turned around so he could insert himself into her once again. They had sex all night long. Moving in unison to the beat of the music. At 8 o'clock they ordered a twelve pack of beer. At midnight they were worn out from all the sex that they had shared. She really loved his sexual appetite and started to regret her decision to dump him. Little did she know that her time with him was already numbered.

Felecia had half of the beers that they had ordered. She had only intended on having a couple but the night had been a long one so she had the extra beers that she had sworn off for the night. She decided that she should probably stay the night since she probably wasn't okay to drive. "Well cowboy, when will Christopher return?" She asked.

"I don't know, I assume he is at Chelsea's house. Can you stay until tomorrow?" Randy asked into the darkness.

"Of course, we can spend the whole night together if you want. Tomorrows Saturday, I'm off on Saturday and we have that date with Christopher and Chelsea tomorrow night." She replied.

"Why don't we spend the whole night and day laying around the hotel room ordering room service?" He asked

"That sounds good to me, now c'mere and make me feel like a real woman again, and again." She said as she let out another slight moan.

"Here I cum tiger. And don't you worry about the small detail of Christopher showing up. He's with Chelsea and he wants to be with her as much as I want to be with you."

"Well that sounds wonderful cowboy, I'll be happy to stay the night with you here in your hotel room." She replied

"Well I love spending as much time with you as possible." He left those words hanging in the air.

She got uncovered her nudity and pulled him closer then kissed him gently. "I see your ready for me again. God I love those boots of yours." She said with a giggle.

"Oh it makes me very happy that you do. I love that they turn you on." And with that said they began another round in his bedroom. They drank all the beer and at midnight they fell fast asleep in each others arms. She never made her way out of the Regency hotel that night but she was totally satisfied from the passion that they shared.

Chapter Twenty

DINNER AT CHELSEA'S PARENTS

Chelsea delighted in the fact that her parents would finally meet Christopher tonight. She was very excited. She went into the bedroom and changed out of her work clothes into a cute pair of shorts and a tank top. She noticed Misty was not in the house but time was running short. So she decided to let her cat have her way tonight. At 5:30 pm a knock came at the door. It was her prince charming.

"Just a minute." She said as she went to the door. She opened it to find two bouquets of flowers with another poem in hers. This one was a little sexy, which took her by surprise.

"Oh my, I hadn't expected that. Thank you very much, and I agree. It's like we were made for each other. Come in sweetheart. Dinner will be about an hour. Mom's a great cook, I'm sure you will love it." She said to him as he came in while he let her go on and made himself at home.

She put her flowers in a vase and read the poem again. She melted with his words.

"I love it, you write so well."

"Well I try, what time is dinner at your parent's house?" He said with a smile.

"Well we said 6 o'clock so we have just enough time to make it there and visit a little bit before dinner."

"Sounds great, how is your mother?"

"She's great, and she's a very good cook."

"Well I bet she is, you look great in shorts babe." He commented.

"Thank you baby," She cooed. She told him that her mother had planned on making her famous meatloaf roll.

"So what's a meatloaf roll?" He asked with a grin.

"Well you steam some broccoli, then you make the meat mixture for meatloaf just like you would any other meatloaf, then you spread out some cling wrap on the counter when the broccoli is done, and you spread the meat out over the cling wrap, then you spread thinly sliced ham over the meat, then you spread the cooked broccoli over the ham. Then you use the edge of the cling wrap to roll the meat into a loaf. Cook it about an hour, then about five minutes before its done you put slices of white cheese over it and let them melt. And you serve it with mashed potatoes, but mother loves to make bread so she will also make either cornbread muffins or biscuit's to go with it. She really is a good cook. I have learned a lot from her but I am in no way as good a cook as she is. But I'm trying."

"Wow, sounds delicious. I can't wait to dig in." He said as a craving hit him hard. He would have to excuse himself to the bathroom and chew some gum to ward off these cravings for the night.

"Well I hope you like it, I really like it when mom makes it." She replied.

"So do I get to meet your cat tonight?" He asked.

"Yes of course if I can find her. She got out again and I can't find her tonight."

"Oh no I hope she's alright."

"Oh she'll be fine, she does this sometimes. I'll find her or let her in when we get back. No problem."

They headed out the door and he led her to the passenger side of his rented SUV. He wanted to make love to her so bad, she looked so good in her shorts but he wanted to keep up the image that he was a perfect gentleman so he kept his thoughts at bay.

Another craving hit him hard so he rode it out until it passed. He knew that if he had a craving hit while at Chelsea's parent's house he would have to excuse himself to the bathroom. While there he would open a new pack of nicotine gum and insert a piece into his mouth. He would carefully place any evidence of the nicotine gum in his pocket so that she wouldn't find it in the garbage. He would just suck on it so that she wouldn't see that he was chewing gum. But he had the regular gum just incase she noticed and wanted a piece. He was excited to be able to gain her trust enough to get invited over to her parent's house. Although Elise McQuire's report wouldn't be a good one.

They hopped in the SUV and he started the engine. Even though she was so excited about introducing him to her parent's he was leary of getting too close to them and her. He wished he were doing anything else in the world but this tonight. When they got to her parent's house he smelled the aroma of something good cooking. Chelsea opened the door and let them in.

"Mom, are you here?" She called out into the air.

"Yes I am dear, here I come." Elise entered the living room and held out her hand to Christopher in a kind greeting.

"Oh hi mom, this is Christopher Fields. He's the reason that I didn't see you last weekend."

"Yes of course I missed you last weekend dear. Nice to meet you Christopher." Elise McQuire said to him.

"Pleased to meet you too ma'am. Dinner smells great. Here I brought these for you." He added as he handed her the bouquet of flowers.

"Oh how lovely Christopher, thank you very much, let me just put them in a vase and give them some water. Then why don't we sit on the couch and chat until the biscuits are done? I just took the meatloaf out and I'm letting it cool right now. Dinner should be about 15 minutes."

"That sounds great Mrs. McQuire." Christopher returned.

"Please, come and sit. What do you do for a living Christopher?"

"Well I have a partner and we sell precious gems. When we met Chelsea here she helped us secure some of our inventory."

"Do you travel much? It seems like you would have to travel a lot for that kind of job."

"Well yes ma'am, we do travel a lot."

"Mom. Why don't we sit and get a little more comfortable." Even though Elise McQuire had directed them to sit on the couch, she hadn't followed through yet. Christopher was still standing in wait for them to sit. Chelsea was getting uncomfortable with this conversation and wanted to put Christopher at ease.

"Yes of course, come right in. Sorry where are my manners tonight. Christopher come right this way and have a seat." Elise said.

"Thank you ma'am, I have looked forward to this dinner all week." Christopher told her.

Elise got a funny feeling that he wasn't what he said he was. And she didn't like the fact that he was a traveling salesman. She was on high alert with this one. This made her uncomfortable to have him charming her daughter like this. She would have to have a long talk with Chelsea when she got the chance.

Chelsea's dad had joined them and sat down in his chair in the living room. Chelsea introduced them and they continued chatting for about 10 minutes, then Elise announced that dinner was almost ready and she excused herself to the kitchen. Chelsea stood and told her mother that she would help set the table. Christopher made small talk with Mr. McQuire. This made Christopher a little uncomfortable because he got the impression that Chelsea's father didn't approve of him either.

They made small talk while they ate dinner. Elise was pleasant to Christopher. Just because she had these feelings didn't mean that she had to lose her manners. Because George McQuire had a funny feeling about him as well, he simply kept his opinions to himself until he could get his daughter alone and talk to her about Christopher. A fact that he would share with his wife as soon as possible. He didn't say much during the meal. He just ate his wife's good cooking and bit his tongue for the evening.

"That was wonderful ma'am. Thank you for inviting me over and serving such a delicious meal." Christopher commented after they finished eating.

"Well thank you Christopher. But please call me Elise." She pleaded. But he refused to call her by her first name. When dinner was finished, Christopher came up with an excuse to leave early. He didn't like the feeling he was getting at her parent's house. So he became very anxious to get out of there as soon as possible.

"Well sweetheart, I have an early business meeting tomorrow so I had better get going." Christopher said.

"Oh do you have to? Do you have to go so soon? Tomorrow is Sunday, its supposed to be a day of rest." Chelsea exclaimed quietly.

"Yes sweetheart I really have to go. It was so nice meeting you tonight Mr. and Mrs. McQuire."

"It's a shame you have to go so early Christopher. But business before pleasure. Have a nice evening and a pleasant meeting tomorrow." Elise told Christopher.

Chelsea and Christopher left her parent's house. Christopher was relieved to be out of there. Chelsea was a little disappointed that they couldn't stay longer but she understood that he kept odd hours with his job. Christopher just wanted to get out of there so he could put an end to the interrogation.

Chelsea was taken by surprise by his behavior but she went with it and just figured he was too nervous about meeting her parents. She thought that he was just being shy. She would have a good talk with her mother in the morning.

He had had to remove his gum for dinner, so another craving hit him again after dinner and this one was a big one. He held his composure until he could rip off the patch and smoke freely. This would end soon and he could have all the cigarettes that he wanted. On the way home he commented on how good of cook her mother was a few times. Chelsea said that she only hoped that she could be as good of a cook as her mother was for him.

Then she said "Well she taught me how to cook so we both should have a knack for cooking. That would be a nice trade off on the chore of cooking every night."

"I would like that princess."

"Do you want to come in for a night cap?" She asked as they pulled into her driveway.

"Yes let's do that. I want to spend as much time with you as possible." He was pleased that she wanted to be with him more. The closer he got to this woman the better. He wondered how Jonathan was making out tonight. The gum did the trick. He would just suck on it the rest of the night.

They made small talk as they drank their wine. It was closing in on 10 o'clock and Chelsea was getting tired. She was also getting concerned about her beloved cat, and worried that something might have happened to her.

"I do hope Misty is alright." She said as a little yawn came out.

"I'm sure she's fine, let's go call her." Christopher said as he got up from the couch. He went to the door and Chelsea followed him. He opened the door and Chelsea called out Misty's name. She called to her cat and finally after about 15 minutes she came strolling up the drive way.

"Where have you been missy?" Chelsea scolded her cat. She bent down to pick her up but Misty was too quick for her. She darted into the house and rushed into the bedroom.

"Well I guess that answers that," Chelsea said.

"At least we found her." Christopher replied with concern in his voice. Chelsea didn't even notice that he was chewing gum. Christopher thought to himself 'Well I guess the gum is the trick then.' And he stuck the gum between his cheek and gum and sucked on it some more.

"Well it is getting late, I better call it a night." Chelsea said with a slight yawn.

"You do seem tired sweetheart. I should go and let you get your beauty rest. When can I see you again?" He asked.

"Well I had hoped we could spend the weekend together." She answered.

"What about dinner tomorrow. We could go to the restaurant in the hotel. What do you think?"

She got excited with that said. "Oh that sounds wonderful, I love that idea."

"Okay then how about if I come pick you up around 6 o'clock and we will have dinner and meet Jonathan and Felecia for drinks and dancing after dinner?" He said with hint of anticipation in his voice.

"I can't wait." She said with excitement.

"Then its set, I will see you tomorrow night around 6 o'clock then. I will also talk to Randy about is so that him and Felecia can join us, what do u think?" He asked.

"That sounds wonderful, I look so forward to it. Until tomorrow night then." She said.

Then he gave her a light kiss and headed for the door. She was sad to see him go but she had had a long week and she really was tired. They said their goodbyes and he left for the evening. As soon as he got out of eye sight he ripped the patch off, spit the gum out the window, and lit a cigarette. He headed for the apartment because he knew that Jonathan was at the hotel room with Felecia. He didn't want to interrupt them.

He got a head rush once again when he took the first drag of his cigarette but it felt so good. He was getting used to these head rushes every time he went without his beloved habit but he knew he had to quit eventually. He stripped down to nothing and hopped into bed when he got back to the apartment. He then dialed the number to Chelsea's cottage.

"Hello sweet prince." Came the voice on the other end.

"Hello sweetheart, just tucking you in before you go to sleep."

"I know and I love that you do this every night." She cooed into the phone. "I'm tired so I will say goodnight to you sweet prince,"

"Oh don't worry about it princess. I just wanted to say good night."

"Well thank you sweetheart, I hope you had a good time tonight?" She asked

"Yes it was a pleasure meeting your parent's." He said into the phone.

"Well I had hoped we could have had a little more time but I understand about your work schedule."

"Yeah it can be a crazy schedule at times, why don't I let you get your beauty rest and I will call you in the morning." Then they said their good byes and hung up the phone.

Misty jumped up on the bed for some affection. "And where were you tonight missy?" Chelsea asked her cat. She pet her because she loved her so much.

"Next time you're not getting out of my sight. I want your opinion on Christopher." She said to her cat. "He's such a nice man, why have you been avoiding him?" Chelsea asked as she rubbed her head. Then she wondered again as to whether or not Christopher was everything he presented himself to be. That nagging feeling crept up on her again. She would tell Felecia about the cat's actions tomorrow and she would have a talk with her Mother on Sunday. Then she would put it to rest.

Christopher would be in her house alone with Misty tomorrow. She simply had to get to the bottom of this. She turned her alarm on and drifted off to sleep. Oh yes she would get to the bottom of this tomorrow.

Frank drifted off to sleep knowing that he wouldn't see his brother until the next day if he saw him at all. He wondered how he was doing with Felecia but the hotel room wasn't tapped. So he would have to count on Jonathan to fill him in on the events of the evening.

Jonathan slept soundly in his clean sheets in the hotel room holding Felecia for the night. He was totally satisfied and dreamt of her while he slept. She was really getting under his skin. He would have to keep his mind about him if he wanted to finish the job they were there to do.

Chapter Twenty One

FELECIA MEETS DAVID

At 10:30 am Felecia stirred next to Randy. She needed to get a move on because she wanted to work out today and she needed to stop at the store on the way home. When Felecia got home she ate some soup fresh out of the can and waited for the clock to strike noon, she stuffed her work out gear into her gym bag and left her house being sure to lock it up tight. She drove to the gym and changed into her work out gear in the locker room. She then made her way to the mirrored room that held the held all the workout machines. She was sweating in no time. It was just what she wanted. When she was finished she headed for the doors and left. She didn't like using the showers at the gym and only used them when she had plans after her work out. Today she wanted to relax. She didn't have any plans until tonight so she would shower after she got home. She then left the building and headed for the store to pick up something to eat. She grabbed a deli sandwich at the deli counter at the store and picked up some coffee and a few other things to keep her alive for a few more days.

As she was walking around shopping she noticed a man was following her. At first she got scared, then she approached him to find out why he was following her.

"Hi how are you?" She asked.

"Well hello, my name is David. I'm sorry that I followed you but I can't help but notice how beautiful you are." David said.

"Well Hello, my name is Felecia."

"Nice to meet you Felecia. I was just wondering if you would be interested in a date sometime?"

"Oh wow, I didn't expect that. Here let me give you my phone number so that we can talk about it on the phone."

"That sounds terrific. Thank you." He replied.

She reached in her purse and pulled out a business card and a pen. Then she wrote her cell number down on the back of the card. Then she handed him her card.

"Here you go, give me a call sometime." She said as she grabbed the last of the things on her list and told him that this was a nice surprise.

Then she said "See ya soon" Then she headed for the checkout stand then home to eat her sandwich. *'Boy that guy was just my type. I hope he is what he seems.'* She thought to herself.

When she got home there was a message from David on the answering machine. It said, "I really liked meeting you today, I hope we can see each other really soon. I'll talk to you as soon as you call me back. Here's my phone number, 555 1392 call me back anytime, well hope to see you soon. Bye Bye"

Felecia got excited when David called. She didn't really like to see more than one guy at a time so she decided to see what David was like and see where it goes. After all she already had plans to dump Jonathan on Sunday.

"Good morning Bro. It's me Jonathan." Jonathan said into the phone. Christopher was at the apartment and Jonathan had called the phone there to give him the news about Felecia dumping him.

"Good morning to you." Frank said to Jonathan "Why are you calling so early? I'm busy getting ready to see Chelsea. I was going to surprise her and take her to breakfast." Frank told his brother.

"Well I can't believe that I'm getting replaced. This is just great, more complications. Why did Felecia have to meet someone else. Now I have competition. What do we do now?" Jonathan went on to say, totally ignoring Franks needs at the moment.

"We just have to wait, and see what happens. I'm more worried about that Cornwell. Why do you have to be so anxious to use that hand cannon?" Frank said to change the subject.

"Because I can't stand him. Besides I thought you were on board with this."

"Yes I am, we have to do it, but I don't have to like it." Frank said to Jonathan

"I'll be doing the dirty work, so just relax, okay?" Jonathan replied.

"Okay, I will leave it up to you." Frank spat into the phone.

"Just let me handle it, Okay?" Jonathan said as he scowled at Frank through the phone.

"Okay, I'm gonna jump in the shower. I have to call Chelsea, so I will talk to you soon."

Jonathan put on his holster and then holstered the gun. "I'm wearin my gun from now on." Jonathan said into the phone.

Frank commented from the phone, "What the fuck are you bringing that for?" Frank said angrily.

"Just incase, I want to be prepared. What if this idiot does something else while with us. You have to admit it would be helping the girls as well as us. You put your friend in place and bingo we're back in business again. I can't stand this uncertainty." Jonathan replied.

"Well just keep it holstered, we won't be needing that tonight. We have to wait." Frank demanded.

"Okay I will keep it in the car at the restaurant, but I aint promising anything after we leave."

"Well I'm driving so I will decide if he goes out tonight or not." Frank said rethinking the situation.

Jonathan threw on his signature snake skin boots and got ready for the day.

Frank left the recorder on in the apartment just incase David called Felecia as he headed for the hotel.

At 11:30 am Frank pulled up to the Regency hotel and parked near the door. He called up to Jonathan using his cell phone. He told Jonathan to get a move on and get down there now or they would be late picking Henry up. Jonathan hurried down to Frank and jumped into the SUV. They arrived at Henry's apartment. Frank hit the horn to let Henry know they were there. Henry was expecting them so he came right out

"Hi guys, ready for lunch?" He said in a chipper voice.

"Just get in the damn car," Jonathan spit out at him from the passenger side window.

So Henry opened the back door to the SUV and hopped in the seat behind Frank.

"Where are we going today?"

"Don't bother yourself with those details." Frank said to Henry. "Just be ready to spill the beans at lunch." Frank demanded.

"Yes of course, I have a lot to tell you." He replied. Jonathan smiled a little knowing that this could be the last meeting with this idiot.

They rode the rest of the way to La Comida in silence. When they arrived at the restaurant Frank parked the SUV in the back lot. He had picked this restaurant because he knew the girls wouldn't be going there anytime soon based on the conversation they had at lunch the other day. Henry was a little nervous because it was so unlike Jonathan to speak to him let alone call him. He wondered if Jonathan was warming up to him. This put him at ease for the moment.

They exited the SUV and walked up to the door of the restaurant. Frank opened the door and let himself in and Jonathan and Henry followed him into the restaurant. They were greeted by the hostess. It was the same waitress that had helped the girls that week was waiting on customers when they arrived, but she was in a better mood tonight plus she took a liking to Frank. She was eager to wait on them tonight so she put a smile on her face and treated them totally different than she had treated the ladies.

"I hope this place is good." Henry said.

"It will be fine, don't you worry about it." Frank said with authority while the hostess took them to their table. Frank slipped her a $100 to keep the area clear of other customers while they ate. She was more than happy to oblige.

The waitress appeared and asked what they wanted to drink. Frank once again ordered iced tea for all of them. He didn't want his brother getting drunk today. Jonathan was not pleased with this fact. The waitress winked at Frank then turned to let them be.

"So what do you have to say for yourself today Henry?" Frank asked.

"Well I think you will be pleased with what I have today." Henry replied. "Like for one, Ms. Grey and Ms. McQuire take their work home with them frequently. They each have a home computer that has the banks information on it so that they can work from home. Their computers are hooked up to the network for the bank. It's a security measure, because they want to make sure that they can always have access to the banks books and records. Say an employee is having trouble with their duties. Well One of the ladies can access their home computers and work from there without having to go into the bank when its closed. I learned that they do this, this week when I was having some trouble with my duties. Ms. McQuire took the time with me the other night to walk me through some of the procedures that I need to know. It's a good set up and they have an open door policy to ensure that all employees are taken care of and understand the procedures." He went on to say.

"That's good information. We have been seducing the ladies at night lately. Jonathan and I have been able to get a copy of their computers data from saving it to this little device here." Frank said as he pulled out the flash drive that held all of the banks information.

This was news to Henry but he just went with the flow and listened to what Frank had to say. "Oh that was a good idea, I wish I had thought of it." Henry commented.

'I sure hope that this guy knows how this works, he may be sleeping with the fishes soon enough if Jonathan has his way' Frank thought to himself before he replied. Then he went on to say, "That's good information, Keep it up Henry. You might just make it out of this alive after all," Frank said as he let out a little laugh.

"No one said anything about dying." Henry replied. "I never would have taken this job if I would have known that you wanted me dead."

"Don't worry about it, that was a joke. Lighten up wouldja?"

"Okay, I will. Just please don't even joke about that."

"Okay, I will keep my jokes to myself. That information is helpful. What else?" Frank asked.

"Well once you have access to the banks funds it should be as easy as transferring the money to your own account. It's really easy to do. Probably the next thing that you should do is go into the branch and open an account so that you can transfer the funds when the time is right."

"Very good," Frank said with approval. Henry relaxed a little bit with that said.

"How tight is the security on the banks website?" Frank asked.

"Well as long as you have all the passwords and security codes, you should have no problem getting exactly what you want. You should have all that information on the flash drive that you just downloaded." Henry replied.

"What else?" Frank asked.

"Well I was thinking, I umm would like a bigger piece of the pie." Henry said to Frank. "I mean I'm doing a lot of work here. I am really trying to help you to have access to the banks backdoors and security codes and passwords. That's a lot of information. I could go to jail if I get caught giving this information. It will take a little bit of research to decipher these codes and passwords but I have a good program to quickly decode all of that information. So I thought I deserved a little more than we agreed on."

Jonathan scowled at Henry and spit out at him. "No way asshole, we are doing all the heavy lifting and you are just our inside man. You don't deserve any more than you are getting." To this Henry cringed and closed his mouth about the subject for the night. He was nervous again and it showed.

The waitress came to take their order. Frank said they would have three enchilada platters. The waitress scribbled on her note pad and said, "Will that be all?"

Frank said, "Yes that's all ma'am. Thank you for your time." And he winked at her before she left them. Then the waitress winked at him and turned to walk away to put in their order.

"I think we have heard enough, if you screw this up Henry you're history, Got that tough guy?" Jonathan scowled at Henry as he said this.

Henry began to sweat and said, "I will sir, I got your back on this."

The food arrived and they dug in. Jonathan ordered a beer with his dinner when the waitress brought them their meals. Frank scowled at his brother for ordering alcohol this time. *Couldn't he go one night without drinking.* Frank thought to himself, *'But then again he does have a point about my smoking so I will leave it at that.'* As the thought continued. Frank commented that the waitress didn't seem so bad here. And Jonathan agreed. His tiger must have had another waitress because this one had done nothing to upset them.

They ate their dinners and kept the conversation on the subject. Henry noticed that Jonathan was watching his every move. So, he got even more nervous.

"You know," Frank said to Henry "We have those bugs that you planted yourself in both of the ladies offices. And Jonathan and I have gotten very close to the ladies lately. We know about you screwing up at the bank. What are you going to do about that? You can't be late again." Frank said with authority.

"I couldn't help it, there was an accident." Henry said almost crying by now. He was shaking with fear.

"Yes we know, but an accident didn't make you miscount your drawer or have trouble with that customer the other day." Frank replied.

"Yes I know, I have had a hard time keeping things straight lately. The closer we get to the robbery date the more nervous I get. I promise to do better. You can count on me." Henry said in between bites.

"Well you better, we need you as our inside man." Frank replied as he lit a cigarette.

Jonathan chimed in with "Yeah you better watch out from now on Mister or I will make you regret it." Henry cringed at the tone in Jonathan's voice. He knew he meant business.

"Honest I will do better guys, c'mon what's a couple of little mistakes anyway?" He said with a nervous smile at Jonathan.

"I don't trust you, asshole, so you better get it right!" Jonathan said with disdain in his voice. Jonathan couldn't wait to take this joker out. He was just itching to use his revolver on this asshole.

The waitress brought them the check and asked if they would like desert. They said no and Frank picked up the receipt book to put his credit card in it to pay for the meals. This was a mistake he would regret later. Jonathan decided that they would have to have had another waitress than the ladies because this one was treating them really good. They finished their meals in silence. Frank was not pleased to have to bring up Henry's incompetence.

"You sure you don't want some desert gentlemen?" The waitress asked as she approached their table.

"No that will be all for today. Thank you though." Frank replied.

Then the waitress turned on her heel and headed to her station to pick up another tables meals. Henry was happy that the lunch was almost over and he could be rid of these two for the day and night. Jonathan took a long pull of his beer and burped.

"So when do we meet again?" Henry asked Frank,

"We need to get closer to the ladies so next week some time. Nothing will get in our way." Frank said to Henry. Jonathan had a smirk on his face as he stared down at Henry.

"Well just let me know when we meet again and I will be ready." Henry said with as much enthusiasm as he could muster.

They left the restaurant and walked to the SUV together. Frank unlocked the car and let them in. Franks hopped in the driver's seat. Henry was in the back seat but he could see the butt of the revolver sticking out from the console in the front of the SUV. He got nervous all over again. He didn't know if he should say something or not. So he kept his mouth shut. He had a feeling that Jonathan wanted to use that gun on him. And he was right.

They pulled out of the restaurants parking lot and headed for Henry's apartment to drop him off. Henry kept his mouth shut the entire ride home. When Frank pulled up in front of Henry's apartment he turned to him and said,

"Remember we know everything that goes on at that bank. And we are closer than ever before to the ladies. You just do your job and everything will be fine. Got it!"

"Yes sir, I will make sure I don't make anymore mistakes. Goodbye." Henry said as he opened the door and hopped out of the SUV. He had no idea how close he came to losing his life tonight.

Chapter Twenty Two

---◆◆◆---

REALLY BAD GUYS

F rank and Jonathan Snow were really bad guys. And Henry knew this well. He had known this when he hooked up with these two in the first place and had had reservations about helping. But Frank had given him no choice in the matter. Henry owed him from a previous job that they had pulled together. So he went along with it. Even though he had never been a bank teller before, he tried his best to perform his duties at the bank well. He had always had a hard time with money. But he was beginning to fear for his life and contemplated walking away from the whole thing. But he was already committed so he went into his small apartment and sat on his couch to watch a little TV.

When Felecia got home she let herself in and put the groceries away. She then took her sandwich to the table and gobbled it up. She had a soda with her sandwich and finished in no time. She didn't realize how hungry she was until the sandwich was gone. She thought of David and couldn't wait for his call. Then she thought of Randy and couldn't wait to see his hotel room and jump his bones once again tonight. She was so horny that it was almost time to take care of it herself. But she wanted to save it for her cowboy or maybe David. So she held off and would wait for one of them to satisfy her soon.

She went to her bathroom and turned on the water to take a shower. She undressed and stepped under the water. She soaped up and washed the sweat off of her body. Then she rinsed off the soap and turned the water off. She stepped from the shower and grabbed the towel on the rack next to the shower. She dried off and heard the phone ringing in the bedroom. She stepped out of the shower and grabbed her silk bathrobe then ran for the phone. It was Mrs. Eldridge with news about her husband.

"Hello" She said a little out of breath.

"Hello Ms. Grey, this is Eleanor Eldridge. I wanted to give you an update on Joseph."

"Oh how is he?" She asked with genuine concern.

"He saw the doctor today and was put on restricted duty. The doctor said it was indigestion but I know my husband so I insisted on the light duty. So he won't be in for a few days and when he returns he will only work a 4 hour day. He will probably be back on Monday. I suggest he works from 10 am to 2 pm. I was just hoping you could help me keep him on track with that." Mrs. Eldridge explained.

"Of course I will, you can count on me Mrs. Eldridge." Felecia said with a little sadness in her voice.

"I can tell you're concerned about my husband and you are his most trusted employee next to Alice, but he seems to respond to you better than her so I need the help. He is a workaholic you know." She said into the phone.

"Oh yes I know how much he likes to work. I will make sure he takes it easy when he returns. Just take care of him now so he can come back soon. I really miss him when he's away and his health really concerns me." Felecia said to Mrs. Eldridge.

"Thank you sweetheart, you're a doll. I knew I could count on you." Then they said their good byes and hung up the phone.

Felecia was upset that Mr. Eldridge wouldn't be in until next week at the earliest because she was worried about her boss, but this also meant that she would have to put up with Anthony Alvarez for another weekend at the very least. *'Maybe he will be back on Monday and I will be able to fire Anthony then.'* She thought to herself. This made her a little more upset that she had to wait. So she decided to read her book for a little bit and then fell asleep taking a little nap before tonight. She would fill Chelsea in about Mr. Eldridge later.

Jonathan's recorder caught the entire conversation. When they returned from lunch Jonathan couldn't wait to hear what his tiger was saying on tape. So when he entered the apartment he went straight for the recorder. He put on the headphones and listened in on the latest conversation at Felecia's. He heard the whole thing and relayed the message to Frank.

"Well at least we have an idea about when the boss will return. When he comes back, we will take Henry out to Bayou Rd., pop him and dump the body in the bay. Then we will put the plan into action on this upcoming Friday before Labor Day." Frank told his brother.

"What about Henry?" Jonathan asked.

"I just told you, would you pay attention." Jonathan had his mind on others things like his tiger and he missed part of the conversation.

"We will take him out after the girls fire him on Monday. Then we will put Charlie into place and we will be good to go. I will mention Charlie when we see them for drinks this weekend."

"Sounds good to me bro, I can't wait to hit him."

"I know seems like that's all you think about. Aren't you the least bit scared of killing someone?" Frank asked with a touch of fear in his voice.

"I have been waiting to take this character out since we hired him. I'm very happy to kill him." Jonathan continued.

"Well just stick to the plan woudlja?" Frank spit back.

Jonathan was getting tired of his brother barking orders at him. But he kept his mouth shut because he knew his brother was distracted and they needed him to be on his toes for the up coming robbery.

Christopher showed up to pick up Chelsea at 6 o'clock. "Hey Princess," He said to her when she answered the door. Chelsea was beaming with pride and she thought that this man really was what she was looking for.

"Hello sweetheart. I can't wait for tonight with Felecia and Randy." Christopher replied.

"Well I'm looking forward to it as well."

"Sounds good to me. Let's go then. I'm ready when you are."

They left the cottage with Misty hiding in the bedroom as usual. Chelsea still didn't understand why her cat was acting so strange. But she would find out tomorrow night. Tonight was all about them.

She grabbed her purse and said, "I can't wait to eat at the Regency restaurant." She had never been there before and she had herd good things about it. It was a dinner that she would live to regret.

They had dinner at the restaurant in the Regency. Christopher wanted her to try the menu at the hotel. So he invited her to have dinner with him in the hotel's restaurant since they hadn't gotten close enough yet to spend the night together at the hotel.

"Hello will that be two for diner?" The hostess asked.

"Yes just two tonight." Christopher replied. Then the hostess took them to their table and asked if she could get them anything to drink. Christopher ordered a shaken martini with two olives. Chelsea ordered her signature long island iced tea. The hostess told them that their waitress would be right there to take their orders. They waited patiently for the waitress to approach their table while they decided on what to eat.

They made their order and when dinner arrived they dug in and ate it up. They made small talk between them while they ate their dinner. When they were finished eating the waitress approached their table and placed the receipt book on the edge of the table and asked if they would like anything else. They thanked the waitress but declined desert.

Christopher put his credit card in the slot this time as well. Once again it would be a mistake he would regret later because each time he used his credit card he was leaving a paper trail to follow. They left the restaurant satisfied for the evening. She had ordered the fillet minion and she was really impressed with it. She told him that she really enjoyed having him meet her parents last night. Now she just wanted to spend more precious time with him. *'Maybe we can take advantage of the time we spend together this weekend and make love Saturday or Sunday after she got her Mothers opinion of him,'* He thought to himself. He kissed her lightly and told her that they had better get a move on if they wanted to meet Randy and Felecia in the bar. This would get him not only closer to her but it would make her trust him as well.

She recalled the conversation that she had had with her mother earlier in the day. Chelsea had called her Mother to get her opinion of Christopher. She thought about this conversation while they waited for Randy and Felecia.

When she had called her mother she said hello into the phone and greeted her mother. "Hello dear, how are you today." Her mother asked her.

"I'm good mom, how are you?" She asked her mother.

"Well I am good. I enjoyed meeting your friend last night." Elise McQuire said to her daughter.

"Well mom what did you think of him? You know how much I value your opinion." She commented.

"Well I am a little worried that he's a traveling salesman. When will you ever find the time to raise a family with him on the road all the time." Elise said into the phone.

"Well I had hoped you would have another report for me. He is just such a dream come true." Chelsea cooed. Elise could tell she had lost her daughter to this guy.

"Well honey, just be careful. Okay?" Elise said

"Of course momma. I trust your opinion and I will take it slow so with him. Okay?" Chelsea said to her mother.

"Well as long as you're happy." Elise replied.

"I am mom. Thanks for your input. I will talk to you soon, I'm making him dinner at my place on Sunday and we have plans to go dancing tonight. Misty has me kinda scared though. She wont come out when he is here." Chelsea admitted into the phone.

"That doesn't give you reason to pause honey? I mean she really is a good judge of character." Her mother said to her,

"Yes I know and that's why I'm taking it slow. I really want him to be the one though." Chelsea said to her Mother.

"Well just don't get hurt honey, I know he's special to you, but be careful." Chelsea's stomach lurched at her Mothers words. She was very close to her Mother and she trusted her opinion.

"You're right mom, I will take it slow and I won't get hurt. I really like him though. I will see you soon then okay?" Chelsea told her mother.

"That sounds good dear, I will see you later" Elise said to her daughter.

"That sounds great mom, I'll keep you posted as to where it goes. I'm making him your famous Chicken Casserole next week. That is a good recipe and I really think he will like it." Chelsea reported

"Oh he will like that honey, I will see you soon." They said their good byes and they told each other how much they loved each other and hung up the phone. Chelsea began to have regrets about just how true to her Christopher was. She would have to get to the bottom of it after the evening was finished.

Even though Chelsea was having these thoughts she still didn't want to spoil the evening for Randy and Felecia. So she banished the thoughts for the night and focused on spending time with Christopher. Chelsea couldn't wait to get the night started. Even though she was having these thoughts she still believed in Christopher. So she let the thoughts pass and waited for Randy and Felecia to arrive to get the night started. She was filled with excitement in anticipation for the night to begin.

Chapter Twenty Three

ELISE'S OPINION MATTERS

E lise McQuire had provoked thoughts that scared Chelsea. She didn't want to dump Christopher but her mother was usually right about these things. The first thing in the morning the phone rang. She rushed to pick it up. "Hello mom, how are you?" She asked, as she recognized the number on the caller ID.

"I'm pretty good sweetheart. How are you doing darling?" Elise McQuire said consciously.

"Thank you for calling mom, please give me your opinion about Christopher, it really matters to me."

"Well he's nice looking and he seemed to treat you pretty good."

"Thank you mom, but I really wanted to know what you truly thought of him. Misty has been acting strange around him. I don't know what to make of it. I need your opinion to think straight about him. Please tell me what you thought at dinner last night?"

"Well I just had a feeling that he was off a little bit. I don't think a traveling salesman would make a good boyfriend let alone a husband. I don't mean to be burst your bubble, but he didn't give me a good impression."

"Really, but he's such a gentleman. He really treats me good mom"

"But honey, what will you do when he leaves town for work and you have two kids running around your feet. You won't care that he's a gentleman then, you will be lonely and tired. You will not be happy my love. But it's your choice." Elise told her daughter.

"Well thank you mom, you have given me something to think about. And I'm sure that you are right. I just fell for him hard and wanted you to say you liked him. But I know that your intuition is on the mark most of the time. Thanks mom. I really appreciate your honest opinion." Chelsea said goodbye with a heavy heart. She didn't want to stop seeing Christopher. She thought he was perfect for her. She would just have to see how it played out now and be more cautious. She knew that she was ignoring her mother's opinion but she really believed that he was her prince charming and that her mother would come around eventually. She would just keep her dating Christopher to herself for a little longer. This was a mistake that Chelsea would regret.

On Monday Mark Patterson told Felecia that loans were up from the last week because of the low interest rate loans that Mr. Eldridge had put in motion before he got sick again. Mark Patterson reported to Felecia that because the loans were up and they would need to up the amount that the armored truck delivers to keep up with demand. Felecia tucked this information away for next weeks drop. The next drop would be on Tuesday. She started to make her order for money drop this week. Labor Day weekend was coming up in just under two weeks and they would need extra money to meet the demand of the customers of Trinity bank then. Felecia tucked that information away for the week before Labor Day so that there would be enough money to get through that week.

Felecia called for $200,000 to be delivered on Tuesday morning so the bank would be covered for this week. Jonathan heard it all. He knew the money count would be up for next two weeks of armored truck deliveries. He also knew that the weekend before Labor Day there would be a larger drop to replenish funds for the weekly drop and the drop would be on Wednesday in two weeks as was the rotation. She would have to double that with the Labor Day weekend approaching. She popped her head into Chelsea's office and filled her in on the increase that she would need to call in for the next two weeks. Jonathan took it all in while he listened in on the recorder. He knew he needed to get to the hotel, but he wanted to catch any last detail that his tiger might give him through the wires in her office.

When the week was over and the bank was locked up tight for the weekend Chelsea walked Felecia to her car and they chatted about what the weekend might bring. Felecia told Chelsea about David. She had grown board with Randy and she was excited about what David had to bring to the table or bed as it were. She told her that she was going to make plans with David for Sunday. She thought that she would invite him over to her house to see how he was in bed. They still had plans with Christopher and Chelsea for dinner and dancing for Saturday night. Felecia wasn't one to spread herself so thin between two guys. However she would just say goodbye to Randy after they went out tomorrow night and see David on Sunday.

Chelsea was excited about the evening's plans. In the morning Misty was waiting on the end of the bed for Chelsea to feed her. She rubbed up against her feet and demanded attention. Chelsea gave her the attention she begged for freely. She just wondered why her cat made herself scarce every time Christopher was near. But she pushed those thoughts aside for now. She knew that dinner with a new guy at her parent's house was a challenge. So she had put her big girl panties on so she would be ready to face him after the interrogation from her parents last night. She readied herself for the evening before Christopher got there.

After dinner with her parents she always got a report from her mother. Elise McQuire had a way of telling if Chelsea's dates were good for her or not. Chelsea was not sure of Christopher at all now. Chelsea would make anyone a great wife and would be a great Mother when the time came. But that nagging feeling came back about Christopher that Misty had provoked and now her Mother's opinion added to that feeling. However, she wasn't going to let anyone interrupt her night with her prince tonight even if he was a little off. 'Nobody's perfect,' she thought to herself.

At 5:30 pm the phone rang. She rushed to pick it up.

"Hello," She said into the phone as she answered it.

"Hello princess, how are you?"

"Hi babe, I'm good. I just talked to my mother and I can't wait to see you tonight."

"Me either princess. What did your mother say? I mean did she like me?" He cooed into the phone.

"She liked you, she's just not sure about a few things about you is all."

"Really, what kind of things?"

"Well she is leary that you are a traveling salesman."

"Well sweetness that's my job. I can't help that." He told her.

"Have you talked to Randy about dinner yet for tomorrow night?" Chelsea asked to change the subject.

"Yes, he is on board, we can spend the whole weekend together." He told her.

"Oh I would like that," She cooed right back.

"Well I hope Misty likes me, I will see you later and maybe we can go see a matinee. What do you think about that?" He asked. "I really enjoyed meeting your parent's." He continued before she could answer.

"Thank you for coming. I realize my father can be gruff sometimes. I hope he didn't scare you away."

"Well he acted l like he loves his daughter and wanted to be sure that she wouldn't get hurt. I can't wait to see you tonight princess, what do you think, should we have brunch at the hotel?"

"Yes that sounds great. I can't wait to see you." She told him.

"Well that's why I suggested brunch, what do you think?" Christopher asked again.

"Oh brunch sounds great." She replied.

"Great I will pick you up in about an hour. Does that sound okay?"

"Of course. I will be ready for you when you get here."

"Sounds good to me then. I will see you when you get here." She said into the phone.

"Great I will see you soon then." He replied. They said their good byes and hung up the phone. He had managed to make the call without smoking a cigarette. Maybe Jonathan was right and it was the girl that was making him so nervous.

He lit another cigarette and went into his bedroom with a cigarette hanging out of his mouth. Jonathan had stayed at the hotel with Felecia last night so his bed was empty and Christopher had the apartment to himself. He spent a few minutes taking in Chelsea's beauty through the pictures that they had tacked up on all the walls of that dingy little apartment.

He had heard the conversation that Chelsea had had with her mother and he wasn't upset about it. Frank just shrugged it off and told his brother to mind his own business and stick to the plan. Frank finished his cigarette, and put it out in the ashtray. It was almost time for him to pick her up for brunch then they would have dinner and dancing together at the hotel with Felecia and Randy.

Chelsea decided she was ready to go after she freshened up her makeup and she heard a knock at the door. "Just a minute, I'll be right there." She yelled from the bedroom. Then she made her way to the door and opened it to see her prince charming with yet another bouquet of flowers.

"Oh they are lovely, I love lilies. You're so sweet," And she gave him a peck on the lips. "Just let me put these in some water and we can go. I can't wait to eat at the restaurant I have never eaten there before." She went on absently.

"Well we have had a few meals there and it seems to be a good restaurant." He chimed in. He was happy that she was so preoccupied with the flowers that she didn't notice him chewing the gum he had put in his mouth just before knocking on the door. He would discard the gum before they entered the restaurant.

"Ready to go then?" He asked as Chelsea put the flowers on the table in a vase.

"Yes just let me get my purse." She replied.

"You look beautiful this morning by the way. As usual." He told her.

"Why thank you kind sir, you always know how to make me feel beautiful."

"You are beautiful, I can't help it," He replied as he opened the door to let them out of the cottage. "Where's your cat?" He asked as they left.

"Oh she is in the bedroom, I don't know what's gotten into her. She is usually so friendly to the people that I bring home."

"Well maybe she is scared of me. Most animals don't like me." He said with a tiny bit of concern in his voice.

"Oh I'm sure she likes you, she's just being difficult, don't worry sweetheart she will warm up to you." Chelsea said with a little bit uncertainty in her voice. Christopher picked up on her tone of voice when she talked of her beloved cat. He really hated that a cat was dictating how things would go between them.

It was almost 11 o'clock when they got to the hotel, he pulled up to the front doors and dropped her off. "Stay right here, I'll just park and be right back." He told her and hopped back in the SUV and drove off to find a parking space. She waited for him and he came walking up in just a few short minutes. He had spit out the gum in the parking lot on the way to the front doors. "Okay, ready princess?" He asked as he approached her.

"Why yes, I can't wait." She replied. He had had the car detailed so the smell of stale smoke wouldn't bother her tonight.

They entered the restaurant and were greeted by the hostess. "Will that be two for this morning Mr. Fields?" She knew his name by now as him and Randy had patronized the restaurant a several times during their stay and she knew that they had rented a room on the 5th floor. Since they were seducing the girls under assumed names they used these names at the hotel as well. He smiled and told her yes they would be dining alone today. So she led them to their table and gave them two menus and told them that the waitress would be along shortly. Then she turned on her heel and returned to her post at the front door.

"Oh this all looks so good," Chelsea said as she looked over the menu.

"What do you feel like having princess?" He asked.

"I think I'll have the eggs benedict, it sounds delicious." She said as the waitress came up to them and asked if she could get them anything to drink.

"I'll have a coffee with 2 creams and 4 sugars" Chelsea said happily.

"I'll take a coffee as well but make mine black." They told the waitress when she approached their table.

"Are you two ready to order yet?" The waitress asked.

"I think I need a couple more minutes, but thanks." Christopher said.

"Very well, I'll be back in a couple of minutes with your drinks. Take your time sir." She said to Christopher. Then the waitress turned and left them to get their drink orders.

"I see your coffee is sweet just like you." He commented to get her attention.

She blushed and said thank you, then went on to comment on the restaurant. "It's such a nice restaurant, I really like it. Thanks for suggesting it."

"Oh you bet, we have eaten here several times and I knew you would like it." He replied. She could tell this from the way the hostess had greeted him.

"I can't wait to go dancing tonight. It's one of my favorite things to do." She told him with a grin on her face. The waitress returned with their coffee and asked if they had made up their minds yet. Chelsea waited for Christopher because he hadn't decided yet. Christopher picked up his menu and pointed to the steak and eggs on the cover of the breakfast menu. A craving hit him hard just then. He held it at bay because he didn't want to show his hand to Chelsea.

"Yes sir. How would you like that cooked sir?"

"I'll take the steak medium rare and the eggs sunny side up, and could you add as side of hash browns?"

"Yes sir." The waitress then asked. "And for you ma'am?"

"I'll have the eggs benedict." Chelsea told the waitress.

"Would u like anything more to drink?" The waitress asked.

"Yes I will have a cup of hot chocolate with lots of whipped cream and a glass of water, and thank you." Chelsea said. She would finish her coffee before the hot chocolate got there. It looked busy in that restaurant this morning and although she already had coffee in front of her, she always loved hot chocolate with eggs benedict.

"Very well, I will be back with you meals shortly." And she turned and walked to another table to take their order.

They made small talk while they waited for the waitress to return with their food. The waitress brought them their water and handed Chelsea her cup of hot chocolate complete with a large dose of whipped cream. About 15 minutes later the waitress showed up with their meals.

They dug in and Chelsea said "This is wonderful, I have to make this for you."

The waitress returned to their table and put the bill on their table when they were done. "Here's your check." She told him.

Christopher tucked his credit card in the slot in the receipt book, he was so wrapped up in Chelsea's beauty that he forgot to bill the meal to his room. He had made yet another mistake with that credit card.

They enjoyed their brunch while they ate it. When they were finished the waitress approached the table again and picked up the receipt book with Christopher's credit card in it. He never gave a second thought to this mistake. It would be back to bite him in the ass when they did the bank heist.

On the ride home Chelsea noticed that the smell of stale cigarettes was still there faintly, but still there nonetheless. "Why can't you get that guy to quit smoking in your car?"

"Does it bother you? I had the SUV detailed today, are you sure you can smell it?" He asked her.

"Well just lightly, it would be nice if he didn't smoke in your car but it's your vehicle."

"Well if it bothers you I can ask him to not smoke in my car. But I have to tell you that he does what he wants whether I like it or not, so I can't promise anything until I talk to him about it."

"Well that's up to you my prince, but if it were me I wouldn't let him smoke in my vehicle." Chelsea replied. Christopher tucked that information away for the future. He would have to try to not smoke in the SUV in the future. However, he always wanted a cigarette after he had spent time with her, that's the reason why he gave her such a weak response.

Another craving hit and he missed the gum. Christopher had found an air freshener to cover the smell of cigarettes in his rented SUV and he bought an air freshener spray that would hide at least some of the smell, but apparently that wasn't enough. He really didn't want her to know he was a smoker. So he took great measures to cover this fact up for the future. He would keep smoking in his vehicle but he would just blame it on this third partner like before.

Chapter Twenty Four

DINNER AT THE REGENCY

Randy and Felecia played sex games until 5 o'clock. They finished off two six packs of beer which they ordered from room service. They were beat by the time it was time to go eat. They had lost count of how many times they had climaxed. All they knew was they fit together very well and they enjoyed each others company. Randy was not sure he wanted to lose this one. But the plan was in place. They would have to introduce the idea of Charlie Wright at dinner tonight. Then maybe the plan would work in their favor. Jonathan so didn't like that Cornwell. He was happy that he got to take him out soon.

They had worn themselves out with their sex games. But they would take a nap and be ready for more later. Dinner with Christopher and Chelsea wasn't for another couple of hours. So they had time to rest a little before dinner. Randy looked forward to it. He was happy that they rented this hotel room so that he could stay with his tiger as long as he wanted. This was something that Felecia was happy about as well. She wanted to spend the entire weekend with her cowboy. She only hoped that she could keep the visions of David from creeping back into her head while she was with Randy.

Randy had stashed a couple of beers in the fridge for later. She would be pleasantly surprised in the morning. A beer will sound really good then after all this beer tonight and the drinks they will have later with Christopher and Chelsea. He thought a little hair of the dog would do the trick when they woke.

At 6 o'clock Chelsea opened another can of cat food before she left for the hotel. Just then, she heard a knock at the door. "Who is it?" She said from the inside of the door.

"It's me Christopher." Chelsea opened the door with a surprised look on her face.

"I thought I would surprise you and give you a ride to the hotel so you can drink tonight." He finished saying as she let him in. She was ready to go and was so excited that he surprised her so nicely. She opened the door while he explained what he was doing there.

"Well what a nice surprise. I really appreciate that." She cooed. "You take such good care of me, I really like that." She continued. Then she hugged him and gave him a fiery kiss. She liked Christopher so much that she threw caution to the wind and kept seeing him for now, even though her mother and cat said he was a bad guy. She decided she would trust her mother's opinion with reservations. He started to get hard from that kiss. He thought to himself, *'Maybe Jonathan is right and the time is right to seduce her.'* He thought to himself. He responded to her kiss and held her tightly. Misty ran for the bedroom again. He caught a glimpse of her as she ran away.

He pulled away and commented "Well there she goes again."

"Oh don't worry about Misty, she'll warm up to you. Just wait." She replied.

"Ready to go then?" He asked.

"Yes, I can't wait to have dinner at the hotel again. Maybe I'll try the steak tonight."

"It's really good princess, you should try it." He replied.

"Good I will then, let's go sweetie." And she headed for the door with her purse in hand. She had thrown on a tight black mini skirt dress and black heels. Christopher was a tall man and she could wear heels without feeling insecure.

They left her cottage and he commented on how beautiful she looked again tonight. She thanked him and blushed. He let her into his vehicle and walked around the front of the car to the driver's side and hopped in. He started the engine and backed out of the driveway as a craving hit him hard. He shook it off and pulled it together so that she wouldn't notice. She noticed that the car smelled like stale cigarette's again but she decided not to comment about it this time. After all it was his business and maybe this partner that he had smoked a lot and he couldn't get him to stop smoking in his vehicle. They drove to the hotel and he let her out at the curb as usual. She was getting used to his gentlemanly ways. And she loved it.

Felecia threw on a pink sparking tank top with no bra. Then she threw on a black mini skirt with no panties, just like the first night they had spent with their gentlemen. She slipped into her black heels and styled her hair. She then called a cab and had them deliver her to the hotel at 5:40. The cab pulled up to the hotel at 5:50 pm. Just enough time to go get her cowboy and meet Christopher and Chelsea for dinner. She paid the driver and entered the hotel. She pushed the button to the 5th floor on the elevator. She went straight to room 504 and wrapped on the door three times.

"Be right there." Came the voice on the other side of the door. Randy opened the door to see his tiger all dressed up. "Well hello tiger, don't you look simply edible tonight." He said with a grin.

"Wait till you see what I'm NOT wearing." She said as she walked into room 504.

"Oh I can't wait. Do we have time for some fun before we meet them for dinner?" He asked.

"I don't think so, but it will be worth your while to wait tonight." She said as she kissed him. He started to get hard just thinking about her nudity under that skirt.

"Well let's get down to the lobby then tiger." He said as he pulled away from her.

"Okay lets go cowboy, and thanks for wearing the boots." She replied. Then they headed out of the hotel room and went straight to the elevator. They rode the elevator to the lobby to find Christopher and Chelsea waiting by the entrance to the restaurant.

"Hi you guys, sorry if we're late." Randy said to them as they walked up to them.

"Don't worry about it, we have only been here a few minutes." Christopher and Chelsea had talked about their childhoods while they waited for Randy and Felecia. This was to keep Chelsea interested while they waited, which wasn't a hard thing to do since they seemed to have so much in common. He would regret letting her go and betraying her when the time came.

"Let's eat." Chelsea chimed in.

"Sounds good to me, I'm famished." Felecia said.

"Okay dinner is served ladies, right this way." Christopher said.

"Will that four for tonight Mr. Fields?" The hostess asked as they walked into the restaurant.

"Yes a table for four will do perfectly." Christopher replied. Randy couldn't take his eyes off of his tiger's boobs. He knew they were just laying there waiting for him to suck on them. The hostess led them to their table and handed them four menus.

"Your waitress will be along shortly, enjoy your meal Mr. Fields" She said as she turned and walked away.

"Chelsea here tried the chicken last time we ate here Randy, I know how much you like chicken."

"Oh that sounds great, maybe I'll have that." Randy replied. He was getting a little tired of his brother dictating what he would eat. But if Christopher wanted him to have chicken, he would have chicken, if it looked good to the ladies. The waitress approached their table and asked if she could get them anything to drink.

"I'll have a rum and cola, is that what you want too tiger?" He turned to Felecia and asked.

"Yes of course, it's my favorite. Make that two rum and colas." She replied.

"And for you sir?" The waitress asked Christopher.

"I'll have a dry martini shaken two olives. And a long island iced tea for the lady, is that okay sweetie?" He asked Chelsea.

"Yes of course, you are getting to know me so well." She said as she blushed.

"I'll be right back with your drinks then." The waitress said as she turned to leave.

"I hear they have a bar and it has a live band tonight in the hotel. We don't even have to go anywhere tonight." Randy said.

"Oh that sounds great," Chelsea chimed in. "I can't wait to dance." She added.

"Well we will be dancing as long as you want princess." Christopher said.

To change the subject and drop his little bomb shell he asked Felecia "So I hear you have an employee who's messing up?"

"Yeah we have to fire him. He really has no business being a teller." Felecia said with disdain in her voice.

"When are you going to fire him?" He asked her.

"Just as soon as Mr. Eldridge comes back to work. Probably Monday." She responded.

"Well if you're looking for someone to fill in in a pinch, I know a guy who would work out well."

"Oh really, who are we talking about." She asked.

"Well his name is Daniel Fields. And he's my cousin. He has banking experience. If you need someone in a hurry." He suggested.

"Well I will think about that. It sounds good, but I'd have to see his resume and meet him. How much experience does he have?"

"Well he worked as a teller for a bank in South Carolina for about 5 years, but he recently got laid off. That's where he is now. I could call him tomorrow and see if he's available."

"Thank you Christopher. That sounds wonderful, I can't wait to fire that guy Alvarez. I changed my mind about Ken firing him. I want to do the dirty work and fire him myself. So he's off the hook. Now no more business, we are here to have fun." She commented further.

"Oh okay Felecia, I'm sure Ken will appreciate that."

"Okay then its settled, now no more talk of business. Agreed?" Felecia asked. And they all nodded their heads in agreement. Christopher was satisfied that he had planted the seed of Charlie Wright successfully in Felecia's mind. This would make the plan go so much smoother.

The waitress returned with their drinks. "Have you decided on what you want for dinner yet?" She asked.

Christopher chimed in and said. "We would like the Fillet Mignon. Is that okay sweetie?" He asked Chelsea.

"Oh yes, that sounds delicious." She replied.

"And what was that chicken dinner you ate Chelsea?" Christopher added.

"Oh its right there, the sauce is awesome." She replied as she pointed out the meal on the menu.

"Then I will have that." Randy said. "What would you like tiger?" He asked Felecia.

"Oh that Fillet Mignon sounds wonderful, I'll take one of those too."

"How would you like that cooked ma'am?" The waitress asked her.

"Rare I want to see it move." She said with a little giggle.

The waitress turned to Christopher and asked him how they would like their steaks cooked.

"I'll take mine medium rare, how would you like yours sweetie?" He asked Chelsea.

"Oh well done. I don't like to see the meat red."

"Sounds good sweetie. She'll have hers well done." He said as he looked up from the menu and told the waitress.

"And what kind of salad dressing would you all like?" The waitress asked.

Christopher chimed in and said "I will have blue cheese." Chelsea wanted ranch and Randy and Felecia wanted Italian. The waitress took their order and turned on her heel to put their order in.

They talked about things to come while they waited for their food. Christopher excused himself to go to the bathroom, he was having a very hard craving hit him. He popped a piece of gum in his mouth on the way to the bathroom and chewed feverishly. He used the restroom and flushed the urinal. He washed his hands and left the bathroom then tossed the gum in the trash on his way out. The gum had done the trick for now. He would watch his drinking so he would be able to drive Chelsea home and keep the nicotine cravings at bay.

When the meal was ready the waitress delivered it to them at the table. They all dug in. Randy was miffed that everyone else was having steak when his brother had set him up to have chicken. He would remember this when the time came. But he played it up all the same.

"Oh this sauce is terrific," Randy said. As he choked down the chicken. He would just order a steak with Felecia tomorrow.

"The steak is great," Chelsea chimed in.

"Oh yes it is," Felecia said. "We will have to have this again cowboy."

"Sounds good to me tiger." He replied. They ate their dinner together and enjoyed each others company. Both ladies were showing cleavage and Christopher was starting to think his brother was on to something with Chelsea. So he would try to seduce her tonight when he took her home.

They finished their meals and were all ready to do some heavy duty dancing. Another craving hit Christopher hard after the meal, so he excused himself again to chew on some more gum. He left for the bathroom and popped another piece of gum in his mouth. He would suck on this piece to keep the cravings at bay as the evening progressed. He was already wearing the patch, but it wasn't doing the trick. So he had to rely on the gum as well to keep his cravings at bay tonight.

When he returned to the table the check had been delivered. He knew Randy wasn't going to pay so he told the waitress to bill it to room 504. When the time came the police would follow him through his credit card transactions. He tried to not use the card very much. But he forgot and paid with his credit card once again. He thought that he was safe from the long arm of the law. But with the previous bank heists he had used his credit card then as well. The cops already had him in their crosshairs.

Chapter Twenty Five

DANCING AT THE REGENCY

It was almost 9 o'clock and the band would start soon. So they made their way to the bar and found a booth that they could all fit in. The ladies scooted over to the middle and the guys sat on the outside edge. The band was getting ready to start. There was a new waitress attending to the bar. The new waitress came by and asked if they would like something to drink?

"I'll have a dry martini shaken with two olives." Christopher said. "Would you like another iced tea princess?"

"Yes that sounds terrific, sweetie," She cooed.

"And a long island iced tea." Christopher added.

"Two rum and colas," Randy grunted to the waitress while he watched his tigers boobs bounce with every move she made.

"Okay, be right back with your drinks." The waitress said as she turned to let them be while she went to retrieve their drinks.

The band introduced themselves and began to play. The dance floor was empty at first but the beat brought out the dancer in everyone. Soon the dance floor was filled with dancers. Christopher turned to Chelsea and asked if she wanted to dance. She happily agreed and jumped up from the booth. They headed for the dance floor and began to move their hips to the music. The waitress arrived with their drinks. Randy told the waitress to bill the drinks to room 504. Now the police would be able to follow the paper trail and tie the transactions to Christopher Fields aka Frank Snow. The police were closing in on the Snow brothers.

"You want to dance tiger?" Randy asked Felecia

"I'd love to, cowboy, let's go." She exclaimed and jumped up from the booth. They joined Christopher and Chelsea on the dance floor and had a ball moving to the beat of the music. Felecia's boobs bounced with each move. Randy loved this and he was growing harder by the second. He had to sit the next one out to regain his composure. They had a ball dancing to that first song. When it was over, Christopher and Chelsea stayed for the next song, and Randy whispered into Felecia's ear, "You are turning me on, I'm getting hard, we need to sit the next one out."

"Okay cowboy. Control yourself, we will be in your room in no time." Felecia replied and said to Chelsea. "We're gonna sit this one out."

"Okay" Chelsea said while she bounced around on the dance floor.

Felecia and Randy went back to the booth and ordered another round of drinks. Chelsea had a small chest, so wearing her top without a bra didn't expose her to the same kind of attention that Felecia's breasts commanded. Chelsea's breasts didn't bounce around while she danced like Felecia's did. Randy wasn't sure how his brother planned to get Chelsea into bed so he didn't order more drinks for them while they danced.

When the second song was finished Christopher and Chelsea returned to the table. Chelsea took a big drink and exclaimed, "Wow these are strong. I think I'm gonna get drunk tonight. Thanks for picking me up sweetie." She said to Christopher.

"No problem sweetness. Drink all you want. I will stop at this one so I can drive you home safely." He replied. They sat the third song out while Chelsea finished her drink.

The fourth song was one that Chelsea knew very well. "Oh I love this song. Let's dance." She said to Christopher.

"Lead the way." He said as he hopped out of the booth.

"Would you order another drink for her Randy while we are dancing?" Christopher asked Randy. "And I'll have a soda." He added.

Chelsea scooted over and jumped up and headed for the dance floor moving her hips to the beat of the music along the way. Christopher loved how good she looked in that little black skirt. It reminded him of the first night that they had met. She was wearing a similar skirt that flared with a shimmering blue top because it was his favorite color. She had picked this outfit out on a recent shopping trip this week. Chelsea had picked it out to turn him on. He had another craving hit him hard again, so he bit his lip and rode it out until he could suck on the gum later.

She knew he was a gentleman and she wanted her cat to like him, so she decided that she would have to sleep with him to get her beloved cat to like him. She figured that if she had a few of her favorite drinks so she might loosen up and be ready to seduce Christopher when they got to her cottage that night.

Randy called the waitress over to the table and ordered another round. Christopher and Chelsea danced to the music and stayed on the dance floor when the next song began. It was a slow song so he pulled her close and started swaying slowly to the beat of the music. He held her hand and put his other hand on the small of her back and led her in slow dancing. She enjoyed the dancing so much. She loved being with Christopher this way. Back at the table Randy and Felecia were making out because he couldn't keep his hands off of her.

"What do you say we dance to this song?" She whispered to him, "We could hide him in between us." She said with a slight giggle. She was happy that she turned him on so much.

"Let's go then," He replied. So they got up from the booth and made their way to the dance floor. He pulled her close and started moving to the beat of the music as well. He grew even harder while holding her.

"Tiger I'm gonna need a lot of drinks to keep the snake under control."

She giggled and said, "Okay lets get drunk then." And they headed to the booth once again. He finished his drink and waited for her to finish hers then the waitress arrived with more drinks. The song was over so Christopher and Chelsea returned to the table just as the waitress arrived.

"Thank you ma'am" Christopher said to the waitress.

"Sure no problem, enjoy your drinks." The waitress said then she turned and walked away.

They sat the next song out and drank their drinks. Christopher watched Chelsea closely. He wanted to make sure that tonight went well so that he could seduce her later. They were almost finished with their drinks when Chelsea took another big drink. "Wow I think I'm getting drunk." Chelsea exclaimed.

"Do you want another one princess?" Christopher asked.

"Maybe a soda in between will do." Chelsea replied.

"That sounds good to me, sweetness." So he called the waitress over and ordered two soda's.

"Make mine a diet," Chelsea chimed in.

"What are you guys not drinking now?" Randy asked Christopher.

"No just taking a little break. I'm driving." He said sternly to his brother.

"Well I'm not going anywhere tonight so I'll take another, you want another one tiger?" He turned to Felecia and asked.

"Yes I'll have another." She returned with a seductive smile.

"So that's one diet soda, one soda, and two rum and colas?" The waitress said.

"Yes that will do," Christopher replied. Then the waitress turned and put their drink orders in at the bar.

Chelsea was feeling dizzy so she asked if Christopher didn't mind going outside for a few minutes. He was happy to go with her. This left Randy and Felecia alone for a few minutes. He started to kiss her again, but she pulled away.

"Now you're making me wet, we have to stop unless you want to go up to your room right now." Felecia said,

"Okay tiger, I can wait." Then they took another drink of their drinks. They were getting low again, so Randy called the waitress over again. Felecia was growing irritated with Randy's desires for her. He was acting like he owned her. He would find out about David tomorrow when she went home. He would make a trip over to the apartment and listen in on all the conversations that she had had within the confines of her home.

"Those drinks are really strong but I love them so much." Chelsea said as they walked outside.

Randy and Felecia talked about what they were going to do to each other while Christopher and Chelsea were away. When they returned Chelsea was feeling a little better. She finished off her soda. Christopher finished his as well so he called the waitress over once again.

"We will have one soda and a long island iced tea." He told the waitress when she returned.

"And do you two want another?" She asked Randy

"Sure that sounds perfect." Randy said. As Christopher pulled out $100 to tip her.

The waitress said "Thank you sir, will that be all then?"

Christopher said "Yes for now, thank you."

"Okay then, I'll be right back with your drinks." Then she turned and left them alone at their table.

Another song played that Chelsea loved so she told Christopher that she wanted to dance again.

He let her out of the booth and said, "Lead the way princess." They made their way to the dance floor.

"Do you think you can hold yourself back long enough to dance once more cowboy?" Felecia asked Randy.

"I think I can manage. Those drinks are helping me to keep the snake under control. Let's go." He hopped up from the booth and said, "Lead the way, I love to watch you walk away." She giggled and led them to the dance floor.

They moved their hips back and forth to the beat of the music once again. They joined Christopher and Chelsea on the dance floor. Felecia let out a whoop and showed everyone her dance moves. Randy loved this side of Felecia. He just wished he could keep her. Christopher was certain that Chelsea wanted him as much as he wanted her no matter what her mother and cat thought of him. So he played on that all night long ignoring the cravings that hit him regularly.

At 1:30 am the lights came on and the bartender called for last call.

"It's time to call it a night ladies and gentlemen." The bartender said with anticipation of getting off of work.

Christopher told Randy that he would be a while before he got back from Chelsea's.

Randy said, "That's cool, we can entertain ourselves." And he let out a slight laugh with an evil grin.

They finished their drinks and got up from the table. Randy planned to spend all night and at least part of the morning with Felecia in the hotel room. He only hoped that Christopher would be able to seduce Chelsea and stay the night with her at her cottage. Otherwise he would have to spend the night at the apartment to give Randy and Felecia some privacy.

Felecia and Randy said good night and headed up to room 504. They got down to business right away. He was so excited by her that he almost couldn't contain himself. He was just glad that he would be inside of her soon.

When they got to the hotel room he fumbled with the key card while she ripped at his shirt and explored his chest with her tongue. She made tiny circles with her tongue around his nipples to turn him on. He was filled with desire for her.

She pushed him up against the door while he fumbled with the lock kissing him the entire time passionately. After she ripped at his shirt and exposed his chest she tore at his pants. He let her have her way with him because it felt so good. Suddenly the door gave way and flew open and they fell into the room. She landed on top of him in the heat of the passion. She reached for his engorged member while he kicked the door shut with his boots again. They seduced each other right there on the floor in front of the door.

He responded by pushing up her skirt to reveal her delicate womanly parts. Then he pushed her top up to expose her breasts in the heat of passion while they were on the floor. He gave her a passionate kiss that got her motor running. He moved down to her nipples and sucked on them once again. She climaxed from this alone. He then picked her up and carried her to the bedroom, then laid her gently on the bed. He then slipped out of his ripped shirt as she tore at his pants. They were both very drunk and they were clumsy this time but they got the job done all the same. He was engorged from the evening of trying to ward off the feelings that she had provoked in him and in anticipation of their upcoming night of passion. He slipped out of his pants then he removed his boxer shorts and she began to suck on him.

He said, "Let me cum inside of you." She responded to his words and scooted up to get into position. He climbed on top of her and inserted himself into her. She was as wet as she could be. They began to move together like they had done so many times before. They began having sex like only they liked. Almost instantly she began to climax again. She clenched him while he was inside of her this made him cum as well. Then he collapsed on top of her and passed out. She fell fast asleep as well.

Christopher drove Chelsea home. He had slipped another piece of gum in his mouth before they left the bar. She was so drunk that she didn't notice that he was chewing gum this time. But he had plenty of regular gum just incase she asked for some.

"How mannny grinks do you tink I had thweetheart?"

"Well it was enough, but don't worry, I will take good care of you tonight princess."

"Oh I'm tho happy dat you are in sharge." She mumbled. He knew that she was drunk and he didn't want to take advantage of her but he had to get close to that cat. So he went ahead with his plan to seduce her tonight.

Christopher drove Chelsea home and parked in front of her cottage. He told her to wait for him to open the door for her. She was a little woozy but felt as though she could maintain in front of Christopher for the evening.

"Otay" She cooed to him as he hopped out of the SUV. He went around the front of the car and when she got to her door he opened it for her. He let her out of it and helped her to the front door. She looked so beautiful tonight to him. She fumbled with her keys and finally found the right one.

She opened the door and said, "Mithty, Oh Mithty. We're home thumb and meet prince tharming." And she giggled. "I don't think the's coming out donight either. Lets have a glass of wine and thee if the'll come out dis time." Chelsea was becoming hard to understand, but Christopher was up to the challenge.

"It's alright sweetie, she just needs to get to know me." Christopher said, "Why don't we just sit down on the couch." And he took her arm and led her to the couch. They sat down and kissed lightly. He put his arm around her and she cuddled up to him.

"I want to dake thove to you." She whispered into his ear.

"Well are you sure sweetie?"

"Oh yes I'm rrrreally thure." She said as her head swayed to the music in her head.

"Oh sweetheart I don't want to take advantage of you."

"You're not thilly, I'm willing and thapable. C'mon lets go to bed. I put freth theets on the bed just this morning."

He just laughed and said. "Lead the way princess."

So she got up from the couch and grabbed his hand to take him to her bed.

When they were in the bedroom Chelsea clumsily lit some candles and turned on some mood music very low. She held the lighter too close and she got s slight burn from it.

She called out "OUCH!!!" In the room.

"Oh sweetie you burned yourself. Come here and let me tend to that."

"No I Will thake thare of it." And she stuck her finger in her mouth to suck on it. This turned Christopher on.

"Do you have clondoms?" She asked clumsily.

"Yes of course sweetie. Don't worry about a thing." She turned out the lights and pulled her dress over her head. Christopher was surprised to see her so forward but he went along with it all the same.

"You look stunning. You're everything I thought you would be. C'mere princess I can't resist your charms." He told her.

Then he cupped his hands around her face and gave her a gentle kiss. Next he reached out to her in the dimly lit bedroom and held her tight. He kissed her on the neck then he made his way to her mouth again. They embraced and kissed passionately.

Misty just stuck her tail in the air and left the room, they were so involved in passion that they didn't notice she left. He removed her top and exposed her breasts. He rubbed his thumb over her nipple and made her feel like a woman. He slowly removed his shirt as she worked at his belt.

Having no luck, he said "Here baby let me," He undid his pants and pushed them off of his hips to let them fall to the floor. He then took his boxer shorts off and they stood there naked embracing each other. Then he picked her up and carried her into the bedroom, next he laid her on the bed gently. He ran his hand gently down her body and found her delicate parts. He put his fingers inside of her and she moaned. She scooted up on the bed to get into a better position. He positioned himself so that he could easily enter her. She reached for him and found that his manly member was engorged in anticipation of her touch.

She stroked him gently and said, "I want to feel you inthide of me." He moved closer and pushed himself up to get on top of her. He told her to wait just one second while he put the condom on. He rolled the condom over himself and he was ready for her. He then moved to her breasts and sucked on her nipple and she moaned again.

"Oh I love that," She said in the throes of ecstasy. He inserted himself inside of her gently and felt her grow wet with anticipation. He moved in and out of her and gently licked her nipples while they made love together.

He said, "I think I'm falling in love with you princess. You're the best I have ever had." They enjoyed each other in the throes of ecstasy, then she climaxed and she squeezed him gently with her private parts. It had been a while since he had had sex so when she climaxed she squeezed him hard with her womanhood, then he came as well right along with her. He exploded and let out a passionate moan. Then he fell to the bed and wrapped his arms around her and fell asleep.

They slept together all night long not even noticing that Misty had left the room once again. Chelsea passed out in Christopher's arms and stayed there all night long. She would deal with Misty in the morning. Christopher was happy that he had finally gotten her into bed and knew that she trusted him now. It would be only a short time before he would betray her. He fell fast asleep with visions of the money that he would have when they hit Trinity bank. The plan to hit Trinity bank was a simple one. He so didn't want to betray his princess but he decided it was worth it in the end.

------⧓------

Chapter Twenty Six

FELECIA DUMPS RANDY

Felecia and Randy stirred around 9 am in her bed. They were both hung over and felt the effects of the night's events. Felecia woke first this time and unwrapped her arms from Randy's chest, hopped out of bed and threw on a hotel robe then headed for the kitchenette for a couple of beers. Randy woke to an empty bed this time.

"Hey, Tiger, where'd ya go?" He said into the morning air.

"I'm right here cowboy, just wanted some hair of the dog and thought you might like some as well." She said returning to the bedroom with two beers in hand.

"You read my mind, I think I'm falling in love." He told her.

"Whow that's not what I expected to hear. It's way too soon for that cowboy. We've only known each other for a week and a half." She said. "Here ya go, have a beer and lighten up." She continued as she handed him the beer.

"I'm sorry, I know we are just having fun." He returned cautiously. He wanted to hold her interest for at least until he decided to dump her, not the other way around. Little did he know his hours were limited and David would take over her bed soon enough.

"Don't go getting any ideas." She replied.

He knew that she would pull away if she felt pressured. *'I shouldn't have said that,'* He scolded himself privately.

"Well just keep you mind on the sex. Its fun and I don't want to mess it up." She said. Little did he know this would end today. He knew what she meant by that.

"What do you say we play a little this morning." He replied.

"Let me get this hangover under control then I have plans to do chores around the house today. Do you have any aspirin?" She asked as thoughts of David popped into her head.

"Yeah, I'll just call room service and have some delivered."

"Great I will be ready for ya in a bit cowboy. And I can't wait to feel you inside of me again." She told him seductively. She wanted one more encounter with Randy before she left to go meet David and spend the day with him. They sipped their beers and made small talk until the aspirin arrived. They ordered another six pack of beer also so they could have more hair of the dog and hopefully feel better soon.

The hotel bellboy knocked on the door and said "Room Service."

Randy pulled on his boxer shorts and answered the door. He tipped the attendant $100 and brought Felecia the aspirin and a beer. All the big tips in the world couldn't stop Felecia from changing her mind about dumping Randy today. She swallowed the pills and took a swig of beer.

"You looked wonderful last night tiger." He said to her.

"Well thank you, so did you." She told him. "I just love your boots."

"How's the headache babe?"

"Give it ten minutes and I will be ready to go." She told him.

When the aspirin started to take effect, she took off the hotel bathrobe and hopped back into bed. She had finished her beer and wanted another. She planned on leaving by 10 o'clock so she could get cleaned up for David. Randy asked if she would like another and she declined this time. She told him that she wanted to have a clear head while she did her chores this afternoon. So he got out of bed and left for the kitchenette. He grabbed a beer for himself and headed back to the bedroom being sure to close the door just incase Christopher came by.

Felecia was getting wet watching him walk around in his shorts all the time.

She said "C'mere cowboy, let me suck on you." He grew hard in an instant. He approached the bed and she grabbed him with one hand and began stroking him gently. He took a swig of beer and kicked back and enjoyed her touch.

"Oh that feels so good tiger." He said into the morning air. She then put him inside her mouth. She began moving back and forth making him cum quickly. She licked up his sweet nectar and swallowed it.

"There ya go cowboy. Now I have to go before 11 o'clock. You took all my time up last weekend and I have some chores to attend to. I have to tell you though I have enjoyed our time together but I have met someone else cowboy." She said as she got ready to leave. Randy already knew this was coming so he took it well.

"Okay, who is he if you don't mind me asking?"

"Just someone I met. I'm sorry I have to break it off but I'm not looking for a boyfriend." They fit so well together and he was surprised but it was something that he was expecting. They both enjoyed having sex in the morning, but it was to end today after one last encounter. He was disappointed that she wouldn't be sharing his bed anymore but the plan came first and this would only help them in the end.

"It's a good thing Christopher hasn't shown yet. When do you expect him?" She asked to change the subject. She wanted to get out of there as soon as possible after all she had just dumped him. He was taking it quite well. *He must have been expecting this.* She thought to herself while she got dressed.

He was curious about his competition but there was nothing that he could do about it since she had already met someone else and she had just dumped him. So he decided that he would just listen in on her through the wires at the apartment.

"I don't know. I suspect he's with Chelsea. I know they have plans today and he will need to change his clothes. So he should be stopping by soon"

Just then they heard the door to the hotel room open and Christopher yelled out, "Hello, is anyone here?"

Randy jumped from the bed and threw on his boxer shorts again, and went out into the living area. "What's up, we're busy. Besides I don't have much time left with her because she met someone else and just dumped me" Randy replied as he walked into the room closing the door behind him.

"Well I needed to change for my date with Chelsea. The good news is the cat let me feed her and pet her."

"Geeesh what are you doing?" Randy said in a hushed tone. "She's right in there." He continued. "I don't have much time left with her. Did u hear me? She dumped me this morning." Jonathan replied angrily because it seemed that Christopher was not listening to him.

"Oh no, well don't let it interfere with the plan okay. And don't worry I'm just here to get a change of clothes, I'll be on my way in a sec." Christopher said in between bites of his precious gum. He couldn't have a cigarette there because Felecia was there. He had had a couple on the way over to the hotel. But Felecia kept herself behind closed doors today so she couldn't smell him. Christopher went to his bedroom and changed into jeans and a button down shirt. He threw on some tennis shoes and left the bedroom.

"Cya later." He said as he left. "Good luck. With that."

Randy went back into the bedroom and said "He's gone now, want to take a shower, we could fool around in there one last time? What do you think?" He asked

"Well its time for me to go. But I could use a shower lead, the way." She replied.

He reached out for her and grabbed her hand and pulled her close. "Right this way tiger." He told her.

She was surprised and a little suspicious that he was taking the break up so well. But she just went with it because she loved the sex so much. She only hoped that David was as good in bed as Randy was. She followed him and he turned on the water and slipped out of his boxers to reveal his swollen member once again.

"Are you always ready like this?" She asked, she only asked because she was having doubts about letting him go. But David had entered the picture and he would be her next conquest.

"Only for you," He replied.

She was already undressed so she stepped under the water. He followed her into the shower. They soaped each other up and she reached for him for the last time. She washed him up then lifted her leg so he could insert himself into her. He slid inside of her and began to move back and forth. She moaned again and moved right along with him. She climaxed in a matter of seconds. When she came she set his wheels in motion. He came too, right after her. *Even a quicky was fun with him,* She thought to herself.. They cleaned themselves up and stepped from the shower. They dried each other off and she left for the bedroom the throw some clothes on. He followed and threw a clean pair of boxers on.

"Do you have to go?" He asked.

"Well if I'm gonna have the strength to fire that guy tomorrow I had better get some rest. Plus I have chores to do. So yeah I'm heading out. Sorry cowboy. Gotta go." She explained.

"Well do we have time for one more tiger?" He asked as he reached for her and pulled her close. He really didn't want to lose her and hoped he could persuade her to stay with him and forget about this other guy. If she left he knew it would be for the last time.

After Christopher heard the news that Jonathan had broken it off with Felecia he realized that Frank would be listening in on them from now on. After Jonathan gave him the news he headed for Chelsea's cottage for their date.

When he arrived at Chelsea's he knocked on the door. She opened the door to him and she greeted him with a kiss. Then they embraced. He noticed that Misty was staring at him when he came in the door. So he unwrapped his arms from around her and leaned down to pet the cat.

Getting close to this cat was an important task, one that he had to master. "Has she eaten yet today?" He asked.

"Not yet, do you want to try. It may get her closer to you." Chelsea replied

He walked into the kitchen and opened the cabinet that he remembered Chelsea getting the cat food from. He found a can of cat food then dug through the utensil drawer for the can opener and opened it the can of cat food. Misty came up to him meowing and weaving in between his legs in anticipation of her meal. He put the cat food into the food dish, and put it on the floor for Misty. She dug in and purred as she ate. He reached down to stroke her, but she pulled away.

"Okay you little scamp, thank you for eating for me." He said to Misty as she began eating again.

He went back to Chelsea and asked if she was ready to go to the beach to ride the horses.

"Yes of course I can't wait to try riding a horse. I have always wanted to try this."

Because they had had their first intimate encounter last night she was feeling a little insecure that she had broken one of her most important rules about getting to know a man. The door had woken Chelsea up. She was still in her robe when she answered it to Christopher. Chelsea's head was pounding. She felt like a truck had hit her twice. She was embarrassed that she couldn't remember their first time together.

"How are you feeling sweetheart?" Christopher asked innocently. He didn't realize that she didn't remember their first encounter.

"I feel terrible. But I will be fine just as soon as I get some aspirin and water in me." She said to him as she rummaged through the cupboard for her bottle of aspirin. He helped her find it and he handed the bottle to her.

"Oh thank you sweetie, I can't believe how bad I feel."

"Well we tied one on last night. You were so wonderful to make love to though." He replied.

"I'm so sorry I got so drunk last night."

"Oh don't worry about it."

"But I don't remember our first time." She said as she began to sob.

"Oh sweetheart, it's alright, you were wonderful. Why don't we do it again, I think our plan worked. Misty let me feed her, that's progress." He told her. They sat down on the couch and he scooted close to her.

He asked if she had had her coffee for the morning yet. "No, I haven't even made a pot yet." She admitted.

"Well why don't you let me make you a pot of coffee so that you can have a cup before we go. I'm sure that will make you feel better along with the aspirin and big glass of water that you just had. I hear that water helps because alcohol dehydrates you really bad. Does that sound good sweetie?" He asked

"Oh that sounds wonderful, maybe I should get a wet cloth to put over my forehead too while I wait for the coffee to get ready. You are so sweet to me and you take such good care of me. I'll just go get that wash cloth."

After she got the washcloth and got it wet with cool water she rested on the couch while she waited for the aspirin and water to kick in and waited for the coffee to finish percolating. When the coffee was done he asked if she would like a cup.

"Yes, that sounds wonderful. My headache has gone away too so I should feel better real soon. Thank you sweetie." And he brought her a cup of coffee just the way she liked it.

She took a sip of her coffee that he brought to her, "Oh I was feeling a so dizzy, thank you sweet prince." She said to him as they sat down. "What did you have in mind for today anyway?"

"Well we could make love again this morning before we go horseback riding. What do you think? I want you to have good memories about our time together."

"We could do that." She cooed and she scooted a little closer to him and cuddled up next to him. He wrapped his arm around her and she felt so secure in his arms.

They began kissing and it turned into a wonderful exploration of each others bodies. She pulled away and grabbed his hand to lead him to the bedroom. When they got there he gently picked her up and laid her on the bed. Christopher wanted to leave a good impression.

She asked. "Do you have condoms?"

"Yes of course sweetie. Don't you worry about a thing." And he grabbed the package that held the condom up to show her. He unbuttoned her shirt and she shook it off. Then he unzipped her pants and slipped them down her legs and tossed them on the floor. He then gently felt her breasts and rubbed her thigh. He moved closer to her and sucked on her nipple.

"Oh I love that." She exclaimed.

"I know sweetie, that's why I'm doing it. Just relax lay back and let me do all the work." He told her. She was happy to follow his lead. She reached for him and found he was stiff for her. She began stroking him and felt him grow harder with each stroke. He found his way to her womanly mound and inserted his fingers. She moaned again and moved gently to his motions while he moved his fingers in and out of her.

"You make me feel so special." She whispered into his ear. Then she kissed his neck and said, "Put that thing on so I can feel you inside of me."

He didn't waste time putting the condom on. The next thing she knew he was inside of her. Only this time she would remember. He moved in and out of her gently. She was easy to please and he loved this. They made love tenderly for the next half hour, they both climaxed several times. Then he told her he wanted to taste her, so he climbed off of her and scooted down between her legs. She opened her legs and invited him to enter her with his tongue. He licked her private parts and inserted his fingers once again. She felt like climaxing the second before it came. It was a slow moving climax. It hit her hard when she let go. She gripped his fingers with the climax and he let go too. She was stroking him as well. They wore themselves out so they just laid there for a few minutes to catch their breath.

Chapter Twenty Seven

CHRISTOPHER AND CHELSEA GO FOR A RIDE

"Well that was wonderful," Chelsea said after they made love. She remembered it this time. And Misty jumped up on the bed. "Well hello missy, did you decide to join us? C'mere sweetie and let mamma cuddle with you." She cooed to her cat.

She was pleased that it had worked. Misty was responding. This made it alright that she had broken her rules and slept with him so soon. Misty walked up to her and rubbed up against her. It appeared as though Misty was accepting Christopher as well. But as soon as he tried to pet her, she ran away.

"Oh well, it's a start." Chelsea said from under the covers. She was embarrassed to be naked in front of him even after what they had shared together.

"Well what time did you want to go horse back riding?" He asked her.

"I need some aspirin to kick in first then I need some water to get rid of this hangover. I had way too much to drink last night. But soon I promise" She reassured him.

"I know sweetie but I took care of you and look Misty's acting different towards me now. So it worked and I feel closer to you than ever before." He said to her.

"Yes that did make me feel closer to you as well, which is what I wanted. I just hope it wasn't too soon."

"I think that as long as we are good with it, then it should be fine."

"Yeah you're right. I am falling for you by the way." She replied sweetly

"Well I feel the same way sweetheart." He returned.

"Well then lets get out the phone book and look up that horse rental place and go for a ride today then." She said as she pecked him on the lips once again. "That sounds great, here let me get the phone book." She got out of bed and exposed her nudity just for a second. She quickly slipped on her bathrobe and reached into her night stand for the phone book.

"Here it is. I'm gonna go throw a bagel in the toaster. Do you want one?" She asked.

"Sure that sounds great. I'll find the horse rental beach."

"I believe it's just a few blocks away." She said as she headed for the kitchen.

She popped a bagel into the toaster. She was disappointed that she didn't remember their first time together. But it was her own fault for getting drunk. She waited patiently while the bagel popped up. She put a second bagel in the toaster after the first one popped up and she slapped some cream cheese on it. Then she poured herself a big glass of water to ward off the hang over. She knew she would be feeling better soon. The second bagel popped up and she spread some cream cheese on it as well. Then she put the bagels on a plate and headed for the bedroom.

"Okay thank you very much, we look forward to it." And with that he hung up the phone. "Well you were right, the beach is just a few blocks away." He had remembered seeing horses on the way while watching her when he was spying on her one day.

"They said they rent horses by the day, and by the hour. Which would you prefer sweetie?" He asked.

"Here's the bagels, dig in sweetheart. I don't think I'm in any condition to ride all day, besides the morning is half over, why don't we just rent by the hour?" She said then she took a bite of a bagel and set the plate on the nightstand.

"Sounds good sweetie whatever you would like is fine with me."

"I just don't want to fall off of the horse feeling this way. I just had some aspirin and water which should do the trick on my hangover. Would you like some aspirin?" She asked.

"No sweetheart I'm okay. So what time do you want to go?"

"Well I could pack a picnic and we could eat on the beach say around noon, what do you think?"

"Sounds good to me, I'm ready when you are?"

"Then let me finish my coffee, I will fill the picnic basket with the necessities and we can go."

"Sounds good to me princess I will hurry and finish my coffee so we can go. Do you need any help with the picnic basket?" He asked.

"Naw, I got it. Just give me a few minutes to finish my coffee and I will get started."

He had hoped for closeness and she was backing off. This could be a problem. So he decided to leave her alone for a bit to let her gain her composure. He waited patiently for her headache to pass and for her to pack the picnic basket, he made small talk with her while he waited.

Her headache began to subside and the dizzy feeling was going away. She decided a shower would make her feel better.

"I need to take a quick shower before we go, do you mind?" She asked.

"Sure sweetheart, take your time. I will wait out here with Misty and get to know her better."

Misty hopped up on the couch and demanded attention. Christopher pet her cat and loved on her until he heard the water turn off. She put on her jeans and the button down shirt once again to wear during their ride. She would put the picnic together after her shower. She stepped from the shower and reached for the towel to dry off with. She wrapped the towel around her and wiped the mirror clean. He was lucky that Chelsea was drunk last night and this morning so that she didn't notice the patch that he had on his shoulder. *'If he wanted to get close to her, he would have to put up with these cravings.'* He thought to himself.

Christopher was making nice with Misty in the living room while he waited for her to finish her shower. She was actually letting him pet her without growling. He was impressed by this. Misty had betrayed her owner.

Christopher decided that he would take it really slow with her from now on. He had planted the remaining bugs and he had conquered the issues with Misty so he gave her a peck on the cheek and she responded by rubbing against his cheek. He knew that he had won Misty over, now he had to work on her mother.

"Well we better get going," He reminded her from the living room, as she was getting dressed.

"I look forward to riding today. Lets get going." She said as she came out of the bathroom all freshened up. Then they left her cottage and headed for the horse rental beach.

With her mom having a hard time accepting Christopher, Chelsea was beginning to get worried that she had made a big mistake getting mixed up with Christopher and Randy. So she made plans to call Felecia and run it past her as soon as they got back from horseback riding and Christopher left.

"Ready to go kind sir? You look like you are ready for our date. Let me just get my purse and we can go." She told him

"Sounds good to me princess, ready when you are." He replied. Then they headed out the door to the horse ranch to go riding on the beach. Although Chelsea felt terrible she thought she could carry on through their new adventure on the horses.

"You look great princess." He told her. He had brought a change of clothes with him. "May I use the bathroom next my lady?" He was excited to be spending so much time with his victim.

Chelsea was impressed that Christopher had won Misty over. It made her relax a little bit more. Little did she know that he would betray her in the end. And the end would be very soon.

He had freshened up the SUV last night so it would not smell like stale cigarettes today. He just kept a piece of gum in his mouth at all times. She had asked for a piece of regular gum several times because he seemed to like fresh breath and that's what she noticed the most. Or so she thought. She was ready for him still being a little hung over. When they were ready to go to ride the horses they got up from the couch and embraced and kissing passionately. She pulled away and commented on how nice it was that Misty was warming up to him. He was pleased that she felt good about that.

"Well are ya ready to go riding?" He asked,

"Yeah lets go." She replied and they left her cottage and she locked it up tight. They hopped into his car and headed for the horse ranch down the street just as a hard craving hit him.

The horses were beautiful and Chelsea didn't mince words about how excited she was to be riding today. The horse handler explained the basics to them, then sent them on their way. He pointed out the way to the beach. Chelsea had attached the picnic bag to the side of her saddle. She had asked for a horse with saddle bags. She put a blanket in one saddle bag. Then she put her picnic bag into the other saddle bag. Then they were on their way. The horses were well behaved and walked slowly to let them get used to being on top of them.

"Which way to the beach did he say it was?" She asked as she trotted up to him.

"Right this way princess, wanna race?" And he kicked his horse in the sides to make it go faster.

"No, I want to get there in one piece." She said with a giggle. They rode along until they found the white sand of the beach. They made it to the surf and she said, "Race ya now." And she took off running down the beach.

"Hey no fair, you cheated." And he kicked his horse to make it go faster. But he only got a trot out of his horse. Another craving hit him hard again. He let Chelsea get far ahead of him so that he could pull out a piece of gum. He slipped a piece of nicotine gum in his mouth and kicked his horse again, no luck, he could only get a trot out of his horse.

Chelsea's horse ran ahead. "I win then." She shouted as she ran ahead of him. He tried to keep up but his horse just wasn't that fast.

This was exactly what Chelsea had wanted. They made it to the end of the beach where there wasn't anyone around to bother them.

"Oh let's eat here, this is a good spot, and look a tie down for the horses. They can eat grass while we eat. I love this place." She said with excitement.

"You looked great running on the beach like that. You looked like you do this for a living."

"Well I have been on a horse before, but I wasn't sure at first. It all came back though." She replied.

"Well you looked like a pro out there."

"Thank you kind sir," She said. Then she tied her horse up to the post and let it graze.

He tied his horse up as well. She grabbed the picnic bag out of the saddle bag then took the blanket out of the other saddle bag. Then they went over to the sand and Chelsea laid out the blanket so they would have somewhere to sit. Then they sat down and started to fix a couple of plates. She handed him the wine and asked if he would open it. She also handed him the cork screw so he could open the wine. A craving hit him hard again but this time he just bit down on the gum and the craving passed. Then she pulled two glasses out of the bag to be filled with wine. Then she reached in the bag and pulled out two sandwiches and some cheese and crackers. She put the food on the paper plates and handed him one. He ditched the gum on the sly because they would be eating.

Then he sat down beside her and said, "This looks great, you really know how to treat a guy. I really like it." He was careful to stay away from the "L" word because she had pulled away after what he had said before. "This is great, what a good idea this was." He told her.

"Well I'm glad you're having fun. What's wrong with your horse anyway?"

"Well I suppose because I told them I was a first timer they gave me the slowest horse possible. She only trots."

"Oh how silly," She said with a giggle. She took a drink of wine and a bite of her sandwich. He ate his sandwich and took a sip of wine and enjoyed the light breeze that over took them.

"Ya know I really enjoyed our time together this time. And I'm really glad that Misty is warming up to you."

"Well most animals just don't like me, but I guess she likes me after all. Maybe that's what's wrong with my horse." She giggle again and said, "Well that's good thing." And she took another bite of her sandwich and took another sip of wine. "I love drinking wine on the shores of this beach. It's so relaxing." She said.

"Well I'm enjoying myself and a little hair of the dog doesn't hurt either." She laughed and took another drink of wine.

When they had finished the bottle of wine and the food they decided to get back to the horse ranch. They untied the horses and mounted them and took off down the beach. They took it slow this time because they wanted to enjoy every moment they had together on the horses. He didn't like his horse trotting anyway so he was happy that they took it slow on the way back. Then another craving hit him hard. He just smiled and rode it out. When they got back to the ranch they thanked the cowboy who had handled their horses and went on their way.

When they got back to her cottage he told her to wait for him this time. He got out of the SUV and walked around the front and arrived at her door in a flash. He opened the door for her and let her out.

"I had a great time this weekend sweetheart. But I'm gonna leave you be for now. We have some business to tend to tomorrow so I want to get some rest before then." He pulled her close and kissed her passionately. Then he said good bye and turned to leave.

"When will I see you again?" She asked as he started to walk away.

"Oh this is a busy week, but I will make time for you sweetness. Don't worry I will call you tonight. I am gonna miss you though." He said as he walked away. He jumped in his car and waved to her as he backed out of the driveway.

She fumbled for the key but found it and let herself in. Misty came up to her in no time demanding attention. She bent down and pet her beloved cat. "Well it's about time you came around missy, see he really is a good guy." Misty just stuck her tail in the air and strutted off at the mention of Christopher. *'Oh well, at least she's warming up to him.'* She thought to herself. She was worn out. It had been a long weekend and she actually was happy that Christopher had left her on her own for the night. She had to work tomorrow and she wanted to be in peak shape. She was happy that Felecia had decided that she wanted to do the dirty work with Anthony. She only wished it didn't have to happen. She could only hope that the guy that Christopher suggested would work out. She decided on what she would have for dinner and settled in for a night alone.

Chapter Twenty Eight

JONATHAN MAKES PLANS TO TAKE ANTHONY OUT

Felecia got dressed in Randy's hotel room. She had neglected to throw in an outfit to wear home so she just threw on her mini skirt from the night before. She kissed him passionately and said goodbye to him at 10:30 am. She had to hurry or she would miss David since he had asked that they meet up at 11 o'clock this morning. Randy was upset that she left so early, he was planning on another couple of rounds before she left for home, or where ever she was going. Jonathan decided to go to the apartment and listen to the tapes that had taken place at her house and Chelsea's house while they spent time with the ladies.

They really needed to get to that apartment to hear what was said in their absence. As Jonathan entered the apartment he saw that the light was blinking. Which meant there was precious information passing through the wires in Felecia's house as well as Chelsea's house. They had them right where they wanted them. Jonathan Snow heard the conversations that came through the wires.

Jonathan listened in on the tapes that delivered every conversation that the girls had in their houses. Felecia was meeting David later at her house. Jonathan would hear it all through the wires. After Christopher and Chelsea were finished riding the horses for the day, Chelsea asked if she could have some time to herself this afternoon to finish her chores around the house. So they said their goodbyes and he headed for the apartment to see what was being said through the wires. He had no idea that Felecia had dumped his brother for another guy.

Frank drove to the apartment and let himself in to find his brother listening in on the tapes again. "Well look what the cat dragged in, wouldja?" Jonathan said to Frank as he walked in the door.

"Well hello to you to brother of mine. How was your weekend?"

"Well she met someone else and dumped me this morning. What do you think about that?" Jonathan remarked.

"Well she is not one to be tied down. You knew that goin in. Are you okay?" Frank asked.

"Yeah, I will just miss her that's all."

"By the way, I slept with Chelsea last night. So that's taken care of. I just hope her cat and mother don't affect how she responds to me now. I hoped I would get closer to her after we made love but she pulled away a little bit. I think I made my move too soon." He admitted to Jonathan.

"Well now that you have picked that cherry, we can put our plan in motion on Monday."

"That sounds good to me bro." Jonathan agreed.

At 6am the alarm went off next to Felecia's head on her night stand. She reached for the snooze button and hit it just once. She laid there thinking of the day's events to come. The alarm went off again and she decided to get up. She threw on her silk robe and headed for the kitchen to start pot of coffee. Then she went into the bedroom to choose an outfit for the day. She wanted to look professional when she fired Alvarez. She only hoped that Mr. Eldridge would show up for work today so she could get this over with.

She laid her outfit, a dark grey pant suit, out on the bed and went into the bathroom and turned on the water to the shower. She showered and rinsed off then stepped from the shower. She reached for the towel and dried herself off. Then she wrapped the towel around her hair and went back into the bedroom to get dressed. She got dressed and went back into the bathroom to style her hair and apply her makeup. When she was satisfied that she looked her best she headed for the kitchen for some coffee.

She poured herself a cup of coffee and slipped a piece of bread into the toaster. Just then she heard the phone ring. "Hello" She said as she answered the phone.

"Well hello, Ms. Grey, its Mr. Eldridge. How are you this morning?" He asked.

"I'm doing great Mr. Eldridge, how are you feeling?" She asked him.

"Oh I'm fine the Mrs. just likes to baby me. I will be in the office this morning. I just can't stand being doted over all the time." He replied.

"Well as long as you're up to it boss. I wouldn't want to see you push it." She said into the phone.

"I'm fine, it was just a little indigestion. So it will be business as usual today. I will however be leaving at 2pm to make the Mrs. happy."

"Well I understand Mr. Eldridge. We all want to see you feeling better." "I will see you at 10 o'clock then Ms. Grey. Have a good morning." He said into the phone.

"Thank you for calling and letting me know boss, there is something we need to go over today. But you just take your time and make sure you're up to it. I will see you at 10 then." And she hung up the phone satisfied that the day would bring her everything that she wanted.

She picked up the phone and dialed the hotel room at the Regency. When the operator came on the line she told her to transfer her to room 504. Christopher had returned to the hotel last night, Randy hadn't. Jonathan had spent the night at the apartment listening in on the girls. He laid sound asleep when Felecia called Christopher. So he didn't know that Mr. Eldridge would give Felecia the green light on firing Alvarez today.

Frank was excited now and decided to head over to the apartment to fill his brother in on this new development. With nothing further going on Jonathan went to bed and was fast asleep when Felecia called the hotel. "Hello this is Christopher Fields."

"Hello Christopher, It's Felecia."

"Oh hi Felecia. I'm sorry but Randy is asleep."

"Oh that's ok, I wanted to talk to you. I will be firing that employee today. So I was wondering if you could call your cousin and have him fax his resume over to me."

"Well I will give him a call just as soon as we hang up. What's your fax number." "800-555-3090" She told him.

"Thanks, I'm sure he will be able to help you. Let me give him a call."

"Thanks Christopher, I really appreciate it. Talk to you soon, Goodbye then."

"Goodbye Felecia, Thank you, I'll get him to get right back to you." And they hung up the phone.

Frank dialed Henry's number and told him that they needed to meet for dinner tonight. Henry was taken aback by the early morning call. But he agreed all the same. He was just heading out the door so he wouldn't be late again. Frank hung up the phone and lit a cigarette and stepped out on the balcony. He was pissed that they had to take this measure but it had to be done. He then brought the phone out on the balcony and called Charlie Wright.

"Hello" Came the groggy voice on the other end of the line.

"Hey Charlie, It's Frank, We need your help."

"Yeah, what's goin on?" Charlie replied.

"Well we have this bank job that we are working on and the inside man just got himself killed. So I need a stand in. You will need to use your banking skills for this one. You will pose as a teller and when the time comes for us to rob the place you will help us keep the hostages under control. You will be paid $20,000 for your services."

"Well that sounds easy. When do you need me?"

"Well you need to fax your resume to Felecia Grey at the Trinity Bank, the fax number is 800-555-3090. Oh and your name is Daniel Fields and you are my cousin."

"On whose side?"

"Who cares, you're just my cousin you got that?"

"Yes yes, I got it."

"So change the name on your resume and send it to the bank right away. Okay?" Frank demanded.

"Will do, will I be receiving a phone call from the bank or how will I be in touch with you?"

"I'm sure Felecia Grey will be calling you. Now just send the dam resume." And he hung up the phone. He took a long drag on his cigarette then made his morning call to Chelsea.

"Hello" She said into the phone as she picked it up. "Well hello beautiful, how are you this morning?" "I'm late, I can't talk right now but I'm glad you called all the same. How are you?"

"I just have some more business plans for tonight is all, but I'm fine."

"Oh really, well you'll have to tell me all about it tonight." She said. "I really have to go though. Thanks for calling and it was nice to talk to you this morning."

"Well I can't go a morning without talking to you sweetness, I'll let you go then, have a good day."

"Oh thank you sweetie, bye for now." And they hung up the phone. Frank smashed his cigarette into the ashtray on the balcony and went into his bedroom to get dressed. He had to get over to the apartment to discuss the Charlie Wright situation with Jonathan.

He hopped in the shower and washed himself up. He reached for a towel and dried himself off. Then he wrapped the towel around his waist and headed for the bedroom to pick out an outfit to wear. He chose a pair of black slacks and a light blue button down long sleeved shirt. He decided he was ready and left room 504. He rode the elevator to the lobby and exited the hotel through the big glass doors. He went straight for his SUV and hopped in. He loved this car. It was one of the better perks of the job. He drove out of the parking lot of the hotel and headed for the apartment. When he got there he let himself in to the little two bedroom apartment. He heard snoring coming from Jonathan's room. "Wake up cowboy," He said as he kicked the bed. "We got work to do."

"Wait, what, what the fuck are you doing here? Leave me alone and let me sleep."

"No we have got work to do, Felecia called me this morning and asked if I would have Charlie send her his resume. Apparently she plans to give Alvarez the ax today."

"Oh my little tiger, I can't wait to take that asshole out. Great I'll be right there." He said as he sat up on his bed.

"Hurry up, this has to go off without a hitch." Frank spit out at Jonathan.

"What's up with you bro?" Jonathan asked angrily still whipping the sleep out of his eyes.

"You know I don't want to do this. I just don't like killing."

"Don't worry, we'll just take him out to dinner and take a drive down Bayou Rd. and finish him off."

"I know I just don't like thinking about it let alone doing it."

"Well leave it all up to me then bro." Jonathan said to reassure his brother.

"Don't worry this one's all you." Frank replied.

Jonathan hoped out of bed and got dressed. "When did all this happen anyway?" Jonathan asked.

"Well I was just getting up at the hotel and the phone rang and it was Felecia and she asked me to have Charlie or Daniel to her, send her his resume. It's all on the tape, just go listen."

"Okay, alright, that's what I will do, just calm down."

Frank lit another cigarette and took a big drag. He blew grey smoke into the air. "When do you see Felecia again?" Frank asked Jonathan.

"We didn't say, but whenever you want us to." Jonathan knew better than to cross his brother when he was in this bad of a mood. So he just went along with it. He went over to the tape recorder and listened to the conversation that Frank had had with Felecia this morning.

"Don't worry I'm on it." Jonathan said as he got out of bed.

"You're sure in a sour mood this morning. What's gotten into you?" Jonathan asked.

"I just don't like killing. We are bank robbers not murders."

"I know but this is a necessary evil of the job. Don't worry bro I got this under control." Jonathan said. As Jonathan got dressed he brought his revolver because they would be able to take Henry Cornwell out tonight.

Chapter Twenty Nine

ANTHONY'S LAST DAY

Felecia hopped out of bed and got dressed in Randy's hotel room. She had neglected to throw an outfit in a bag to wear home, so she just threw on her mini skirt and top from the night before. She kissed him passionately and said goodbye to him at 10 am. She had to hurry because she needed to shower before she met up with David. She would meet David at 11 o'clock this morning. She would not have enough time to shower if she didn't leave right then. Randy was upset that she left so early, he was planning on another couple of rounds in the sack before she left for home, or where ever she was going. Jonathan decided to go to the apartment and listen to the tapes that had captured the conversation at her house and Chelsea's house while they spent time with the ladies.

As Frank entered the apartment he saw that the light was blinking on the tape recorder. This meant there was precious information passing through the wires in the ladies houses. They had them right where they wanted them. Frank Snow heard the conversations that came through the wires. He decided to call his brother at the hotel and tell him he really needed to come by and hear what was said this weekend. Jonathan had no idea yet that Felecia had met someone new and she was contemplating dumping him.

When Frank called Jonathan from the apartment, he told him that he should get over there right away. Frank had left Chelsea's around 10 o'clock. Jonathan told Felecia that something had come up and he needed to call a cab and head to the Regency Hotel to meet with his business partner. They really needed hear what was said in their absence, because it would change the plan.

"What the hell was so important? I was planning on spending the day having sex with Felecia."

"Would you please keep the events of your evening quiet. We have got a problem."

"Alright, what's going on then?" Jonathan asked.

"You might get the boot before we rob the Trinity Bank. That's all. Hear it for yourself. Felecia met some guy at the grocery store and she is spending time with him right now as we speak."

"What? That can't possibly be true. I thought I had all of her attention."

"Well she's dating a guy named David this afternoon. Go listen for yourself."

"Alright but this was supposed to be temporary anyway, so I really don't see what the problem is. I was planning on dumping her before the heist. If she wants to see another guy, there is literally nothing I can do about it." Jonathan replied.

"Okay, we have her house wired up so if she dumps you we will just have to listen to the conversations in her house and office. No big deal bro. I got it handled."

"You better have it handled or we may have a hard time robbing her. But I suppose if she wants another guy you can deal with it then. I just thought you should know. By the way, I slept with Chelsea last night. So that's taken care of. I just hope her cat and mother don't affect how she responds to me now. I hoped I would get closer to her after we made love but she pulled away a little bit. I think I made my move too soon." He admitted to Jonathan.

"Well now that you have picked that cherry, we can put our plan in motion on Monday."

"That sounds good to me bro." Jonathan agreed. They both said their goodbyes and hung up the phone. Then Jonathan called a cab to get over to the apartment to listen to the tapes that had recorded every conversation that they had had while at the ladies houses. Frank and Jonathan spent the rest of Sunday afternoon and night going over the plan.

At 6am the alarm went off next to Felecia's head on her night stand. She reached for the snooze button and hit it just once. She laid there thinking of the day's events to come. The alarm went off again and she decided to get up. She threw on her silk robe and headed for the kitchen to start a pot of coffee. Then she went into the bedroom to choose an outfit for the day. She wanted to look professional when she fired Alvarez. She only hoped that Mr. Eldridge would show up for work today so she could get this over with.

She laid her outfit, a dark grey pant suit, out on the bed and went into the bathroom and turned on the water to the shower. She felt the water to check the temperature and felt that it was perfect so she slipped out of her robe and stepped under the water. She showered and rinsed off then stepped from the shower. She reached for the towel and dried herself off. Then she wrapped the towel around her hair and went back into the bedroom to get dressed. She got dressed and went back into the bathroom to style her hair and apply her makeup. When she was satisfied that she looked her best she headed for the kitchen for some coffee.

She poured herself a cup of coffee and slipped a piece of bread into the toaster. Just then she heard the phone ring. "Hello" She said as she answered the phone.

"Well hello, Ms. Grey, its Mr. Eldridge. How are you this morning?" He asked.

"I'm doing great Mr. Eldridge, how are you feeling?" She asked him.

"Oh I'm fine the Mrs. just likes to baby me. I will be in the office this morning. I just can't stand being doted over all the time." He replied.

"Well as long as you're up to it boss. I wouldn't want to see you push it." She said into the phone.

"I'm fine, it was just a little indigestion. So it will be business as usual today. I will however be starting the day at 10 am and leaving at 2 pm to make the Mrs. happy."

"Well I understand Mr. Eldridge. We all want to see you feeling better."

"I will see you at 10 o'clock then Ms. Grey. Have a good morning." He said into the phone.

"Thank you for calling and letting me know boss, there is something we need to go over today. But you just take your time and make sure you're up to it. I will see you at 10 o'clock." Then she hung up the phone satisfied that the day would bring her everything that she wanted.

She picked up the phone and dialed the Regency Hotel. When the operator came on the line she told her to transfer her to room 504. Christopher was in the hotel, Randy was not. Randy had spent the night at the apartment listening in on the girls. He lay sound asleep when Felecia called Christopher. So he didn't know that Mr. Eldridge would give Felecia the green light on firing Alvarez today. Christopher was excited now and decided to head over to the apartment to fill his brother in on this new development.

With nothing further going on Jonathan had gone to bed that night and was still fast asleep in the morning when Felecia called the hotel. "Hello this is Christopher Fields." Christopher said when he answered the phone.

"Hello Christopher, It's Felecia."

"Oh hi Felecia. I'm sorry but Randy is asleep."

"Oh that's ok, I wanted to talk to you. I will be firing that employee today. So I was wondering if you could call your cousin and have him fax his resume over to me."

"Well I will give him a call just as soon as we hang up. What's your fax number?" He asked

"It's 1-800-555-3090" She returned.

"Thanks, I'm sure he will be able to help you. Let me give him a call."

"Thanks Christopher, I really appreciate it. Talk to you soon, Goodbye then."

"Goodbye Felecia, Thanks I'll get him to get right back to you."

"Thanks again Christopher," She said, then they hung up the phone.

Frank dialed Henry's number and told him that they needed to meet for dinner tonight. Henry was taken aback by the early morning call. But he agreed all the same. He was just heading out the door so he wouldn't be late again. Frank hung up the phone and lit a cigarette and stepped out on the balcony. He was pissed that they had to take this measure but it had to be done. He then brought the phone out on the balcony and called Charlie Wright.

"Hello" Came the groggy voice on the other end of the line.

"Hey Charlie, It's Frank, We need your help."

"Yeah, what's goin on?" Charlie replied.

"Well we have this bank job that we are working on and the inside man just got himself killed. So I need a stand in. You will need to use your banking skills for this one. You will pose as a teller be our inside man. We will be using the software that the bank uses that we downloaded onto the flash drive this weekend when we were at the ladies houses. Are you familiar with BankSecure software?" He asked."

"Well yes I have used that software before, is that the software that Trinity Bank uses?" He asked.

"Yes that's the one. When the time comes for us to rob the place you will give us the crucial information that we need for this software. We have made a note of your password so we should be able to access the banks backdoors with that, but we will need the ladies passwords to browse through the site at will when we are ready. You will be paid $20,000 for your services."

"Well that sounds easy. When do you need me?"

"Well you need to fax your resume to Felecia Grey at Trinity Bank the fax number is 1-800-555-3090. Oh and your name is Daniel Fields and you are my cousin."

"On whose side?"

"Who cares, you're just my cousin, you got that?"

"Yes yes, I got it."

"So change the name on your resume and send it to the bank right away." Frank demanded.

"Will do, will I be receiving a phone call from the bank or how will I be in touch with you?"

"I'm sure Felecia Grey will be calling you. Now just send the dam resume." Then Frank slammed the phone down in frustration. He took a long drag on his cigarette then made the call to Chelsea to calm his nerves.

"Hello" She said into the phone as she picked it up.

"Well hello beautiful, how are you this morning?"

"I'm late, I can't talk right now but I'm glad you called all the same. How are you?"

"I just got some more business plans for tonight is all, but I'm fine."

"Oh really, well you'll have to tell me all about it tonight." She said. "I really have to go though. Thanks for calling and it was nice to talk to you this morning."

"Well I can't go a morning without talking to you sweetness, I'll let you go then, have a good day."

"Oh thank you sweetie, bye for now." And they hung up the phone. Frank smashed his cigarette into the ashtray on the balcony and went into his bedroom to get dressed. He had to get over to the apartment to tell Jonathan about the recent events.

He hopped in the shower and washed himself up. Then he turned the water off and stepped from the shower. He reached for a towel and dried himself off. Then he wrapped the towel around his waist and headed for the bedroom to pick out an appropriate outfit to wear. He chose a pair of black slacks and a light blue button down long sleeved shirt. He decided he was ready and left room 504. He rode the elevator to the lobby and exited the hotel through the big glass doors.

He went straight for his car and hopped in. He loved this SUV and wished he could keep it. It was one of the better perks of the job. He drove out of the parking lot of the hotel and headed for the apartment. When he got there he let himself in to the little two bedroom apartment. He heard snoring coming from Jonathan's room. "Wake up cowboy," He said as he kicked the bed. "We got work to do."

"Wait, what? What the fuck are you doing here? Leave me alone and let me sleep!" Jonathan said angrily.

"No we have got work to do, Felecia called me this morning and asked if I would have Charlie send her his resume. Apparently she plans to give Alvarez the ax today."

"Oh my little tiger, I can't wait to take that asshole out. Great I'll be right there." He said as he sat up on his bed.

"Hurry up, this has to happen tonight." Frank spit out at Jonathan.

"What's up with you bro?"

"You know I don't want to do this. I just don't like killing."

"Don't worry, we'll just take him out to dinner, ply him for any last bit of information and take a drive down Bayou Rd. and finish him off."

"I know I just don't like thinking about it let alone doing it."

"Well leave it all up to me then bro." Jonathan said to reassure his brother.

"Don't worry this one's all you." Frank replied.

Jonathan hoped out of bed and got dressed. "When did all this happen anyway?" Jonathan asked.

"Well I was just getting up at the hotel and the phone rang and it was Felecia and she asked me to have Charlie or Daniel to her, send her his resume. It's all on the tape, just go listen."

"Okay, alright, that's what I will do, just calm down."

Frank lit another cigarette and took a big drag. He blew grey smoke into the air. "When do you see Felecia again?" Frank asked Jonathan.

"We didn't say, but whenever you want us to." Jonathan knew better than to cross his brother when he was in this bad of a mood. So he just went along with it. He went over to the tape recorder and listened to the conversation that Frank had had with Felecia this morning.

"Don't worry I'm on it." Jonathan said as he got out of bed. "You're sure in a sour mood this morning." "Whats gotten into you?" Jonathan asked.

"I just don't like killing. We are bank robbers not murders."

"I know but this is a necessary evil of the job. Don't worry bro I got this under control." Jonathan said. As Jonathan got dressed he brought his revolver because they would be able to take Henry Cornwell out tonight.

Chelsea arrived at the bank at 7:55am. Felecia was already there waiting for her. When the time locks released the doors they would enter the bank. "So how was your weekend with Randy?" Chelsea asked innocently.

"It was great. We had a ball, I really like his hotel room." Felecia said with a slight giggle.

"How'd you do, how's Misty getting along with Christopher?" She asked.

"Well we did it and Misty has warmed up to him. So no problem anymore."

"Oh you did, did you? How was it?"

"I don't kiss and tell but he is fantastic." Chelsea said with a grin. Just then they heard the click of the locks opening the doors to their great bank. Harold the security guard, Alice and Cheryl had just arrived and were waiting for the doors to open as well. They had arrived at their usual time. Felecia and Chelsea greeted them and said a happy good morning to all of them. Then Felecia opened the front door at 8 am precisely.

Charlie Wright did a back ground check on Daniel Fields. He found a guy by that name who fit his description online. He looked into his back ground further and found that he worked as a bank teller as well. He was satisfied that he could fool the banks bosses. He would use this guys social security number when he was hired at the bank. He doctored his resume and faxed it to Felecia Grey at Trinity Bank as Frank had ordered. Frank had also done a background check on Daniel Fields and knew he would pass the background check that Felecia would do.

Felecia let them all in and Harold took his post by the door. Chelsea and Felecia headed for the vault to open it and pass out the money bags as the tellers arrived. Cheryl headed for her desk to settle in for the day. And Alice headed for the elevator to go to her office upstairs. When the vault was open, Chelsea went out to the front door to let the rest of the employees in. They all filed in one by one and Chelsea and Harold greeted them as they came in. Cheryl had made her signature pot of coffee and almost the entire staff headed for the break room at one point or another to get a cup of her coffee.

Anthony Alvarez was the last one to arrive and he was 5 minutes late. Felecia was steaming mad at him and did not hold it back. "You're late Mr. Alvarez, again."

"I know Ms. Grey, I'm sorry. My car wouldn't start this morning."

"That sounds like an excuse to me, I want to see you later privately."

"Okay, I'll be right here when you need me." He said with a heavy heart. He tried to hold his fear at bay but he was nervous and it showed.

"I will call you when I am ready for you." She told him. Then she climbed the stairs to her office. She still had a few minutes to wait for

Alvarez to count his drawer. The rest of the tellers were ready to go for the day. At 8:45 am Anthony called to Felecia to let her know he balanced and was open for business. Somehow he thought this would save him. But his fate was sealed.

Chapter Thirty

⟨※⟩

ANTHONY'S DEMISE

Felecia found a fax from Daniel Fields on the fax machine. It was his resume. She looked it over and typed his name into the background check software that she had on her computer. He passed with flying colors so she decided that she would give Christopher's cousin a try. When Anthony called up to her office to let her know he was finished she climbed back down the stairs and opened the blinds above the picture windows. The rest of the employees had showed up and Harold and Chelsea said good morning to all. At 9 o'clock sharp Chelsea open the doors to the public. There were a couple of customers waiting for service at the door. Chelsea let them in and thanked them for using Trinity Bank.

At 10 am Mr. Eldridge arrived and said good morning to Harold. He made the rounds to everyone this morning to let them know he was alright. He stopped in Richard's office to chat for a minute. "How are you getting along son?" He asked Richard.

"I'm shadowing Mark like you asked. I'm learning a lot. He's a good teacher."

"Well I'm glad it's working out then. I would like to see you for lunch, what do you say we go to lunch today."

"Yes dad that sounds good, it's good to see you up and about. Mom really does care about you." Richard told his dad.

"Yes I know but I'm fine. It was only indigestion!" Mr. Eldridge said in frustration.

"I know but you can't be too careful. Just take it easy today, okay dad?"

"Will do son. Be ready at noon for lunch, I'll see you then." And he turned and left Richards office and headed for the elevator.

He rode the elevator to the 2nd floor and said good morning to Chelsea as he walked by her office. He then stuck his head in Felecia's office and said good morning to her as well. "I will meet with you in a few minutes Ms. Grey. Just let me get settled in." He told her.

"Sure thing boss, we just have a couple of pressing matters."

"Okay then, I will call you when I'm ready for you." And he turned and walked to Alice's office. He popped his head in Alice's office and said good morning to her. Then he settled in behind his desk. Alice hopped up and headed straight down to the break room to get him his coffee. Cheryl had kept a fresh pot of coffee going so that everyone would have a chance to have a cup when they arrived.

She returned with the coffee and said. "One lump of sugar just how you like it Mr. Eldridge. Will there be anything else this morning sir?" She asked.

"No but you could tell Ms. Grey that I'm ready for her now."

"I will get right on that sir. Enjoy your coffee." And she turned on her heel and left his office.

Alice popped her head inside of Felecia's office and told her that Mr. Eldridge could see her now. Felecia thanked her and grabbed Daniel's resume and headed for Mr. Eldridge's office. When she got to his office she stepped inside knocking on the door slightly, "Hello, Mr. Eldridge, Alice said you were ready for me. Is now a good time?" She asked,

"Yes of course I told Alice to send you in. Come, sit down. What's on your mind Ms. Grey?" He asked her.

"Well we have an employee who is not doing well. As a matter of fact he's been late several times. He's also having trouble balancing his drawer on a regular basis. We hired him a couple of months ago and I think he lied on his resume about his experience. So I want to fire him. This guy has been making so many mistakes I really can't stand him, so I would like the chance to fire him with your approval of course. I have a friend who suggested his cousin who is a bank teller and out of work and here's his resume. We could get him in right away and train him in a weeks time. So I just need the green light to fire Mr. Alvarez."

"Well what else has he done?"

"He is constantly not balancing on his drawer and he has trouble keeping the high end customers happy, Chelsea had to go to smooth things over with him and Mr. Gordon, and I know that Mr. Gordon is a good friend or yours. I just don't want anymore mistakes."

"Well if he has you convinced then do what you have to do. What about this Daniel? How does he look?"

"Well I ran a back ground check on him before you came in and he has worked as a teller before, he has no criminal record and he looks good to me." She explained.

"Well if you say he's the one, then let's get the ball rolling." He said.

"Thank you Mr. Eldridge, I will keep you posted as to the progress of Daniel Fields." And with that she stood and left his office to go to Chelsea's office to tell her to cut Anthony's last check. She would fire him as soon as Chelsea was finished.

Frank listened in on the recorder when Felecia told Chelsea to cut the final check for Henry. He had a knot in his stomach. He didn't like what came next. He knew that Henry was getting the boot soon. So he called Charlie and told him to be ready to take the call from Felecia.

Felecia headed back to her office and called Daniel. She dialed the number on his resume which was a disposable cell phone number. "Hello" came the voice on the other end of the phone.

"Hello, May I please speak to Mr. Fields?"

"That's me. Who is this?"

"Well your new employer if all works out. I received your resume and a recommendation from your cousin Christopher."

"Oh yeah Chris, how is he? I haven't seen him in a while."

"He's doing great as far as I know. I looked over your resume and with Christopher's recommendation I would like to give you a try. Would you be available to work tomorrow?"

"Yes I would. Just give me the address and tell me what time you would like me to be there and I will be there on time."

"Great, the bank is Trinity Bank and we are on the strip in near the beach in Tallahassee. We're at 1360 Bald Point Rd. in Tallahassee Florida. Can you be here by 8:30 am?"

"Yes I will be there in the morning. Thank you Ms. Grey. I will see you tomorrow." His phone number had a South Carolina Prefix, so Felecia questioned whether he would make it on time to work for tomorrow. But she decided to take a chance on him.

"I will see you in the morning then Mr. Fields. Thank you." They hung up the phone and Felecia went into Chelsea's office with Daniel's resume.

"Here's the new hire that will start tomorrow. He's Christopher's cousin so I figure that he would be a good fit. I did a back ground check on him and there was no surprises. So I called him in for tomorrow morning."

"That sounds great I just wish you would give Anthony another chance." Chelsea said with a slight tone of regret.

"He's a screw up and he has to go. Just let me know when you have his check ready."

"Oh its right here, I paid him through today. You can let him go anytime now." Chelsea replied as she handed Felecia the check.

"Great, thanks I will let him go right now then." And she left to go to her office.

Felecia called down to Cheryl and asked her if she would send Anthony up to her office. Cheryl relayed the message to Anthony who started to get nervous at the sound of going upstairs. He said thanks to Cheryl and locked his drawer up then headed for the elevator.

When he got to Felecia's office he sheepishly said, "You wanted to see me Ms. Grey."

"Yes come in and sit down Mr. Alvarez." She punched a few keys on her keyboard while he sat down. Then she turned her attention to Anthony. "You have been late several times and you have had a hard time keeping your drawer straight. Quite frankly Mr. Alvarez I believe you may have lied on your resume. Here is your final pay check. You are fired." She said as she handed him his check.

"I tried really hard Ms. Grey, can't I have one more chance?" He whined.

"My mind is made up, Mr. Alvarez. Go clean out your station and leave the premises." She said harshly.

To this he said "Okay, I understand, I will leave and clean out my station. Thank you for giving me a chance." He told her as he stood and left with his check in hand. He rode the elevator to the first floor with a somber look on his face. He went to his station and put his sparse belongings in a box and left the bank. Felecia watched him from the hallway upstairs.

After Anthony called Felecia to tell her he was ready for her, she came back down to enormous staircase and met him at his station. He had placed the money from his drawer in his money bag again and handed Felecia the bag when he was finished. "It's been a pleasure working here." He said to Felecia when he handed her his money bag.

"Just leave the premises please Mr. Alvarez. I really just want you gone."

"Okay I just wanted leave on a happy note." Anthony said to Felecia.

"Well this is not the place for you Mr. Alvarez. You just need to move on. I hope you do well on your own god luck to you in the future." She said to him as he handed the bag to her.

"Well that's it then. Good bye and thank you again for giving me a chance." He said to Felecia as he headed out of the door.

Frank and Jonathan heard the whole thing on the recorder. "Now we step it up. I know your anxious to kill Henry but just don't make me watch."

"Okay bro, no problem. He's fish bait." Jonathan said with an evil grin on his face. Just then the phone rang in the apartment.

"Hello" Frank said as he answered the phone.

"Hey it's me Charlie. She wants me to be at work tomorrow at 8:30 am. I have to catch a plane to get there tonight. You gotta cover the airfare I'm broke." Charlie said into the phone.

"Don't worry about it, just use this credit card number, do you have a pen and paper?" Frank asked

"Yes go ahead"

"Okay the credit card number is 4490 6382 4906 5520 expiration date February of 2020. If you need the code on the back it is 324 and the name on the card is Frank Snow. Anything else?" Frank asked Charlie

"No that will do, I should be there shortly. I'll have to use this credit card to get a cell phone and pay for the hotel room when I get there as well so I can call you when I get there so I will know where you are."

"No problem use it for whatever you need."

"I'll see ya when I get there then."

"Okay see ya then," Frank said into the phone and then hung it up.

"Well Felecia's a good girl. She already wants Charlie to work. We should be seeing him shortly."

"Sounds great bro, see it's all falling into place." Jonathan said.

"Yeah I just wish we didn't have to get blood on our hands." Frank said while he blew grey smoke into the air.

"Man I can't wait for this to be over and I don't have to breathe in your second hand smoke."

"Oh shut up about my smoking would ya? Let's just get this done." Frank spit back at his brother.

Felecia came down stairs at 4 o'clock to let the tellers count their drawers and put the money away. Chelsea wasn't far behind. It had been a long day at Trinity Bank. Chelsea just wanted to get home and talk to her prince charming. Felecia was heading to Clark's aerobics class tonight after work again. Felecia began collecting the money bags from the tellers and let them go for the day. Chelsea had locked the doors at 4 o'clock and let the teller's out as they finished for the day. Chelsea had already let the loan officers out for the day. She was beat and just wanted to get home. She said goodnight to Alice and Cheryl as they left the bank. Then there was only Felecia, Chelsea and Harold in the bank. Felecia closed the blinds and let them all out for the night. They said their goodbyes and left for the evening.

At 6 o'clock. Frank and Jonathan stopped by Henry's apartment and honked the horn to let him know they were there. Frank chain smoked while they waited for him. Henry was scared to tell the brothers that he had been fired. He should have remembered that both of his bosses offices were bugged and that he had planted the bugs, but this information had had escaped him since he was so nervous tonight.

He locked up his little two bedroom apartment and hopped in the car. "Hi guys, how are you tonight?" He asked both of them.

Jonathan turned and told him to shut up until they got to the restaurant. Henry was afraid of Jonathan so he did as he was told.

They arrived at the restaurant and hopped out of the vehicle. "Oh seafood, my favorite." Henry said trying to lighten the mood a little.

"I said shut the fuck up you asshole, we know what happened today."

Henry's face went pale and he swallowed hard. "I tried but I had no experience in banking, I told you that from the start." He whined.

"I said shut the fuck up." Jonathan demanded. Then Henry decided he would just listen from now on tonight unless he was told to speak. Frank smoked feverishly before they got into the restaurant. When they were seated Frank asked if Henry had anything new to tell him. Henry told them that he didn't have any new information for them because he was so nervous about how Jonathan was treating him that he forgot everything that he was going to tell the Snow brothers tonight.

Frank lit another cigarette. The waitress trotted up and brought Frank an ashtray. Frank ordered dinner and drinks for all of them. He made sure no one had alcohol so they didn't mess anything else up. Frank chain smoked all through their meal.

He lit a fresh cigarette when his meal arrived. Jonathan finished his dinner first. "Well I'm ready to go. Call that pretty little waitress over here and get the check, let's get this done." Jonathan said.

"Don't be so impatient Jonathan, we got time." Frank told his brother.

Henry asked, "What's going on later?"

"You just don't worry about it, you got a free meal tonight be grateful." Jonathan spit back at him. Henry didn't say another word in the restaurant.

They finished their meals and called for the waitress to bring the check. She came rushing up and left the receipt book on the table and said. "I'll be you cashier too, so just wave when you're ready."

"Thank you sweetness." Frank said. And he put his credit card in the receipt book, leaving a nice trail for the cops to follow. Then he waved for the waitress to come back and smashed his cigarette out in the ashtray. She arrived in a flash. Frank gave her an extra large tip because she had been so efficient. She thanked him and trotted off to process his credit card.

She returned a few minutes later and said "Thank you for coming tonight, come again anytime,"

"We will and thank you ma'am." Frank said to her. Then they left the restaurant.

As soon as they got into the SUV, Frank lit another cigarette. Henry noticed that Frank was smoking more than usual but he didn't say anything about it. They headed for Bayou Rd. Which was in the opposite direction of Henry's apartment.

"Where we goin now guys?" Henry asked.

"You just keep your mouth shut and we will do the thinking. You know you almost ruined the job for us today. That's just not acceptable. What do you think we should do about that, you're a liability to us now." Jonathan said with disdain in his voice.

"What do you mean liability?" Henry asked.

"Just shut the fuck up and enjoy the ride. You idiot!" Jonathan spit back. Frank had determined that he couldn't take anymore of the bantering that was going on between Jonathan and Henry. They had made it to Bayou Rd. so he pulled down the next side road. It took them to a secluded spot in the marsh. Frank stopped the car and hopped out.

Jonathan said to Henry "Get out now asshole,"

"Why what are we doing here?" He asked with fear in his voice.

"Just get out now. And stand over there." Jonathan said as he pointed out where Henry should stand. Henry was getting a really bad feeling about this. Frank got back in the SUV and rolled up the windows. He lit another cigarette. Frank had thrown the last cigarette butt out of the window and left it behind in the sandy road of the marsh. He didn't want to hear Henry plead for his life. This was a mistake that would lead the police straight to then when the time came.

Jonathan said. "Now turn around asshole,"

"Why, what are you going to do?" Henry said almost peeing himself because he was so scared.

"Because I said so, now do it." Jonathan said with authority.

Henry turned around slowly, his knees knocking the whole time. Jonathan took out his colt 45 revolver and cocked it.

"I hear a gun, what are you going to do to me, I can keep my mouth shut just give me a chance." He pleaded. Pop the gun went as Jonathan pulled the trigger and Henry fell to the ground in a slump. Frank winced in the car when he heard the gun shot. Then he tossed his second cigarette butt out of the window because he didn't want any cigarette butts stinking up the car that he drove Chelsea around in. Jonathan took too much pride in killing Henry. When this was over Frank would put some distance between his trigger finger hungry brother and himself.

Henry laid there on the ground dead and bleeding all over the place with one bullet to the back of his head. The bullet had blown off the back of his head and he was bleeding profusely. Jonathan grabbed him by the feet and dragged him into the marsh so as not to get any blood on himself. Then he left him there to be fish food. He then hopped in the SUV and told Frank to put some distance between this asshole and them. Frank started the engine and drove off. He headed back to the apartment to see if the girls were chatting on the phone and to call his princess.

He puffed on another cigarette whole they drove back to the apartment. When they returned they listened in on the recorder and found that there were no conversations going on. So he called Chelsea.

"Hello" She said into the phone when she answered it. He had made this number a private number so that she couldn't tell where he was calling from. "Hey princess how are you?"

"Oh Christopher how nice to hear from you so early. It's only 9 o'clock. Are you okay?" She asked.

"Oh yes, we just finished another business dinner and I missed you so I wanted to talk to you now. That's all." He cooed.

"Well how was your dinner then?" She asked innocently. He cringed because he didn't want to think about what just happened.

"Oh it was just business princess. How was your evening?"

"Well I spent it doing chores so not very exciting. Thank you for asking."

"No problem sweetness, I just miss you." He said again.

"Well when can I see you again." She asked,

"I'm free for dinner tomorrow. What do you say I cook you dinner again at the hotel."

"Oh that sounds great. I'll be there. No drinking though, I have to work the next day."

"Okay princess whatever you wish. Can I pick you up again or do you want to drive?"

"Oh I can drive, I know where the hotel is, what time did you have in mind." She asked.

"Well how about 6 o'clock. I will cook you some chicken cordon blue. It's an old family recipe."

"Oh that sounds wonderful, I can't wait. I'll see you tomorrow then."

"Sounds good princess, see you then." And they hung up.

"Now we have an alibi. Chelsea will back up that he had been at a business meeting and that he had called her at 9 pm precisely." He said to his brother. And he lit another cigarette to calm his nerves.

Chapter Thirty One

───── ❖ ─────

CHARLIE'S WRIGHT BECOMES THE THIRD PARTNER

A t 6am Felecia woke up to the sound of music flowing through her bedroom. Felecia was in a good mood today. She thought of David. She couldn't wait to see how he was in bed. Since she had dumped Randy he made plans for another business meeting tonight with his brother and Charlie Wright to find out how his first day went. It was the meeting that would change their plans.

Felecia hopped in the shower and washed up. She picked out a professional outfit to wear for the day and laid it out on her bed. She thought maybe she would call David later then went into the bathroom and applied her makeup and styled her hair in a professional manner. She then got dressed in her black dress suit. She threw her hair in a bun on her head and headed for the kitchen to make coffee and toast. When they were ready she finished them quickly and left her house. She hopped in her sports car and left for the bank at 7:50 am. She knew there was no sense being there any earlier than 8 am because of the time locks.

The phone woke her up. She had over slept again and was running late. It was 7am when Chelsea heard the phone ringing, she reached for the phone and said a hurried "Hello"

"Well hello princess, you sound upset, are you okay?"

"Well I have no time to talk, I'm late again and I must get to the bank before 8 o'clock."

"Well I will let you go then, I just wanted to say good morning. But I don't want to hold you up so I will let you go and I will call you tonight after our meeting."

"Sounds good, gotta go, love you sweet prince, bye." Then she hung up the phone regretting the words that she had just said to him. It was too soon for such nonsense just yet. Her alarm had failed to go off again. She would need to look into that for tomorrow. She pushed the covers away and hopped out of bed.

Misty wrapped herself around Chelsea's feet. "Not now sweetheart," Chelsea said to Misty as she pet her once and left the bedroom for the shower. She wouldn't have time to make a pot of coffee today, but she would get a cup at work. She just needed to shower and eat. So she turned on the hot water and slipped out of her nightie then she stepped under the water. She showered so that she would be clean for the day. She hurried as fast as she could because there was no way she could be late. She turned off the water when she was finished and reached for the towel. She dried herself off and wrapped the towel around her hair. She then headed for the kitchen to open a can of cat food for Misty. Buzzzz the can opener went and Misty hurried over to her for her breakfast. Chelsea put the can of cat food in Misty's bowl and headed for the bedroom to get dressed. At 7:30 she was almost ready to go. She just had to get dressed. Then she would throw a bagel in the toaster and eat it before she left the house.

She picked out a professional looking dark grey suit dress, and put it on. Then she braided her hair and headed for the kitchen to toast her bagel. 'I can't be late' She thought to herself. The bagel popped up and she lathered it with cream cheese then put it on a plate to hold it so that she could eat it quickly. She ate her bagel and declared that she was ready to go at 7:45 am. She then picked up her purse and got ready to leave her cottage. She said good bye to Misty and opened the door and left the house, then locked it up tight. She hopped in her sedan at 7:50 am. She would just make it in time. She started her car and backed out of her driveway and headed the Trinity Bank.

Felecia arrived at 7:55 am. Chelsea wasn't far behind at 7:58 am, she was relieved that she had made it on time. They said their good mornings to each other and made small talk while they waited for the time locks to release the doors.

"So what did you think about Daniel yesterday?" Felecia asked Chelsea. "I think he's a God send." Felecia continued.

"Yes he worked out great yesterday. I was surprised to see him so early in the morning. But that's a good thing so I like him." Chelsea replied.

"Well speak of the devil," Felecia said as Daniel arrived then walked up to the banks entrance. The locks made a loud click and Felecia opened the doors. "Well hello Mr. Fields, You're right on time. I'm impressed. But I thought you said you lived around here? Why the cab?" Felecia asked.

"Well good morning ladies. Yes I do have an apartment and I live around here, as a matter of fact I live just down the street. But I'm in between cars at the moment. I will have one soon. Hopefully by tomorrow." He replied as he climbed the steps to the front door. Daniel was a handsome man and Felecia thought she could see the family resemblance in him and Christopher. He was a tall 6'3" and looked as though he worked out regularly. Felecia made a mental note to mention Clarks aerobics class to him later.

Harold and Cheryl had arrived early as usual. It was Harold's job to arrive by 8am. And he was punctual every day. Harold nodded good morning to Chelsea as she let him in the door at 8 am sharp, and he took his place beside her. Cheryl said a happy good morning to everyone and headed for her desk to put her purse away. Then she made her way to the break room to make everyone coffee. When the coffee was done Chelsea asked Cheryl if she would get her a cup while she was in the break room. Cheryl gladly did as Chelsea had asked her to do. She quickly went to the break room and made Chelsea a cup of coffee and brought it to her at the door. Chelsea couldn't leave the door unattended because the employees needed to be let in when they arrived.

Alice showed at 8:10 am and Chelsea and Harold let her into the bank as well. She was a few minutes late today, but she didn't have to be at work until 8:30 so she didn't fret about it. Then Felecia and Chelsea went to the vault and opened it up with their keys. Felecia opened the door to the money and began counting Daniels money bag. She wanted to hurry so that he would have something to do while they waited for the doors to open at 9am. Daniel has been waiting in the break room for the coffee to get ready. He made small talk with Cheryl as she tidied up the break room. They made fast friends.

Felecia finished Daniels bag and popped her head into the break room to tell Daniel that she was ready for him. Daniel said "I will be right there Ms. Grey. And thank you for counting my bag first."

"Oh it was my pleasure Mr. Fields. You are making great progress here. I do not regret hiring you." She told him as they walked back to his station with his coffee in hand. She watched as he counted his money bag.

"$500 exactly" He said as he put his money in his drawer.

"Good job Mr. Fields. Now just get comfortable, you did a great job yesterday, I expect the same for today. Mr. Stevens should be here soon. Then he can finish training you, although you seem like you don't need training. I'm impressed again Mr. Fields. Keep up the good work" She said with authority.

"Yes ma'am," He said. Then he said good morning to Mathew Burch as he arrived at 8:15. They had being male in common and made small talk after Mathew counted his drawer and put his money away.

"Finished Ms. Grey" Mathew said to Felecia.

"Very well, Mr. Burch. Thank you." She replied. Daniel chatted with Mathew as the other tellers arrived. Daniel wanted to make everyone trust him so that when the Snow brothers downloaded all that money he could keep everyone distracted during the heist. They would be taken by surprise for sure.

At 9 am all of the employees at the Trinity Bank were in place. There was a line forming outside the door of customers. The bank would be busy today. Chelsea knew by the early birds that it would be a long day. She only hoped Christopher's cousin could impress Felecia enough today as well. As far as she knew he was just another employee that was related to someone she cared for. So she gave him special treatment when he had a question for Ken Stevens and Felecia was away.

The day went well and Felecia was impressed with Daniel's performance yesterday and that made her expect him to do the same today. Daniel handled the customers that he waited on with respect and made no mistakes. Felecia really liked him. She did not miss Mr.

Alvarez one bit. Around noon Felecia let Daniel go to lunch. She said take advantage of the break and eat something because the afternoon should be busy based on the mornings activities. Daniel thanked Felecia and left the bank to have lunch.

He called for a cab to take him to the Mexican restaurant down the street. He really needed a car. Frank better be prepared to provide one soon. He couldn't wait for their meeting tonight. He finished lunch and called the same cab company to pick him up from the restaurant. He rode in the taxi cab back to the bank and arrived at the same time that Chelsea got back from lunch as well.

He said a cheerful hello to Chelsea and she returned with "Hello Mr. Fields, did you have a good lunch?"

"Yes I did, all full. Thank you for asking."

"Well we like our employees to be happy and you seem to be working out rather well. I'm glad that Christopher recommended you." She replied.

"Well my cousin helps me out once in awhile. He is a stand up guy."

"Oh I know I really like Christopher. We have spent some time together." She admitted.

"Well he's a good choice in a man, if you don't mind me saying so."

"No not at all. He is very special to me. Thank you for saying so."

"No problem Ms. McQuire. You two make a good couple."

"Well thank you Mr. Fields." She said as they walked into the bank.

Daniel took his place at his station and began helping customers right away. *Ms. Grey and Ms. McQuire were right, it is busier this afternoon* He thought to himself as he settled in.

"I'm going to take lunch now Mr. Fields, do you think you can manage with Mr. Stevens until I get back?" Felecia asked Daniel.

"Yes I think I have got it, Ms. Grey. Thank you for giving me a chance. I think Mr. Stevens can cover me now"

"You're welcome, if you have any questions just ask Mr. Stevens and he will help you while I'm gone."

"Okay ma'am, I won't need the help though."

"That's good to hear Mr. Fields." She said as she turned to climb the stairs to her office to get her purse. Normally Chelsea and Felecia would have lunch at the same time, but with Daniel being so new they wanted to make sure he had someone to help him while Chelsea and Ken Stevens were out.

The first person Daniel helped was a good friend of Mr. Eldridge's. Daniel didn't know this but he was being tested by Mr. Eldridge. If he handled this transaction well, he was a good find. If not, Mr. Eldridge might have to step in and fire him. Daniel handled Mr. Eldridge's friend with no errors. He had passed Mr. Eldridge's test. This pleased Mr. Eldridge. Daniel watched as Mr. Eldridge stepped out of the elevator and greeted the customer. He then knew that he was in good, because if he could handle the big boss's friend he could handle anyone.

At 4 pm Chelsea locked the doors and the tellers began wrapping things up. The loan officers all left for the day. There were three customers in the bank so Chelsea had to wait by the doors with Harold tonight to let them out when they were finished with their duties. Daniel was free of customers so Felecia told him to count his drawer and run his tape for the day. He needed his drawer to balance to impress Felecia even more. Thankfully he had made no mistakes and his drawer balanced. At 4:15 pm Chelsea let Daniel out of the bank to go home. There was a cab waiting for him outside. He rode the cab to the Regency hotel to get ready for his business meeting with the Snow brothers tonight.

At 6 o'clock Charlie knocked on room 504. "I'll be right there." Came the voice on the other side of the door.

Frank was still in his boxer shorts because he had just taken a shower and was running late. He opened the door and greeted Charlie. Jonathan was dressed in a button down cowboy shirt, his signature snake skin cowboy boots and black jeans. He was sitting in the living area going over the newspaper for current events. He wanted to see if there had been any bodies turn up lately unclaimed. Charlie said hello to Jonathan and Jonathan just grunted at him, not being one to mince words.

"So where are we going tonight?" Charlie asked Frank.

"Just down to the restaurant here. We need to keep our distance from you for now."

"But you're posing as my cousin. What does it matter if we go somewhere that they can see us together. That doesn't make any sense." Charlie complained to Frank. But it fell on deaf ears.

Frank just told him again that they would be eating at the hotel restaurant. And that was the end of it. Frank always had the last word.

The ladies think we are having a business meeting tonight so they won't bother us. Here take these. The car is that big grey Buick out front." He said as he tossed Charlie the keys.

"Thanks man, now I can just drive to work."

"It's only a rental. So don't wreck it." Frank said as he blew grey smoke into the air from the balcony. Charlie had joined him and lit a cigarette as well.

"I don't see what the problem is if we just say I'm your cousin." Charlie replied. While they smoked their cigarettes Frank told Charlie to stick to the plan and let them handle any information that they told the ladies. They discussed their meeting plans before going down to eat.

"Are you two ladies ready, I'm fucking starving." Jonathan spit out at them.

"Oh shut up, we will eat when I'm ready." Frank spit back. Jonathan just grunted and frowned. He wasn't sure if he could trust this one either. But dinner tonight would prove that Charlie was indispensable.

Chapter Thirty Two

CHARLIE'S REPORT

At 6:30 pm Frank got dressed and declared himself ready to go. "Finally," Jonathan said sarcastically. Charlie wasn't quite sure how to take Jonathan, but he knew that he had a trigger happy finger and when Frank had said they had to take someone out, he only assumed it was Jonathan was the who did the bidding.

"Let's go then," Frank said as he headed for the door. They all left the hotel room and headed for the elevators. They rode the elevators in silence until the elevator stopped in the lobby.

"The food is great here," Frank told Charlie.

"I know I've been eating it for two days now. I kinda thought we could go somewhere else tonight." Charlie commented.

"No we will just stay here. Do you need me to point out the car for you?" Frank asked as they walked towards the restaurant.

"Yes could you. I mean a grey Buick is kinda vague." Charlie replied.

"Let's walk out here then before we eat. See that grey boat over there?"

"Yeah, that's it?"

"You bet. It's all yours for a week."

"Okay that will do." Charlie replied.

When Frank was finished filling Charlie in, they went back into the lobby and headed for the restaurant.

The hostess asked "Will it be three for dinner tonight, Mr. Fields?"

"Yes, and could we have a booth in the back?" Frank asked her and slipped her $100 as a tip.

"Sweetness, do you mind keeping our area clear of others tonight?"

"Sure sir, no problem, and thank you. Right this way." And she led them to a booth in the back. There were five other booths in the area where they were seated. But the restaurant was slow tonight so keeping the area clear should be no problem for her.

The waitress came up to the table and asked, "Can I get you gentlemen something to drink to get started."

"Yes we will all have iced tea."

"No sugar in mine." Jonathan spit out at the waitress.

"Yes sir, no sugar. Will there be anything else before I get your drinks?"

"Yes would you bring me an ashtray, sweetness? Thank you." Frank replied as he lit a cigarette. Charlie followed suit and lit a cigarette as well. Jonathan just frowned, now he would have to put up with two smokers. The waitress trotted off to get them their iced tea. Jonathan was miffed that Frank had ordered non-alcoholic drinks once again but he kept his mouth shut and fidgeted with his napkin while he looked over the menu.

"Do I at least get to order dinner for myself?" He asked Frank sarcastically.

"Order what you want bro, and don't be so edgy."

"I wouldn't be edgy if I had a beer to drink." Jonathan said angrily.

"Well not tonight, just drink your tea when it gets here." Jonathan just grunted and looked over the menu.

Charlie was taken aback by the banter between the Snow brothers. But he knew that he shouldn't ask questions if he wanted his piece of the pie.

"So what are you having tonight, the fillet mignon is to die for," Charlie asked to change the subject.

"Yes, the steak is pretty good," Frank agreed.

Charlie blew grey smoke in to the air. Charlie already knew this but he went along with the order that Frank had given as he was the boss of this little operation. "Well I think I will have the fillet mignon then,"

"Sounds good." Frank replied. Just then the waitress came back with their drinks.

"Here you go gentlemen, have we decided on what we want to eat yet?" She asked.

"We will take the fillet mignon." Frank said as he pointed to Charlie and himself.

"And I'll take the t-bone" Jonathan added.

"Great and how would you gentlemen like those steaks cooked?"

"I'll take mine rare." Jonathan chimed in.

"I want medium rare for mine," Charlie told the waitress.

"And I will take mine medium rare as well sweetness." Frank said.

"And would you like a baked potato or rice?" She asked Frank,

"I'll have a baked potato" Frank replied

"And I'll have the rice," Charlie said.

Then Jonathan added "And I'll have a baked potato."

Then the waitress asked. "What kind of salad dressing would you like, gentlemen?"

"Well I'll have blue cheese," Frank replied.

"I'll have ranch." Charlie chimed in.

"And I'll have ranch dressing as well." Jonathan said.

"Okay I will be right back with your orders." She replied then she trotted off to fill their orders.

The waitress arrived with their drinks and scurried off to fill their dinner order. The hostess had kept her word and left the area that they sat in free of other customers. They had the entire area to themselves. "So is there anything that we should know about Charlie? I mean do you have anything to report?" Frank asked as he lit another cigarette, Charlie followed suit and lit another cigarette as well.

"Well I'm getting close to the other employees so that they will trust me, and Ms. Grey is very nice to me. I think she likes my performance." Charlie replied.

Jonathan got hard at the mention of his tiger. It was a good thing that they were sitting down and he could hide his manhood from the others.

"That's good then." Frank replied.

"Then there's the locks. Were you aware that the bank is locked down every night with time locks? I heard them click open when I arrived early my first day. Ms. Grey said that none of the other tellers knew about the time locks. So I was wondering if you knew as well."

"We didn't know about that but, we won't be entering the bank before it opens since we have downloaded the software for the bank and have your password. That should be enough to get us started. Then all we have to do is crack the code to the main password that secures the BankSecure software that the bank uses." Frank explained.

Jonathan was prepared to break into the banks deepest crevices with the information on that flash drive that he had on his person at all times.

"What time do the doors open?" Frank asked Charlie.

"8 am sharp." Charlie said between drags.

"That's great Charlie. This is good information. Henry obviously wasn't the right guy. But Charlie here fits in very well. Is there anything else?"

"Well my station is by the vault. And when the tellers all count there drawers and are done Ms. Grey opens the picture windows above the doors." Charlie went on to say.

Then he continued. "I'm not sure why, but the owner Mr. Eldridge shows up at 10am and the first thing he looks at is those windows. You can tell when he climbs the banks steps as he comes in." Charlie said as he blew grey smoke into the air.

"Great information Charlie. Thanks for your insight. This really helps us out a lot."

"We know that the armored truck will show at about 8 am we just didn't know why. Now we do. That means we are ahead of the game. We just wait until the truck arrives and then leaves. The we wait for Felecia to update the banks software with the money that is delivered before we download the it from the Trinity Bank. We will need your help to navigate and teach us how to use the banks software and to get into it." Frank explained.

"Okay I can do that. I can't believe you didn't know about the time locks. Who did you have in my place before?" Charlie asked.

"Nevermind about that. He's out of the picture." Frank said with authority. Jonathan just smirked at the mention of the killing.

The waitress arrived with their meals and asked if there was anything else she could bring them. "I'll have some steak sauce." Charlie chimed in.

"I'll be right back with that sir." Then she trotted off to get Charlie his steak sauce.

They started eating and the chatter ended. Frank ate his meal and thought of the changes that they would have to make with Charlie in the picture. First they would leave cracking the BankSecure software passwords to Charlie. They would need Chelsea and Felecia's passwords and Charlie was the best in the business for cracking into password protected software.

The waitress came by with the steak sauce and Charlie said thank you to the waitress then poured some on his steak, then took a bite. He felt that he was in cahoots with two men who might just be able to get away with this. The money didn't mean as much to Charlie as the fun of breaking into that software. After all his cut was only $20,000 plus a vacation and the amenities. He knew how the Snow brothers worked, so he didn't push it when they told him about his cut.

They talked more about the timing and when Charlie Wright would be able to break the codes to the BankSecure software. When they were finished with their meals the waitress brought them the check and placed it on the table in the receipt book. Frank picked up the receipt book and told the waitress to bill the meals to room 504. Then she took the receipt book to bill the room. After she processed the payment she went back to their table and returned his receipt to him and thanked him for the generous tip. As soon as the bill was settled they went back to their rooms.

Charlie had to work the next day so he stripped down to his briefs and watched a little TV, then went to bed early. Frank and Jonathan went up to room 504 and talked about the plan.

"Well it's a good thing we took that Henry out. What an idiot. No big loss there." Jonathan said as they let themselves into the hotel room.

"Well now that we have Charlie in place it will go smoother. I just can't believe Henry missed the time locks." Frank said to Jonathan.

"Well it's a good thing he was an idiot and showed up to work late and got fired." Jonathan retorted.

"Don't worry about it. The problem is solved so we can just get on with the plan with a few changes." Frank replied.

"How long have you known this guy anyway?" Jonathan asked. "It seems like we should have gone with Charlie from the start."

"Yeah you're right bro, but it's fixed now, so stop worrying and just do your part."

"What do you mean do my part, I been doing my part all night long if you don't remember." Jonathan said angrily.

"Don't get your panties in a twist, I just meant that we all need each other to make the plan work."

"Oh okay, I gotcha." Jonathan said as he regained his composure.

Frank needed to call his princess and one of them needed to get to the apartment. They had decided that one of them would stay in the hotel room and one of them would stay in the apartment each night. That way they could monitor what was being said at the girl's houses and in their offices. "Well I'll see you tomorrow, go hop in that pretty SUV that you love and get over to the apartment, I've done it two nights in a row. I need a break. Plus I want to call my tiger so I want to be alone." Jonathan told his brother.

"Okay I'll take the apartment tonight, its better anyway, I can smoke there."

"You and those damn cigarettes, why don't you just quit?"

"Oh mind your own business wouldjya."

"Okay, okay, smoke all you want, just don't let them rest without us knowing it."

"You got it," Frank said as he left the hotel room and headed for the apartment.

A jogger was jogging along Bayou Rd. with his dog when he came across a dark stain in the sand with dark stain trailing off into the marsh. He then noticed that there were drag marks in the dirt leading to the marsh as well. His dog started off into the marshy waters and began barking. The jogger followed the sound of his barking dog and found out what he was barking at. There was a body back in there.

"Oh my." He said out loud. He then pulled his cell phone out of his pocket and dialed 911. He reported the dead man and called his dog back so as not to disturb the crime scene. He waited along side the road until the police arrived. When they got there the jogger told them that he had noticed this dark stain and then the drag marks. Then he explained how he walked over to what his dog was barking at and found the dead man. The police checked him for a weapon and the body looked like it had been there for a couple of days. They asked the jogger for his name, phone number and address so that they could check with him later. He had a solid alibi so he was soon eliminated as a suspect.

The police investigated the scene and found that the dark spot was blood. Then about ten feet away they found a couple of casings to a 45 caliber bullet. Next they found two cigarette butts on the ground next to the tire marks left in the soft sand of the marsh. They collected the casings and the cigarette butts so that they could analyze them when they got back to the station. They marked off the crime scene and called the coroner. They also took castings of the tire impressions left in the sand by the marsh on the road. When they took castings of the tire marks they discovered they belonged to some sort of SUV. There were footprints left in the sand near the marsh where Jonathan walked and had dragged Henry's body into the marshy waters.

The boot impressions looked like cowboy boots. The cops took impressions of the boots too to further their investigation. It would be hard to tell the size of the cowboy boots, but they could get a rough idea about the size from the castings that they took. The police would have to check the data base to see who had vehicles matching these tire marks and since the cigarette butts were found near the driver's side of the vehicle they would have them analyzed in the lab for DNA. Little did the police know that the vehicle was rented and would be easy to find. The Snow brothers did not know that the jogger had found Henry yet. This is why Jonathan had been checking the newspaper for current events lately. He wanted to see if Cornwell had turned up yet.

While the police investigated the crime scene they noticed that the deceased was missing the back of his head. This could only mean that he was shot at close range with a 45 caliber gun based on the casings they had found. They were also not far from where they found the drag marks in the sand. Jonathan Snow loved his Colt 45 and his snake skin cowboy boots.

Frank opened the door to the apartment and lit a cigarette. He then turned on the tape recorder and listened in on the two women they had seduced. There wasn't anything going on at the moment so he decided to call Chelsea. He turned off the recorder and called her.

"Hello" came the voice on the other end.

"Well hello princess. How was your day?" He asked

"Oh hi Christopher, it's so nice to hear from you. I really miss you."

"I miss you too baby."

"My day was good, and your cousin is working out really well." She said. "When can I see you again?" She added.

"Well tomorrow night is free. What do you say we go to dinner and a movie."

"Oh that sounds wonderful, what movie did you have in mind?"

"Well I thought I would let you decide that this time. Just name the movie and we will go see it."

"Well there is a new mystery movie that sounds scary and good, do you like scary movies?"

"Yes I do, what's it called?"

"I think its called 'I Hear You Sleeping' it sounds really scary." She replied.

"Well lets go see it then, what time does it start?" "I think there is a show at 8 o'clock" She replied.

"Then we will have dinner at 6 o'clock and a movie at 8. Sounds good to me, then I'll see you tomorrow sweetness."

"Oh I can't wait sweetheart." She cooed.

"It is getting late though and you have to work tomorrow so I will let you go until tomorrow night sweetness." He told her before he hung up.

He then turned the tape recorder back on and heard his brother talking to Felecia. He listened in and heard that his brother was doing great gaining her trust and she would be putty in his hands in no time. Jonathan was worried about this David guy taking over with his tiger. He wanted to just beat the shit out of the guy, but he had no cause to do that because he was just having a good time with his tiger.

Frank went into his bedroom and stripped down to nothing then lit a cigarette and hopped into bed. He smoked his last cigarette of the day then he smashed it out in the ashtray beside his bed. He decided that he would spend at least some time cleaning up this place before he went back to the hotel. The least he could do was wash the dishes and take out the garbage. *'I will address that in the morning.'* he said to himself. Then he drifted off to sleep.

Chapter Thirty Three

THE TIME CLOSES IN

F rank was staying at the apartment tonight, so he drove to the apartment at 5 o'clock so that he could get call Chelsea. It was Jonathans turn to stay at the hotel and he was looking forward to spending time with Felecia. He called her and got her answering machine. He figured that she was out with that David character. So he left her a casual message and hung up the phone. He would just order room service for one tonight.

Just then a knock came at the door. It was Charlie Wright coming to give them a full report about the contents of the banks software that he had access to. He opened the door to Charlie and invited him in. He explained that Frank was out for the night and that they would need to go over this with him. So Jonathan, not wanting to get too close to Charlie told him that he was tired and needed to get some sleep then sent him on his way.

Frank called Chelsea at her house at 6 o'clock. Frank was excited that he would be able to have dinner with Chelsea at 6:30 tomorrow night. They told each of the ladies that they had another business meeting tonight so dinner would have to be for tomorrow tonight. Felecia was unhappy about not having enough time to play with Randy tonight, so she gave David a call and asked him to come over to her house. Jonathan was disappointed to hear this. However they did need to go over the plan with Charlie and hear how his day went at the Trinity Bank. Charlie was an easy study when it came to nefarious business. Frank was very pleased with the way that Charlie understood the plan inside and out already after their meeting that night.

When Frank settled in after he had dinner in room 504 he made a phone call to room 410. The voice on the other end said "Hello"

Frank said "Hello Charlie, It's Frank, I needed to talk you tonight. What are your plans for tonight?"

"Well I was seducing Kristen from the bank. I just got back from dinner with her, she's in the bathroom now. I can't talk right now, okay boss" He said to kiss ass a little bit.

"That's good, you need to get as close to them as possible. We only have a week for you to get to know the bank employees so that they will trust you." Frank said into the phone.

"Don't worry about it boss, I am getting to know both Thomas and Kristen very well. I will soon get to know the rest. Just give me a little bit of time to gain their trust."

"Very well, you are doing great so far. Just don't be late and keep doing what you are doing. You are a charmer and that's an asset for us." Frank told Charlie.

"Well thank you boss I try. Don't worry I will have all of them trusting me before this Friday."

"You are doing good Charlie, keep up the good work. How about if we have a drink in the bar downstairs at 9 o'clock?" Frank asked.

"That sounds great. I will see you then at the bar." Then they said their goodbyes and hung up the phone for the night.

The police were curious about the tire marks and the next of kin for Anthony Alvarez, so they started an investigation into this Henry Cornwell which was the name on the identification on the man found on Bayou Rd. He was resting in the morgue at the moment. They were having a hard time placing him anywhere based on the ID's in his wallet. His real name was Henry Cornwell. Because the police had found a wallet with two ID's in it on the body in the marsh they decided to check into Henry Cornwell's whereabouts as well.

They were looking into all possibilities to identify the body. Officer Hamilton had gone over the jogger's statement several times and he was certain that he had nothing to do with the crime. He tried all the known relatives based on the application that Ms. Grey had given him at the bank. He had come up short on information. He gave a statement to the media saying that there had been a man found dead out on Bayou Rd. a few days ago and he pleaded for more information about the murder. He released the information to the local media and left out a few details just incase they ran across the murderer by mistake.

They neglected to tell the press that two casings were found and that they had size 13 cowboy boot footprints in the sandy ground by the marsh. They left out that the shoe impressions as well. He was curious about the tire marks found by the body. There was no shortage of sport utility vehicles in the area. Officer Hamilton knew that the chase would be a hard one. He also wondered about the murder weapon. There had been two casings for a .45 caliber pistol near the body on Bayou Rd. He was looking into that as well.

Jonathan was reading the local newspaper when he noticed the story about Anthony Alvarez aka Henry Cornwell. He started to get nervous. He decided that he would mail the murder weapon to the apartment in New York. Jonathan had called their neighbor to ask her to sign for the package and hold it until he returned. She had no idea what was in that package.

Frank let himself into the dingy little apartment and turned the recorder on. He would meet with Jonathan and Charlie at 9 o'clock as they had said this morning. Frank just wanted to talk to Charlie and make sure he understood how this was going to go down. With Charlie Wright on the job Frank felt as if everything was in place and they would be rich by the end of the week. Felecia had pulled away this week because she would be spending time with David, she had dumped Randy and felt no lasting loyalties to him.

Charlie arrived at room 504 to greet Frank for another meeting at 9 o'clock. He decided that he didn't need to impress anyone tonight except Charlie so he dressed casually. Thoughts of his princess danced around in his head. Ever since he had made love to Chelsea he could keep his mind on little else. It was a good thing that this was the last job that they would pull because they had made too many mistakes on this job for his comfort. All the other jobs hadn't included such beautiful women to seduce and he was starting to have serious feelings for Chelsea. Jonathan was feeling the same way about his tiger. But the plan came first and they had made it this far so they only needed three more days and it would all be over.

Frank and Charlie met in the bar in the hotel. They chatted about the two bank tellers that Charlie had gotten close to during his short time at the bank. When the waitress came by Frank told her that he wanted his signature martini. Then he asked Charlie what he would like to drink.

"Oh I'll take a beer," Charlie said, "Anything you have on tap is fine." He added.

Jonathan would arrive shortly. It was looking like Frank had made the right choice getting rid of Henry and bringing in Charlie. They had made plans to have Charlie meet with Frank and Jonathan at 9 o'clock tonight for a nightcap in the bar. Frank wanted to go over any last details before the day of the heist. Frank was really preoccupied, which wasn't a good thing.

Frank asked Charlie how it was going at the bank?

"Well I went to lunch with Thomas Underwood today. Thank you for the credit card again."

"No Problem. Anything we need to worry about with him?" Frank asked.

"Well no he seems harmless. He's just a bank teller."

"That's good, keep up the good work."

"Then I took Kristen, another teller, to dinner tonight, again thank you for the credit card, much appreciated." Charlie added.

"Very good Charlie. You fit right in with us, keep up the good work."

Frank wanted to get a feeling for how things were going at the bank. "Where's Jonathan?" Charlie asked innocently.

"Don't worry about him. We will meet up with him tonight and fill him in. I was just worried about you getting enough rest so that you will be sure to be on time at the bank in the morning." Frank said with authority.

"Then on Friday, we will hit the bank after the armored truck arrives."

"Yes you told me this." Charlie replied.

"I just wanted to settle up all the details for the next three days. It's time and we will be set up to rob the bank on this Friday, the day before Labor Day weekend."

"I got it, don't worry you can count on me."

"I hope so, because I don't want to be held responsible for what happens if you don't." Frank retorted.

Charlie was taken aback by this comment. He assumed that that meant he would be in a very dangerous position if he didn't come through for the Snow brothers. He was a little scared by the comment. But that was the reason for the meeting in the room.

Frank wanted to steady up the plan with Charlie before Jonathan got there and got a chance to intimidate Charlie with dirty looks. He knew how his brother could be. "How much money are we talking about?" Charlie asked innocently.

"Well if we add the armored truck and the money that we will get by robbing them too, It should be at least $500 grand, we have it all planned out now. I will up your portion to $30,000. Okay?" This was a charity gesture towards Charlie for coming on such short notice.

"That sounds great." Charlie replied. They both lit a cigarette and headed out to the balcony.

"Okay, what do we know about the time the armored truck arrives?" Frank said to Charlie.

"It arrives at 8am sharp on Friday the same time the locks open the doors at 8 am the day of the heist. We will be right behind it." Charlie reassured Frank.

"And you're sure you can break the software password codes?" Frank said has he took a sip of his martini. He took a long drag of his cigarette and blew out the grey smoke. Charlie followed suit and took a drag of his cigarette as well. They smoked their cigarettes in the bar of the restaurant while they went over the last details of the heist.

They talked more about the plan and at 9 Frank and Charlie met Jonathan in the bar. They moved to a secluded booth when Jonathan arrived. The bartender came up to Frank and asked if he would like another martini to drink. Frank told her that he would like a refill. Then she asked Charlie if he wanted a refill as well. Charlie said yes to for another beer. They waited on Jonathan who was running late. This upset Frank, he liked everyone to be punctual on his team. The bartender brought them their drinks.

Jonathan showed up at 9:15 pm. Frank had had time for two drinks while he waited. "Well look whose here." Frank said sarcastically to Jonathan as he approached.

"Oh nevermind. The girls were having a conversation and I was trying to get any information that we might have missed. That okay with you!" Jonathan spit at Frank.

"Okay already, you're late and I just wanted to know why. Let's get a table." So they got up and grabbed a table in the back. "I was just going over the last of the plans with Charlie" Frank said to Jonathan.

Jonathan ordered a beer before they moved to the table. Frank was not as demanding this night because he was loosened up by the two drinks and the fact that Charlie turned out to be such an asset to them.

They found a secluded booth in the back and made themselves comfortable. "I just wanted to go over any last details that we might need to go over before the heist. Because we have never taken from an armored truck before." Frank said as he sat down at the table. "I want to get it right the first time." Frank said with enthusiasm as he tipped his drink to Jonathan because their plan was almost a reality. They were sure that they had everything in place that they needed to get the job done. This meant that the job would go smoothly on Friday the day of the heist.

"Okay then, we are all set." Frank grabbed his drink and took another sip.

"Charlie said he had overheard his boss Ken Stevens telling Felecia that the money will be delivered on Friday due to the rotating drops at 8 am. I thought that's why we were hitting it on this Friday. Plus the Labor Day weekend is this weekend."

"That's correct. No backing out now." Frank added with authority. "Charlie why don't you go upstairs to you room to get some rest." Frank added. Then Frank sent Charlie back to his room so he would be fully rested when he goes to work in the morning." Charlie's plan was to follow any lead that these guys threw at them. And he was doing great keeping up with them.

"Alright then, we will meet up again on Friday morning in this room before you go into work. Charlie, you just keep up the good work and

Thursday will be your last day at the Trinity bank. You got it?" Frank said with authority.

"Of course I got it. I made the plan with you remember." Jonathan said sarcastically.

"I know you did, I was just tying up all the loose ends." Frank retorted. "And I was mostly talking to Charlie."

"Got it bro." Jonathan said as he took a sip of his beer.

"I just don't want any mistakes that's all Jonathan." He told his brother. Frank was really nervous because the plan was almost a reality some things had changed and the plan had changed so drastically.

"Don't worry about it. I got this. Okay?"

"Okay, I'm gonna turn in then, I will go now so that I can stay at the apartment tonight again just incase the ladies say anything else on the recorders."

"Sounds good. I love the bed in that fancy hotel. Gotcha bro." Jonathan said. He so didn't like that cramped dirty little apartment. But it was a necessary evil of the job. He could put up with it for one night to keep up with the plan.

They broke their meeting up at 9:30. Frank was anxious to talk to Chelsea. Frank went up to room 504 and settled in. Thoughts of Chelsea were running through his mind ever since they started seducing the ladies and he knew that he only had two more weeks to be with her. He grabbed a newspaper on his way to the hotel room. He wanted to look over the paper for any information on the murder that Jonathan had committed.

Jonathan had grabbed a newspaper as well to read at the apartment when he got settled in. He was a little uneasy when he read the story that said they had tire tracks that could lead them to the killer. Officer Hamilton had left out the part about the two .45 caliber shell casings that had been left behind at the crime scene. Frank decided that they needed to get the hell out of dodge as soon as possible after the heist. He also decided that they needed to ditch Frank's vehicle before the cops found them. He would ditch it somewhere in town when this was all over.

Officer Hamilton had just received the results of the tire tread marks test found at the murder scene. They definitely were from an SUV. Most SUV's normally used the same tires. So he started the tedious task of looking for the vehicles that matched that tire tread. The rented vehicles were the easiest to chase however it was easy to just drop a rented vehicle any place and leave it behind if they needed to. He came up with three possible vehicles, but none were the vehicle that Frank had driven that night. There had been no witness's and no one had heard the gun shot in the marsh that night.

Officer Hamilton continued with his investigation. He had called the next of kin listed on Anthony Alvarez's application. But the second license made him wonder. The leads on Mr. Alvarez's application took him nowhere. So he decided to call it a night for now. He would follow the leads to the vehicle and his next of kin for Henry Cornwell tomorrow. It had been a long day for Officer Hamilton.

Frank lit another cigarette on the balcony when they got back to room 504. Jonathan grabbed a beer that he had stashed in the fridge. He drank the beer fast and asked Frank about the new twist on the plan. They were both happy that the plan was coming along so well now that Charlie Wright was on board. That dam Henry had cost them. And he wasn't done paying the bill yet.

Jonathan said goodnight and headed out the door for the apartment. It was his turn to listen in on the ladies in through the wires in their homes. Jonathan dialed Felecia's number and got the answering machine. He figure that she must have gone to her favorite aerobics class and would try her again later. He would be in for a big surprise when he tried to get ahold of her later. She was spending time with David tonight.

When Frank got to the apartment he picked up the phone and dialed Chelsea's number as he knew it by heart by now. "Hello" came the voice on the other end of the line.

"Well hello sweetness, how was your day babe?"

"Well hello baby. Not too bad I'm really impressed with Daniel." Chelsea replied.

"That's great, I had hoped that he would be a good fit." Frank said into the phone.

"I couldn't wait to talk to you." She cooed. "Your cousin is really impressing both me and Felecia. I really think he is going to work out well. How was your day?" She asked.

"I had a great day. Thank you for asking."

"It's nice to hear from you like this every night." She replied.

"It's nice to talk to you as well sweetheart." He cooed.

"Why don't we start the weekend with a dinner date tomorrow night?" She asked.

"Well I can't believe our luck that we have met such nice ladies. I just don't know how long we will be available. But I will come up with something soon." He replied. He wanted to string her along until the robbery so that she didn't get suspicious.

"Okay that sounds good." She cooed.

"Where do you feeling like eating tomorrow night?"

"How about I make you something special this time. How does a big juicy steak sound. Do you like to barbeque?"

"Well yes that sounds great. We could cook together at my house. I like that idea. Say about 6 o'clock?

"That sounds terrific." He replied

"I'll pick up a couple of steaks on the way home tomorrow. And I'll come up with something to go with it." She said into the phone.

"Sounds good sweetness. I look forward to it. Talk to you tomorrow then. Good night sweetheart, sleep well."

"Good night sweet prince, I will see you tomorrow night then." And they hung up the phone with plans for tomorrow night.

Jonathan called Felecia again to see if she was back yet. She wasn't and he was beginning to wonder where she was. He heard Chelsea talking to her mother again and turned it off to give her some privacy. He dialed Felecia's number and waited for her to answer. *'Hello, I'm not here right now, please leave your number and a message and I will call you back.. beep.'* Came the answering machine on the other end. "Hey tiger how are you tonight?" He said into the answering machine. "I hope to be alone with you tomorrow night in my hotel room." He said. Then he went on to say, "Christopher and Chelsea asked if we wanted to have dinner with them and then dancing and drinks afterward on Saturday night. What do you think tiger? Do you want to join them on Saturday night? Well I better let you go I will see you tomorrow night." Beep the machine went after he left this message.

Felecia was out with David and had no thoughts of Randy tonight. He hung up the phone leaving the message on her answer machine. When she got home she heard the message, but she wasn't sure if she wanted to spend the night with Randy or not. She really liked David and had already let Randy go since she was bored with him. She decided to get together with David on Sunday afternoon.

On Saturday morning Felecia picked up the phone to call Chelsea to tell her they were on board with the plans for tonight. "Hello" Came the voice on the other end of the line.

"Hello Felecia how are you?" She asked.

"Pretty good, I have plans with David this weekend." Felecia replied.

"David will be good for me. It will be good for me to put some distance between Randy and myself. I mean he's satisfies me but I am having feelings for him. So I will had to let him go last weekend."

"Well I hope you know what you're doing. Have fun tonight then."

"Good bye, talk to you soon." Chelsea said into the phone then they hung.

Officer Hamilton had found something with Henry Cornwell. He had a criminal record in New York. What Officer Hamilton wondered was first of all where was he now and second who was Anthony Alvarez. The bank offered no help where Mr. Alvarez was concerned. But Mr. Cornwell had spent time in jail for armed robbery. While Henry was incarcerated he learned about the Snow brothers and he had learned about bank robberies as well. He was a really bad guy at heart. He hoped they would call on him to help them on their next heist.

Officer Hamilton wondered if there was a connection with the Charlie Wright. And he wondered if there was a bank in danger of being robbed with him on the loose and with Henry Cornwell ending up dead like that. His job now was to figure out who his partners were and get to them before they struck again. Little did he know that he only had 2 days to solve this crime before the event happened.

He thought about the upcoming Labor Day weekend and what a bank would have to prepare for in the event of such a big weekend. He put two and two together and decided that he would pay Ms. Grey a visit at the bank tomorrow to tell her about his thoughts. Though he would be closer to the killer if he could only figure out who Mr. Cornwell's partners were and who killed him. He thought he may just thwart a robbery attempt by talking to Ms. Grey tomorrow because he had a feeling the two were connected.

Chapter Thirty Four

———— •❦• ————

TIME WITH DAVID

Felecia received another message from David while she was out. The message asked her if she would like to have lunch together on Sunday. He also left a phone number for her to return the call. She dialed the number and he answered the phone on the second ring.

"Hello" He said into the phone.

"Well hello to you too. It's me Felecia. I thought I would return your call and find out about the lunch plans that you asked about in your message."

"Well I would like to see you, is Sunday a good day to have lunch?" He asked into the phone.

"Well yes that sounds fun, What time did you have in mind?

"How about noon."

"Sounds good to me. Where did you have in mind?"

"Well I was thinking that the new seafood restaurant that they just opened down the street. What's it called? Do you know? I only know where it is." She asked.

"It's called 'Captains Quarters'. And I hear they are really good."

"Sounds good to me. I will be ready at noon then on Sunday then. I look forward to seeing you. Let me tell you where I live so you can come and pick me up."

"That sounds terrific." And she gave him directions to her house. Then they said their good byes and hung up the phone. Felecia decided that she needed to put fresh sheets on her bed in anticipation of some sex games with David. Her libido was doing backflips in anticipation of meeting with David today.

Officer Hamilton reviewed the castings, casings, the bullet that they had found in Henry Cornwell's head and the castings of the cowboy boots that were at the forensic lab. They found out that a Frank Snow had rented an SUV and they just needed to find him and take a look at the tread marks left in the sand on the vehicle that he had been using. When Officer Hamilton checked with the rental agency, he found that one Frank Snow had rented an SUV and he knew that Jonathan Snow wore snake skin cowboy boots all the time.

He checked with the agency to find that Frank had used his credit card to rent the car in question. He now had Frank Snow's credit card information to follow. He would follow the paper trail until he was able to tie Frank and Jonathan Snow to the murder on Bayou Rd. They analyzed the boot impressions that were made in the sand on the road of the marsh. The forensic lab found a DNA profile from the two cigarette butts that they had found in the moist sands of the road leading to the marsh. The forensic lab just needed a swab between Frank's teeth and cheeks to make an identification of the DNA left at the scene. But Frank Snow would refuse to submit to a DNA test.

So Officer Hamilton would have to use all of his skills to tie Frank and Jonathan Snow to the murder of Henry Cornwell. He did have Frank's finger prints from a previous bank robbery that the Snow brothers had done. But there were no finger prints left at this crime scene. He now had DNA from the cigarette butts that he found at the crime scene. Officer Hamilton was closer to catching them than he thought. He would make an arrest as soon as he could catch the Snow brothers off guard. He was able to tie them to an apartment at the Deluxe Arms Apartment Complex in New York. Apartment number 125 belonged to the Snow brothers. So he made plans to visit their address in New York. This is where the murder weapon was hiding. But he had no way of knowing that. He had enough evidence to have the judge issue an arrest warrant in New York. But the problem was that the Snow brothers were not even close to New York or their apartment there. They were in Florida about to pull off another bank robbery. However, Officer Hamilton had no idea about the heist planned at the end of the week.

This murder didn't make much sense but Officer Hamilton knew he would have his man just as soon as he tied down the vehicle tread marks and an identification of the footprints left in the marsh. It was hard to tell the size of the boots but they guessed based on the length of the impressions that they were close to a size 13. All they needed was an identification of the boots and tread marks to tie it all together.

Based on the forensic evidence and the fact that Jonathan Snow was very fond of his snake skin cowboy boots, which were a size 13, Officer Hamilton started to think that the Snow brothers were involved in the murder on Bayou Rd. that night. The Snow brothers were responsible for many of the bank robberies that had taken place over a period of about ten years along the east coast. He knew that they were brazen about their robberies. But they never been involved in a murder before. Since then they were tied to the robberies there was a lone finger print of Jonathan's left behind at one of the banks that they had robbed. Officer Hamilton gathered this information because he now had DNA as evidence to tie them to the murder of Henry Cornwell.

He had felt bad about Henry's death ever since he had to tell Mrs. Cornwell that her son had been murdered. It was always hard when he had to break a death to the family members who were left behind. Officer Hamilton traced the tread marks to a rental place in the city. The person who had rented the vehicle was one Christopher Fields which was an alias for none other than the notorious Frank Snow. However he couldn't tie him to the murder just yet. He knew that Jonathan Snow liked to wear his snake skin cowboy boots. So he felt like he was on the right track when it came to the Snow brothers from New York. He just couldn't understand why they had traveled to Florida for this murder.

Felecia was really growing bored with Randy. She felt like he had overstayed his welcome. Frank was upset with his brother for not being able to keep her happy. Felecia loved the sex games that they played but she didn't like the way he was acting towards her now. He was being too clingy and Frank could hear it in the tapes that were wired into her house and phone. This is why Felecia had made plans to see David. Jonathan was steaming mad at himself for acting that way towards her. He knew that he had pushed too hard where Felecia was concerned. However, he really didn't need to be with her any longer because even though he loved the sex, it really was the only thing that they had in common. So he wasn't surprised when she met and went for this David character. The only thing he could do now was listen in from afar through the wires in her walls. But he had gathered all the information that she had to offer and they had Charlie in place as the inside man.

Felecia had spent the night in the hotel room with Randy. They woke up at around 9 o'clock. She was anxious to get home so that she could spend some time with David. She told Randy that she had chores to do today, so she had to go home early and get them done. He knew this was a lie but he decided not to call her on it. Felecia wasn't aware that Randy knew all about David. Randy knew exactly what she would be doing and when and where she would be doing it. He decided that waiting on her to come back to him would be the best thing to do. After all he had her house, office and home phone tapped so the he could keep close tabs on her while she spent time away from him. If she knew that her entire life was being recorded she would have been steaming mad. But since she had no idea she being taped she just went about her business as if nothing was out of place.

At 10 o'clock she told Randy that she really needed to get home to do her chores. She told also him that she had met someone else and she did not want to see him anymore. She said good bye to Randy and left the hotel satisfied by him. As she went out of the hotel lobby then she went to her sports car and hurried home. She wanted to be there when David called to come over. She picked up some provisions at the store on her way home so that they wouldn't go hungry while they spent time at her house. Jonathan was content to listen in on her through the wires in her house.

At 10:30 she was ready to meet David. She had taken a shower to wash Randy off of her and then slipped into a negligee and waited for David to arrive. She wanted to get right down to business when he got there. David was punctual. He arrived at her house at 11 o'clock sharp. He knocked at her door and she said "Be right there" Into the air. Then she answered the door dressed only in her skimpy nightie and her silk bathrobe. She was ready for David to show her how good he was in bed.

"Well hello, how are you today. You look fabulous, have you been waiting long?" He asked as she answered the door.

"No not at all, you are right on time. Come on in. Let me show you around." She told him. He followed her around as she pointed out every room except the bedroom. She wanted to save that room for the last room that she showed him. When he has seen all of the rest of the house she asked seductively, "And this is my bedroom. Would you like to play around a little while before we have lunch?"

He wrapped his arms around her and kissed her passionately. She was taken by surprise by the kiss but she was ready for him all the same. She got wet from the kiss alone. This gave her the feeling that he would be a great lover and that trading Randy in because was the best idea she had had in a long time. It was a simple decision, Randy was great in bed but he was dispensable.

As they made it to her bedroom he picked her up and carefully laid her down on the bed. He slipped out of his pants and pulled his shirt over his head, to expose his nudity to her. She liked what she saw. He was muscular and she loved a guy who kept himself up. This was something that Randy couldn't offer her. Randy was handsome and he did have muscle structure but he was lazy about exercise so she decided that if David was good in bed, she would just keep David.

She then slipped out of her bathrobe and showed him her negligee. He liked what he saw as well. She was ready for him to ravage her body. He told her how beautiful she looked and started stroking her leg. He made it up to her womanhood and inserted his fingers. She reached down to find him hard as a rock for her, he responded to her touch. He was a bit smaller than Randy, but she liked him just the same. She scooted down off of the pillows to get comfortable. He slid in beside her while they explored each others body's. She was wet for him. She knew he would be different than Randy, and she tried not to think of him while she was with David. However, she couldn't get Randy out of her head. This concerned her because she didn't want to be tied down to anyone. David began to move his fingers while she climaxed for the first time. It was a big one. "Whao that was awesome. Are you okay to continue?" He asked in the air. "Absolutely, don't you worry about me. I'm great here right beside you." She cooed.

"Well let me show you how it's really done." And he made his way up to her womanhood. He licked her while he had his fingers inside of her. This made Felecia climax again. He was impressed with her response to him. She couldn't believe that he was so good in bed. He climbed on top of her and inserted himself into her then began to move in and out of her body. She climaxed again and he could feel her womanhood responding to him. When she climaxed he did as well. They had sex for about an hour, then she asked, "Would you still like to go out to eat?"

"Well I think I have enough to eat right here. We could order a pizza if you're like though?"

"Oh I like the way you think. And I can't believe how good you make me feel. You're awesome. I only hope that you enjoyed it as well."

"Oh yes you're fantastic. You are so easy to please. I can't wait to spend the day with you. Go ahead and order anything you like on your pizza. We can take a break to eat."

"Get over here and make me cum again, the pizza can wait, I'm not that hungry."

"Okay, what ever you want to do is good with me." And they started round two.

Jonathan was steaming mad at Felecia for not being true to him. He listened in on them as they had sex all day long. He was upset that his tiger seem to be seducing another guy while she should have been seducing him. Just then Frank walked in on him listening to what was going on at Felecia's house. "What are you doing. Don't you realize that we have all we need from Felecia through these wires in her home and office."

"Yeah I realize that, I just thought that I had her under my spell. Like you have with Chelsea. I just don't like sharing her is all, I'm not getting attached yet. She just turns me on and I enjoy her company. Is that such a bad thing?"

"You're torturing yourself by listening in on them. Turn that dam thing off and let's go get something to eat. What do you think?"

"Alright, let's go, I was getting tired of listening to them having sex any way. He doesn't seem to be a good lover but only time would tell about that."

They left for the restaurant called 'Captain's Quarters'. Jonathan needed to get the images of his tiger having sex with that David that she had met out of his mind.

"Yeah let's get out of here. I'm starving and seafood sounds wonderful. Let's get going." Jonathan said as he turned the recorder to Chelsea's house so that he wouldn't have to listen to David and Felecia having sex any longer.

They left the apartment and headed for the restaurant. Frank lit a cigarette and headed for his car. They hopped in the SUV and drove out of the parking lot. They headed for the restaurant and they chatted along the way about what to do about Felecia and her new boy toy. Frank smoked his cigarette down to the numb and threw it out the window. He lit another right after he finished the last one. "When are you going to cut back on those damn things?"

"When I'm ready. That okay with you." Frank said sarcastically.

"I guess, but you should quit all together, I mean what happens If you get lung cancer. What will you do then?"

"Don't worry about it, I will quit when I'm ready. Can we just drop it and go eat without the commentary?"

"Yeah whatever bro, I just wish you would quit those nasty things."

"I will when I can rest easy, I will rest easy when this job is over and I can stop seeing Chelsea. She wont want anything to do with me after we rob her. Okay?"

"Whatever bro, it's your life. Do what you want, just please do something about smoking in the apartment."

"No that's the only place that I can smoke freely. I will not make that deal with you. Just mind your own business." Frank said with authority.

"Then you will be taking more time at the apartment than the hotel room. But that's okay because I like the hotel bed so much better." Jonathan said.

They headed for the restaurant and when they got there Frank parked his car and they walked to the doors of the 'Captains Quarters'.

The hostess greeted them and asked if there would be anyone joining them tonight. Frank told her that it would be just the two of them tonight. So she led them to a booth in the corner of the restaurant. Since the plan had changed they needed some privacy in the restaurant. "Here take this sweetness, and could you please keep this area free of others while we are here?" He asked her just the same as he had asked at every other restaurant that they had ate at. He tipped her $100.

"Sure sir, don't worry about it. I will tell your waitress. And thank you sir." And she said to them. Then she asked if they wanted anything to drink and Jonathan said he wanted a beer. Frank ordered his signature martini. They talked about anything but the man who was upsetting Jonathan at the moment. Jonathan enjoyed seafood so he was content to enjoy the meal in peace for one night. However visions of his tiger kept coming into his head. Frank did his best to keep Jonathan happy. What he really needed was a night with his tiger. But it seemed to Frank that Jonathan's time with her had ended.

Frank didn't feel the same way at all. He wanted to keep Chelsea. But he knew he couldn't so he just kept his mouth shut about it for the moment. When they finished their meal Jonathan asked if he could be alone in the hotel room tonight again? He needed some time to soak in what was happening to his relationship with Felecia. He knew that she was only temporary but it still hurt that she chose to be with this David character above him. It made him steaming mad with jealousy.

Dinner had helped to calm Jonathan down. He was full and ready to watch a little T.V. and turn in. Frank would erase all of the conversation that Felecia had had with David on the recorder. He wanted to save his brother any further embarrassment. Jonathan's heart was crushed. Which wasn't how he normally acted with women. He got attached to Felecia and she tossed him to the curb as soon as she got bored. He knew she was the love em and leave em type of woman but it still stung that she was having sex with a new partner. She was so good in bed and she had such a healthy appetite for sex he just didn't want to let her go. She was like no other that he had had in the past. But she was disposable. So Jonathan just kept his feelings to himself. He would get even during the heist.

Chapter Thirty Five

OFFICER HAMILTON INVESTIGATES ANTHONY

fficer Hamilton picked up the bullet from the medical examiner that he had found in the back of Henry Cornwell's head off. He put it in a bag and labeled it as evidence. He hoped that at least one of the slugs were a match for the casings that he found. He asked the medical examiner if she had found any bullets in the body. Jonathan had shot off an extra round after he had shot Henry. This is why Officer Hamilton had found two casings in the sandy road by the marsh. He knew that at least one of the bullets went into Henry's head and hadn't exited. He had no idea that Jonathan had used two bullets that day. He had shot off the second bullet into the air to celebrate the death of a liability to them. So Officer Hamilton worked the case as best he could based on the evidence that he had. Ms. Green the medical examiner did find a partial bullet buried in Henry's skull. Apparently the fact that the back of his head was gone and he was mostly unrecognizable based on the time he spent face down in the waters of the marsh made him a hard sell for Ms. Green. She did her best to attend to this autopsy in a professional manner.

Frank tried to talk his brother about the fact that these women were only pawns in the game that they were playing with the Trinity Banks money. They were going to lose them anyway, so he reassured Jonathan that they were simply that. A pawn to get them what they wanted. He reminded Jonathan that he couldn't keep Chelsea either. Jonathan stayed at the hotel tonight to recover from the pain that Felecia had caused. Frank agreed and went to the apartment with that said. The he proceed to erase anything that he heard at Felecia's house until she let Jonathan go. Then she would become the liability that they had planned on. He also told Jonathan that time was on their side and this would all be over tomorrow. Jonathan agreed and that got his head back in the game where he could focus on playing his part without error. Jonathan decided that he was much better off without Felecia. She had betrayed him, so why was he upset about it. He would just think of her as the pawn she was. Chelsea on the other hand would be a much harder for Frank to betray. They had made a crucial error in judgment when they had set this heist up. Jonathan decided that this would afford him a bird's eye view of the events that were about to take place at the Trinity Bank.

When the medical examiner pulled the partial bullet out of Henry's skull, Ms. Green said that it was definitely part of a .45 caliber bullet. Apparently the bullet exploded and broke into fragments when it was discharged from the gun. Ms. Green wondered if the gun that had shot it was still intact. The only way that Officer Hamilton was able to identify the caliber of the bullet was by the casings that he found at the murder scene. It would match the bullet that that had come from the gun that had been fired that night and that they had found in Henry's skull. Ms. Green showed them the partial round that had taken Henry's life.

Then Officer Hamilton followed up on the tire castings that they had recovered from the murder scene. He had tied the tire marks to the SUV that Frank was using at the moment. With that information Officer Hamilton was able to tie Frank Snow to the murder. Jonathan would be identified by the boot prints left in the sandy road. These placed Jonathan at the murder scene. He had sent the murder weapon to their apartment in New York. There would be no gun to turn to, when they went to compare the bullet to the casings. It would be a much harder job because it was only a partial bullet and would be hard to track down because of this. Officer Hamilton had no idea that the notorious Snow brothers were about to strike again the next morning.

When Chelsea got off work she went by the outlet stores to replace her alarm clock. She had had it for most of her adult life. It was a gift from her father one Christmas. But it was time to retire it. She looked around when she got to the store and found one that would suit her needs. She went to the checkout stand and paid for her new alarm clock. *'She wouldn't wake up late tomorrow'*, she thought to herself.

Felecia had a great time with David in the afternoon. She decided that he was just as good as Randy if not better in bed. She didn't like to sleep around with more than one man at a time so she decided that David was the one for now. She had been alone for quite some time now and for now she was just enjoying the sex games that they played when she spent time with Randy and David. However she was happy that she had met David and she enjoyed how much he turned her on. He was decidedly direct and got straight to the point about everything that they talked about. David told her that he was a professor at the local college. He taught a class that would come in handy to Felecia in the very near future. He taught all about forensic science. She liked that he did this and nick named him Professor.

She called Chelsea and said "Hello" into the phone when she picked it up.

"Hey there Chelsea, it's me Felecia. I really need to talk to you. What do u say we have lunch together tomorrow."

"Well that sounds great, what's goin on?" Chelsea asked.

"Well do you remember that guy I told you about that I met last week at the market?"

"Yeah I remember what happened?" She asked Felecia.

"Well we spent the morning together and you know how I don't like to be with more than one man at a time."

"Yeah that can lead to problems." Chelsea replied.

"Well I dumped Randy and wanted to make sure that this wouldn't affect your relationship with Christopher. For some reason Randy became very clingy. I told him that I didn't want to see him any longer and I dumped him this morning before I met with David. You know how much I hate that?"

"Yeah, I'm sorry you are going through this."

"Well I would like to have lunch together tomorrow so that we can talk about it."

"Yeah that sounds good. Where do you want to go?"

"Well maybe we could take a picnic lunch and eat it on your beach that you like so much. Just for something different to do. I will walk with you if you like." Felecia responded.

"Well that sounds good to me. Do you think Daniel will be okay without one of us there?"

"Oh yeah, he's making fast friends with the rest of the employees and he is working out wonderfully. Besides Ken will be there with him. I think he will be fine under the supervision of Ken. What do you think?"

"Well he's been doing great. I think Ken can handle it. Sounds good to me." Chelsea replied.

"I just need to talk to you as soon as possible. I have chosen David but Randy keeps filling my thoughts. I need help trying to decide which guy suits me better, Randy or David? I hope you can help before Randy is gone forever."

"Oh yeah that sounds like quite a quandary. I will be happy to have lunch with you tomorrow." So the date was set for Chelsea and Felecia to have lunch together at an unknown restaurant at noon the next day. Little did they know that their latest beau's would betray them during that lunch date.

Jonathan was livid. He thought for a few minutes and wished that she would just pick him. But he knew that he would betray her soon enough. So he kept his mouth shut about it. Frank was right. They would lose these two women tomorrow. Time was moving swiftly. Felecia decided to call it a night after she read more of her book again to help her get sleepy. David had left her satisfied and she liked that. But Randy satisfied her as well. She really didn't know who to pick. It had been awhile since she had had this problem. She would sort it out at lunch with Chelsea tomorrow. She was beginning to have doubts about dumping Randy.

When Chelsea got home she set up her new alarm clock. She set the alarm for 6 am and set the time. That would give her enough time to eat, shower, and get dressed without incident. She would even have time for her beloved cat before she left for work in the morning. She was pleased with her selection and it was closing in on bed time. She had had a deli sandwich after she found out that Christopher had plans for the evening as well so she waited patiently for his call when he got home.

At 9 o'clock the phone rang at Chelsea's house. "Hello" she said into the phone.

"Well hello princess how was your day?" He asked her.

"Well I spent training your cousin but I always look forward to your call to say good night and tuck me in."

"Well I'm here to save the day. Are you ready for bed yet?" He asked.

"Yes I'm really tired and I know it's early but I had a long day." She said to him with a slight yawn.

"Oh don't worry about it princess, we will have other nights to spend together."

"Oh thank you sweetheart. You really are prince charming." She cooed.

"Well I try. I better let you go so that you can get your beauty rest."

"Oh thank you kind sir, I will do just that. I will talk to you tomorrow."

"Good night sweetheart, sleep well." He cooed back to her. Then they hung up the phone.

In the morning the alarm went off on time. At 6 am she woke to soft rock playing from her new alarm clock. The song that was playing reminded her of Christopher. Lately it seemed that everything reminded her of Christopher. She just couldn't get him out of her mind. She decided to take Clark's aerobics class tonight to try to forget about Christopher for just one night. It wouldn't be easy but she would try all the same.

Officer Hamilton arrived at the station house at 6 am sharp. He had gone home to shower and shave but was pulling an all nighter because he was trying to solve the murder and find then arrest the murderer, who he assumed was one Jonathan Snow of New York. He had been aware that he Snow brothers were in town for the past few weeks. He knew something was up. He just didn't know when and where a crime was going to happen.

Mr. Cornwell's death was helping him solve the case and at least identify the perpetrator. He decided to check the local hotels to see if he could find the Snow brothers in his small town. He was aware of the many alias's that the Snow brothers used when they committed crimes. He would put Deputy Parsons and Deputy Andrews on it as soon as they come in at 6:30 am. They were due to arrive soon. Then he would have a direction to go in while looking for the Snow brothers. Little did he know he would be too late save the Trinity bank.

Felecia would give David a call when she got up to see if he had plans for dinner tonight. After all it was Friday and it was the beginning of a long 3 day weekend. She hadn't been eating well for a while again. Putting distance between her and Randy was harder than she thought it would be. And Randy wasn't done with her yet.

Felecia wanted to call Randy. However, when she woke up she called David. She got the answering machine and sunk. She left a message and hoped that he would call back tonight. Then she called Randy to find out how he was this morning. He was her second choice but she chose him nonetheless.

"Well hello tiger." Randy cooed into the phone while he wiped sleep from his eyes.

"What time is it Tiger?" He said into the phone. He thought to himself '*I have a chance now. I will just pour on the charm.*'

"Hello there. What are you doing tonight?" She replied.

He did everything he could to keep her interested. But since sex was all they had in common they didn't really have anything to say to each other. So she again grew bored with him and told him that she just wanted to say good morning. She had accomplished just that, so they said their goodbyes and hung up the phone. She had chickened out. Felecia would just have to do without companionship for the night or hope that David would return her call. She had stripped down to nothing and hopped into the shower to get ready for the last day that she would want Randy. Then she made a quick meal of a bowl of cereal and headed for the bank to start her day. At least she thought she would be ready for her day at the bank.

It was 9 am, Deputy Parsons and Deputy Andrews had been searching for the Snow brothers all morning. Deputy Parsons had hit the jackpot when he called the Regency hotel. He found a Christopher and Randy Fields in room 504. He reported this back to Officer Hamilton and asked if he could accompany him to the hotel to check things out.

Officer Hamilton agreed to take both Deputy's along, as he would probably need the backup.

Since Frank and Jonathan Snow were staying at the Regency hotel under the alias's of Christopher and Randy Fields, Officer Hamilton hopped in his cruiser with the two Deputy's in tow in their police cruiser to head for the hotel to further investigate the situation. When they pulled into the hotels parking lot Officer Hamilton parked his cruiser near the front entrance. They were closing in on the Snow brothers. However little did they know that these two men were clever with an assortment of disguises as well as their many alias's. They also didn't know about the apartment that they had set up specifically for the heist of the Trinity Bank. Frank was at the apartment and only Jonathan was at the hotel. Jonathan had grown a few days stubble so he looked like a range cowboy.

Frank had just picked up a police scanner radio at the local electronics store so that they could monitor where the police were at the time of the heist this morning. Frank overheard the words Regency hotel fill the air coming from that police scanner. He realized that Jonathan was in trouble and needed to know that the police were there as soon as possible. So Frank dialed the Regency hotel and asked to be patched through to room 504.

The phone in room 504 rang several times before a groggy Jonathan picked up the receiver and said a gruff "Hello"

"Hello to you too brother. We got a problem. You are about to be visited by the police. The scanner told me so just a minute ago. Whatever you do bro, you need to get the hell out of there as soon as possible. I will be there in 5 minutes. Wear you cowboy hat and boots to look the part of a city slicker cowboy. Then leave the hotel and meet me in the south lot." Frank told his brother.

"Okay bro, I will get out of here. This place was only a resting spot and a place to seduce Felecia. Now that she is gone there really isn't any point in staying here. See ya in 5 bro." Jonathan replied then hung the phone. He threw on a cowboy shirt complete with snaps that held it together down the front and decorative fringe across the shoulders. He really did look like a city slicker cowboy. Once the elevator doors opened to the lobby, Jonathan pulled his cowboy hat over his eyes and made his way past the commotion in the lobby and parking lot then headed for the south lot as per his brothers instructions.

Jonathan recognized the SUV that Frank had decided to keep until this was over and headed for it. He was now in the clear. They would head to the apartment as their time with the women was over now. Jonathan hopped into the vehicle and greeted his brother. Then Frank started the engine headed for the apartment. This is where they would pull off the heist.

The Deputy's parked their cruiser behind Officer Hamilton's cruiser. Officer Hamilton approached the front desk with a warrant that Judge Hiemelin had ordered in his chambers and had had it hand delivered by his clerk before Officer Hamilton had left for the Regency hotel. Officer Hamilton showed the clerk the warrant and asked if she would call up to room 504 to see if the Snow brothers were in. When the clerk replied that there had been no answer in that room, he said they must still be asleep then. At least he hoped they were. He then asked where the elevators were so that they could exercise the warrant on the Snow Brothers if they were still in the room. Little did he know that Jonathan had just slipped past them, walking right beside of Deputy Parsons unnoticed. Deputy Parsons was a rookie and hadn't picked up on the art of observation just yet.

Officer Hamilton was aware of Jonathan Snow's penchant for killing and how much he loved to wear those snake skin cowboy boots of his. He was sure that the boot impressions found in the marsh next to the body would be linked to Jonathan Snow that morning. He was also certain that Jonathan was the murderer because he had made that mistake in the past on previous jobs. He was a killer that Officer Hamilton would love to arrest and put behind bars forever. But he would not get the chance today.

Chapter Thirty Six

THE HEIST

I t had been a long week at the Trinity Bank. Home loans were up and many customers were getting personal loans and auto loans for the holiday weekend specials. It was Thursday night and Felecia and Chelsea were beat. They had no idea what would happen in the morning. Felecia had dumped Randy. He took her dumping him in stride and spent the week listening to the conversations that the lady's had in the confines of their homes and offices. He was ready to do this job together with Charlie and his brother Frank.

Chelsea was tired but she had to forge on because it was Friday and in the morning Christopher would betray her. She will be devastated when she realized that her bank was robbed right under their noses. Christopher had called her every night and every morning to keep her in check. Frank made one last call to Chelsea so that she wouldn't get suspicious before he stole all that money from her and Felecia.

However Jonathan had mixed feelings about the situation with his tiger. He wanted her but he knew from the start that she was the love um and leave um type of woman. So this wasn't unexpected. He just kept his feelings for her at bay and focused on the upcoming morning so that he could focus on the heist.

At 7 am the phone rang in Frank's bedroom at the Regency hotel. "Hello" He said groggily into the phone.

"This is just your wakeup call Mr. Fields. It's time to get up." The chipper voice said on the other end of the line.

"Yeah thanks." Frank said as he hung up the phone. He then called the operator to put in a call to room 410.

Charlie picked up the phone on the first ring. "Hello this is Charlie Wright."

"Good morning Charlie, it's me Frank. Are you ready to join us?"

"Yes of course, I will be right up. I was just getting out of the shower and getting dressed" Charlie said.

"Alright then. See you in a few minutes."

"See you then." Charlie said before he hung up the phone.

Frank then made the wake up call to Chelsea. The phone rang at Chelsea's house and Chelsea answered the phone with a sleepy "Hello".

He kept it brief because it would be the last call he made to her. He had a job to do today. One that would set them up for a very long time. Jonathan had done the math. With this pull they would have enough to last a very long time. He wasn't even upset about the measily $50,000 going to Charlie.

Frank then walked into the other bedroom and slapped his brother on the leg and said "Get up cowboy, It's time."

"What the....Why don't you find something to do while I wake up,"

"No cowboy, it's time. Charlie is on his way up. Now get up!"

"Alright already, you don't have to be a jerk about it. I'm getting up. Just give me a second."

"We don't have a second. It's time to go. Get up and get dressed we have to meet with Charlie." Frank demanded again.

Frank left his brother to get dressed and wake up a little before they joined Charlie. At 7:15 am Jonathan was ready to take on the day. Jonathan came out of his room with his signature cowboy boots on, a pair of black jeans and a snapping cowboy dress shirt. He wanted to look his best for this morning so that if Felecia saw him she would like what she saw.

"Let's get started, I'm ready to get this over with." He told his brother while he booted up the high powered satellite powered laptop that they had purchased for this job.

Frank had stayed in his bedroom that night. They decided to abandon the apartment since the job was almost complete. Frank had awoke in room 504 at the Regency hotel. By 8 am Frank woke his brother so that they could follow through with the plan. As Jonathan came to life he slowly got out of bed and got dressed. Frank had packed up all the pictures that had decorated all the walls in the living room of apartment. They would be left behind in room 504 when this was all over. Little did he know that this would be the key that tied the Snow brothers to the bank heist and the murder on Bayou Rd. He also packed up the listening devices that they had at the apartment. That part of the job was over as well. He waited anxiously while his brother came to life in his bedroom.

Charlie had a copy of a very powerful software program that was stored on another flash drive. This program did a search of all possible passwords until it found the correct one so that the banks money can be downloaded and transferred to the unnumbered account in Switzerland.

After Frank woke Jonathan up he called in an order for breakfast and coffee. Their breakfast arrived at 7:30 am, it was delivered directly to room 504. The smell of coffee brought Jonathan to life. Charlie was anxious to get moving on the heist. But he knew that the money would be in his account in Switzerland soon. He was ready to boot up the laptop and the BS program that they would hack into. He had all that he needed at that time. They could download all that money soon.

They had to wait until 8:15 am to make a move because they needed to wait for the armored truck to pick up the week's receipts. The armored truck also delivered the banks wire transfer of money for the long holiday weekend and the next week ahead. The bank had beefed up security for this labor day weekend. This was a new way of banking. One that protected the armored trucks. As soon as Felecia received the wire transfer, she downloaded all the money that the bank would need for next week. The bank would be closed on Monday for the holiday weekend. Chelsea was anxious to see Christopher for the entire three day weekend that lay ahead. Chelsea was missing Christopher so badly at the moment. He would betray her within the hour. She wouldn't have a clue what was going on after Charlie locked up the computers at the bank with the virus. He would use the password software to decipher the password that allow the Snow brothers to steal from Trinity bank.

The armored truck didn't transfer actual money anymore because over the years they had found it was just too risky. Many people had tried to rob the armored trucks no matter where they were or how careful they were. They only received the receipts from the banks that they visited now. The Trinity bank was all set up to electronically move the money around until it was lost in the foreign banking system in Switzerland. The Snow brothers and Charlie expected that this pull would be at least $250,000 based on their research. This meant that each of the brothers would take $100,000 and Charlie would receive his $50,000 when the heist was over. They would complete their plans of robbing the Trinity bank soon. Jonathan was ready to download all that money and transfer it into the offshore account with Charlie's help. Jonathan would download the money after Charlie set the virus in motion at the bank. This was a temporary job for him. At 7:45 am he then proceeded to get dressed and head out for work at the Trinity bank as Daniel Fields.

At 7:55 am Daniel arrived at his normal time and walked up the large set of steps to the bank that would help him to gain access to all that money. He would assist the Snow brothers, by freezing up the banks computers with a virus while they heist took place. Only the Snow brothers knew the code that would release all that money while Felecia fought with tech support to fix the problem. She had found that the money in the bank was at risk and Jonathan would download all the banks money soon. Ms. Felecia Grey and Ms. Chelsea McQuire would just think that their banks computer system must have had a virus. Which was true.

Daniel was a computer guru. He had copied the virus onto yet another flash drive that he could insert into his computer to download the virus onto the banks software.

Meanwhile Jonathan would be swiping the money that the Trinity had received from the armored truck delivery while the banks employees waited for the go ahead from Felecia, this would not come today. Jonathan had the skills he just didn't have any common sense. That's why he shot Anthony Alvarez. He had no ill feelings for what went down that night.

After Felecia downloaded the money she thought that it was safely secure behind the banks firewalls. Daniel had downloaded the virus after Felecia had entered the money transfer that the armored truck had dropped off. Jonathan had successfully hacked into the banks computers and security software. He downloaded all that money and wired it to the unnumbered account in Switzerland with ease. By 8:45 the transaction was complete. That computer class that Jonathan took at the local Junior college and this had helped him with this heist.

It was a very annoying virus to say the least. Felecia noticed the virus first when she tried to log into the banks computer software at her desk after all the employees had arrived for the day. Chelsea didn't have a clue as to what to do to fix it. Felecia and Chelsea were chasing their cursors. Felecia was relieved that the money for the tellers would be safe until the next armored truck delivery.

Daniel made his move. Felecia could not log in no matter how hard she tried or how patient she was. She would need someone that could get rid of the virus that was infecting the computers in the bank. The cursor simply wouldn't allow her to log in. Every time she wanted to open a new page the cursor would malfunction when she tried to move it. And no matter how many times she cussed at it, it simply wouldn't allow her access because of the virus that Daniel had downloaded. Who ever tried to use the cursor found that it quickly move around wildly and would never let anyone in. There was simply no way to open anything on the banks computers. The cursor wouldn't click to anything and it would not open anything. Felecia's cursor was chasing its targets when she moved the mouse while she tried to gain access to the banks software. But it would not respond to any commands. This rendered the mouse useless. Since the mouse was useless, Felecia wondered if the vault security had been compromised as well.

After a few minutes spent fighting with the computers mouse, Felecia and Chelsea went down the stairs and unlocked the vault with their keys to inspect the situation. The vault was still locked up so Felecia opened up the room to that held the money with her combination. The bank kept the money that they needed and received from its patrons each week behind this door inside the vault. This is why the armored truck had stopped by. They had to pick up the banks deposits for the week, and to give the bank their password protected software that Jonathan would hack into. They would transfer the money that the bank had received that week. The amount that the Trinity bank received at this drop was $500,000. She opened the door that held the money for the tellers. She had given the tellers $500 each to start the day. The tellers money was kept safely in the vault behind that barred door.

Amanda Stevens spoke up first after they had all received their money for the day. "Excuse me Ms. Grey, but I cannot log into my computer. Every time I try to use my mouse the cursor jumps away from the log in page. What do u want me to do?" Amanda asked.

"Yeah I can't log in either, my mouse is doing the same thing." Daniel said with a hint of satisfaction.

"I can't log in either. Mines doing the same thing." Thomas Underwood said in frustration.

Chelsea spoke up first because she was closer to the tellers than Felecia was. All of the tellers were having the same problem. She informed Ken Stevens of the situation and offered to help inform the tellers. "Okay everyone, we seem to be having some computer problems. I will call tech support immediately." Felecia told them.

"What do you want us to do in the meantime." Mathew asked. And waited for patiently for an answer.

"Well I will get tech support to help us with the computers. Why don't you all have a cup of coffee and wait for me to get tech support on the line to have them come here and fix the issue. I will get started right away" She told her employees.

"I have a great antivirus software package and I dabble in fixing situations like this from time to time. I could help you get back online and destroy the virus. Would you like me to try?" Daniel asked. "Why don't you let me run home, I am only a few short minutes away from my house." Daniel added.

"Well Daniel that sounds better than waiting on tech support to arrive. That could take hours. Yes Daniel give it a try." Felecia said. "We will open when we have recovered all the money."

"I will be right back then. Don't worry about a thing, I will be back in about 10 minutes." Daniel said. Then he left the bank for the Regency hotel.

Amanda Stevens used the time to catch up with her husband while the bank lost all its money. Kristen Mayes and Thomas Underwood were chatting by their stations innocently. The rest of the tellers met up in the break room waiting on the coffee to finish percolating that Cheryl had made when she heard the commotion about the vault. The loan officers would still be able to work because they had other assignments that didn't include the computer for the time being. Cheryl had snuck into the break room and started another pot of coffee. Kathy and Mathew made small talk in the break room while they waited to gain access to the banks software.

After the armored truck picked up the deposits that week and transferred the next week's money Felecia had transferred the money for the bank for next week and locked it down while the tellers set up their drawers. She made an entry in the journal that showed the amount that was supposed to be in the bank at the moment based on her order from the armored truck. Little did she know that it was long gone now to parts unknown to her. Frank liked to run the show. Jonathan had gotten into the banks backdoors to download the all of banks funds.

Daniel was a computer guru. He had copied the virus onto another flash drive that he inserted into his computer to download the virus. He also had the means to kill the virus on yet another flash drive. Meanwhile, Jonathan would be swiping the money that they had received from the armored truck delivery. He had the skills he just didn't have any common sense.

After Felecia added the deposits from the week and the armored truck delivered the money tickets that would give the Trinity bank the funds to stay in operation on the computer. Felecia went upstairs to her office to look over the banks reports for that day. Daniel would clog the banks computers with the virus that would disable the mouse so that no one could access the banks money online, not even Felecia.

'The money that we will take away from this heist will allow us the freedom to live comfortably for many years, if we invest wisely and live frugally. Maybe the Bahama's or the Carribean. We will decide after we retrieve all the money.' Jonathan thought to himself excitedly. He was unsuccessful with the password so he resorted to his new software that they had bought for this job. He tried a few little known passwords that didn't work so he then resorted to his trusty password decoding software 'Password Unlock' to unlock the computers software when he was able to.

The program was entering the banks back doors and had set the download of all the banks money in motion to head for the Swiss Bank account. This is where the Snow brothers intended on visiting when the heist was complete. They would just take a little trip to Switzerland. Little did they know they had left a paper trail for Officer Hamilton and Officer Brooks to follow under the alias Christopher Fields.

Felecia liked Daniel. She could see that he was an experienced teller by the he acted at the bank. He was the first one to try to deposit his money in his bag and put it away. At precisely 8:15 am the Officer Hamilton and his partner Officer Brooks made a drive by and checked on the Trinity Bank. He left the parking lot without incident because everything seemed to be in order. Chelsea had waved her hand at officer Hamilton and he thought that the bank was secure as well. He was expecting men in trench coats, not cyber thieves.

'The money that we will take away from this heist will allow them the freedom to live comfortably for many years, if they invested wisely and lived frugally.' Jonathan thought to himself. When he was unsuccessful he resorted to his new software that they had bought for this job. He tried a few little known passwords then resorted to his trusty password decoding software 'Password Unlock' to unlock the computers software when he was able to.

After Daniel had secured his $500 to start the day, he turned on his computer to downloaded the virus then he left for the break room. Then Daniel met Kristen in the break room. She asked him if he liked Trinity bank. He agreed that the Trinity bank was a good place the work. After they finished their conversation, he made it back to his station. After Jonathan finished he had taken every last penny from the bank.

After the money was gone Daniel had made a few clicks of the keys and had unleashed the virus that was a distraction until Jonathan could download the all that money.

The program was entering the banks back doors and had set the download of all the banks money in motion to head for the Swiss Bank account. Jonathan was busy at work trying to decipher the password. I Ie was successful in securing the fire walls until the money was transferred. No one would be able to get in with Jonathan blocking them with his secure firewalls.

'*Look at all those zero's. Ha, we did it! Now it's all ours. Thank you Charlie Wright.*' Jonathan thought to himself while he used the powerful laptop accomplish this mission. Normally the Snow brothers would just take a lower amount and go into the banks that they robbed and sporting guns to keep the people under control. But this time they knew they could access to the banks software with this simple device and take every last penny that they could get their hands on. Their take was a lot of money this time, they hoped that they would be able to retire after this one. He was counting on this virus attacking the banks activities. He downloaded a virus that only he knew how to override so that could download the banks money into an unnumbered account in the swiss alps. They used three flash drives to save the data and programs on the banks computers after they downloaded all that money.

With the click of a key Jonathan had the banks money in his sights. In two seconds the bank software transferred the money to their unnumbered account half way across the world. Frank had neglected to call Chelsea this morning. He had to dump her to finish the job. As soon as the tellers reported that they couldn't access their accounts Daniel went to work using his trusty password decoding software. He would have complete control of the money in just a few short minutes. Daniel left the bank with his keys in his hands. He simply jumped in the boat of a car that Frank had given him. He left the banks parking lot in a hurry because he was anxious to get this over with.

While he was out he was in a hurry so he was speeding. At the intersection nearest to the Regency hotel, Daniel was t-boned by an SUV. The SUV had just rolled over his boat of a car and Daniel was trapped in his crushed car. However that boat saved his life because it was built so strong that it held together and Daniel's life was saved. He was met by

The bank would have to open a little late because of the interference that the robbery caused. However, Jonathan was growing wary of the unsuccessful passwords that he had tried. The unknown passwords for the data base of BS software was nearly impossible to break. Each new screen was password protected. There were three tiers to the banks security in all. Jonathan would need at least a half hour to 45 minutes to download the money after he got through all the passwords. This meant that they would start locking up the banks computers around 8:30 am, that is if they couldn't retrieve the money. The banks employees were locked out by the virus. Felecia Grey got on the phone for tech support immediately, just incase Daniel couldn't figure it out with his software. But he had to download the virus that would lock them out of their computers. This is the reason why the bank would open late today. Felecia left the blinds above the doors closed to signal Mr. Eldridge that the bank had been compromised and there was trouble going on at the Trinity bank.

At around 8:15 Jonathan began the process of downloading the virus to the banks computers. By 8:20 am the banks computers were locked up curtesy of the new virus that Daniel had download onto the system after he finished counting and putting away the money that he managed for the day. All of the tellers had shown up by then. So they were just cooling their heels. Jonathan began downloading all that money and transferring it to the unnumbered bank account. After the download was complete and the money was secure behind the new firewalls that Jonathan had created, Jonathan deleted the transaction history that had taken the banks money out of the accounts of the tax payer's hands who patronized the Trinity Bank

"Okay done." Charlie said with as satisfied smile on his face at 9:15.

"Thank you Mr. Fields. I really appreciate your help." Felecia said. With that said it seemed like they could finally open the bank. Felecia checked various accounts for errors and found that the money was simply gone. Felecia Grey made the decision to call the police and report the crime. She dialed 911 and the lady at the other end answer in a pleasant tone, "What is your emergency?" The calm voice on the other end of the line.

"Hello this Felecia Grey with the Trinity bank and we have been robbed." Felecia said into the phone. Then she proceeded to report that there had been a robbery, and she needed an officer to respond immediately. She could replace the money based with their insurance. The bank would be operational shortly.

When the transfer was completed, Jonathan hit a few more keys and the money was on its way to its next destination. "Great, the deposit that was taken was deposited $2,000,000 less your $50,000." Frank said. "Did you take your cut when you made the transfer?" He continued.

"Yes my $50 grand was transferred into the offshore account that you gave me. It will rest here in this numbered account until we need it" He said this while handing Frank a piece of paper with the account identification and the bank name with the location on it.

"Now we should head to parts unknown." Frank told Charlie.

"Gotcha, I will head for to Bermuda, I like the sights there. Bikini's on a white pearly beach. I can live cheaply there for a very long time. I'll catch the next plane out of here. Thanks guys for including me. I will be around if you need further assistance. Here's my throw away cell phone number when you need my help again"

"Thanks Charlie, you were a big help. We will see you around." Then Charlie booked the next flight to the sunny beaches of Bermuda.

Charlie Wright left with his take in hand. He already had almost a million saved totaling the $900,000 that he had saved from the last heists that he had pulled with the Snow brothers. He had hoped that there would be more jobs to pull soon. He had been living frugally to save as much as he could. So he just decided he would wait until they called again.

The Snow brothers booked the next flight out of town to the Switzerland to recover the money that had been deposited in their unnumbered account, under another assumed name. Frank used The First Bank of Switzerland another alias to deposit the money. His newest alias was Tom Redford. Frank had made up this name recently to honor his only remaining relative of the Snow family besides his brother. His uncle was Tom Bellows and he was his mother's brother, and he had been very close to him in past years.

Tom decided to fly alone when they got the money settled in a bank account that was protected by foreign laws. They each had nearly

$975,000 each to add to their previous heists and keep them happy for a little while longer, or maybe retire all together.

Felecia returned to her office where she would find out that the bank had been robbed. There simply wouldn't be any money in the Trinity bank today, at least in the morning air. When Felecia noticed that the bank accounts were empty, she felt a panic set in. How had this happened on her watch. Mr. Eldridge would take it the hardest. She immediately called 911. The 911 operator took her information and dispatched Officer Hamilton and his partner to investigate. The officers knew that the Snow brothers were involved somehow. They knew Jonathon liked to wear his snake skin cowboy boots. The boot impressions were a size 13. It said so in the prints that he left in the sand that night with Henry Cornwell in the marsh.

Daniel had betrayed them. Christopher and Randy had betrayed them as well in the worst kind of way. Now all they had to show for it was an empty bank for the week. Felecia immediately got on the phone to the insurance and gave them all the particulars that they would need to transfer the limit of $500,000.

Chapter Thirty Seven

------ ❧❧ ------

THE HEIST

Felecia liked Daniel. She could see that he was an experienced teller by the he acted at the bank. He was the first one to try to deposit his money in his bag and put it away everyday. At precisely 8:15 am Officer Hamilton and his partner Officer Brooks made a drive by and checked on the Trinity Bank. They left the parking lot without incident because everything seemed to be in order. Chelsea had waved her hand at Officer Hamilton and he thought that the bank was secure as well. He was expecting men in trench coats, not cyber thieves.

The driver if the SUV had gotten the worst of it. Daniel would be out of commission for now, but that was okay because Daniel had completed his part of the job. Officer Hamilton and Officer Brooks arrived at the accident scene. They did not know that Daniel was a thief in disguise, and the one who would help the Snow brothers take all of that money. As soon as the ambulance arrived the paramedics worked with the police to

'The money that we will take away from this heist will allow us the freedom to live comfortably for many years.' Jonathan thought to himself. He planned on moving the money around until it was lost in the banking system. When he was unsuccessful with the passwords he had tried, he resorted to his new software that they had bought for this job. He tried a few little known passwords then resorted to his trusty password decoding software 'Password Unlock' to unlock the computers software when he was able to.

After Daniel had secured his $500 to start the day, he turned on his computer to download the virus then he left his station for the break room. Daniel met Kristen in the break room. She asked him if he liked

Trinity bank. He agreed that the Trinity bank was a good place to work. After they finished their conversation, he went back to his station. When Jonathan finished he would take every last penny from the bank.

While the tellers got situated Felecia walked back up the stairs to her office to start her day. After the money was gone, Daniel tapped a few keys and unleashed the virus that was a distraction to everyone who tried to use their computer for work. Jonathan downloaded all the money and transferred it immediately to the designated unnumbered account. The program was entering the banks back doors and had set the download of all the banks money in motion. It headed for the Swiss Bank account. Jonathan was busy at work trying to decipher the password. He was successful in securing the fire walls until the money was transferred. No one would be able to get in with Jonathan blocking them with his secure firewalls.

'Look at all those zero's. Ha, we did it! Now it's all ours. Thank you Charlie Wright.' Jonathan thought to himself while he used the powerful laptop to accomplish this mission. Normally the Snow brothers would just take a lower amount and go into the banks that they robbed and sporting guns to keep the people under control. But this time they knew they could access to the banks software with this simple device and take every last penny that they could get their hands on.

They had downloaded all of the banks money and their take was a lot this time, they hoped that they would be able to retire after this one. Daniel was counting on this virus attacking the banks activities. He downloaded the virus that only he knew how to override so that he could download the banks money into an unnumbered account in the Swiss Alps. They used three flash drives to save the data and programs on the banks computers after they downloaded all that money. Daniel numbered the flash drives so that he would know the order in which to download the money.

With the click of a key Jonathan had the banks money in his sights. In two seconds the bank software transferred the money to their unnumbered account half way across the world. Frank was distant with Chelsea this morning. He had to dump her to finish the job. As soon as the tellers reported that they couldn't access their accounts, Daniel offered to help. He left the bank and drove his boat of a car to the Regency hotel so that he could seek and destroy the virus that was infecting the banks computers.

He would have complete control of the money in just a few short minutes. Daniel left the bank with his keys in his hands. He simply jumped in the car that Frank had given him. He left the banks parking lot in a hurry because he was anxious to get this over with.

While he was out he was in a hurry so he was speeding. At the intersection nearest to the Regency hotel, Daniel was t-boned by an SUV. The SUV had just rolled over his boat of a car and Daniel was trapped in his crushed car. However that boat saved his life because it was built so strong that it held together and Daniel's life was spared.

The driver if the SUV had gotten the worst of it. Daniel would be out of commission for now, but that was okay because Daniel had completed his part of the job. Officer Hamilton and Officer Brooks arrived at the accident scene. They did not know that Daniel was a thief in disguise, and the one who would help the Snow brothers take all of that money. As soon as the ambulance arrived the paramedics worked with the police to extract both drivers from their cars. Daniel was unconscious at the moment. But Officer Hamilton recognized him as an employee of the Trinity bank.

The bank would have to open a little late because of the interference that the robbery caused. However, Jonathan was growing wary of the unsuccessful passwords that he had tried. The unknown passwords for the data base of BS software was nearly impossible to break. Each new screen was password protected. There were three tiers to the banks security in all. Jonathan would need at least a half hour to 45 minutes to download the money after he got through all the firewalls and passwords. This meant that they would start locking up the banks computers around 8:30 am.

The banks employees were locked out of the computer by the virus for the moment. They patiently waited for Daniel to return. No one knew that Daniel was involved in an accident while he was retrieving the password software. Felecia Grey got on the phone for tech support immediately, just incase Daniel couldn't figure it out with his software. He had downloaded the virus that would lock them out of their computers so he should be able to delete the virus.

Felecia left the blinds above the doors closed to signal Mr. Eldridge that the bank had been compromised and there was trouble going on at the Trinity bank. Around 8:15 Jonathan began the process of downloading the money from the banks computers. By 8:20 am the banks computers were locked up curtesy of the new virus that Daniel had download onto the system after he finished counting and putting away the money that he managed for the day.

All of the tellers had shown up by then. So they were just cooling their heels. Jonathan had used the alias John Alabaster to set up the unnumbered account. After the download was complete and the money was secure behind the new firewalls that Jonathan had created, Jonathan deleted the transaction history that had taken the banks money out of the accounts of the tax payer's hands who patronized the Trinity Bank

Thomas Underwood was computer savy, so he offered to help with the virus that was holding his place of employment hostage at the moment.

"Okay done." Thomas said with as satisfied smile on his face at 10:15 am.

"Thank you Mr. Underwood. I really appreciate your help." Felecia said. With that said it seemed like they could finally open the bank. Felecia checked various accounts for errors and found that the money was simply gone. She made the decision to call the police and report the crime. She dialed 911 and the lady at the other end answered in a pleasant tone, "Hello, what is your emergency?" Said the calm voice on the other end of the line.

"Hello this Felecia Grey with the Trinity bank and we have been robbed." Felecia said into the phone. As calmly as she could. She proceeded to report that there had been a robbery, and she needed an officer to respond immediately. She could replace the money with their insurance. The bank would be operational shortly. When the transfer was completed, Jonathan hit a few more keys and the money was on its way to its next destination.

"Great, the deposit that was taken was $250,000 less your $50,000. Leaving us with $100,000 each." Frank said. "Did you take your cut when you made the transfer?" He asked.

"Yes my $100,000 grand was transferred into the offshore account that we set up under John Alabaster. It will rest here in this unnumbered account until we need it" He said this while handing Frank a piece of paper with the account identification and the bank name with the location on it.

"Now we should head to parts unknown." Frank told Jonathan. The Snow brothers would not know that Daniel had just been involved in a car accident.

Charlie Wright wanted his take, but he would just have to wait until he got out of the hospital. He would finally be comfortable with his take in hand. He already had almost a million saved totaling the $500,000 that he had saved from the last heists that he had pulled with the Snow brothers. He had hoped that there would be more jobs to pull soon. Charlie had been living frugally to save as much as he could. So he just decided he would wait until they called again.

The Snow brothers booked the next flight out of town to the Switzerland to recover the money that had been deposited in their unnumbered account, under the assumed name John Alabaster. Frank used The First Bank of Switzerland and another alias to deposit the money. His newest alias was Tom Bellow's. Frank had made up this name recently to honor his only remaining relative of the Snow family besides his brother.

His uncle was Tom Bellows and he was his mother's brother. He had been very close to him in past years. This was yet another part of the trail that would lead Officer's Hamilton and Officer Brooks right to them.

Frank decided to fly alone when they got the money settled in a bank account that was protected by foreign laws. They each had nearly $500,000 to add to their previous heists and keep them happy for a little while longer, or maybe retire all together.

Felecia returned to her office. She was really upset that a robbery had happened during her shift. She didn't know that Jonathan was the robber who had taken all of the banks money. When she got to her office she made the call to the police to report the robbery. She was relieved that Mr. Eldridge had called and told her that he would not be coming in today. As ordered by Mrs. Eldridge.

There simply wasn't any money in the Trinity bank today, at least in the morning. When Felecia noticed that the bank accounts were empty, she felt a panic set in. How had this happened on her watch. Mr. Eldridge would take it the hardest. She immediately called 911. The 911 operator took her information and dispatched Officer Hamilton and his partner to investigate. The officers knew that the Snow brothers were involved somehow. They did not know that the notorious Snow brothers had robbed the Trinity bank that morning. They knew Jonathon liked to wear his snake skin cowboy boots. The boot impressions were a size 13. So were the prints that he left in the sand that night with Henry Cornwell in the marsh.

Daniel had betrayed them. But there was nothing that anyone could do about him at the moment. Christopher and Randy had betrayed them as well in the worst kind of way. Now all they had to show for it was an empty bank for the big holiday weekend. Felecia immediately got on the phone to the insurance and gave them all the particulars that they would need to transfer the limit of $250,000 immediately. The bank would be operational soon and could open their doors for business.

At precisely 8:15 am the Officer Hamilton and his partner Officer Brooks made a drive by and checked on the Trinity Bank. They left the parking lot without incident because everything seemed to be in order. Chelsea had waved her hand at Officer Hamilton and he thought that the bank was secure as well. He was expecting men in trench coats, not cyber thieves.

'The money that we would take away from this heist will allow them the freedom to live comfortably for many years.' Jonathan thought to himself. He planned on moving the money around until it was lost in the banking system. When he was unsuccessful with the passwords he had tried, he resorted to his new software that they had bought for this job. He tried a few little known passwords then resorted to his trusty password decoding software 'Password Unlock' to unlock the computers software when he was able to.

The Ambulance delivered Charlie Wright to the local hospital. He was in bad shape. But he was new to the area and Officer Hamilton had no idea that he was involved with the Snow brothers. The officers had no idea that their newest hire was a bank robber.

With the click of a key Jonathan had the banks money in his sights. In two seconds the bank software transferred the money to their unnumbered account half way across the world. Frank was distant with Chelsea this morning. He had to dump her to finish the job. As soon as the tellers reported that they couldn't access their accounts.

The banks employees were locked out by the virus for the moment. They patiently waited for Daniel to return. However Thomas had saved the day. Felecia Grey got on the phone for tech support immediately just incase Daniel couldn't figure it out with his software. But he had to download the virus that would lock them out of their computers until the heist was complete. The lady at the other end answered in a pleasant tone, "What is your emergency?" Said the calm voice on the other end of the line.

"Hello this Felecia Grey with the Trinity bank and we have been robbed." Felecia said into the phone. She needed an officer to respond immediately. She could replace the money with their insurance. The bank would be operational shortly.

When the transfer was completed, Jonathan hit a few more keys and the money was on its way to its next destination.

"Great, the deposit that was taken was $250,000 less your $50,000. Leaving us with $100,000 each." Frank said. "Did you take your cut when you made the transfer?" He asked.

"Yes my $100,000 grand was transferred into the offshore account that we set up. It will rest here in this unnumbered account until we need it" He said this while handing Frank a piece of paper with the account identification and the bank name with the location on it.

Because of foreign laws the banking system would reward them with tightly sum. They each had nearly $900,000 to add to their previous heists and keep them happy for a little while longer, or maybe retire all together. With this latest heist they would have a cool million each. And Daniel would receive hiw $50,000.

For the banks employees, there simply wouldn't be any money in the Trinity bank today, at least in the morning. When Felecia noticed that the bank accounts were empty, she felt a panic set in. How had this happened on her watch. Mr. Eldridge would take it the hardest. She immediately called 911. The 911 operator took her information and dispatched Officer Hamilton and his partner to investigate. The officers knew that the Snow brothers were involved somehow. They knew Jonathon liked to wear his snake skin cowboy boots. The boot impressions were a size 13. So were the prints that he left in the sand that night with Henry Cornwell in the marsh.

Daniel had betrayed Felecia and Chelsea, but the ladies didn't know that he had been in an accident on the way to the Regency hotel. Which was where home was at the moment. Christopher and Randy had betrayed Felecia and Chelsea as well in the worst kind of way. Now all they had to show for it was an empty bank for the next week. Felecia immediately got on the phone to the insurance and gave them all the particulars that they would need to transfer the limit of $250,000 immediately. The bank would be operational soon and could open their doors for business.

Chapter Thirty Eight

THE MONEY TRAIL

By 9 am the bank was surrounded by police cars. Each employee gave their details as to what happened. But no one knew anything except that they had been robbed and the only that they had control of was the initial $500 that they were given each day. Officer Hamilton and Officer Brooks were on the job trying to be helpful to Ms. Grey and Ms. McQuire who had never lost any money on their watch. He questioned them and asked for the information that would lead them to the bank robbers.

"Are you sure Henry Cornwell wasn't involved with this?" Officer Hamilton asked Felecia.

"Well I don't know a Mr. Cornwell. All I know is his what you told me about him. His ID was found on the dead man found on Bayou Rd. He must be involved though. I think there were three of them. They used an inside man this time. Daniel Fields was his name and there were two others and I'm ashamed to say I had a relationship with one of them." Felecia reported. "I just hired Daniel Fields er um Christopher or whatever his name is was."

"You were involved with them you said? Was any other employee involved with them that you know of?" He asked.

"I had just hired Christopher's cousin Daniel Fields last week. I guess that was a mistake too. They obviously had an inside man. And he his absent at the moment."

"So can you describe them?" He asked.

"Well Randy, they one who I was seeing, was about 6 ft. tall with brown hair and he wore snake skin cowboy boots where ever he went. He called himself Randy Fields"

"Okay there may be a correlation with Henry Cornwell's murder. I found cowboy boot foot prints in the sands of the marsh last week when I found the body." They got lucky and found an impression of the cowboy boots in the sandy marsh of the bay. The impression was so good that is showed there was an impression the number 13 left in the marsh as well in the boot impression. So they knew what size the killer would wear. "Do you know where they were headed? I mean since you got to know them, Did this Daniel Fields put in for a vacation or talk about one?"

"He was only here for a week so he didn't have time to set up for a vacation."

"What about this Christopher and Randy, you said you were seeing them, did they mention going anywhere soon?"

"Well we spent the weekends together with Randy and Ms. McQjuire spent the weekends with Christopher for the past three weeks. But Randy didn't say anything to me about taking a trip"

"Okay, then what can you tell me about this Daniel Fields." He replied.

"I don't know, Christopher just recommended him and I hired him almost immediately. I suppose I played right into their hands."

"Well Ms. Grey, they used you. You were vulnerable and they seduced you. Don't beat yourself up about it. We will find them. Don't you worry. I have a lead on the car they liked to drive and we have the boot impressions to go on. We also have tire impressions found in the sand of the marsh that we can compare to the vehicle that they used regularly. Christopher drove a rented an SUV to get around in right?"

"Yes that's correct." Felecia said. The police officers knew that it was only a matter of time before they would put two and two together and tie the Snow brothers to the murder and the bank robbery.

"I believe the three men involved are career criminals. We will find them and get your money back Ms. Grey. Don't you worry. They used an inside man, they used your vulnerability against you and if there was three of them. They couldn't have gotten far yet."

"Well I'm just glad no one was hurt. I can't believe I let my guard down with these guys. I'm not supposed to do that. I guess I got caught up in the moment." She admitted.

"I wonder if they went back to their hotel room? They could be there."

"What hotel were they staying at?"

"They Regency." She answered reluctantly because she was embarrassed that she had slept with Randy.

"Okay what room number?"

"We stayed in room 504. Do you think they are there?"

"Lets hope so ma'am." Officer Hamilton called in to send two units to room 504 at the Regency hotel. He sent the first officer to room number 504 and the other one to watch over the lobby until he got there. They would find that Frank and Jonathan Snow checked out this morning when they left to commit the heist.

"Lets start with this. What kind of car were they driving today?"

"Well Daniel showed up today and every day that he worked here except for the first day, in a big grey Buick." She explained. "It was Daniels car. He was a transplant from South Carolina. He did really well learning his duties and making friends with the other employees. I so hoped he would work out." She said with a hint of sadness in her voice.

Do you really think they had something to do with that man's murder?"

"Well it all fits. We will check with the rental agency to see if there was a credit card used to rent the vehicles that Frank, I mean Christopher drove around. Christopher Snow is the name that he gave you."

"When Henry Cornwell was murdered we found cowboy boot impressions in the sand and we found tire marks that match an SUV at the murder sight. I think your employee Anthony Alvarez crossed them somehow and got himself killed. That's where Henry Cornwell comes in. He has a criminal record and has banking experience. So if we can just find out who rented that grey Buick I think we may have our man." He told her.

"Don't worry Ms. Grey. We are on it and have a way to find out who they are." Officer Brooks said to reassure her.

"Well that's good because I don't think the owner of the bank can take any more bad things happening to his bank."

"We will get them Ma'am. Don't worry."

"Oh I do hope so, I don't know what to tell Mr. Eldridge. He doesn't come in until 10 o'clock. I think I should call him and tell him not to come in today." Felecia told the Officer after they rode the elevator upstairs to her office.

"Well Ms. Grey we will need his statement for the investigation."

"Okay, but please don't upset him, he recently had a heart attack."

"Don't worry Ms. Grey we will be as easy on him as possible."

"Let me break it to him. He needs to hear it from me. It happened on my watch. I want to do something to make it up to him." She returned.

"Okay, you can break it to him. But we will need to talk to him afterwards."

"No problem he will be here at 10 o'clock. It's almost 10 now. He should be here any minute." She told Officer Hamilton. Just then Cheryl buzzed her with a call from Mr. Eldridge. "Okay thanks Cheryl. Can you please hold on a second Officer Hamilton this might be helpful" She said. "Okay thanks Cheryl." She said as she picked up the receiver of the phone and Cheryl told her that the boss was on the phone.

Officer Brooks was consoling Chelsea at the moment. She felt like the biggest fool for being taken by Christopher or whoever he was. She knew that Misty was on to something when she reacted that way. She also knew that her parents were on the mark as well when they told Chelsea about their feelings about Christopher. Felecia was kicking herself for getting involved with Randy.

The cop cars told everyone that something had happened at the bank before they got there. There were many customers waiting to fulfill their banking needs. The customers were told that there had been a robbery. Then the customers were told that the bank would be closed today But they would reopen on Monday. This put a crimp in many of the banks customers plans. They were waiting patiently while they worried about their bank accounts and wondered if they would get their money back when the bank reopened on Monday.

Chelsea just cried through the whole thing. Harold stayed calm and tried to reassure the rest of the employees to keep them calm. Alice and Cheryl were crying as well. Ken and Amanda Stevens consoled each other. They couldn't believe their beloved bank was robbed. Mark Patterson wore his self assured hat and tried to calm his employee's. When the transfer was completed, Jonathan hit a few more keys and the money was on its way to its next destination.

"Great, the deposit that was taken was deposited in the first of many bank accounts until it disappeared in one of the foreign bank accounts. We will take $500,000 less your $50,000." Frank said. "Did you take your cut when you made the transfer?" He asked.

"Yes my $50 grand was transferred into the offshore account that you gave me. It will rest there in this unnumbered account until u get to the next destination." He said this while handing Frank a piece of paper with the account identification and the bank name with the location on it.

"Now we should head to parts unknown." Frank told Jonathan,

"Yes lets get going. Where is Charlie?" Frank asked. "We were supposed to meet up with him here."

"I don't know brother of mine." Jonathan replied. Little did they know that Charlie was resting in the local hospital unconscious right now. He was headed to Bermuda with his take before he was in the accident. Jonathan commented that he would make himself comfortable in the Caribbean islands and never be caught. Or so he thought.

He had mentioned that he liked the sights there. Bikini's on a white pearly beach. He knew that he could live cheaply there for a very long time. He was set to catch the next plane out of here. But the accident had rendered him useless, but he still earned his $50 grand. Then they heard the local news about an accident that happened just a few minutes ago. The other driver of the SUV had gotten the worst of it. Daniel would be out of commission for now, but that was okay because Daniel had completed his part of the job.

Officer Hamilton and Officer Brooks arrived at the accident scene. They did not know that Daniel was a thief in disguise, and the one who would help the Snow brothers take all of that money. As soon as the ambulance arrived the paramedics worked to get both drivers out of their vehicles.

Frank was getting worried about Charlie because he hadn't touched base with Frank yet. He immediately hopped in his SUV to head for the accident scene. It wasn't far from the Regency hotel. This was the break that the police needed.

Charlie had an ID that said he was Daniel Fields. So the hospital referred to him as Daniel Fields. Frank called the hospital to see if he had been admitted. The nurse on the phone told him that there was a Daniel Fields in the ER and then she asked if he was a family member.

"Yes ma'am. He's my cousin." Frank told her.

Then Frank told Jonathan to stay put until he could get to the hospital. Frank jumped into his favorite car and headed for the hospital with that said. When he arrived he told the hospital staff that his cousin had been in an accident and that his name was Daniel Feilds. Then the nurse told him that he had was unconscious and gave him Daniels room number. "Well I will be right there." He told the nurse on the other end of the line.

Felecia immediately called 911. The 911 operator took her information and dispatched Officer Hamilton and his partner to investigate. The officers knew that the Snow brothers were involved somehow. They knew Jonathon liked to wear his snake skin cowboy boots. The boot impressions in the marsh were a size 13. It said so in the prints that he left in the sand that night with Henry Cornwell in the marsh.

Charlie spent the better part of the morning recovering in the ER. He had almost a million saved totaling the $500,000 that he had saved from the last heists that he had pulled with the Snow brothers. He had hoped that there would be more jobs to pull soon. He had been living frugally to save as much as he could. So he just decided he would wait until they called again to tell him that they were at the Regency hotel and the money was secure.

The Snow brothers booked the next flight out of town to Switzerland to recover the money that had been deposited in their unnumbered account. Frank used The First Bank of Switzerland. His newest alias was Tom Bellows. Frank had used this name recently to honor his only remaining relative of the Snow family besides his brother. His uncle was Tom Bellows and he was his mother's brother, and he had been very close to him in past years.

Frank decided to fly alone to parts unknown when they got the money settled in a bank account that was protected by foreign laws. They each had nearly $975,000 now to add to their previous balance and keep them happy for a little while longer, or maybe retire all together.

Felecia returned to her office to lick her wounds. There simply wouldn't be any money in the Trinity bank for at least a couple of hours when the insurance covered the loss. When Felecia saw that the bank accounts were all empty that feeling of panic set in again. How had this happened on her watch. Mr. Eldridge would take it the hardest.

Daniel had betrayed them. Christopher and Randy had betrayed them as well in the worst kind of way. They had no idea that Christopher and Randy, and Frank and Jonathan were one in the same. Now all they had to show for it was an empty bank for the week. Felecia immediately got on the phone to the insurance and gave them all the particulars that they would need to transfer the limit of $500,000.

By 9 am the bank was surrounded by police cars. Each employee gave their details as to what happened. But no one knew anything except that they had been robbed and the only that they had control of was the initial $500 that they were given each day. Officer Hamilton and Officer Brooks were on the job trying to be helpful to Ms. Grey and Ms. McQuire who had never lost any money on their watch. He questioned them and asked for the information that would lead them to the bank robbers.

"Are you sure Henry Cornwell wasn't involved with this?" Officer Hamilton asked Ms. Grey.

"Well as I said before, I don't know a Mr. Cornwell. All I know is his ID was found on the dead man found on Bayou Rd a week ago. He must be involved though. I think there were three of them. The notorious Snow brothers and the gentleman who was resting at the hospital at the moment. They used an inside man named Daniel Fields, and there were two others who I'm ashamed to say I had a relationship with one of them." Felecia reported. "I just hired Daniel Fields a week ago."

"You were involved with them you said? Was any other employee involved with them that you know of?" He asked.

"Yes, I think Christopher was the ring leader. I had just hired his cousin Daniel Fields last week. I guess that was a mistake too."

"So can you describe them?" He asked.

"Well Jonathan, they one who I was seeing, was about 6 ft. tall with brown hair and he wore snake skin cowboy boots where ever he went. He called himself Randy Fields"

"Okay, there may be a correlation with Henry Cornwell's murderer. I found cowboy boot foot prints in the sands of the marsh last week when I found the body. Do you know where they were headed? I mean since you got to know them, Did this Daniel Fields put in for a vacation or talk about one?"

"He was only here for a week so he didn't have time to set up for a vacation."

"What about this Christopher and Randy, you said you were seeing them, did they mention going anywhere soon?"

"Well I spent the weekends with Randy and Ms. McQuire spent the weekends with Christopher for the past three weeks. But Randy didn't say anything to me about taking a trip"

"Okay, then what can you tell me about this Daniel Fields."

"I don't know, Christopher just recommended him and I hired him almost immediately. I suppose I played right into their hands."

"Well Ms. Grey, they used you. You were vulnerable and they seduced you. Don't beat yourself up about it. We will find them. Don't you worry. I have a lead on the car they liked to drive and we have the boot impressions to go on. We also have tire impressions found in the sand of the marsh that we can compare to the vehicle that they used regularly. They had rented an SUV to get around in right?"

"Yes that's correct." Felecia said. It was only a matter of time before Officer Hamilton put two and two together and tied the Snow brothers to the murder and the bank robbery.

"I believe they were career criminals. We will find them and get your money back Ms. Grey. Don't you worry. They used inside man, they used your vulnerability against you and there was probably three of them. They couldn't have gotten far yet."

"Well I'm just glad no one was hurt. I can't believe I let my guard down with these guys. I'm not supposed to do that. I guess I got caught up in the moment." She admitted.

"What hotel were they staying at?" He asked.

"They Regency."

"Okay what room number."

"We stayed in room 504. Do you think they are there?"

"Lets hope so ma'am." Officer Hamilton thought about it and wondered if they would find that Frank and Jonathan Snow checked out this morning when they left.

"Lets start with this. They may have used a credit card to secure room 504? What kind of car were they driving today?"

"Well Daniel showed up today and every day that he worked here in a big grey Buick. I have the license plate number on his application. Let me just get that for you." She explained while she stood and retrieved his application.

"It was Daniels car. He was a transplant from South Carolina. He did really well learning his duties and making friends with the other employees. I so hoped he would work out." She said with a hint of sadness in her voice. "Who do you think they are Officer?" She continued. "Do you really think they had something to do with that man's murder?" She continued to say.

"Everyone in the banking industry knows about the notorious Snow Brothers. I can't believe that the Snow brothers could be behind it." She went on to say.

"Well it all fits. We will check with the rental agency for a credit card that they had to use to rent the vehicles. If there was a credit card used to rent the vehicles under the assumed names. We will find them ma'am. We aim to protect and to serve."

"When Henry Cornwell was murdered we found cowboy boot impressions in the sand and we found tire marks that match an SUV at the murder sight as well." He added. "I think your employee Anthony Alvarez crossed them somehow and got himself killed. That's why I think that is where Henry Cornwell comes in. He has a criminal record and had some banking experience. So if we can just find out who rented that grey Buick I think we may have our man." He told her.

"Don't worry Ms. Grey. We are on it and have a way to find out who they are." Officer brooks said to reassure her.

"Well that's good because I don't think the owner of the bank can take any more bad things happening to his bank."

"We will get them Ma'am. Don't worry."

"Oh I do hope so, I don't know what to tell Mr. Eldridge. He doesn't come in until 10 o'clock. I think I should call him and tell him not to come in today." She replied. "I think I'm going to call him. Then she picked up the phone and dialed Mr. Eldridge's phone number.

Mrs. Eldridge answered the phone. "Hello this is Mrs. Eldridge" Felecia answered then waited for the reply. "Is this Felecia?" She asked.

"Yes Eleanor, This is Felecia. I was wondering when Mr. Eldridge might be coming in today."

"Oh hun, he is having more indigestion, at least I hope its indigestion. He wont be making it in today." She said with authority, then she said good bye and hung up the phone.

"Well Ms. Grey we will need his statement for the investigation."

"Okay, but please don't upset him, he recently had a heart attack."

"Don't worry Ms. Grey we will keep it as easy on him as possible."

"Let me break it to him. He needs to hear it from me. It happened on my watch. I want to do something to make it up to him." She continued.

"Okay, you can break it to him. But we still need to talk to him."

"No problem. That was Mrs. Eldridge. She is keeping him home again today. He maybe retiring soon." She told Officer Hamilton.

Officer Brooks was consoling Chelsea at the moment. She felt like the biggest fool for being taken by Christopher or whoever he was. She knew that Misty was on to something when she reacted that way. She also knew that her parents were on the mark as well when they told Chelsea about their feelings about Christopher. Felecia was kicking herself for getting involved with Randy.

The cop cars told everyone that something had happened at the bank before they got there. There were many customers waiting to do fulfill their banking needs. The customers were told that there had been a robbery and they would be closed until Monday. The customers worried about their bank accounts and wondered if they would get their money back when the bank reopened on Monday.

Frank and Jonathan used the big grey Buick to make their escape. Charlie was in pretty bad shape at the hospital. Frank had called the hospital and didn't find a Daniel Fields there yet, but he knew about the accident. He was just waiting for Charlie be admitted. They would just have to wait patiently for the call from Charlie. Chelsea was having a hard time holding her composure. With Charlie in the hospital only Frank and Jonathan would meet up in room 504 to wait on Charlie. They made their plans to go their separate ways while they counted up the money that they had just stolen in room 504 at the Regency hotel.

Chapter Thirty Nine

ANTHONY ISN'T GOING AWAY THAT EASY

Anthony's face was bloated from being in the murky waters of the marsh for two days. He was mostly unrecognizable. Officer Hamilton found Anthony's wallet in his back pocket. It had his Driver's license in it and a check from the Trinity bank with a pink slip attached. It also had an ID for a Henry Cornwell which gave Officer Hamilton reason to pause. He didn't know which ID trust. He assumed that Mr. Alvarez had been an employee and had been fired recently based on the check in his wallet. Luckily the check didn't get ruined because he was laying on his face. The check was in his wallet which had not gotten wet because it was in his back pocket. Officer Hamilton decided to investigate the check and headed for the Trinity bank.

Officer Greg Hamilton showed up at Trinity bank with Anthony's last check in hand. He went up to Cheryl and asked if he could speak to the manager.

Cheryl said, "Sure officer just let me call her down to the lobby. Go ahead and have a seat over there and she will be right down" She dialed Felecia's extension and told her that the police were here to see her.

"That's okay, I don't need to sit." Officer Hamilton told Cheryl while she called up to her boss. Felecia told Cheryl that she would be right down. Then she went down the stairs to the lobby to meet Officer Hamilton.

"Hello I'm Felecia Grey the banks president." Felecia said to Officer Hamilton.

"Hello Ms. Grey, I have some bad news for you. Is there somewhere we can talk privately?" He asked.

"Of course, we can go to my office, come right this way." She replied. Then she headed for the elevators so they could ride them up to the 2nd floor. She walked him to her office and sat behind her desk while she motioned for him to have a seat across from her.

"Thank you Ms. Grey. I'm afraid I have some bad news. Do you know this man?" He said as he showed her a picture of Anthony's Driver's license.

"Why yes, I just fired him about a week or so ago. He was working for me for about 2 months but he just didn't work out. Why what has happened to him?"

"Well a jogger found his body in the marsh on Bayou Rd. yesterday. He was barely recognizable but we were able to make an ID based on this check and ID in his back pocket." He said as he showed her the check that she had just given Anthony.

"Oh no, I didn't like him, but I never wished him dead. This is awful. Who did it?"

"We don't know yet. We were hoping you could be of help with that. Is there anything in his file that would give us a next of kin or some way to contact someone who knows him? Otherwise we have to hold his body for 30 day or until his next of kin identifies him."

"Well I don't think I can be of help, I think he lied on his resume. I don't think anything on it is true."

"That's a shame Ms. Grey. We really need to contact his next of kin."

"Here's his resume, and application. There's a contact in case of emergency person on his application." She said as she stood and reached into her file cabinet and pulled out the forms. "But like I said I think he lied on his resume and that would mean he lied on his application too." She replied.

"At least it's something to go on." Officer Hamilton said.

"Well I hope it helps you in your investigation."

"So if you don't mind me asking, why was he fired?"

"Well it looked like he was going to work out then he started making stupid mistakes and being late. Things I just couldn't stand for. I expect my employees to be here on time and balance. He had trouble with both of those things."

"Okay Ms. Grey I will look into his application and see if I can come up with a next of kin."

"How did he die, if you don't mind me asking?" Felecia asked.

"He took a bullet to the back of the head. He was found by a jogger and his dog. He was face down in the marsh and the water made him almost unrecognizable. We really have to find his next of kin and the killer."

"Well I hope you do find the killer, I didn't wish him dead. I just couldn't keep him on here after the mistakes he had made." She answered feeling a little sick to her stomach because Randy may have been one of the bank robbers. She went into Chelsea's office to tell her the news after Officer Hamilton left the building.

"Do you know a Henry Cornwell?" Officer Hamilton asked Felecia

"Well no I have never heard of him." She replied. "Why do you ask?"

"Well we found a second ID on the body so we are just trying to follow all leads." He continued "Very well Ms. Grey, Thank you for your time." He said as he stood to leave.

"My pleasure, I'm just sorry it had to be under these circumstances." She replied. Then she walked him to the elevator and rode down to the lobby with him. When he was gone Felecia went back up to the 2nd floor by climbing the stairs. She was confused and wanted to talk to Chelsea about Anthony's demise.

"Hey, do you know who that was about?" Felecia said as she popped her head in on Chelsea.

"No. What was that all about?" Chelsea replied.

"Anthony Alvarez was found with a bullet in his head out on Bayou Road yesterday." "Oh My God, how awful. I wonder what happened to him?" Chelsea asked.

"I don't know but the officer had his last check that we gave him when I let him go and he had his drivers license and he had a second ID on him that claimed he was Henry Cornwell. What do you make of that." Felecia asked Chelsea.

"Well I don't know. Didn't you say you thought he lied on his application and resume?"

"Well yes, that's what I suspected, I wonder who this Henry Cornwell is." Felecia continued

"Wow that's awful." Chelsea said. "What did the cop want with you then?"

"Oh he just wanted to see if we knew about his next of kin. So I gave him his application to investigate. I told him that I thought he lied on his resume and application."

"Oh no, now they won't be able to find out who needs to claim the body. This is awful," Chelsea exclaimed. "Is there anything we can do to help?"

"I gave them everything I had, so we have helped as much as we can."

"Okay, I guess that's all we can do then." Chelsea replied.

"Yes I guess you're right, I just hope there isn't a killer on the loose." Then Felecia left Chelsea's office to go to hers. Little did Felecia know she was sleeping with the killer.

Jonathan was busy playing with his revolver at the hotel room when the conversation between the cop and Felecia took place. Jonathan had moved the surveillance equipment to room 504. Frank over heard the conversation. He then lit a cigarette. '*Oh shit, what do we do now*' he thought to himself. He would need to speak to Jonathan before dinner tonight. They just wished they could do something about it. So he phoned the hospital room to speak to Charlie Wright.

"Hello" Frank said loudly, Wake up cowboy we're on." Frank told Jonathan.

"Leave me alone. I did what I was supposed to do. Now we have all the amenities that we need. I'm tired. I just want to take a small cat nap." Jonathan said into the morning air." Frank had woke him up abruptly again.

"Yeah we got problem. You need to listen to this."

"What's goin on?"

"Just get up and get out there." Frank demanded.

"Alright Alright, I'll be there in a little bit then. Just let me shower."

"There's no time for that. Just get in here now please." Frank demanded again.

"Okay bro, don't flip out, whatever it is it will be alright. I'll be ready soon." Jonathan told Frank. Jonathan jumped out of bed and got dressed.

"You cleaned up apartment but you won't quit smoking, you're a joke bro." Frank had picked up and did the dishes, but he had chain smoked the entire time. The little two bedroom hotel room smelled awful from the stale smoke. But Frank had tried to smoke out on the balcony.

"Just come in here and listen to the tape." Frank spit out at his brother. So Jonathan went out of his bedroom and readied himself to hear what was so important. He sat down in front of the tape recorder and listened to the conversation that his tiger had had with Officer Hamilton.

"Oh Shit, what do we do now?" Jonathan said with a hint of fear in his voice.'

"Well we aren't going to be here for very much longer, our plane leaves in an hour, so we just lay low until the its time to go and then we get the fuck out of dodge." Frank said with confidence.

Jonathan sat back and took in what just happened. He had sent the gun that had killed Henry Cornwell aka Anthony Alvarez to their apartment in New York. It would only be a matter of time before the signs pointed to them. They had to come up with a story that would keep them out of jail if the cops came knocking on their door.

Jonathan had strong feelings for Felecia. He had decorated the hotel room with those same pictures. "We need to get these pictures down now. Come on, we can't take the risk of them figuring out what we are doing here."

"Oh don't freak out on me now bro we don't need to do anything. There is nothing tying us to this murder."

"Did you pick up after yourself?" Frank asked.

"What do you mean?" Jonathan spit back.

"The bullet casing, they can trace it back to you. You're gonna have to get rid of the gun."

"I already said that I sent it to the apartment in New York, I called our next door neighbor to ask her if she would accept the package when it came."

"Then mail it to yourself or something like that, just get rid of it. We don't want any attention regarding this at all."

"Alright already. I sent it home just to make sure that the murder weapon is hidden well." Jonathan replied.

"I'm glad you did something with it so they can't tie it back to us."

"I can have Mrs. Mathews our next door neighbor pick up the package. No problem."

"That sounds good to me, bro. That's what I did with it. They wont tie that weasels death to me. Okay, so stop worrying."

"Okay, that's one thing down. Now what else could they do to tie us to the murder."

"Well I didn't see anyone on that road that night. It was dark and no one saw us, I'm sure of it. It will take the cops a long time to tie anything to us. We will be long gone before they find us." Jonathan replied.

"I sure hope you're right bro." Frank said a little unsure.

They spent the day going over all the possibilities that could come of this latest news. "I will be seeing her soon. "Sounds good. I hope she lets you in on what she is thinking about Alvarez."

"She's just a loose end that I need to forget and tie up."

"Oh I'm sure she will, don't worry bro, I got it under control. I have to call a cab right now"

"Yeah like you had Anthony under control." Frank said sarcastically.

"That's not fair. How was I supposed to know there would be a jogger come by and find him this soon?"

"I don't know, I just want this to be over." Frank said as he lit another cigarette. He smoked his cigarette down quickly and then hopped in the shower. Then Christopher went over to the apartment and used his nervous energy to clean up the rest of the apartment since. '*They have become a liability.*' He thought to himself as he began to clean the living room. He wanted the apartment to be presentable if the cops came knocking on his door. Had spent the day at the apartment.

"Be right there." Came the voice on the other side of the door.

"Hello prince charming," She cooed as she opened the door. She was wearing a white short sleeved dress with white sandals. She had thrown her hair into a French braid again.

"You look stunning, I know I'm in love now." He exclaimed.

"Why thank you sweet prince. The feeling is quite mutual." She replied. Then she moved and she kissed him gently on the lips. He responded to her touch and held her tightly. "You smell great too baby."

"Thank you sweetheart." She replied.

"Are you ready to go?" He asked.

"Yes just let me get my purse."

"What do you feel like having for dinner?"

"Oh I'm in the mood for Chinese tonight." She replied.

"Sounds good to me princess. Let's go then." They left her cottage and she locked it up tight.

They arrived at the 'Chinese Banquet' and entered the restaurant. He opened the doors for her and once again treated her like the lady she was. The hostess asked "Will that be two for dinner?"

"Yes ma'am" Christopher said just as a craving hit him hard. He bit his tongue and rode it out. He paid for two dinners and they picked a table that was in the back. The waitress came by and left two glasses and two plates on the table for them. "Can I get you something to drink?" She asked,

"I'll have a soda. What would you like sweetness?"

"Oh I'll have an iced tea." She told the hostess. "I will be your waitress and I will bring those drinks right away. And you can fill your plates whenever you're ready" Then she turned and left them alone.

"It all looks so good." Chelsea commented.

"You look so good." Christopher said to her.

Chelsea blushed and smiled. "What would you like to eat sweetness."

"I'm thinking Chicken Chow main and Jumbo fried shrimp with some sweet and sour pork. What do you feel like having?" She asked.

"Well that all sounds good, but how about some egg rolls too?"

"Sounds good to me," She replied. They got up from their table and filled their plates at the buffet. Christopher scooted over on the seat and snuck a kiss on Chelsea's neck. He so wanted to make things work out with her. It was too bad that he had to betray her in the end. She cooed back to him and they snuggled at the table as much as they could without getting caught. The waitress showed up with their drinks and left them to cuddle. "Are you excited about the movie?" He asked her.

"Yes, it is supposed to be really scary. I'm just glad that I'm going with you. You wouldn't believe what an awful day it has bee, You can protect me." She said with a slight giggle.

They ate the food and they shared everything right down the middle. "I love Chinese food," She commented in between bites.

"Me too, it's really good." He replied as another craving hit him. He shook it off and kept eating. He would have to put some gum in for the movie. When they were finished eating Christopher left a generous tip and they left the restaurant. They didn't want to be late for the movie.

When they got to the movies 'I Hear You Sleeping' was playing in two theaters. They chose the 8 o'clock movie and bought tickets. Then they waited in line at the concession stand for their snacks. When they got up to the snack bar he told the cashier that he wanted a large popcorn and a large diet soda. Then he asked, "Is there anything else you want sweetness?"

"Yes I'll have some milk duds." She replied. "And some milk duds." He told the cashier. Then they headed for the theater that was playing their movie and they found a seat. They enjoyed their treats and the movie throughout the night.

Randy showed up at Felecia's house at 6 o'clock. She was wearing her signature silk robe with nothing on underneath. The knock came at the door and she said "Coming" Then she opened the door to find her cowboy in his signature snake skin cowboy boots.

"Oh those boots turn me on." She said as she reached for him and wrapped her arms around his neck and began kissing him. David popped into her head and she had a hard time getting him off of her mind. He responded right away to her kiss. She slipped out of her robe and hopped on his hips and he kicked the door shut then he took them into the bedroom. "You look delicious tiger." He whispered into her ear.

"You make me wet." She whispered back.

They made their way to the bed and she scooted up to the pillows. "I want to feel your tongue on me." She whispered to him in the dimly lit room.

Again David slipped into her head. Jonathan was jealous and he was having a hard time keeping those thoughts at bay. He slipped out of his boots first then took off his shirt then slipped out of his pants and boxers. No matter what she did when he was gone he still wanted to keep her. He knew that she was disposable to him and that he would dump her in the morning. He just wanted one more romp in the hay before he disappeared. He then climbed on top of her and reached for her womanhood. He slipped his fingers inside of her and began to move in and out. She began to move to the rhythm of his movements. She climaxed almost instantly. She really did have a strong libido. He almost came when she did. She then scooted around and said "Your turn." Then she began sucking on him. She put his manhood inside of her mouth and licked him as she moved him in and out of her mouth. He came almost instantly when she did this. She drank up his man juice and giggled a little.

"We really fit well together cowboy."

"Yes we do tiger."

"Do you want to order a pizza, I picked up some beer today on the way home."

"Oh that sounds great. Let's order and go at it again. Let's see if we can have another round before they get here."

"Sounds good to me," She replied as she handed him the phone book. "Same as before?" He asked her.

"Yes that sounds good." She replied. He picked the phone and ordered the pizza then asked her if she wanted a beer.

"Yes that sounds great cowboy."

So he hopped out of bed and headed for the kitchen to get two beers. He didn't even get dressed. She stayed in bed while he went to the kitchen. He came back with two beers in hand and asked "Ready for round two?"

"Get over here cowboy, and make me cum." She demanded.

"Here I come tiger." He handed her the beer then climbed into bed with her. He rubbed her leg and felt his way up to her womanhood. He found her mound and inserted his fingers. She reached for him and began stroking him to make him hard. When he felt his manhood responding he climbed on top of her and inserted himself into her. They moved back and forth together and she began to cum first. Her womanhood gripped him and squeezed out his man juice inside of her. They laid there in the throes of ecstasy and made small talk until the pizza arrived.

When the doorbell rang she hopped out of bed and said, "Just a minute." She threw on her robe and grabbed her purse from the night stand. She pulled out $50 and headed for the front door. She opened the door and paid the pizza guy. He handed her the pizza and she handed him the $50 and told him to keep the change. Then she shut the door and headed back to the bedroom. Randy was hiding under the covers but she could tell he was ready for round three. "Want some pizza?" She asked.

"Of course tiger. Bring it over here. And don't forget the anchovies."

"I won't, let me just get settled." She returned to the bedroom with two plates. She handed him a plate and he loaded it up and dug in. He put the anchovies on his slices and took a bite.

"How can you eat those things?" She asked with a disgusted look on her face.

"They're good. Why don't you try one?"

"No way, I don't like them." And she turned away.

They finished their pizza and laid in bed to relax for a bit. They made small talk while they rested.

"You'll never guess what happened today." She said to him.

"What tiger?"

"Well the police came by and they had Mr. Alvarez's wallet with them. It still had his last check in it from this week. They said he had been murdered down on Bayou Road. Some jogger found him in the marsh."

Of course Randy already knew this but he went along with it just incase she got suspicious. "Really, wow, poor guy." He said to her in the dark.

"Yeah it was a big surprise to me. He lied on his application and they wanted to know who his next of kin was. Since he lied on his application they had no way of knowing who to contact. They didn't seem like they had any leads. But he did tell me that they found an ID that had a guy named Henry Cornwell on it." She went on.

"Oh that's terrible. Sorry you had to find out that way. Did the cop come to the bank?"

"Yes we talked about it in my office." "Oh okay. Well I hope they find out who did it." He said secretly regretting killing Anthony for the moment. He knew it was only a matter of time before the police came knocking on his door now.

They moved on to other subjects and came back around again to sex. They began to kiss and feel each others bodies again. She wanted to break it off with Randy and spend more time with David. But she enjoyed Randy just as much. So she went along with him because she couldn't resist those damn cowboy boots. He ran his fingers across her nipples and she shivered. Then he licked her nipple and she came again. They went at it until 10 o'clock. Then she said that she had to call it a night because she had to work tomorrow. He had to go because she had to work in the morning. So he called the cab company from memory and ordered the cab to pick him up. He had betrayed her but she didn't know that he was involved in the robbery. So he was happy to have this last night with her.

He got dressed and put on his signature boots that she loved so much. She got wet again just seeing his boots on him. Then she put her robe back on and walked him to the door. Tomorrow was Friday. The end of the week was coming tomorrow. That meant they could spend some uninterrupted time together.

She walked him to the door and wrapped her arms around him and kissed him passionately. "When can I see you again?" She asked. "How does tomorrow night sound? We could stay at the hotel and order room service again. What do you think?"

"Sounds great to me I can go one more day without you I'll just go work out. But don't make me wait any longer, Okay?" She replied as the horn of the cab honked outside the door.

"I better get going then tiger."

"Okay I will see you again tomorrow night at 6 o'clock?"

"Sounds great to me see ya then." He opened the door and headed for the taxi cab. She had no idea that she had just slept with a murderer and the man who would turn her life upside down. It was the Friday before Labor Day. It was time to Chapter Forty Two

Anthony Isn't Going Away That Easy

Anthony's face was bloated from being in the murky waters of the marsh for two days. He was mostly unrecognizable. Officer Hamilton found Anthony's wallet in his back pocket. It had his Driver's license in it and a check from the Trinity bank with a pink slip attached that said final paycheck on it. It also had an ID for a Henry Cornwell which gave Officer Hamilton reason to pause. He didn't know which ID trust. He assumed that Mr. Alvarez had been an employee and had been fired recently based on the check in his wallet. Luckily the check didn't get ruined because he was laying on his face. The check was in his wallet which had not gotten wet because it was in his back pocket. Officer Hamilton decided to investigate the check and headed for the Trinity bank.

Officer Greg Hamilton showed up at Trinity bank with Anthony's last check in hand. He went up to Cheryl and asked if he could speak to the manager.

"Sure officer just let me call her down to the lobby. Go ahead and have a seat over there and she will be right down" Cheryl said, then she dialed Felecia's extension and told her that the police were here to see her.

"That's okay, I don't need to sit." Officer Hamilton told Cheryl while she called up to her boss. Felecia told Cheryl that she would be right down. Then she went down the stairs to the lobby to meet Officer Hamilton.

"Hello I'm Felecia Grey the banks president." Felecia said to Officer Hamilton.

"Hello Ms. Grey, I have some bad news for you. Is there somewhere we can talk privately?" He asked.

"Of course, we can go to my office, come right this way." She replied. Then she headed for the elevators so they could ride them up to the 2nd floor. She walked him to her office and sat behind her desk while she motioned for him to have a seat across from her.

"Thank you Ms. Grey. I'm afraid I have some bad news. Do you know this man?" He said as he showed her a picture of Anthony's Driver's license.

"Why yes, I just fired him about a week or so ago. He was working for me for about 2 months but he just didn't work out. Why what has happened to him?"

"Well a jogger found his body in the marsh on Bayou Rd. yesterday. He was barely recognizable but we were able to make an ID based on this check and ID's in his back pocket." He said as he showed her the check that she had just given Anthony.

"You said ID's. May I see the second ID?" She asked.

"We are still sorting that out ma'am." Officer Hamilton replied.

"Well, I didn't like him, but I never wished him dead. This is awful. Who did it?"

"We don't know that yet. We were hoping you could be of some help with that. Is there anything in his file that would give us the next of kin or some way to contact someone who knows him?"

"We may have to wait to identify him until we find his next of kin." Felecia said. "Quite frankly I don't know what to tell you. He didn't work for me long enough to know that about him. But it is unusual to carry two ID's in his pocket isn't it?" She continued. "I don't know if I can be of help, I think he lied on his resume. I don't think anything on it is true."

"That's a shame Ms. Grey. We really need to contact his next of kin."

"Here's his resume, and application. There's a contact in case of emergency person on his application." She said as she stood and reached into her file cabinet and pulled out the forms. She kept the documents of ex-employee's in her office. "But like I said I think he lied on his resume and that would mean he lied on his application too." She replied.

"At least it's something to go on." Officer Hamilton said.

"Well I hope it helps you in your investigation."

"If you don't mind me asking, why was he fired?" Officer Hamilton replied.

"Well it looked like he was going to work out then he started making stupid mistakes and being late. Things I just couldn't stand for. I expect my employees to be here on time and balance. He had trouble with both of those things."

"Okay Ms. Grey I will look into his application and see if I can come up with a next of kin."

"How did he die, if you don't mind me asking?" Felecia asked.

"He took a bullet to the back of the head. He was found by a jogger and his dog. He was face down in the marsh and the water made him almost unrecognizable. We really have to find his next of kin and the killer."

"Well I hope you do find the killer, I didn't wish him dead. I just couldn't keep him on here after the mistakes he had been making." She answered feeling a little sick to her stomach because she realized that Randy may have been one of the bank robbers.

"Do you know a Henry Cornwell?" Officer Hamilton asked Felecia

"Well no I have never heard of him." She replied. "Why do you ask?"

"Well his name was the other ID on the body so we are just trying to follow all leads." He continued

"Well no I do not recognize that name." She said

"Very well Ms. Grey, Thank you for your time." He said as he stood to leave.

"My pleasure, I'm just sorry it had to be under these circumstances." She replied. Then she walked him to the elevator and rode down to the lobby with him. When he was gone Felecia went back up to the 2nd floor by climbing the stairs. She was confused and wanted to talk to Chelsea about Anthony's demise.

When she got to the top of the stairs, she made a detour into Chelsea's office. "Hey, do you know who that was about?" Felecia said as she popped her head in on Chelsea.

"No. What was that all about?" Chelsea replied.

"Anthony Alvarez was found with a bullet in his head out on Bayou Road yesterday."

"Oh My God, how awful. I wonder what happened to him?" Chelsea asked.

"I don't know but the officer had his last check that we gave him when I let him go and he had his drivers license and he had a second ID on him that claimed he was Henry Cornwell. What do you make of that." Felecia asked Chelsea.

"Well I don't know. Didn't you say you thought he lied on his application and resume?"

"Well yes, that's what I suspected, I wonder who this Henry Cornwell is." Felecia continued

"Wow that's awful." Chelsea said. "What did the cop want with you then?"

"Oh he just wanted to see if we knew about Anthony's next of kin. So I made a copy of his resume and application and gave it to him so that he could locate Anthony's next of kin. I told him that I thought he lied on his resume and application."

"Oh no, do you know that for sure. I mean he passed all the entrance tests and he did work out for a couple of months. Now they won't be able to find out who needs to claim the body. This is awful," Chelsea exclaimed. "Is there anything we can do to help?"

"I gave them everything I had, so we have helped as much as we can."

"Okay, I guess that's all we can do then." Chelsea replied.

"Yes I guess you're right, I just hope there isn't a killer on the loose." Then Felecia left Chelsea's office to go to hers. Little did Felecia know she was sleeping with the killer.

Jonathan was listening in room 504 when the conversation between the cop and Felecia took place. Jonathan had moved the surveillance equipment to room 504 when they cleared out of that dingy little apartment. They didn't need the apartment anymore now that they had achieved their mission. Frank over heard the conversation. He lit a cigarette and took a long drag to calm his nerves. *'Oh shit, what do we do now'* he thought to himself. He would need to speak to Jonathan before dinner tonight. They just wished they could do something about it. So he phoned the hospital room to speak to Charlie Wright.

"Hello" Frank said loudly, Wake up cowboy we're on." Frank told Jonathan.

"Leave me alone. I did what I was supposed to do. Now we have all the amenities that we need. I'm tired. I just want to take a small cat nap." Jonathan said into the morning air." Frank had woke him up abruptly again.

"Yeah we got problem. You need to listen to this."

"What's goin on?"

"Just get up and get out there." Frank demanded.

"Alright Alright, I'll be there in a little bit then. Just let me shower."

"There's no time for that. Just get in there now please." Frank demanded again.

"Okay bro, don't flip out, whatever it is it will be alright. Can you at least let me wake up a little bit?" Jonathan asked Frank.

"No, just get out there."

"Okay, I'm coming, I will be right there." Then Jonathan jumped out of bed and headed towards the tape recorder to listen in on whatever his brother was freaking out about.

"You cleaned up that apartment but you won't quit smoking, you're a joke bro." Frank had picked up and did the dishes, but he had chain smoked the entire time. The little two bedroom hotel room smelled awful from the stale smoke now. But Frank had tried to smoke out on the balcony, however this little glitch would cost them and Frank was fight his nervous energy.

"Just come in here and listen to the tape." Frank spit out at his brother, he then left him to get up.

Jonathan then listened in on what the ladies had said that had his brother so worked up. When Jonathan got up, he threw on his cowboy boots for luck and headed for the other room. He didn't look much like a bank robber when he came out of his room. He readied himself to hear what was so important. He sat down in front of the tape recorder and listened to the conversation that his tiger had had with Officer Hamilton.

"Oh Shit, what do we do now?" Jonathan said with a hint of fear in his voice.'

"Well we aren't going to be here for very much longer, our plane leaves in an hour, so we just lay low until the it's time to go and then we get the fuck out of dodge." Frank said with confidence.

Jonathan sat back and took in what just happened. He had sent the gun that had killed Henry Cornwell aka Anthony Alvarez to their apartment in New York. It would only be a matter of time before the signs pointed to them. They had to come up with a story that would keep them out of jail if the cops came knocking on their door within the next hour.

Jonathan had strong feelings for Felecia. He had decorated the hotel room with the same pictures that he had posted on the walls of the apartment. "We need to get these pictures down now. Come on, we can't take the risk of them figuring out what we are doing here."

"Oh don't freak out on me now bro we don't need to do anything. There is nothing tying us to this murder."

"Did you pick up after yourself?" Frank asked.

"What do you mean?" Jonathan spit back.

"The bullet casing, they can trace it back to you. You're gonna have to get rid of the gun."

"I already did. I mailed it to the apartment and Mrs. Green said she would accept it. It's resting in her apartment for now. She agreed receive it, so stop worrying about that."

"Just get rid of it. We don't want any attention regarding this at all." Frank demanded.

"Alright already. I sent it home just to make sure that the murder weapon is hidden well." Jonathan replied. "Now what do u want me to do? The cops don't know about the apartment. So just relax." Jonathan said with false certainty.

"I'm glad you did something with it so they can't tie it back to us. But we need to destroy it. We will just have to leave it in the hands of Mrs. Green until we get back from Switzerland."

"That sounds good to me, bro. That's what I did with it. They won't tie that weasel's death to me. Okay, so stop worrying."

"Okay, that's one thing down. Now what else could they do to tie us to the murder."

"Well I didn't see anyone on that road that night. It was dark and no one saw us, I'm sure of it. It will take the cops a long time to tie anything to us. We will be long gone before they find us." Jonathan replied.

"I sure hope you're right bro." Frank said a little unsure.

They spent the day going over all the possibilities that could come of this latest news. "I will be seeing her soon."

"Sounds good. I hope she lets you in on what she is thinking about Alvarez."

"She's just a loose end that I need to forget and tie up." Jonathan returned

"Oh I'm sure she will, don't worry bro, I got it under control."

"Yeah like you had Anthony under control." Frank said sarcastically.

"That's not fair. How was I supposed to know there would be a jogger come by and find him this soon?"

"I don't know, I just want this to be over." Frank said as he lit another cigarette. He smoked his cigarette down quickly and then hopped in the shower. Then Frank went over to the apartment and used his nervous energy to clean up the rest of the apartment. *'These ladies have become a liability.'* He thought to himself as he began to vacuum the living room. That thought didn't set well with Frank. He didn't want to hurt Chelsea any more than he already had. He wanted the apartment to be presentable if the cops came knocking on his door.

After he was finished cleaning up the apartment, he decided to make his last visit to Chelsea. So he left the keys to the apartment laying on the counter as this would be the last time he would set foot in that apartment. He would crush all of her dreams.

Chapter Forty

---◆◆◆---

CHARLIE GETS GROUNDED

By 9 am the bank was surrounded by police cars. Each employee gave their details as to what happened. But no one knew anything except that they had been robbed and the only thing that they had control of was the initial $500 that they were given each day. Officer Hamilton and Officer Brooks were on the job trying to be helpful to Ms. Grey and Ms. McQuire who had never lost any money on their watch. He questioned them and asked for the information that would lead them to the bank robbers.

"Are you sure Henry Cornwell wasn't involved with this?" Officer Hamilton asked Felecia.

"Well I don't know a Mr. Cornwell. All I know is his what you told me about him. His ID was found on the dead man found on Bayou Rd. He must be involved though. I think there were three of them. They used an inside man this time. Daniel Fields was his name and there were two others and I'm ashamed to say I had a relationship with one of them." Felecia reported. "I just hired Daniel Fields or Mr. Cornwell or whatever his name is was."

"You were involved with them you said? Was any other employee involved with them that you know of?" He asked.

"I had just hired Christopher's cousin Daniel Fields last week. I guess that was a mistake too. They obviously had an inside man. And he his absent at the moment."

"So can you describe them?" He asked.

"Well Randy, they one who I was seeing, was about 6 ft. tall with brown hair and he wore snake skin cowboy boots where ever he went. He called himself Randy Fields"

"Okay there may be a correlation with Henry Cornwell's murder. I found cowboy boot foot prints in the sands of the marsh last week when the body was found." They got lucky and found an impression of the cowboy boots in the sandy marsh of the bay. The impression was so good that is showed there was an impression the number 13 left in the marsh as well inside the boot impression left behind by the killer. So they knew what shoe size the killer would wear. "Do you know where they were headed? I mean since you got to know them, Did this Daniel Fields put in for a vacation or talk about one?"

"He was only here for a week so he didn't have time to earn a vacation."

"What about this Christopher and Randy, you said you were seeing them, did they mention going anywhere soon?"

"Well we spent the weekends together with Randy and Ms. McQjuire spent the weekends with Christopher for the past three weeks. But Randy didn't say anything to me about taking a trip"

"Okay, then what can you tell me about this Daniel Fields." He replied.

"I don't know, Christopher just recommended him and I hired him almost immediately. I suppose I played right into their hands."

"Well Ms. Grey, they used you. You were vulnerable and they seduced you. Don't beat yourself up about it. We will find them. Don't you worry. I have a lead on the car they liked to drive and we have the boot impressions to go on. We also have tire impressions found in the sand of the marsh that we can compare to the vehicle that they used regularly. Christopher drove a rented SUV to get around in right?"

"Yes that's right." Felecia said as she regained her composure. The police officers knew that it was only a matter of time before they would put two and two together and tie the Snow brothers to the murder and the bank robbery.

"I believe the three men involved are career criminals. We will find them and get your money back Ms. Grey. Don't you worry. They used an inside man, they used your vulnerability against you and if there was three of them. They couldn't have gotten far yet."

"Well I'm just glad no one was hurt. I can't believe I let my guard down with these guys. I'm not supposed to do that. I guess I got caught up in the moment." She admitted.

"I wonder if they went back to their hotel room? They could be there."

"What hotel were they staying at?"

"They Regency." She answered reluctantly because she was so embarrassed that she had slept with Randy.

"Okay what room number?"

"We stayed in room 504. Do you think they are there?"

"Lets hope so ma'am." Officer Hamilton called dispatch to send two units to room 504 at the Regency hotel. He sent the first officer to room number 504 and the other one to watch over the lobby until he got there. They would find that Frank and Jonathan Snow had checked out this morning when they left after they committed the heist.

"Lets start with this. What kind of car were they driving today?"

"Well Daniel showed up today and every day that he worked here except for the first day, in a big grey Buick." She explained. "It was Daniels car. He was a transplant from South Carolina. He did really well learning his duties and making friends with the other employees. I so hoped he would work out." She said with a hint of sadness in her voice.

"Do you really think they had something to do with that man's murder?"

"Well it all fits. We will check with the rental agency to see if there was a credit card used to rent the vehicles that Frank, I mean Christopher drove around. Christopher Snow is the name that he gave you right."

"When Henry Cornwell was murdered we found cowboy boot impressions in the sand and we found tire marks that match an SUV at the murder sight. I think your employee Anthony Alvarez crossed them somehow and got himself killed. That's where Henry Cornwell comes in. He had a criminal record and had some banking experience. So if we can just find out who rented that grey Buick I think we may have tied up all the loose ends." He told her.

"Don't worry Ms. Grey. We are on it and have a way to find out who they are." Officer Brooks said to reassure her.

"Well that's good because I don't think the owner of the bank can take any more bad things happening to his bank."

"We will get them Ma'am. Don't worry."

"Oh I do hope so, I don't know what to tell Mr. Eldridge. He doesn't come in until 10 o'clock. I think I should call him and tell him not to come in today." Felecia told the Officers after they rode the elevator upstairs to her office.

"Well Ms. Grey we will need his statement for the investigation."

"Okay, but please don't upset him, he recently had a heart attack."

"Don't worry Ms. Grey we will be as easy on him as possible."

"Let me break it to him. He needs to hear it from me. It happened on my watch. I want to do something to make it up to him." She returned.

"Okay, you can break it to him. But we will need to talk to him afterwards."

"No problem he will be here at 10 o'clock. It's almost 10 now. He should be here any minute." She told Officer Hamilton. Just then Cheryl buzzed her with a call from Mr. Eldridge. "Okay thanks Cheryl. Can you please hold on a second Officer Hamilton this might be helpful, Okay thanks Cheryl." She said as she picked up the receiver of the phone and Cheryl told her that the boss was on the phone.

Officer Brooks was consoling Chelsea at the moment. She felt like the biggest fool for being taken by Christopher or whoever he was. She knew that Misty was on to something when she reacted that way. She also knew that her parents were on the mark as well when they told Chelsea about their feelings about Christopher. Felecia was kicking herself for getting involved with Randy.

The cop cars told everyone that something had happened at the bank before they got there. There were many customers waiting to fulfill their banking needs. The customers were told that there had been a robbery. Then the customers were told that the bank would be closed today, but they would reopen on Monday. This put a crimp in many of the banks customer's plans. They were waiting patiently while they worried about their bank accounts and wondered if they would get their money back when the bank reopened on Monday.

Chelsea just cried through the whole thing. Harold stayed calm and tried to reassure the rest of the employees to keep them calm. Alice and Cheryl were crying as well. Ken and Amanda Stevens consoled each other. They couldn't believe their beloved bank was robbed. Mark Patterson wore his self assured hat and tried to calm his employee's.

At about 9 am the wire transfer was complete. Jonathan hit a few more keys and the money was on its way to its next destination. Then he called the airport and booked two first class seats on the next plane to Switzerland.

Jonathan had studied how to make a large deposit in the bank in Switzerland. He really knew what he was doing. The deposit that was taken was deposited in the first of many bank accounts until it disappeared in one of the foreign bank accounts. We will take $500,000 less your $50,000." Frank said. "Did you take your cut when you made the transfer?" He asked.

"Yes my $50 grand was transferred into my offshore account that you gave me. It will rest there in this unnumbered account until u get to the next destination." He said this while handing Frank a piece of paper with the account identification and the bank name with the location on it.

"Now we should head to parts unknown." Frank told Jonathan,

"Yes lets get going. Where is Charlie?" Frank asked. "We were supposed to meet up with him here."

"I don't know brother of mine." Jonathan replied. Little did they know that Charlie was resting in the local hospital unconscious right now. He was headed to Bermuda with his take before he was in an accident. Jonathan commented that he would make himself comfortable in the Caribbean islands and never be caught. Or so he thought.

He had mentioned that he liked the sights there. Bikini's on a white pearly beach. He knew that he could live cheaply there for a very long time. He had bought a ticket to the Caribbean Islands. He was set to catch the next plane out of there. But the accident had rendered him useless, however he still earned his $50 grand which was resting in that big grey Buick that had been totaled in the accident.

It was 10 o'clock in the morning. He knew that all hell was breaking lose at the Trinity Bank. He was at a loss as to what had happen to his cut of the money. He was resting while watching the news. At that moment he heard the local news reporting about an accident that happened just a few minutes ago. The other driver of the SUV had gotten the worst of it. Daniel would be out of commission for now, but that was okay because Daniel had completed his part of the job. He decided to call the rental agency where Frank had rented the cars from.

Officer Hamilton and Officer Brooks arrived at the accident scene. They did not know that Daniel was a thief in disguise, and the one who would help the Snow brothers take all of that money. As soon as the ambulance arrived the paramedics worked to get both drivers out of their vehicles.

Frank was getting worried about Charlie because he hadn't touched base with Frank yet. He immediately hopped in his SUV to head for the accident scene. It wasn't far from the Regency hotel. This was the break that the police needed.

Charlie had an ID that said he was Daniel Fields. So the hospital referred to him as Daniel Fields. Frank called the hospital to see if he had been admitted. The nurse on the phone told him that there was a Daniel Fields in the ER and then she asked if he was a family member.

"Yes ma'am. He's my cousin." Frank told her.

Then Frank told Jonathan to stay put until he could get to the hospital. Frank jumped into his favorite car and headed for the hospital with that said. When he arrived he told the hospital staff that his cousin had been in an accident and that his name was Daniel Fields. Then the nurse told him that he had was unconscious and had been admitted. She gave him Daniels room number. "Well I will be right there." He told the nurse on the other end of the line.

Felecia had immediately called 911 after she realized that there had been a robbery. The 911 operator took her information and dispatched Officer Hamilton and his partner to investigate. The officers knew that the Snow brothers were involved somehow. They knew Jonathon liked to wear his snake skin cowboy boots. The boot impressions in the marsh were a size 13. It said so in the prints that he left in the sand that night with Henry Cornwell in the marsh.

Charlie spent the better part of the morning recovering in the ER. Frank and Jonathan were on a plane now headed for Switzerland. Charlie Write had almost a million saved totaling the $800,000 that he had saved from the last heists that he had pulled with the Snow brothers.

When he regained consciousness he wondered what had happened to his cut. He was a little bit foggy about what had just happened to him. He knew that the Snow brothers were gone. He knew that he was alone now. He had been living frugally to save as much as he could. So he just decided he would wait until they called again to tell him that they were at the Regency hotel and the money was secure. That way he might just be able to save a cool million and retire for good.

The Snow brothers had booked the next flight out of town to Switzerland to recover the money that had been deposited in their unnumbered account. Frank used The First Bank of Switzerland. His newest alias was Tom Bellows. Frank had used this name recently to honor his only remaining relative of the Snow family besides his brother. His uncle was Tom Bellows and he was his mother's brother, and he had been very close to him in past years.

When they got the money settled in a bank account that was protected by foreign laws Frank relaxed a little. They each had nearly $900,000 now to add to their previous balance and keep them happy for a little while longer, or maybe retire all together.

Chapter Forty One

—◦◦◦—

THE MONEY TRAIL

B y 9 am the bank was surrounded by police cars. Each employee gave their details as to what happened. Or at least tried to give their account of what had happened. The robbers had hit early, so many of the banks employee's didn't have much to tell. But they were happy to give Daniel a sour review. However, no one knew anything except that they had been robbed and the only thing that they had control of was their initial $500 that they were given each day. Officer Hamilton and Officer Brooks were on the job trying to be helpful to Ms. Grey and Ms. McQuire who had never lost any money on their watch. He questioned them and asked for the information that would lead them to the bank robbers.

"Are you sure Henry Cornwell wasn't involved with this?" Officer Hamilton asked Felecia.

"Well like I told you before I don't know a Mr. Cornwell. All I know is his what you told me about him. His ID was found on the dead man found on Bayou Rd. He must be involved though. I think there were three of them. Daniel Fields was hired last week. And there were two others. Which I'm ashamed to say I had a relationship with one of them." Felecia reported. "I just hired Daniel Fields or whatever his name is was." She told him with as much reassurance that she could.

"They used an inside man this time." Officer Brooks said to no one in particular.

"You were involved with them you said? Was any other employee involved with them that you know of?" Officer Hamilton asked.

"I had just hired Christopher's cousin Daniel Fields last week. Christopher was seducing my colleague, Ms. McQuire, I guess that was a mistake too. They obviously had an inside man. And he his absent at the moment."

"Can you describe them?" Officer Brooks asked.

"Well Randy, they one who I was seeing, was about 6 ft. tall with brown hair and he wore snake skin cowboy boots where ever he went. He called himself Randy Fields"

"Okay there may be a correlation with Henry Cornwell's murder. I found cowboy boot prints in the sands of the marsh last week when I found the body." The police got lucky and found an impression of the cowboy boots in the sandy marsh of the bay that actually showed the size of the boot. The impression was so good that is showed that there was a 13 on the sole of the boot. So they knew what size the killer would wear.

"Do you know where they were headed? I mean since you got to know them, Did this Daniel Fields put in for a vacation or talk about one?"

"He was only here for a week so he didn't have time to earn a vacation."

"What about this Christopher and Randy, you said you were seeing them, did they mention going anywhere soon?"

"No I was seeing Randy, and Ms. McQuire was seeing the one named Christopher. I spent the weekends together with Randy and Ms. McQuire spent the weekends with Christopher for the past three weeks. But Randy didn't say anything to me about taking a trip"

"Okay, then what can you tell me about this Daniel Fields."

"I don't know, Christopher just recommended him and I hired him almost immediately. I suppose I played right into their hands."

"Well Ms. Grey, they used you. You were vulnerable and they seduced you. Don't beat yourself up about it. We will find them. Don't you worry. I have a lead on the car they liked to drive and we have the boot impressions to go on. We also have tire impressions found in the sand of the marsh that we can compare to the vehicle that they used regularly. Christopher drove a rented SUV to get around in right?"

"Yes that's correct, but I didn't know that it was a rental." Felecia said. The police officers knew that Snow brothers were connected to both crimes.

"I believe the three men involved are career criminals. We will find them and get your money back Ms. Grey. Don't you worry. They used an inside man, they used your vulnerability against you and if there was three of them. They couldn't have gotten far yet."

"Well I'm just glad no one was hurt. I can't believe I let my guard down with these guys. I'm not supposed to do that. I guess I got caught up in the moment." She admitted.

"I wonder if they went back to their hotel room? They could be there." Officer Brooks said.

"What hotel were they staying at?"

"They Regency." She answered reluctantly because she was embarrassed that she had slept with Randy there.

"Okay what room number?"

"We stayed in room 504. Do you think they are there?"

"Lets hope so ma'am." Officer Hamilton called in to send two units to room 504 at the Regency hotel. He sent the first officer to room number 504 and the other one to watch over the lobby until they got there. They would find that Frank and Jonathan Snow checked out this morning after committed the heist.

"Lets start with this. What kind of car were they driving today?"

"Well Daniel showed up today and every day that he worked here except for the first day, in a big grey Buick." She explained. "It was Daniels car. He was a transplant from South Carolina. He did really well learning his duties and making friends with the other employees. I so hoped he would work out." She said with a hint of sadness in her voice. "Do you really think they had something to do with that man's murder?"

"Well it all fits. We will check with the rental agency to see if there was a credit card used to rent the vehicles that Frank, I mean Christopher drove around. Christopher Snow is the name that he gave you?"

"Yes that's correct" Felecia replied with a hint of frustration. She was growing weary of all the questions.

"When Henry Cornwell was murdered we found cowboy boot impressions in the sand and we found tire marks that match an SUV at the murder sight. I think your employee Anthony Alvarez crossed them somehow and got himself killed. That's where Henry Cornwell comes in. He has a criminal record and has banking experience. If I showed you a couple of pictures do you think you could identify them? If we can just find out who rented that grey Buick I think we may have our man." He told her.

"Don't worry Ms. Grey. We are on it and we have ways of finding out who they are." Officer Brooks said to reassure her.

"Well that's good because I don't think the owner of the bank can take any more bad things happening to his bank."

"We will get them Ma'am. Don't worry." Officer Hamilton added.

"Oh I do hope so, I don't know what to tell Mr. Eldridge. He doesn't come in until 10 o'clock. I think I should call him and tell him not to come in today." Felecia told the Officer after they rode the elevator upstairs to her office.

"Well Ms. Grey we will need his statement for the investigation."

"Okay, but please don't upset him, he recently had a heart attack."

"Don't worry Ms. Grey we will be as easy on him as possible."

"Let me break it to him. He needs to hear it from me. It happened on my watch. I want to do something to make it up to him." She returned.

"Okay, you can break it to him. But we will need to talk to him afterwards." He repeated. "Can you take a look at a couple of pictures of who we think they are? Would you please take a look at these photo's?" He asked again.

"No problem he will be here at 10 o'clock. It's almost 10 now. He should be here any minute." She told him. Just then Cheryl buzzed her with a call from Mr. Eldridge. "Okay thanks Cheryl. Can you please hold on a second Officer Hamilton this might be helpful" She said. "Thank you Cheryl." She said as she picked up the receiver of the phone when Cheryl told her about the waiting call.

Officer Brooks had gone into Chelsea's officer and consoled Chelsea at the moment. She felt like the biggest fool for being taken by Christopher or whoever he was. She knew that Misty was on to something when she reacted that way. She also knew that her parents were on the mark as well when they told Chelsea about their feelings about Christopher. Felecia was kicking herself for getting involved with Randy.

The cop cars told everyone that something had happened at the bank before they got there. There were many customers waiting to fulfill their banking needs. The customers were told that there had been a robbery. Then the customers were also told that the bank would be closed today, but they would reopen on Monday. This put a crimp in many of the banks customer's plans. Especially over the holiday weekend. They were waiting patiently while they worried about their bank accounts and wondered if they would get their money back when the bank reopened on Monday. Felecia had asked Chelsea to tell the banks employees that they had insurance and would be operational by Monday morning. Then she sent each one them home for the day.

Chelsea just cried through the whole thing. Harold stayed calm and tried to reassure the rest of the employees to keep them calm. Alice and Cheryl were crying as well. Ken and Amanda Stevens consoled each other. They couldn't believe their beloved bank had been robbed. Mark Patterson wore his self assured hat and tried to calm his loan officers nerves.

When the transfer was completed, Jonathan hit a few more keys and the money was on its way to its next destination. He was proud of himself for learning one of the many ways that money could be taken from the banks all across the world. He started to dream about living abroad and taking more money from more banks.

The deposit that was taken was deposited in the first of many bank accounts until it disappeared in one of the many foreign bank accounts that they held. "We will take $500,000 less your $50,000." Frank said to Daniel at the Regency hotel.

"Thanks for my cut, that $50 grand was transferred into the offshore account that you gave me. It will rest there in this unnumbered account until you get to the next destination." He said this while handing Frank a piece of paper with the account identification and the bank name with the location on it.

"Now we should head to parts unknown." Frank told Jonathan,

"Yes lets get going." Frank said to instruct them. "We were supposed to meet up with him here."

"I don't know brother of mine." Jonathan replied. Little did they know that Daniel, or Charlie, was resting in the local hospital unconscious at the moment. He was headed to Bermuda with his take before he was in the accident. Jonathan commented that he would make himself comfortable in the Caribbean islands and never be caught. Or so he thought.

Jonathan couldn't wait to see the sights there. He liked the thought of watching bikini's on a white pearly beach. He knew that he could live cheaply there for a very long time. He was set to catch the next plane out of there headed for Switzerland to retrieve their money at 8:30 am. After all it was their money now. But the accident had rendered Charlie useless. And Frank didn't know about the acidedent yet. Charlie had still earned his $50 grand.

When Charlie came to at about 9 am. He heard the local news reporting that an accident that happened just about an hour ago. He didn't remember anything about the money or the accident he was just in. The other driver of the SUV had gotten the worst of it. Daniel would be out of commission for now, but that was okay because he had completed his part of the job. Charlie didn't even know what day it was, but he had completed his task and had taken his cut that the Snow brothers had given to him. His $50 grand was waiting for him in the bank account that Frank had given to him. Right now the information about his cut was resting in the pocket of his pants that were blood soaked from the accident.

The nurse that was attending to Charlie Wright took good care of him. Slowly Charlie's memory came back to him. "Where are my clothes?" He demanded when nurse Shelly entered his room.

"Now don't you worry about that. We had to dispose of them when you arrived." Nurse Shelly returned. "Your pants were ruined when you got into that accident. There was a whole in them and they were soaked in blood. Can I get you anything?" She asked him. Then she went on to say "When you broke your leg the bone poked through your pants." Charlie was resting his broken leg and licking his wounds at the moment while nurse Shelly reported this to him. He would not see Frank again for a while. He needed to talk to Frank and ask him if he knew what had happened to that Buick that Frank had rented for him after the accident.

He didn't know yet that Frank had set him up with a new account and had deposited his $50 grand in that account.

"No Thanks, I'm fine right now." He returned "When can I get out of here?

"Well at least a couple of days. You were involved in an accident sir. Now can I bring you another pillow? Are you warm enough?" She went on the ask.

"I'm fine, I just want to get out of here!" He demanded.

Nurse Shelly noted his attitude and backed away a little when he yelled at her. "Well if you don't need anything now, I have got a several patients and I need to get back to my rounds. You are in good hands Mr. Fields. We got ur name from your wallet when they brought you in." She added. So if you are okay for now, I need to see my other patients. Just rest Mr. Fields."

"Thanks." He told her. "Did you check the pockets to those pants that you threw away?" He asked sternly.

"Oh yes, I was told that you had some money and some personal belongings that the nurse put in your wallet when you came in." She said this while quickly cleaning up after him. "We put your wallet in the closet over here." She said as she went to the closet in Charlie's room. "Ah here is it. Here's your wallet sir." She said as she handed him his wallet, with the wire instructions in the inside pocket of his wallet. His memory was coming back to him slowly. Just then he remembered about the banking instructions that Frank had given to him. That little piece of paper held his life in the balance. He relaxed a little when she gave him back his wallet. He quickly rummaged through his wallet looking for the banking instructions that the nurses had taken from his pants pocket. The hospital had respected his privacy and he found little piece of gold that had been taken from the discarded pants in the billfold pocket of his wallet. He found what he was looking for quickly. Whoever had admitted him had treated him well. Charlie decided to do as instructed and rest his weary mind. He knew that he would be out of commission for at least 6 to 8 weeks with his leg broken and the head injury that he had sustained. But his money was safely tucked away in an unnumbered account at the moment.

Chapter Forty Two

THEY MEET UP IN SWITZERLAND

After the money was taken, Felecia first called Mr. Eldridge and told Mrs. Eldridge what had happened that morning. Mrs. Eldridge was not helpful at all. She insisted on handling her husband's health her way. So Felecia just went along with what Mrs. Eldridge told her to do. Mrs. Eldridge was a demanding woman. Felecia was wondering how her boss handled being married to that woman. She said thank you and farewell to Mrs. Eldridge and hung up the phone, noting that Mr. Eldridge would not be in that Friday.

The insurance company moved very quickly. They restored the integrity to the Trinity bank with a few clicks of keys. Felecia had asked for a claim of $500,000, which was the banks limit on the their insurance policy. By 10:30 am the bank had enough money to pay the employees for the holiday weekend. Chelsea had told all of the tellers that the bank would be closed for the day but would reopen on Tuesday morning. She also told them that she would be able to pay them today, they just couldn't open the doors to the public just yet.

Felecia had worked feverishly getting the insurance money together so that she could pay her employees before the long weekend ahead. She made sure that all her employees were happy and they trusted Felecia's words. With a few strokes of the keys the Trinity banks funds were restored and Felecia Grey was back in business.

Officer Hamilton and Officer Brooks followed up with the Trinity bank and filed a lengthy police report for the heist. The bank may only get away with staying closed for the long holiday weekend. Many of the banks customers were put off by their bank closing before they could all get their funds for the long holiday weekend. They had faith in the Trinity bank with their money. The customers who were Mr. Eldridge's friends understood and prayed for his welfare and quick recovery.

The police officers had a lead on where Frank and Jonathan Snow were at the moment. They had been following Frank closely by simply following the credit card activity, when he used his card to pay for the hotel room under the alias Christopher Fields.

So they called the authorities in Switzerland and asked if they could assist in bringing these bank robbers to justice. They had to move fast in pursuit of their deposit that was resting in the Switzerland bank. This was only a resting point for the money. The Swiss banking system was changing rapidly. Soon there would be no secrecy laws to protect criminals like the Snow brothers. "You never know when they may strike again." Officer Hamilton said to no one in particular.

"Okay, can we agree that the money needs to be moved around after it rests in the bank in Switzerland?" Frank asked. They knew that banking rules and activities with the Swiss bank had changed and it was only a matter of time before they were not as much of a safe haven for their take. Jonathan had been studying the banking rules and regulations for the banks in the Caribbean Islands for other options. As soon as the money was retrieved by Frank, Jonathan's share was sent to the bank of his choice while Frank did the same. Jonathan had also studied the banks in the Cayman Islands. He knew the final destination had to be the Caymen Islands.

Officer Hamilton and Officer Brooks had followed the credit card activities under the name of Christopher Fields. This had helped them to gain access to all money. The officers were anxious to catch the Snow brothers red handed. So they booked the next flight in coach and headed for Switzerland. They had checked with the Frist Bank of Switzerland to make sure their money was still there and was protected. They had contacted the authorities in Switzerland and they knew that the Snow brothers were on their way and were not wanted in this part of the world.

When they got to Switzerland, Frank settled into their new motel room and quickly pulled out his high tech laptop, powered it up, then pulled up the banks website. He then moved the $500,000 around to a couple of bank accounts, always being careful to keep good track of the money. He then quickly moved the money to an unnumbered account in the Caymen Islands after deciding that the Caribbean banking laws were too tight as well. Since they had been robbing banks, the banking rules had changed so many times that it was hard to keep track of.

The Officers of Marshalls Bay had flown to Switzerland to hopefully recover the Trinity banks money. When the airplane touched down in Switzerland the Officers kept their composure and met briefly with the Switzerland authorities. The officers were told that banking there had changed in the past few months. Luckily the new rules didn't start for a few months. So Frank Snow had to act fast. He was walking a tight rope trying to wrap this up.

The Officers borrowed a police cruiser to get around in while they were there. They knew that if they didn't arrest the Snow brothers while they were there, they may never catch them. Officer Brooks was a rookie but he had learned the ropes rather quickly. He was a good kid and Officer Hamilton had been training him ever since he began working with him.

Greg Hamilton was a seasoned officer. When the officers were finished going over what would happen next with the cooperation of the authorities in Switzerland, they decided to go to the First Bank of Switzerland to watch what was going on there, dressed in plain clothes. They met with the First Bank of Switzerland president Arnold Becken.

While the officers were debriefing Mr. Becken, he filled the officers in on how the Snow brothers had robbed the bank. It was actually quite clever. The robbers had downloaded the money directly out of the hands of Ms. Grey and Ms. McQuire. Officer Brooks was watching the monitors for the cameras in the lobby. They wanted to catch the Snow brothers as soon as possible and take them back to the states to prosecute them to the fullest extent of the law.

Just then Frank and Jonathan Snow walked into the bank. "Hey would you look at that. There they are." Officer Brooks exclaimed.

All of the other cops had left the scene. The only cop car that was left in the parking lot was in the back. Officer Hamilton had parked there for a reason. He wanted to make sure that his cruiser was hidden if the Snow brothers arrived at the bank. And they didn't disappoint. Frank and Jonathan Snow arrived packing heat this time.

"Well will ya take a look here? There they are. Right under our noses. How brazen is that, I ask you?" Officer brooks said rather quietly. Felecia and Officer Brooks studied their movements. Then Felecia called down to Ken Stevens and told him not to let any of the tellers leave.

"Ms. Grey, I will make sure that they are taken care of." Officer Hamilton responded. "Right now we need to arrest them on suspicion of robbery." He replied.

"Okay I guess if that's what you have to do, then it is what it is." Felecia replied.

"I'm going to go into the lobby to help as much as I can. You bank is safe. We will make sure of that." Officer Hamilton told Felecia to reassure her.

This helped to calm her nerves just a little. "Well thank you officer. I really appreciate the help. Now can we move on? We are going to stay closed but its pay day here. We pay the employees every Friday. I called in for the money to be deposited just a few minutes ago. The employees will not go without pay this for this weekend. I just want to make sure my employees are taken care of financially for the long holiday weekend." Felecia said. "I'm really sorry about this." She went on the say.

"Don't worry about it Ms. Grey. It happened so now all we can do is deal with it." Ken Stevens said as the meeting was coming to a close.

"I know, but this happened on my watch and I feel really bad for Mr. Eldridge." Felecia returned. "Besides I will not be the reason that he has another heart attack."

"I will pay the employees their regular wages. Chelsea can you go the weekend without pay? I will do the same." Felecia asked

"Yes. I thought I would be spending this weekend on the beach with Christopher. But he hasn't called yet this morning." Chelsea said from the seat across from her desk. Little did Felecia and Chelsea know that they would never see the Snow brothers again.

Officer Hamilton and Officer Brooks, decided to call the airlines and check to see if any of Frank Snow's alias's had booked a flight. He would find that there were no flights going to Switzerland until after the long holiday weekend. Officer Hamilton knew if they didn't catch them now, they may never have this chance again.

"Are you sure Henry Cornwell wasn't involved with this?" Officer Hamilton asked Felecia.

"Well like I told you before I don't know a Mr. Cornwell. All I know is his what you told me about him. His ID was found on the dead man found on Bayou Rd. He must be involved though. I think there were three of them. Daniel Fields was hired last week. And there were two others. Which I'm ashamed to say I had a relationship with one of them." Felecia reported. "I just hired Daniel Fields or whatever his name is was." She told him with as much reassurance that she could muster.

"They used an inside man this time." Officer Brooks said to no one in particular.

"You were involved with them you said? Was any other employee involved with them that you know of?" Officer Hamilton asked.

"I had just hired Christopher's cousin Daniel Fields last week. Christopher was seducing my colleague, Ms. McQuire, I guess that was a mistake too. They obviously had an inside man. And he his absent at the moment." Felecia explained.

"Can you describe them?" Officer Brooks asked.

"Well Randy, they one who I was seeing, was about 6 ft. tall with brown hair and he wore snake skin cowboy boots where ever he went. He called himself Randy Fields"

"Okay there may be a correlation with Henry Cornwell's murder. I found cowboy boot prints in the sands of the marsh last week when I found the body." The police got lucky and found an impression of the cowboy boots in the sandy marsh of the bay that actually showed the size of the boot. The impression was so good that is showed that there was a 13 on the sole of the boot. So they knew what size the killer would wear.

"Do you know where they were headed? I mean since you got to know them, Did this Daniel Fields put in for a vacation or talk about one?"

"He was only here for a week so he didn't have time to earn a vacation."

"What about this Christopher and Randy, you said you were seeing them, did they mention going anywhere soon?"

"No I was seeing Randy, and Ms. McQuire was seeing the one named Christopher. I spent the weekends together with Randy and Ms. McQuire spent the weekends with Christopher for the past three weeks. But Randy didn't say anything to me about taking a trip"

"Okay, then what can you tell me about this Daniel Fields."

"I don't know, Christopher just recommended him and I hired him almost immediately. I suppose I played right into their hands."

"Well Ms. Grey, they used you. You were vulnerable and they seduced you. Don't beat yourself up about it. We will find them. Don't you worry. I have a lead on the car they liked to drive and we have the boot impressions to go on. We also have tire impressions found in the sand of the marsh that we can compare to the vehicle that they used regularly. Christopher drove a rented SUV to get around in right?"

"Yes that's correct, but I didn't know that it was a rental." Felecia said. The police officers knew that Snow brothers were connected to both crimes.

"I believe the three men involved are career criminals. We will find them and get your money back Ms. Grey. Don't you worry. They used an inside man, they used your vulnerability against you and if there was three of them. They couldn't have gotten far yet."

"Well I'm just glad no one was hurt. I can't believe I let my guard down with these guys. I'm not supposed to do that. I guess I got caught up in the moment." She admitted.

"I wonder if they went back to their hotel room? They could be there." Officer Brooks said.

"What hotel were they staying at?"

"They Regency." She answered reluctantly because she was embarrassed that she had slept with Randy there.

"Okay what room number?"

"We stayed in room 504. Do you think they are there?"

"Lets hope so ma'am." Officer Hamilton called in to send two units to room 504 at the Regency hotel. He sent the first officer to room number 504 and the other one to watch over the lobby until they got there. They would find that Frank and Jonathan Snow checked out this morning after committed the heist.

The Snow brothers had a funny feeling that the heat was on. So they checked out of the luxuries of the Regency Hotel and moved to a Seedy motel on the strip. They would hold up there until Monday and leave on the earliest flight to Switzerland. Little did they know that Officer Hamilton and Officer Brooks were closing in on them and would apprehend them sooner then they thought.

Chapter Forty Three

OFF INTO THE SUNSET

Office Hamilton was trying to make sense of the events that led up to the murder on Bayou Rd. that he had found three weeks ago today. He thought he had everything under control. He knew that the notorious Snow brothers were in Marshalls Bay. This could only mean one thing. Where there was smoke there was usually fire. He had been to the car lot where Frank Snow had used his credit card to secure the big grey Buick that Charlie Wright was driving when he got t-boned by the other car. He had also used that same credit card to secure his SUV while he was in Marshalls Bay.

Officer Clayton had been watching room 504 at the Regency hotel but he hadn't seen the Snow brothers leave or return yet. However, he knew that they were staying there based on the information that he had gathered. Officer Clark was in the lobby of the Regency hotel and would arrest the Snow brothers as soon as he saw them. But what the officers didn't know is that Frank Snow had moved to the Starburst motel to rest his heels for the long weekend. They would take the first flight out of there on their way to the money in the Caymen Islands after the heist Tuesday morning. They would be on their way.

Since Charlie Wright was in the hospital, he would be out of commission while he rested up. Because the Officer's knew this they had at least one of the robbers or the murderer that had killed Henry Cornwell in their sights. The accident that put Charlie in the hospital was a very bad accident. The Buick was totaled. The paramedics had done everything they could to save the other driver but he didn't make it.

Mr. John Mathers was survived by his three beautiful daughters, Haley, Brook and Elli and his beautiful wife, Danielle Mathers. The collision was ruled an accident and it was caused by the dead man in the other car, so Charlie Wright was in the clear for now. He just had to heal and then he could use his cut to live in the Caymen Islands from now on. He would enjoy a steady climate and a beautiful white pearly beach. He couldn't be happier about how this had turned out. He just wished he could talk Frank Snow into giving him a bigger cut. After all he was helping them. His role was just as important as theirs, or so he thought. The Snow brothers liked working with Charlie but not so much that they were willing to give up more money.

It was a good thing that the other driver had gotten the worst of the accident in his big SUV. Charlie Wright was admitted into the hospital as Daniel Fields because that's who his ID said he was. The big SUV had rolled over the Buick that Charlie drove and it was headed to the junk yard now. But it had saved Charlie's life. The paramedics had done everything they could to save the other driver but he had a severe head wound and he had lost too much blood. His big SUV had betrayed him. He had bounced around his big car and lost the battle of his life.

Charlie Wright was a not a smart man and he understood just enough about the foreign banking laws to get himself into trouble. He wasn't very good with his own money either. He was the one who mistakenly thought that the banks in the Caribbean would be changing their laws to a more restricted way of banking next month instead of this month. This would put a crimp in the Snow brother's plans.

Charlie knew that if the money was tucked away Caymen islands, it would be safe from foreign banking laws for the time being. He also knew that the longer the money sat the longer he could avoid the unsavory taxes that he would have to pay otherwise when the new changes took effect. He thought that he should be getting at least more than that twit Henry Cornwell had been promised.

He tried to handle his money well but when it came to his own money he simply found it hard to keep control of what he had collected and deposited it into his bank account. This was one of the only smart things that he would do with his money. The second thing he did was put his eldest son's name on the bank account just incase he didn't make it out of this alive. Hopefully the Snow brothers would call him again to pull another heist soon, so that he could build his wealth further.

His bookkeeper would have to keep track of his money for him. He liked to indulge in the finer things in life, even though he wasn't very sophisticated. After all it was so easy to take this amount of money away like they did this time. He wanted to pull a couple of more jobs because he wanted to have at least a million to live on for the rest of his life. But he was afraid of that Jonathan, just like most people were afraid of Jonathan Snow. Charlie was eager to team up with them and he was the only one in their circle that loved the chase and could help them to rob the Trinity bank.

After they pulled the Trinity bank job, they were gone like a flash in the pan. But the chase would end soon. Officer Greg Hamilton and Officer Brooks met up with Officer Clark and his partner in the Regency Hotel. They readied themselves to take the Snow brothers into custody as soon as Officer Hamilton and Officer Brooks arrived. Over the weekend the Officers held their posts at the Regency Hotel. They had no idea that their criminals had checked out because Officer Clark wanted all the glory of catching these characters himself.

Frank had to appear at the designated bank to move the money on Tuesday morning. He chain smoked feverishly while waiting on that day. The officers once again headed to the Trinity bank because Felecia was the one who had called in the robbery. She went over the details with the officers once again. "Lets start with this. Do you know what kind of car were they driving today?"

"How would I know that. Aren't they gone now? Daniel showed up every day that he worked here except for the first day, in that big grey Buick that was involved in the accident on Friday." She explained. "It was Daniels car. He was a transplant from South Carolina. He did really well learning his duties and making friends with the other employees. I so hoped he would work out." She said with a hint of sadness in her voice. "Do you really think they had something to do with that man's murder?"

"Well it all fits. We have checked with the rental agency to see if there was a credit card used to rent the vehicles that Frank, I mean Christopher drove around. Christopher Field's is the name that he gave you?"

"Yes that's correct" Felecia replied with a hint of frustration. She was growing weary of all the questions.

"When Henry Cornwell was murdered we found cowboy boot impressions in the sand and we found tire marks that match an SUV at the murder sight. I think your employee Anthony Alvarez crossed them somehow and got himself killed. That's where Henry Cornwell comes in. He has a criminal record and has banking experience. If I showed you a couple of pictures do you think you could identify him?" He asked.

"Yes go ahead," She replied

He they proceeded to place pictures of the Snow brothers and 3 other wanted criminals and one other officer. She picked out both Randy and Christopher.

"Don't worry Ms. Grey. We are on it and we have ways of finding out who they are." Officer Brooks said to reassure her.

"Well that's good because I don't think the owner of the bank can take any more bad things happening"

"We will get them Ma'am. Don't worry." Officer Hamilton added.

"Oh I do hope so, I don't know what to tell Mr. Eldridge. He doesn't come in until 10 o'clock. I think I should call him and tell him not to come in today again." Felecia told the Officer after they rode the elevator upstairs to her office.

"Well Ms. Grey we will need his statement for the investigation."

"Okay, but please don't upset him, he recently had a heart attack."

"Don't worry Ms. Grey we will be as easy on him as possible."

"I have already told him what happened. He needed to hear it from me. It happened on my watch. I want to do something to make it up to him." She returned.

"Okay, I understand. But we will need to talk to him afterwards." He repeated.

Just then Cheryl buzzed her with a call from Mr. Eldridge. "Okay thanks Cheryl. Can you please hold on a second Officer Hamilton this might be helpful" She said. "Thank you Cheryl." She said as turned away and picked up the receiver of the phone when Cheryl told her about the waiting call.

Officer Brooks had gone into Chelsea's office and consoled her. She felt like the biggest fool for being taken by Christopher or whoever he was. She knew that Misty was on to something when she reacted that way. She also knew that her parents were on the mark as well when they told Chelsea about their feelings about Christopher. Felecia was kicking herself for getting involved with Randy as well.

The cop cars told everyone that something had happened at the bank before they got there. There were many customers waiting to fulfill their banking needs on Friday morning. The customers were told that there had been a robbery. Then the customers were also told that the bank would be closed today, but they would reopen on Tuesday. This put a crimp in many of the banks customer's plans. Especially over the holiday weekend. They were waiting patiently while they worried about their bank accounts and wondered if they would get their money back when the bank reopened. Felecia had asked Chelsea to tell the banks employees that they had insurance and would be operational after the holiday weekend. Then she sent each one them home for the day.

Chelsea just cried through the whole thing. Harold stayed calm and tried to reassure the rest of the employees to keep them calm. Alice and Cheryl were crying as well. Ken and Amanda Stevens consoled each other. They couldn't believe their beloved bank had been robbed. Mark Patterson wore his self assured hat and tried to calm his loan officers nerves.

When the transfer was completed, Jonathan hit a few more keys and the money was on its way to its next destination. He was proud of himself for learning one of the many ways that money could be taken from the banks all across the world. Frank just blew grey smoke into the air in satisfaction.

Jonathan started to dream about living abroad and taking more money from more banks. He was privately celebrating because it was his idea to take the money from the Trinity bank in the first place. And Felecia Grey was a nice bonus.

The money that was taken was deposited in the first of many bank accounts until it disappeared in one of the many foreign bank accounts that they held. "We took $500,000 less your $50,000." Frank said to Daniel at the Starburst motel when he met with the Snow brothers on crutches after he had been released from the hospital. Now all the bank robbers were in one place. This pleased Frank and he lit another cigarette.

The officers had watched room 504 at the Regency Hotel all weekend and were growing weary of the wait. Officer Hamilton had checked with the clerk when he had arrived. But somehow the trail had gone cold. Greg Hamilton had posted several officers in the Regency over the weekend. It was like the Snow brothers had just vanished into thin air. Just then the clerk answered the phone at the front desk. She had been debriefed as to how to handle this call if it came in. And since the trail had gone cold Officer Hamilton had no idea where they were now.

"Yes Mr. Fields. I will send that right over. That's the Starburst motel, room 110 is that correct sir?' She asked as Greg Hamilton wrote down what the clerk said.

"What a lucky break, Greg Hamilton told his officers, lets get over to the Starburst motel. Room 110, now men." He ordered. "Thank you ma'am, you have been a big help." He said to the clerk as she hung up the phone. An army of patrol cars were dispatched to the Starburst motel.

"Thanks for my cut, my $50 grand was transferred into the offshore account that you gave me. It will rest there in this unnumbered account until you get to the next destination." He said this while handing Frank a piece of paper with the account identification and the bank name with the location on it. Charlie Wright was on crutches now but he had been released from the hospital. So he headed straight to where the Snow brothers had told him they would be on the phone when he called.

"Now we should head to parts unknown." Frank told Jonathan.

Just then Jonathan heard gravel crunching outside. A lot of gravel. So he went to the window and took peek outside. He was baffled by the shear number of police cars that had accumulated in the parking lot of the seedy little motel. "What the…" He said "Would you take a look at this. We are surrounded. This place is crawling with police. Wonder what they are here for."

"Well I don't know brother of mine, but I smell something fishy." Frank replied then he lit a cigarette because he grew nervous. "They're everywhere. We gotta get out of here." He said as he took a drag and took one more look out the cracked curtain. Just then there was a knock at the door.

"Mr. Snow, we know you're in there. Please come out with your hands up!" Officer Hamilton shouted as he banged his nightstick against the door. "We have the keys, and we will use them. We don't want any trouble." He said again sternly.

They had them by the short hairs now. But the Snow brothers had a plan. Charlie Wright was dispensable. So they would give him up first. They would send him out of the motel room with his take in hand and have him arrested coming out the front while Frank hid in the adjoining motel room. Jonathan had discovered this little known secret on the earlier in the day. He had shared the information with Frank who then added it as a possible escape plan. He had picked the lock to that door and found the other room. No one had rented it yet so Frank put that part of the plan into motion. He grabbed his cigarettes a lighter. Then Frank carried the money with him, then Jonathan hopped out the bathroom window into a certain capture. He had he bought a second gun just for such an occasion. He was packing today. Jonathan knew that if he was captured he would only spend a short time in jail before his brother found a way to get him free again.

"Hands up Mr. Snow. We have you surrounded." Officer Greg Hamilton said to Jonathan sternly. "Drop the weapon and step back slowly." Jonathan did as he was told. "That's great Mr. Snow. Now put your hands behind your back." Again Jonathan did as he was told.

One officer handcuffed Jonathan Snow and handed him off to Officer Brooks to take back to the cruiser and bring him to justice. Next the motel manager opened the door to let the officers in to search the premises. Frank had locked the adjoining door behind himself, and he had carefully placed a cleaning ladies smock over the knob of the hidden doorknob. He just watched the commotion next door from the window and snickered about his brother taking the rap again. Luckily this was only his second arrest. And he carried no money with him.

Officer Clark reported that room 110 was empty. "Where do you think he went sir?" Officer brooks asked.

"Well he has to be around here somewhere. Where does this door lead?" He asked the clerk.

"Oh that's just a closet. It's locked because we keep cleaning supplies in there."

"Would u mind opening it?"

"Of Course officer. My pleasure." The clerk was named Shelly. She was a short term employee and didn't know that there was another hidden door just on the other side of the closed door. The doorknob was hidden behind a smock that Frank had hung on it. Thinking that there was no one in the room and not knowing that this was an adjoining room door, the clerk guided Officer Hamilton in searching the room. They came up dry. Frank Snow had disappeared with all that money and Jonathan was in custody but with nothing to charge him with because the evidence was missing. As the cop cars slowly left to attend to other crimes, Jonathan Snow was hauled away to the Marshall's Bay Jail.

Frank waited until the sun went down. Then he left the seedy motel for with their take in hand. He knew that his brother would be pissed that he had to take the fall again. But that's just the way it worked in his family. He was the brains of the operation. He knew when to hide and Jonathan didn't know how to use his head under pressure. So it would be up to him to get his brother out of jail once again.

Frank Snow headed just up the beach to another seedy motel and checked himself in as Mathew Hamilton. A new name in honor of his latest foe. This was a new alias that he had thought of just last night. Not even Jonathan would know it until he bailed him out. So since it was a long weekend and Frank knew that the courthouse would not be opened until Tuesday morning, he hopped a plane under his new alias to the Caymen Islands to hide the money.

Jonathan was not happy being the fall guy again. But he knew his brother would not forget him. They had a plan in case of this contingency. However that was little comfort to Jonathan at the moment. As he sat in the Marshall's Bay Jail, he waited for his brother to bail him out. He was agitated but he held his composure.

Frank spent the long weekend seeing the sights and laying low on one of the many islands of the Caribbean. He enjoyed the tanned bodies and bikinis while sipped a margarita. He thought of Chelsea and how much he wished that she would be the one who helped him spend all that money. But when he came back to reality, he knew that could never be. He would wait until Tuesday morning and free his brother from captivity and they would be on their way again to parts unknown. Frank had booked two first class seats to one of the many islands down there.

Jonathan was spitting mad that he had to spend even 5 minutes behind the bars in the jail in Marshalls Bay. And just like Frank, thoughts of Felecia came to mind frequently. However this was a small comfort from where he was siting now.

"Hey dude, how the hell are ya? It's me Mathew." Frank said loudly so that he could be heard by any stray officers. Officer Hamilton had left orders for his crew to watch the prisoner closely while he searched for his brother.

"Don't you worry pal, I'm gonna git you outta here right quick. Where do ya'll post bail round here?" He shouted to the officer who was new to the case and didn't know that he was remanded until this morning when court could be held.

"Right over here sir." Officer Pent said to Frank,

"Well lead the way officer. My pal here doesn't take to kindly to your menu." He said with a laugh. "How much is this bail anyway, Jonathan buddy?"

"Well its supposed to be around a hundred grand. But they can't find any of this money that I am supposed to have stolen, so I guess I get a get out of jail free card today." Jonathan retorted.

"No now its got to be around here somewhere, now where did I put that file." Officer Pent said as he dug through the file. "Oh here is your paper work. Take this to the court house and pay the $100.000 then come back here with your voucher, and we'll get your buddy out of here right quick. Sir." Officer pent neglected to read the part of the file that said remand. It was stuck to another piece of paper courtesy of a jelly donut eaten but Officer Pent that morning.

"Well thank you sir. Where might that courthouse be?" Frank asked, knowing it was just upstairs and he would have his brother out of is Podunk town quickly.

"Its on the 2nd floor sir. Just take this slip and ride the elevator to room 201."

"Thank you sir. Be right back pal. Don't you worry you head over this little misunderstanding, now that Mathew Hamilton is on the job." Frank said loudly again for affect.

Jonathan knew exactly what Frank was doing. He had made the plan with Frank, so he knew the plan well, except for the alias, which was supposed to be decided on that evening before his release. Jonathan took a breath now. He knew he would be out of there soon.

About a half hour later Frank announced his arrival loudly again. "Hey Buddy, why don't you open that jail door over there and let my buddy out. He has already lost a long weekend to this town. Its time we get the flock out of this town, ya know what I mean?' He said as he laughed.

The officer looked over the paperwork and saw that it was in order. Officer Greg Hamilton had spent the entire weekend beating the bushes looking for the notorious Snow brothers, but had come up short. So he was resting with only Jonathan in jail and Frank with the money in the wind now.

"Here we go, now you just let my buddy go. He aint done nothin wrong." Frank said sarcastically.

"Right away sir." The officer on duty said to Frank. Then he released Jonathan. "Well it's about time, you could serve a decent meal around here ya know. We're outta here buddy, thanks a lot." Jonathan said.

The Snow brothers walked freely out of the Marshall's Bay jailhouse. Jonathan had been freed and the Frank directed Jonathan to the new Cadillac that Frank had rented just for such an occasion. They laughed at the incompetency of his jailer. Officer Greg Hamilton would be pissed when he returned to work on Wednesday. The Snow brothers would already be gone and he would have to continue the chase.

"Hee hee hee, we did it bro. yahooooo." Jonathan shouted as they drove away in that big black Cadillac. "Love the car man. And the color suits me."

"I thought it might. Let's just get to the airport and get the hell out of here." Frank said as he took off the cowboy hat and fake moustache and lit another cigarette.

"Man why you takin all that off, you look great. Just my style bro." He said as he snickered.

"Oh that's your look brother of mine. The money is secure and here are the plane tickets. Off we go, bikinis here we come." Frank said with a big smile on his face. He was once again relieved to be at this point in the game. They had made it with just a few scratches along the way. But hey, what's a broken heart or two. They got away with it, murder and all.

Printed in the United States
By Bookmasters